Robert Derry is in his 50s, is a human resources consultant, living in Somerset, England. He was educated at Lancaster University before moving to London, where he worked in the city, within a stone's throw of the River Thames and the site of his debut novel, *The Waterman*. He is an avid supporter of Aston Villa Football Club, who hail from his hometown of Birmingham, England, and of the NFL, following the Green Bay Packers from a distance. He is married to Tina with two grown-up children and two troublesome cats.

In respectful memory of John Taylor
"The Water Poet"
1578-1653

All chapter quotes attributed to John Taylor.

Robert Derry

THE WATERMAN

Nor all the wit in man or devil's pate,
can alter any man's allotted fate

To Dave

Hope you enjoy
it, but if you
dont no getting
angry about it !

[signature]

AUSTIN MACAULEY PUBLISHERS™

LONDON • CAMBRIDGE • NEW YORK • SHARJAH

A CIP catalogue record for this title is available from the British Library.

ISBN 9781398422032 (Paperback)
ISBN 9781398422049 (ePub e-book)

www.austinmacauley.com

First Published 2021
Austin Macauley Publishers Ltd®
1 Canada Square
Canary Wharf
London
E14 5AA

For my family

Part One: The Crossing

Chapter One
Old Swann Stairs

From our births, unto our graves, our care attends on us in number like our sinnes, and sticks unto us close, as do our skinnes.

I dreamt of stairs again tonight. Twelve ancient steps that rise before me, cold and stagnant in the loosening mist.

This time, it's different. I approach them from beneath. Drawn in by an unseen cord that tightens with each turn of a winding cog, until the vessel's spine splits the soft skin of the shore.

There is no sound. Even the water's gentle sigh is lost as it licks at the final tread on which my foot now leans.

And then I am ashore.

Standing like an errant watchman at the waterside; staring up and up, as the sea salt stings my chapped lips and a rising stench lingers on the ebbing tide.

And now, I am looking down.

Down into the semi-darkness of the hallway, where our cat lies curled, unperturbed by my presence in the early hours of just another Wednesday.

Chapter Two
South Shore Lock

Nor all the wit in man or Devil's pate, can alter any man's allotted fate.

There had been colder nights than this, but such frost-bitten memories were of little comfort at twenty-five minutes past midnight on a freezing winter's morning. It was cold enough.

As the tramp stared downstream, across the hurdle of Tower Bridge and up towards the city's ever improving skyline, he allowed his thoughts to stray once more to his former life—a life that now seemed to have belonged to someone else.

Almost a year had passed since his eviction from a damp South London bed-sit—alone and without a penny to his name, and with the dwindling patience of his friends fully exhausted, he had run out of options. Finally, cast out onto the unforgiving streets of London, he had sunk like a lead weight on a fishing line and slipped unseen into its depths.

On this day, the coldest of the season so far, his routine had begun much like any other. At seven-thirty, he'd bought the cheapest available tube ticket and like some disoriented tourist, had begun a continuous journey around the Circle Line in a vain quest for anonymity. Sleep had come in fits and starts until, worried and weary, he had finally surfaced at Monument station at the end of the morning rush. Unwanted, he'd meandered down towards the river; just another unremarkable beggar cast adrift upon the crowded streets of Wren's resurrected city, one of thousands who had sunk beneath the porous line of poverty that year.

There, amongst the furious swarm of office workers, Terry had whiled away what was left of his morning, but as midday came and went, only a few had stopped to offer their usual portion of pity and disgust in equal measure. He had learned from bitter experience that only a handful of these pin-striped legions could ever be parted from their hard-earned cash, but that had never stopped him from trying.

Something, however small, was always better than nothing.

He had no standard patter prepared to fall upon deaf ears each day; rather he would simply sit and stare in silence, his head lowered in humble deference, his eyes transfixed on the cardboard inscription at his feet:

Homeless and hungry, please help.

"Can I get you a coffee?" one girl had asked him. "Maybe a sandwich?"

It was a kindly gesture, and he was in no position to refuse. He accepted the gift with a nod and a smile, and she had reciprocated, dropping a two-pound coin into the paper carrier bag for good measure. Several others, who had born witness to her simple act of charity, stared at the scene as it played out before them, as if she had just taken leave of her senses.

"It's all organised," he heard one sharply groomed man say to another. "They get dropped off in minivans each morning up at Spitalfields. I couldn't believe how much they make in a day. They make more than me! Don't fall for it, it's all a con!"

Terry smiled as he remembered a time when he'd thought much the same thing. If only it were true. He could always sense the fear and loathing that his presence in their world invoked and whilst he would never be able to come to terms with it, he knew well enough that for those who looked away, he simply did not exist.

The afternoon had been spent pacing the familiar streets of Southwark, one of the oldest quarters of London and the place where he had once lived in rent arrears for six weeks. Now, it seemed like just another ward of an unforgiving city, its walkways paved with forgotten headstones from two thousand years of life and death. One more overboard wouldn't even raise a ripple on the murky surface of the mighty Thames.

After a late lunch at his favoured establishment at Waterloo, he had left the busy soup kitchen and continued to walk with aimless abandon, yet some vague mental path had led him back through the cluttered back streets of nineteenth-century London and eventually to London Bridge station as the evening rush hour waned.

Soon, the same pavements that had been lost beneath an unwavering tide of white-collar workers, would fall prey to the steady shuffle of less well-heeled feet.

It was night.

Through the winter, most of Terry Stubbs' kind are believed to congregate on the Embankment or at Waterloo, but many more keep their own counsel and stay well away from such places. There is no spirit of togetherness there, no sense of camaraderie, no collective understanding. Terry preferred to walk the empty streets alone in a vain search for his own warm corner in which to hide. Sometimes, if the weather was agreeable, he would just wander aimlessly all night, but when the cold became too close, he would be forced to seek shelter.

He was only twenty-two years old, but on those increasingly rare occasions when he could bear to return his reflected gaze from the shining steel of the city facades, he would barely recognise himself. He had always been thin, but nowadays his whole frame seemed to have shrunk and his face had aged a hundred years; a rash of fair stubble had now laid claim to his once boyish features and where no hair grew, his flesh was fractured like ice.

How had it come to this?

His younger years had been so full of promise, and there had never been any doubt amongst his teachers that he would go on to have a successful career. After rising to the post of house captain at school, he had been vice-captain of both the soccer and rugby teams and had gone on to sixth form, leaving two years later with three good 'A' levels. Those results had been good enough to secure him a university place; an unconditional offer that would have set him on the path to a lucrative career in high finance, but by then, the dreams had started.

His parents had been dismayed to discover that he had chosen not to take up the guaranteed offer, but Terry had convinced himself that he wouldn't have fitted in. He had always harboured an intense dislike of the stereotypical undergraduate, complete with their striped scarves and obedient accents. Maybe that was why he'd opted for the job in the city.

The fast track to fast cars and even faster women, or so he had thought.

As it had turned out, it had been a one-way ticket to the scrap heap.

And so, instead of attending seminars and socials, he was to be found alone on a bridge in central London in the middle of the night, watching his breath rise before him and wondering if his feet were still where they had always been. As he hobbled over to the top of the worn stone steps, he was assured that both were still functioning in spite of the cold, but as he peered down into the open stairwell, he was soon left gasping for air, as the river's own breath charged up to meet his.

A single gust that burst out into the deserted street and was no more.

Terry raked his unkempt hair from his face and stared down at the dimly lit path below, as far as the turn in the stairs, which snaked its way down to the water's edge where a huddle of boats would have been moored in years gone by.

"Hello?" he called out, his nerves getting the better of him. "Is anybody there?" He had seen nothing and assured himself that he had heard nothing, but the question had been instinctive and if there was one thing that Terry had learnt from his year submerged in the underworld of London, it was to always trust his instincts! From his lofty vantage point, he could just make out the wide stone-littered riverbank thirty feet below, as it slipped beneath the black waters' white rolling edge.

The tide was close to turning.

The ebb and flow of the Thames was now part of his life, its relentless rhythm pulsing like an artery through the chaotic heart of London. On previous nights he had drawn some strange sense of comfort from it, as if it were an old acquaintance or a familiar friend. Yet on this night, its presence had failed to quell the stalking sense of peril that had slipped unseen like a noose around his neck.

As he strained to see from the top of the stone ramparts, the distant clamour of what sounded like a raucous argument, skated across the bridge on the breeze, and pulled him back from the brink. A drunken mob of city types was edging towards him, seemingly unaware of his presence just a few hundred yards ahead. As they got closer, he could hear the vague outline of an old Christmas classic, unmistakable despite the tuneless rendition.

Parallels with his own past crowded in around him, as he recognised the life he had left behind.

"Spare any change, lads?" he asked shamelessly as they drew near, keen as ever not to miss out on an unexpected opportunity to amass a little extra cash.

It was almost Christmas after all.

Until that moment, these nocturnal revellers had been oblivious to his presence, but having now made his acquaintance, it became all too apparent that the four of them were intent on having some fun to go with their paper hats and party poppers.

"What in heaven's name for?" the tall, well-spoken, but extremely drunk city gent enquired, as he exhaled into his silvery Christmas party blower, the sudden noise of which encouraged a passing motorist to beep his horn in reply. "Merry Christmas!" he screeched at the top of his voice.

"For a cup of tea?" answered Terry, ignoring the spontaneous yuletide greeting.

"Oh yeh, right!" slurred another dishevelled banker, who until that moment had been staring trance-like at his phone, his fingers frozen in dial mode, the object of his intended call lost in his stupor. "You'll be spending it on special brew or somefin, won't ya, you twat?" spat this the shortest member of the entourage, keen to extract some random revenge after a bad day at the office. At that, they all roared in unison, as if some popular comedian had just told them a rip-roaringly funny story.

"Here!" the short one continued. "I'll give you something to drink, old chap!" and he proceeded to unzip his fly and urinate in Terry's general direction, relieving himself of the evening's excess in the process. This proved to be just too funny to the odd assembly of highly educated drunkards, who continued to lean all over each other like some victorious first eleven.

The youngest member of the group was so overcome by the hilarity of the whole situation, that he had slumped to the ground, completely oblivious to the steaming stream of urine that was pooling around his knees. The moment would go down in legend at their small city hedge fund, but by the time they had collectively hauled the damp degenerate to his feet, Terry had taken the opportunity to make himself scarce.

"Oy! Oy!" yelled the dyed blond geezer, the second syllable rolling off his filthy tongue, as he tried his best to break into a trot. "Wait up, you ain't got yer dosh!" and he zigzagged after Terry, waving a twenty-pound note in the vagrant's direction, like a linesman waving frantically for an offside.

It proved too much for Terry to resist.

He paused at the top of the stairwell that was waiting to welcome him like some creature's cavernous jaws and turned to face his soon-to-be assailants.

"That's better!" the toff teased. 'But there's a catch' and he withdrew the twenty just as Terry was about to relieve him of it. It seemed rehearsed and Terry knew that the next act was unlikely to be to his liking. "You've got to give him a blow-job!" the tall drunk ordered, nodding towards the fourth member of the group who was now barely standing, his arm draped around his companion's shoulders for support and his knees close to buckling.

Terry had had enough. "Oh, fuck off," was all that he could think of to say, but he would soon find himself wishing that he had kept his thoughts to himself.

"Who do you think you're talking to, you shit?" the boss man in the made-to-measure suit raged and without warning, his fist landed firmly on Terry's shoulder in a blow that was hard enough to force the tramp to the floor. As Terry struggled to get to his feet, he felt the full fury of the same man's boot as it landed square in his stomach.

He was in trouble.

As the blows began to rain in from all sides, he knew that he had to take his chance when it came, and as a fourth or fifth boot lingered too long in his midriff, he grabbed on for dear life and pulled down hard. It had the desired effect and the man with the imitation cockney accent crumpled to the floor in an undignified heap, his expensive cell phone clattering onto the pavement. In a single movement, and ignoring the tearing pain in his ribs, Terry scooped up the handset and bolted for the darkness.

"He's getting away!" croaked a superior strangled cry, but by then Terry had reached the top of the worn stone steps and had dived into the gloom.

It was then that the blue lights swirled silently into view and for a moment, Terry was sure that the colourful carousel that now swam before his eyes was a prelude to a seizure. Perched on the first turn in the stairwell, he fought hard to regain his breath, half expecting to see the gang re-emerge above him, leering and spitting, bearing down on him to finish the job. He could still hear their voices, but their laughter had ceased and their tone seemed altogether more sombre and more sober.

The police had arrived on the scene and not a moment too soon, but Terry had no intention of making a formal complaint. He had learned his lesson well over the course of the last twelve months that it was he who was the undesirable; they were the city's finest, unwinding after a hard day's trading.

"Just a bit of fun, Guvnor," he heard the fake Londoner plead. "Weren't doin' no 'arm, were we lads?" but the others had passed far beyond comprehension. "I'll see them all home safely, officers, no worries." But the well-chosen words quickly faded as the disillusioned city police ushered them on towards the precarious staircase at Bank station and a long journey home.

Terry sat and waited for the flashing lights to fade and for the night's silence to thicken around him. It could have been a few minutes, but it was probably much longer, when he finally plucked up the courage to clamber to his feet.

A needle-like pain in his knee caused him to cry out as he snatched at the handrail, and his shoulder also hurt like hell, whilst the pain in his side was sharp enough to snag on every intake of breath. As he bent forward, his freezing hands pawing at his wounds through layers of soiled clothes, a passer-by would have been forgiven for thinking that he was busy emptying the contents of his stomach in the privacy of the stairwell. On another night, such an observation may not have been out of place, but on this night, Terry had become engaged in an altogether more portentous pursuit.

He was under the river's spell.

He was tuning into the sound that emanates from the great river, when it is not drowned out by the urban uproar to which most city-dwellers are oblivious. The inconspicuous sound of the river's eternal passage beneath the bridge, was in sharp contrast to that belching fury of traffic, which normally greets any visitor passing within twenty square miles of Charing Cross. It was just a whisper and one that his subconscious must have registered many times before, but this time he grasped it, visibly straining his neck to drag it into earshot.

He could hear the shallows as they chuckled over the shale somewhere beneath his feet, accompanied by an almost rhythmical patter. It reminded him of the comforting clatter that echoes around the confines of a caravan during a midnight downpour. He recalled the times as a child when he'd been tucked up on a cosy sofa-bed, listening in awe to the drumming rain, and even the relentless passage of time had not laid claim to such treasured memories. As he allowed those thoughts to wash over him, his grandfather's voice echoed in his head, as clear as if the words had been uttered only yesterday.

"How many times do I have to tell yer, Tel," he'd scold in his sharp East End accent. "Now go to sleep, boy, I ain't gonna tell yer again!" But the old man's sternest warning was never to be taken too seriously and Terry had to swallow hard, as those few simple words served up another painful reminder that his grandfather was dead.

Yet somehow, the old man just didn't seem dead at all.

It was as if the funeral, which, to Terry's eternal shame, he had failed to attend, had never taken place. It was as if the man that he'd called 'Gramps' to the old man's dying day, had somehow slipped the Reaper's grip, to stay by Terry's side through the darkest days of his grandson's life.

His recollection was cut short as a ship's horn blasted a warning of its presence and Terry rubbed his temples to ward off the throbbing headache that had begun to take hold. As the ripples from the boat's unnatural cry petered out, Terry tried once more to focus on the sound that had breathed new life into those lost years. A metallic tapping that seemed to emanate from the foot of the frozen steps on which he was now stood.

Terry swiped up on his newly acquired iPhone to reveal its torch feature and suitably armed, he turned its beam across the grimy 1970s stonework. He knew that the phone would be of limited use; its battery wouldn't last the night but knowing that he'd be able to make a few quid out of it, he stepped into its illumination with a new-found confidence, and began his tentative descent. As he edged his way down, he could still offer no explanation for the steady pulse from below, which tip-toed up the stone steps to meet him. It was akin to the sound of raised voices in a neighbouring room and although Terry was unable to make out the meaning, he could sense the urgency in the sound.

It was calling to him.

"Hello?" he croaked for the second time, swallowing hard to allow himself a less timid shot at it. "Hello!"

Silence.

For a moment he just stood and listened, certain that there was someone lying in wait beyond the next turn of that dark and brooding stairwell.

"Who's there?"

There was no reply.

There was no one there.

Only the river answered him; it's chilled breath, slipping off its surface like a shroud. He pressed his fingers to his ears; his inner heartbeat throbbing like a double bass, offering its own back beat to the unknown percussionist's rhythm.

An enigmatic sound that refused to be explained.

"Hello!" he called for the third time in quick succession. He had not expected an answer and so he wasn't surprised when none was forthcoming, but the sound of his familiar voice in the gloom offered some small comfort as it reverberated around the arch. Yet he had expected to find someone, hiding deep in the shadows. Someone or something that would object to his intrusion, but nothing stirred to provide substance to that sound. Even the resident pigeons, which are often to be found roosting under the bridges at Cannon Street, Blackfriars and London Bridge, were conspicuous by their absence. Maybe it was the intense cold that had driven them further into town, up onto the ledges of the surrounding office blocks, where a trace of warmth offered a welcome solace.

That, or something else.

When the colder breeze poured in off the river again, Terry almost turned away, as his interest moved once more to his more pressing need for warmth. But even the sound of his grandfather's voice calling to him through the years and dislodging the unwanted memory of a long-submerged nightmare, failed to sound his retreat.

"Don't go too close to the edge, Terry lad. I'm too old to fetch yer out!"

Gramps had never liked water and he was never all that keen on boats. He had never liked to see his only grandson going too close to the side on those numerous occasions when they'd wandered hand in hand across the old bridge at Bideford. Terry could remember one particular summer's day a million years before, when his grandfather's grip had almost become too much.

"That hurts, Gramps!" he'd yelped, but his grandfather had been lost in thought and his hold on the boy grew tighter still as he stared out across the ramparts.

His eyes had been set on some scene at the water's edge below, where the ancient stone pillars of the uneven arches burrow deep into the shifting sand of the estuary.

"Gramps, let go!" the young Terry had screamed, as his knees crumpled beneath him, but still the old man stood like a statue, marooned in his memories.

"Let go of that boy!" came the disembodied order from somewhere nearby. "You're hurting him!"

Had that anonymous woman not intervened at that very moment, Terry may well have passed out on the bridge that day, but when he saw the look on his grandfather's face, he could have forgiven him anything.

Anything at all.

It was a look of absolute terror.

At that moment, a blast of sound exploded in the silence, so loud that Terry dropped the vibrating handset as if its metal casing was suddenly on fire. Some vaguely familiar heavy metal guitar riff dragged him back to reality, but the melody was short-lived. As voicemail kicked in, Terry scrambled towards the light to retrieve his prize, a spoil of war that he hoped could be converted into cash as soon as the shops in Camden opened for business later that morning; no questions asked.

In the subsequent silence, the same sound that had entranced him just moments earlier curled up beside him like smoke, but this time it was more insistent, its point of origin more apparent. He turned away from the pedestrian route in an ever-eager pursuit and moved towards a rusting cast-iron gate, a solitary opening to the final precarious trail that leads down to the water's edge.

Terry hesitated at his first uneasy shiver, but the continuance of the sound spurred him on, despite the words of warning from his trusty old Gramps that seemed to rebound off every stone. "I'm too old, Tel," he heard him say. "Too old to fetch yer out!"

Even then, common sense very nearly prevailed as he came closer than ever to giving up; the fact that he didn't would come back to haunt him again and again in the days that followed. His curiosity had been awakened and for the first time in a very long time, he found that he had something else to occupy his mind, other than the basic instincts that are fed by hunger, fear and cold.

Only two of those had been banished as he began the final plunge.

He clambered up and over the railings, ignoring the fading pain in his ribs and lifting his legs so that his feet came to rest on top of the gate, before allowing himself to fall the few feet onto the next flight. His knee complained again, but he was no longer listening.

Ever more cautiously, he began to make his way down this second set of weathered stones, as the easterly wind slithered along the channel of the river to hasten him on his way. It was still only a breeze, but it swirled around him to deepen the chill that was no longer confined to his feet, face and hands.

His blood and bones now shivered with every step.

His sense of isolation became ever more intense with each stride as he scrambled down in the narrow path of electronic light; a single seam that pierced the darkness at the city's heart. The familiar beacon of the streetlights now cast their comforting spell somewhere above his head, the consoling sweep of a rare passing headlight failed to reach these depths and even the permanent reflection of the uneven office blocks seemed stifled at the river's threshold.

Looking up from the abyss of the riverbed at the rows of jostling back-lit buildings, Terry was surprised at how different the city's skyline looked with the river at its core. The water's expanse dominated the reflected scene, even at such a low ebb, whilst the lights from the opposite bank seemed less regimental than before, their fluorescence flickering in a sicklier shade of yellow that now failed to filter down from the tallest of the office blocks. The murky silt beneath his feet was softer than it had seemed to be from above, and before too long, he could feel the water seeping inside his torn trainers, like icy fingers about his weathered soles.

Then, from somewhere up above him, a soft irregular chime rang out, so clear and yet so calm. The faintest rap of metal on hollowed metal, so quiet that it could have sounded out across the bustling city for centuries and yet still have gone unheard. Terry could recall a similar sound from his schooldays; the distant command of the headmaster's heavy brass bell, which rang out thrice daily, whenever lessons were about to commence.

Each intermittent beat fell like a feather down towards the water's edge, where Terry stood enchanted. As each melodic wave of sound drifted closer, it was cushioned in the grey blanket of mist that was now draped across the river's lap. The regular resonance gained in clarity as its source lurched across the bridge some way ahead of him, but all too soon it faded into the night air and four words wandered aimlessly in its wake.

"Bring. Out. Your. Dead!"

Terry heard the words once and once only and in that subsequent void, his heart weighed heavily, as if in grief. As the words dissipated into the night air, he began to wonder if he had heard them at all, until the bells rang out.

It was as if the full fury of some ancient Celtic God had been brought to bear against the very banks of the river and had that pagan deity's own club struck such a chord, the resulting tremor would have rattled the lingering bones of his long dead disciples.

Terry screamed, but no one was there to hear, and the monotonous peal of the bells continued unabated. The very bed of the river seemed to quiver with every strike, but Terry knew that the nearest church of St Magnus the Martyr could surely not have given rise to such discord. He had failed to keep a tally, but just as he began to think that there would be no end to the aural punishment, the last strike sounded.

Silence followed, except for the serpent-like sound that still rattled from beneath the bridge. There was no question of going back now. It was like a distant light that draws a weary traveller home across the hills.

Except that for Terry, he had no home to go to.

The first of too many arches that spanned the channel was no longer as close as the bridge had once appeared. Jagged buildings protruded from the northern shore to block his view of the roadway approach, and although he scanned the length of the structure from north to south, the gloom had now engulfed much of the southern shoreline.

In just a hundred yards or so, he could still make out more than a dozen tight arches raised high on what looked like wooden platforms and as he turned to look back, he failed to recognise the route that he had just traversed. The stairs behind him seemed of a darker shade and each tread looked uneven, with wooden stakes rising high out of the mud at either side. Above his head, an assortment of lights shimmered closer together, whilst trails of smoke from absent chimneys curled and merged in the faintest glow.

"What's goin' on?" Terry pleaded in desperation, out loud or to himself, he wasn't sure. So, he made sure. "What the fuck is going on?" he roared in anger or in fear, but one thing was for sure, if a figure had slipped from the shadows to answer his aimless question, then his pounding heart would have surely burst.

He was alone, he reassured himself, but still his instincts begged to differ.

He could hear the water as it began to freeze around him, creaking and cracking as it contracted, the sudden ice stretching as far upstream as he could see. An anonymous tributary to his right had been stopped in its tracks and as Terry turned to look the other way, his sight skated off towards the old bridge. The span of arches reflected across the dimly lit surface like the trail of a skimming stone, each darkened curve diminishing as the opposite bank approached. Lost voices whispered across the channel, but their meaning was misplaced somewhere in between and all that reached him was the breath that bore them.

Terry glanced upstream, the phone's light reaching out just a few feet into the night in a frantic bid to find some familiar object to cling to. Dark shapes littered the river; some larger than others; some moving on the surface; some still like the bridge itself.

A noise from beneath it forced Terry to turn once more to peer into the darkness of the first tight arch that was perched, like the others, up high against the rising tide.

Suddenly, the struggling beam of light snagged on some motion in the gloom. The reflection was strong, but fleeting, and whatever was seized in that split second appeared to be moving, like a tiny waterfall whose droplets glint on the slightest flicker of light. For a split second, he was tempted to call out again, to ask who was there, but there was something not quite right about the scene before him and instinctively, he stayed as silent as the early grave that waited patiently for his presence.

The light no longer seemed to be his to command and it darted back and forth in a reflex action, until it came to rest on the stirring again. Terry started forward, ignoring the gathering voices that seemed to be closing in behind him to bar his path to freedom. Its focus flickered and fell as he scrambled across the unpredictable surface, whilst his every limb had begun to shiver violently with the cold, or with his drifting sense of dread, he could no longer tell.

A dark expanse of smoothed wooden boards came into view as the area illuminated in the beam of light expanded with every step. The expertly shaped wooden hull of a boat had nestled a few inches into the once soft mud and Terry could just make out the threads of a mooring rope, trailing beneath its bow like a rodent's ribbed tail.

"Keep away from the edge, son!" Terry closed his eyes tight and then slowly allowed them to open in a vain attempt to wake himself from the familiar nightmare in which he was now immersed, but he knew in his heart that it was futile.

This time he was awake.

Wide awake.

"Keep away from the edge!" his grandfather's voice begged him.

But he had reached the edge. The very edge; where dreams place their Judas kiss on reality's cheek. He stopped dead just three or four feet away from the mesmerising sound. The fading phone remained horizontal in his hand's desperate embrace, illuminating the sight in a pathetic spread of light.

The bells were silent.

The sea fog had lifted.

Gold and silver pieces tumbled again and again through elongated fingers, cascading down in an eternal cataract. But even at this distance, Terry could make out little of substance from the priceless downpour of coins and metal, and the hunched shape that shielded its catch from the onlooker was even more obscure. Its vague ebony limbs swept up and down and in the meagre torchlight, their unflagging motion invoked an image of oil-smeared pistons in some demonic factory. If any trace of flesh were there, it was lost deep beneath the enticing hoard.

And then the movement stopped. Its outstretched hands spread like Our Lord's at the Last Supper.

It was like strangling a sodden cloth until its fabric bleeds dry; the flushing water trickling into seeping moisture, until the last drops plunge to the earth. A single dull coin slipped onto the precious mound, its echo resonating around the stone arch before sinking greedily into the lap of the Thames.

His instinct ordered him to run, but Terry declined the fierce urge to claw his way to safety. Instead, he found himself compelled to listen, as a new sound pierced the darkness. The sorrowful weeping of a woman weaved its way between his heartbeat and his breath as the shape shuffled from its lair. The shroud was torn in two, as the expanse of timeworn leather rose up and back, swelling the belly of the boat, and then the creature burst out from beneath the Gothic arch. A flash of ivory crawled from the gloom as the iPhone tumbled from Terry's hand for the final time and summoned into life the yellow eyes of a thousand river rats that slid and clambered towards him.

**

The phone's light crawled upstream for a while afterwards, beckoning an old Victorian bridge into life, until the muddy bank succumbed to the first flow of returning waters and the fading signal fell victim to its thirst.

Chapter Three
Borough Wheel Lock

I want dissimulation to appeare, a friend to those, to whom I hatred beare: I want the knowledge of the thriving art, a holy outside and a hollow heart.

In this, the last year of his long and eventful life, Edward Gallagher had come to accept that he was completely alone in the world, and up until that moment, he had been settled in his solitude. For most of the morning, he'd been sat in his usual chair, his legs submerged under a patchwork blanket and his hands at rest, neatly perched on each arthritic knee.

Now, just an hour later, his worried hands were in his lap, his fingers woven together like strands of flax in a weather-beaten rope. A fat vein snaked along the rugged valleys of each hand like swollen tributaries, whilst blue blood seemed fit to burst, to flood all but the highest peaks, where thick and battered fingernails protruded.

A sealed envelope lay within his grasp and yet, judging by the way that Ted was staring out across the room, he lacked either the inclination or the courage to open it. The television called to him from a million miles away, but Ted seemed to be paying it no mind. His thoughts had strayed far beyond the confines of those walls many years before. His only wish was that he could have gone with them.

Occasionally a smile would trickle across his face, but memories of happier times were few and far between. He possessed only a few photographs as reminders of the past; one of them, a small portrait of his young wife, was perched on his bedside table in a silver frame, her ebony hair cast across one shoulder and her brown eyes beaming from her sepia features.

Before the war.

Before the dark times.

That he had survived for so many years after his wife was taken, still shamed him to the core. Lucy was just twenty-seven years old when she had died, and they had been married but a few months. He was now a not so sprightly pensioner of ninety-eight years. Almost eighty of those had been spent in purgatory.

A frail lady in a pink dressing gown shuffled into the room, singing quietly to herself as she came, but Edward Gallagher's eyes did not waver. He didn't even flinch as she passed ever so slowly across his line of sight, as if he was simply unaware of her presence, or as if he didn't care.

"Excuse me, Mister Gallagher," she whispered whilst waving weakly at the brooding television set in the corner. "Are you watching this programme at all?"

She stood there for a moment, waiting for his permission to switch channels as the multi-coloured lights on the artificial white Christmas tree flashed in turn. Slowly and without raising his eyes, Ted shook his head, but not a word passed his lips.

"Oh good!" she exclaimed and gradually turned away. "It's time for my favourite programme soon," she announced to no one in particular, "so I'll just turn it over and then I'll get comfy." Esther picked up the remote control and pointed it very deliberately across the room, bringing an unremarkable episode of a dated nineteen seventies comedy to an untimely end.

Her chatter continued unabated and soon received an audience, when she was joined in the dayroom by a congregation of other residents, who descended en-masse into the dishevelled array of armchairs. All four watched like a murder of crows as he shuffled quietly from the room, and as the door closed behind him, Ted heard their voices rise, like boisterous children in an unattended classroom.

For the most part, Ted passed his time without too much company. He never sought out companionship, although on occasions it would find him and so now and again, he would concede to a game of gin rummy or dominoes with some of the more able pensioners.

He sometimes wondered what the others had to say about him, behind his back and what they might say about him when his time finally came. Ted knew his own epitaph off by heart, but they wouldn't have had a clue and he'd passed caring what anyone thought of him anymore.

Still, he was curious, sometimes.

He could usually tell when the others had been chin-wagging at his expense, as too many of them could no longer rely upon the speed of reaction that they had once taken for granted. He would arrive in the common room as the chitchat subsided, until a single someone was nudged in the side to clam up in mid-sentence.

It was by no means just the ladies either, the men were even worse. The room would fall silent as he sat down, but one of them would always fall prey to their conscience and so ask him if he would like a cup of tea, or if he had read the morning newspaper yet. He never read the newspapers or listened to the news. There was nothing out there that could possibly be of any interest to him anymore, or so he had come to believe.

For most of the time, Ted was happy in his isolation and the staff was more than happy to keep it that way. After all, Mister Gallagher was no trouble to anyone, unlike a few of the other residents who were a constant challenge. Ted would often find himself staring into the vacated features of some such old gentleman over dinner and would then spend the rest of the evening inspecting his own reflection in his bathroom mirror, in the hope of convincing himself that no similarities had yet appeared.

Too many of them wanted to talk about the good old days, to relive the war years or to remember the Blitz. Ted just wanted to forget it all; for him, there was nothing worth remembering that wouldn't keep him awake at night.

Lucy was always with him, in his waking thoughts and always in his dreams. Talking to him about normal everyday matters, re-assuring him that there was always something to hang on for. On occasions, Ted would answer her out loud and if he happened to be in the dayroom at the time, then the heads would turn, and the sniggering would start.

When visitors arrived, they would hover awkwardly in doorways or behind chairs. It was as if they were taking tea in some recently discovered country, where the local customs have yet to be mastered and where the natives might yet prove to be more dangerous than they looked. Whenever that time came, Ted would dodge his way out as they filtered in and head for the relative sanctuary of his room, or if the weather was agreeable, to the quiet of the gardens.

Ted never had any visitors and never expected to get any. Lucy had died before they'd managed to have a child and there was never anyone who could have displaced her in his heart. So, there were no children and no grandchildren, although he often recalled with a heavy heart how he and Lucy had longed for a child of their own.

A son maybe, or a daughter, it wouldn't have mattered to them.

But Ted was the last of his line and there would be no more.

He had managed to outlive all of his closest friends and those that lingered on were not up to the journey to visit him, even if they'd had the notion to do so. His generation had packed the pages of history, from the calamity of the Great War, in which his father had fought and died, to the necessity of the World War in which he'd played his part. The last thirty years had seen his world transformed into something that he no longer cared to understand. Yet in spite of the computers and the space travel and the seemingly endless quest for speed, they still did not have an answer to everything.

Some things remained beyond the realms of human understanding.

Joe's death had come as a great shock to him, although Ted had known that his friend was seriously ill for some time. The two of them had been through an awful lot together during the early forties and even the passage of well over half a century, could not sever the link that they had forged. He could hardly believe that his old friend and one-time patient had been gone for over a year and Ted missed his increasingly frequent letters that had stopped so suddenly. They hadn't set eyes on each other in nearly a decade, but Joseph's words were alive with his spirit, even now.

Joe always did have the knack for letter-writing; the time he spent with a rifle in one hand and a pen in the other, had presented him with an opportunity to hone his literary skills, an experience that Joe had put to good use after the war.

On reaching the seclusion of his room, Ted shuffled around and carefully locked the door, so that only someone armed with the master key would be able to disturb him. Even then, should a stray hand have rapped upon the wood, he would have had ample warning of the impending intrusion, whilst they fetched the key. He then slid his hand-me-down cane into the old umbrella stand and hobbled across to the desk by the window. With great care, Ted placed the latest letter on the veneer surface, before lowering his weight onto the stiff wooden chair. Then he dragged his legs unwillingly into place before tugging open the right-hand drawer to retrieve a tightly strung bundle of vellum envelopes held together by a wide black ribbon.

As Ted glanced from the pile of letters to the latest delivery, he was left in no doubt; no doubt at all. He had known all along of course, but this simple comparison meant that there could be no mistake.

It was Joe's handwriting. The same swirling style, the same blue-black ink.

But Joseph was dead.

The bulk of their correspondence spanned a period of ten years, but the frequency had gathered pace towards the end. Ted always felt that Joe had been trying to get something off his chest but had never quite managed it, and his death had put paid to that possibility.

Or so he had thought.

It wasn't as if their letters contained the answers to some dark secret, or that each was packed with some fascinating historical reference. Quite the opposite. The two of them had agreed long ago that the past was gone, the history books had been written and no amount of mental regurgitation was going to change that simple fact.

They just agreed that, when it came down to it, silence was the best course of action.

Instead, their ramblings were just that. Joe talked of his family most of the time and Ted had got to know them all so well that he almost felt that they belonged to him, which was no bad thing. The grandson who was off to university, his wife's frequent illnesses, the successes and failures of the local Cricket Club.

Over the last year, he'd been able to keep up with the cricket team's fortunes but having to get by without knowing how Joe's family were getting on had proved quite hard for Ted to come to terms with. Ted had asked Joe's daughter if she would keep in touch with him every now and again, but nothing had come of it and with hindsight, he realised that his request had been a bit of a cheek.

As Ted stared out of his window across the grounds of the modest retirement home, he tried to imagine the consequences of what he was about to do. The part of his brain that belonged to an old-aged pensioner was certain that he didn't want to know the contents of the letter, but the man that he had been years before knew, that there was no choice to be made.

No choice at all.

For Joe's sake, he had to open the letter.

Methodically, he ripped the corner of the sealed flap and inserted a single bony finger. Then, with a slow and deliberate scissor-action, he tore open the envelope and slipped the letter out into the light for the first time in over a year.

As the first few words passed silently from his moving lips, Ted felt a too familiar chill slither from his heels and sensed the goosebumps rise across the ripples of his limp skin.

Dear Ted,

I don't have long left, Teddy-boy. I know that for sure now. The doc's just been around and he wants me to go in, but I'd rather stay with Annie. For an extra few weeks on the sentence, it hardly seems worth it. I'd rather spend what time we have left together without that lot prodding and poking. You know what I think of doctors (no offence, old pal!).

Annie sends her love (honestly). It's a shame that you two never saw eye to eye, but that's the way it goes, I suppose. She just didn't understand what we knew—and I never really explained it to her. I wanted to keep her out of it. You would understand that more than anyone, Ted. She never really blamed you for it, not really. You weren't to blame, Ted. I want you to know that.

(The style changed at this point, as if he'd taken a break for a while. The ink was lighter from this paragraph onwards and the pressure on the page lessened.)

My grandson is in a bad way, Ted. I think he's going under. I haven't seen him in a year and my girl says that he's not interested in seeing me before I go. That hurts, Ted, but that's not the point. There are things I need to tell him before it's too late, but I can't get to him and his dad's not the man for the job. He wouldn't understand. And I don't want to involve Jackie if I can help it, not after keeping her out of it for so long. I know that what I ask is a lot to ask, Ted, but you're my only hope.

You were a good friend, Ted. My grandson will be at the funeral. Just ask someone to point him out to you. Please, can you talk with him then and try to make him listen? I don't know how far things have gone yet and he's a bit of a hothead (runs in the family, eh?). I know that the dreams have started; Jackie told me that he's not been sleeping too good lately.

Please, do your best. I know you will.

It wasn't a bad innings, was it? It would've been nice to have seen a bit more of this new Millennium, but maybe we've seen enough for one lifetime…what do you think?

The twentieth century was ours. I never much cared for the others!
See you on the other side, I hope.
Always your friend.

Joe

Ted hadn't been able to go to Joe's funeral. He'd been too ill to attend and despite his loud and angry protests, the doctors had refused to let him leave the home. There had been no-one who could have argued the case on his behalf and so he'd fallen silent and had wallowed in self-pity for a long time. When he had fully recovered, he wrote to Joseph's daughter to apologise for his absence and to offer his condolences, for what it was worth.

It was she who had been in touch to tell Ted of his friend's death in the first place; a very short and to-the-point discussion with one of the more considerate carers that had shaken Ted to his very soul. Terminal illness was one thing; the finality of death was something else altogether, and it had been the opinion of at least one of the doctors that the sad news had actually brought on the sudden deterioration in Ted's own condition.

Ted knew that Joe would have impressed on his only daughter the importance of letting his old pal know the funeral details, as there was no way that Annie would ever have been persuaded to get in touch. In the end, none of it mattered, until now.

When Ted had recovered sufficiently to make the journey south, it was all too late and although he had thought long and hard about making the effort, just to pay his last respects, he decided then to let sleeping dogs lie. Had he known the plight of Joe's grandson, he would not have hesitated for a moment, however difficult it may have been to get away. But that fact had been kept from him, until now.

What he failed to understand is why the letter had arrived so long after it had been written. The postmark showed that it had been posted only the day before, in East London. Someone had decided to send the letter on to him over a year after its intended date.

Ted was at a loss to understand why, but he knew that there was only one way that he was going to find out.

The time had come, at last.

Chapter Four

Rock Lock

However others doe esteeme of me, yet as I am, I know my selfe to be.

Terry had been wandering through the streets and alleyways of the city for hours, when he finally slumped to his knees at Victoria Coach station at just a little after seven o'clock in the morning.

It wasn't the first time that he'd been left prostrate on the pavement along with the night's discarded leftovers, but on this morning, he found that he couldn't recall where he'd been since the small hours. The exact time had long since ceased to be of any interest to him, but the streets were already in full flow, packed with people that seemed to come from some higher order of primate than the species to which he now belonged.

His recollection of the previous night's trauma was already beginning to take on the familiar hallmark of a Terry Stubbs' memory: frayed at the edges and fading fast. Today, the effect may well have been intentional, but somewhere inside of him, two and two were slowly being dragged together. Later in the day, the calculation would almost be complete, but for now, those events remained as inexplicable as ever.

He remembered the scuffle on the bridge and could recall clambering his way down to the riverside, but not really why he had done so. Looking back, there seemed to be no plausible explanation as to why he would want to do such a thing, other than as an unlikely means of escape. And yet he had done so. No matter how hard he tried, he just couldn't erase the memory of that face, staring back at him through sunken eyes and taut white skin.

Each black tooth conspiring with its neighbour to smile.

"Are ye all rite, mate?"

One gold tooth. Shining.

"Hey, ahm talkin' ti yer," a fellow sub-human with a Glaswegian accent growled, a tattered string of tinsel around his neck and a discarded festive hat perched on his head.

"Ah sid, are ye all rite?"

"Yes, fine, thank you," Terry answered in the voice that had belonged to him a hundred years before. But it was his no longer and it didn't take him long to remember it. "Yes, now just piss off and leave me alone!"

The drunk wandered away, muttering incomprehensible curses in Terry's direction that were interrupted only to take another mouthful of extra strong lager. Terry watched as the last two cans of a newly acquired four-pack swung this way and that, nuzzling against the leg of the drunk's soiled grey trousers. Like a pendulum. A drunk's timepiece and the only kind that either of them needed anymore.

At that moment, Terry's own urge for alcohol was all consuming. So much so that, ignoring the resurgent pains in his side and knee, he forced himself up from the ground with the sole intention of assaulting his Scottish compatriot, to take from him what he most needed. What they both needed. But something held him there, as if he were bound like a ship in port that shifts with the tide and strains to be free.

It had started to rain.

Cold droplets of winter that threatened to shrink into sleet.

Terry's reaction was to sit back down, in spite of the damp that had begun to form on the littered streets. If you could have stood and watched as the drizzle turned to downpour and seen the clamour of pedestrians slumped beneath umbrellas and crouched behind upturned collars, you might have wondered why anyone would sit and suffer as the weather worsened.

For Terry, the cold rain was his salvation for he had remembered the caravan roof. The revitalised memory that had stirred on the bridge washed over him once more, and it was as if a great dam had burst.

The recollection that he had thought buried forever, until it rose to the surface, hand in hand with the rattle of avarice that had sung like a siren and enticed him down.

"It's only the rain, son," his grandfather had said. "Go back to sleep now." But Terry realised then that he had been asleep for too long.

He reached inside his sodden shirt, wincing at the pain in his ribs as his freezing hands delved frantically beneath someone else's coat to pull out the necklace that he had worn every day and night for the last year. As his fist closed around the object, he tugged at it impatiently, but the chain was caught on his zipper and a few more fumbling moments were consigned to history before the medallion was prised into view. As he stared at the unknown words that were emblazoned in Latin across its silver surface, Terry felt a familiar stab of guilt as he remembered the occasions when he had almost parted with it. A few pounds were all that was ever on offer, but it was worth much more than that to him now.

When his grandfather died, after a long illness, Terry had refused to attend the funeral. His father could not forgive him for that and looking back, Terry didn't blame him. His father had a lot to answer for, but the death of Terry's beloved Gramps was not on the list. When Patrick Stubbs arrived back from the crematorium, not a word had passed his lips, but he tossed a piece of tissue paper onto the sofa where his son lay.

"What's this?" Terry asked, raising the heavy metal object to the light, but no answer had been forthcoming. His grandfather's medal awarded for bravery during the last war had meant more to Terry than he could have ever said, but he never got the chance.

"Just get out!" The last words that Terry ever heard from Patrick Stubbs and the last he ever wanted to hear.

He left home that day, and spent the next month moving from house to house and sofa to sofa until the collective patience of his small circle of friends had been thoroughly depleted, and all outstanding favours had been called in. His job had already gone by the wayside a few weeks earlier, and with it went a lifestyle that he had grown accustomed to in the nine months or so that he had been employed.

The hours had been long, but the salary had been incredible for a fresh-faced school leaver and as for the social life—well, that had been something else! The job had been both mentally and physically demanding and mistakes were punished, as he had found out to his cost. He'd been given a second chance after his error had cost a trader a great deal of money, but another one so soon afterwards was not to be tolerated and he was duly escorted from the building on St Mary Axe, his pass confiscated and his career in tatters before it had really begun.

For a few days, he had managed to keep the bad news to himself, but before too long, his mother had guessed his little secret and Jackie Stubbs was never able to keep anything from her husband. Old Pat always knew when she was keeping something from him, and he had a way of making her talk. And so, before the week was out, Terry's father had read him the riot act.

It wasn't that the job had been too much for Terry, not at all. He'd quickly understood the complexities of the trading floor and had soon picked up the alien technology and rapid reflexes required to make money before the opportunity had passed.

It was the dreams that were his undoing.

Of course, his father had blamed the late nights spent with the traders in the city pubs, celebrating the good days or drowning their sorrows on the bad ones, and the lost weekends, recovering from the inevitable Friday night binges. By Sunday morning, he was always shattered, but so were many of the others who worked on the trading floor. It was all part of the game, but he could never have expected his old man to understand that.

From then on, the gospel, according to Patrick Stubbs had formed the basis of a twice-daily sermon around the family home, the latter of the two usually coinciding with chucking-out time at his local pub, The Mourning Crown.

There was a time when Terry and his father had got along quite well; when they had watched West Ham together and enjoyed family holidays in Devon and Cornwall. Like so many other families though, the cracks had begun to appear as his teenage years progressed and the young Terry began to question the wisdom of his father.

The final nail was hammered into the coffin of their relationship when Terry had finally rejected the offer of that university place. Then Patrick Stubbs had been forced to face the world, or rather the world that sat in judgement at the local pub, to tell them that his prophecy was not to come true after all.

His son was not to be the first in a long line of Stubbs to go to University. Jackie's father had been an educated man, but he was a Wilson, not a Stubbs, a fact that Pat took pains to point out whenever the topic came up. The disappointment might not have been so difficult for Pat to bear, had he not spent two years hailing his prophecy from the rooftops after Terry's straight 'A' performance in his GCSEs. And his fellow permanent fixtures at the Crown might not have rubbed it in quite so frequently and with such glee, had he not been so vociferous in his forecasts.

Eventually, the dust did settle, but it was never to be the same again. Indeed, it seemed that his father was merely waiting for the opportunity to say, "I told you so" and when it came, he did so with a vengeance.

The dreams went on and on, gaining in clarity and intensity once Terry was out of work, but other than scaring the living daylights out of him, they had never reached any meaningful conclusion. And once his life on the streets began, they had stopped as suddenly as they'd started. Maybe it was because he then had something real to worry about. Or maybe he was just so tired when he closed his eyes to sleep that the dreams just couldn't penetrate.

He left home with a single suitcase to his name, but there was no blaze of glory as he walked from the house. He had waited until his mother was out doing the weekly shop and his father was asleep upstairs and just left. No note was written. No phone call was made. He just left his house-keys on the telephone table and walked away.

He took with him just a few clothes; by no means all of them, as he had doubted that he would need his night-clubbing gear for a while. He'd had some savings to fall back on as unbeknownst to his father and thanks largely to his mother's inexpensive hospitality, he had managed to put away in excess of a thousand pounds during those nine rollercoaster months. He had hoped that the money would tide him over until work was found, but a new job proved a lot harder to find than he'd anticipated without a decent reference.

In reality, life had just turned out to be more expensive all round and even a modest bedsit had set him back £600 a month. The choice had seemed a good one at the time but looking back, he could never quite recall why he had chosen to look in Southwark, where rents were typically higher than in the suburbs and where the quality of housing was often poor. He had hoped that Social Security would contribute to some of the cost, but his application for assistance was turned down when he told them his story. A reference from the investment bank, stating the reason for his termination, had also put paid to his unemployment benefit for twelve weeks after which time, he was told, he could re-apply.

Twelve weeks had proved to be too long a wait. After three weeks, Terry's money had already run out and whilst he'd managed to find some casual work on the local market for a few days, it was only enough to support a hand-to-mouth existence. The cash had come in handy though and for two consecutive evenings, he'd been able to enjoy some cheap pub grub and a pint or two, but it wasn't to be repeated.

Some of his savings had been spent on a silver chain to which a jeweller had attached his grandfather's medal. The scruffy old man had taken one look at

Terry and offered him a 'few quid' to take it off his hands, which was declined without a second's hesitation.

"You do know that it will be far less valuable if I bore a hole in it, young fella?" the jeweller informed him, disgust scrawled on his wrinkled face like graffiti on a derelict wall.

Terry had explained that it was of sentimental rather than financial value to him and that it was more important that it wasn't lost, which was a constant danger if he carried it loose in his pocket or left it in his unsecured bed-sit.

The jeweller had shrugged his shoulders. "No skin off my nose," he said. "I just thought I'd let you know! Come back in an hour and I'll have it ready for you."

"I'll wait," Terry replied and to the jeweller's undisguised annoyance, he sat down on a rough old dining room chair and did exactly that. When the old man eventually returned, he looked puzzled. As he held the newly formed necklace up to the light, he pointed out to Terry that, at the core of the silver medal, there seemed to be a smaller bronze-coloured coin, the rim of which was clearly visible in the newly forged hole.

"It's rather unusual, to say the least," the old man frowned, but Terry didn't give it a second thought. He just shrugged, paid the man his dues and left.

Later that day, in a moment of weakness, he had considered going back home. He even dialled the number to speak to his mother and had she answered, everything might have turned out differently, but as fate would have it, it was his father's gruff tone that greeted him. Without taking time to ponder the consequences, Terry had slammed the receiver back onto its hook and pushed his way out of the booth.

He never called home again and before too long, even the number had been forgotten as an irrelevance in his new existence.

Yet now, he had seen the steps.

For a moment, he wondered whether last night had merely been the recurrence of the bad dreams that had once plagued him, but it wasn't the steps that he'd stared down that had featured in those nightmares. It was those that he'd looked back at, as he made his way out towards the bridge through the freezing mist that had blocked the opposite bank from his view.

Wooden steps.

Ancient steps.

The rain had stopped, but it had gone on long enough to soak him to the skin. The last time he'd fallen victim to the weather, he had walked for miles in saturated clothes, but it had been a warm day and before too long they'd fully recovered from the onslaught of that summer storm. Terry knew that in these conditions, the freezing temperatures would not be so forgiving, and a resulting bout of flu would be considerably more serious in his present circumstances, than the few days off work that such an illness might once have warranted.

He headed back to the Underground and spent the last of the week's pitiful benefit money on a travel-card and then headed off towards Tottenham Court Road. As he boarded the crowded commuter train, he could smell the concentrated stench of body odour that the rain had stirred up. Yet, for a split second, he didn't recognise it as his own.

When he caught the accusing eye of a pretty girl, he was left in no doubt as to the cause, and she was not alone amongst the silent few who were forced to remain close by in the fading morning rush. She seemed very familiar to him, but as he glanced at her for a second time and offered up an involuntary smile, her reaction very nearly brought him to tears.

It was a look of fear and not a little disgust.

Not for the first time, he bowed his head in shame, choosing instead to stare at his torn trainers as he resisted the urge to flee, to find another carriage in which to conceal himself. She was the kind of girl that he would once have asked out on a date. The kind he would have been proud to have on his arm. The kind he could have loved.

This was not how it was meant to be and so he did the only thing that he could do. He tried to drift away, to escape into his memories. Recollections of his grandparents crowded closer than the passengers could, and they did not scorn or turn their heads away. But through the image of his grandfather, frozen in time at the ripe old age of ninety-five, another scene rose up before him.

The bridge. The ice. That face.

Up until now, it was the latter that had haunted him and as his ragged clothes began to dry, he thought again of the bridge. Its numerous arches. The strange lights from above. The high buttresses on which each arch linked with the next.

Then there was the ice. The frozen river that had stretched out before him. But Terry knew that the Thames didn't freeze, the tides see to that. But he had walked across the water, right up close to the first tight arch. Of that, he was sure.

Terry changed at Oxford Circus for the Central Line, where a timely and less obtrusive train carried him the short journey to his destination. As he emerged back into the morning air, the rain had dried up and the weak sunlight had done its best to polish the surface of the city.

For the first time in a long time, he found that his life had some purpose again. He strode across the crossroads, ignoring the intrusive horns that blasted from more than one direction, climbed the steps in front of the Centre Point tower and walked into the centre for the homeless.

**

An hour and forty minutes later, Terry Stubbs emerged a changed man. He had taken his first shower in many weeks and had managed to find some half-decent clothes from amongst a pile of charitable donations. To any passer-by, he remained what he was, a down-and-out. But at least he had taken one small step back towards the life that was once his.

And now, on this unremarkable winter's morning, he knew exactly what had to be done. But first he needed a drink, from somewhere.

In the end he had to make do with half a cup of flask-coffee donated by a vendor at one of the tourist kiosks. But it was better than nothing and whilst its bland flavour was not to his taste, it aroused every other sense he possessed.

Terry could see his grandfather as if he was there before his very eyes. Laden like a packhorse in the first light of morning. Striding out three-legged across a summer meadow, with his weary but willing grandson at his side.

In Terry's mind's eye, he could hear the cacophony of a long-dead dawn chorus and could smell the sweet scent of the wet grass underfoot. He could feel the early breath of the day against his legs and could taste that same rich coffee that always accompanied them to the hide. Terry could still recall how nervous his grandfather had seemed that day and how he had looked over his shoulder once too often. Even a child of twelve years could tell that he wasn't just checking to see that his grandson was in close pursuit. Such reassuring comments as 'not far now, son' or 'just around that corner,' had failed to mask the old man's nervousness and his gaze always lingered far beyond the boy, over every gate that they passed and across every stile that they climbed.

His 'gammy leg' never stood in the way of his obsession with birdlife, until the last few years when he could no longer navigate the fields and pathways of the Essex countryside. In those final years, he would sit motionless in his wheelchair with a woollen blanket across his knees and watch the garden birds, his field binoculars strangely redundant at his side.

Rarely did the old man speak of the accident. If anyone asked, which they did less and less as he got older, he would call it his 'war wound' and that was usually enough to satisfy whoever was asking. Over the years, Terry had built up his own imaginative version of events from the few scraps that he'd heard.

His version of the story varied widely, depending on the relative knowledge of the unfortunate recipient, from being shot down over enemy lines to being caught and tortured after a foiled attempt to blow up Hitler. Either way, Gramps was a bloody war hero and Terry had always made sure that everyone knew it. Only nowadays, there was no one around to listen. The reality was quite different, but Terry had never heard the full story. Before the funeral, his father had let slip that it was an unexploded bomb that had 'done for him' but he had declined to elaborate.

Patrick Stubbs was never one for reminiscing, but then again, he never had an awful lot to say.

But there was one occasion when his grandfather had hinted at an incident. That cool summer morning at the hide. There was no one else cooped up in there that day, which was unusual as the woodland was a popular spot for ornithologists all year around.

Not on that day.

On that day the place was deserted, save for an eager young boy and a restless old man. As they settled down on the wooden pew and peered out across the misted lake from where a hundred different birds called, the old man turned to thrust his torchlight into each and every crevice of the hide.

"Rats!" he snarled, with a visible shiver. "You can never be too careful, with rats," he muttered quietly, as if too himself. "Bloody things!" In a sudden lull, when the birdsong was silent and the ticking of a watch was the only sound, the gentle old man was suddenly transformed.

"Make it stop," his grandfather commanded, a fierce voice that was not in keeping with the man or the surroundings.

"Make what stop, Gramps?" the confused boy responded, his breath rising in his chest as he sensed the tension that had sunk its teeth into the silence.

"The ticking, the watch. Stop it!" The order was irrevocable.

"I can't, Gramps," Terry stammered.

"Stop it now, boy!" the old man screamed, raising his hand as high into the air as the low ceiling would allow, at which Terry had pulled the elasticated strap from his wrist and thrown the watch out into the field.

At that, his grandfather cried and those tears had scared Terry more than anything that he could remember and until last night, more than anything that had befallen him since.

"Forgive me, my boy," his grandfather had begged. "But it brought back memories. Memories that are best left beneath that damn bridge."

Nothing more was said, but now those words had returned to him and Terry needed to know more. The link was tenuous, but at least it was something, and his grandmother was now his only hope. Of course, there was no guarantee that she would still be talking to him after what he'd done, but the trip had to be worth a try.

The only problem he now faced was how to get out of London without a penny to his name.

Chapter Five
Fourth Lock

The rarest features, and the fairest formes, must dye and rot, and be consum'd with wormes.

It was before dawn when Ted slipped quietly from his room. He had always been an early riser, but he was long out of practice, and he was surprised at just how tired he felt for the loss of only two hours sleep.

As he pushed and pulled his way through the seemingly endless procession of fire-doors, which lay in wait at the end of each strength-sapping corridor, Ted silently rehearsed his excuse. The one that he hoped would persuade the receptionist that this soon-to-be centenarian wasn't in fact attempting to do a bunk on that fine winter's morning. As he made his way through the final double glass doors and out into the foyer, he breathed a sigh of relief that the home's Chief Administrator was not lying in wait for him.

"Morning, Ted!" hailed the cheerful care assistant from the front desk, where a tiny desktop Christmas tree flashed and played a festive tune at the sound of her voice. "And where do you think you're going at this time of day then?"

Ted smiled and thanked his lucky stars that the girl on duty was one of the more amenable members of the staff.

"Well, Gillian," Ted began in his very best of British accent, as he stifled a cough that may have given the impression that he was about to recite a well-rehearsed explanation. Which, of course, he was. "I found myself wide awake a couple of hours ago and now I'm bored stiff, so I thought, as it is such a beautiful day, that I'd take a short stroll down to the corner shop."

He waited with bated breath for her reply, half expecting his best laid plan to be scuppered before it had even got started. As no response was forthcoming, he thought that he'd push his luck just a little more.

"I want to buy some mints," he went on. "I'm clean out of them and I can't get through the day without my mints, as you know," which he was certain that she didn't. "Can I get you anything while I'm there?"

The middle-aged woman paused and like some mid-West gambler who has just been dealt a losing poker hand, she looked Ted straight in the eye as if to read his true intentions. But Ted's nerve held and with a calm assurance that belied his age, he returned her gaze and smiled his best old gentleman smile into the bargain.

It worked.

"Oh, go on then," the girl conceded. "But don't be too long and get that coat on or you'll catch a chill and then I'll be for the high jump!"

She rounded the high fronted desk and lifted the wad of keys from her waistband to unlock the front door. As she moved into view, Ted tucked his small satchel further out of sight beneath his folded overcoat, which he promised faithfully to put on as soon as he was outside. For one dreadful moment Ted thought that she was about to insist that he was properly dressed before allowing him out into the cold air, a request that would undoubtedly have revealed his true hand and put paid to his little daytrip.

But she didn't, and as Ted negotiated his way down the steeply sloping driveway towards the busy road, he was glad to see that the sky had already turned a lighter shade of blue. As he stooped and shuffled into the waiting taxi that he'd instructed to wait out of sight around the corner, he found himself faced with another unwelcome inquisition, so much so that he was forced to repeat his request.

"Train station!" Ted ordered for the second time, less politely than before.

Again, the driver did not respond, and as he deliberated, he shot the old man a suspicious look before slipping the car into gear.

Ted tried to avoid making any further eye contact, but he could sense the man's unease, as every now and again the driver would stare intently into his rear-view mirror, to heighten his aged passenger's undeniable sense of guilt. The driver was clearly curious as to why an apparently very old O.A.P. would creep unaccompanied from his retirement home at such an early hour, without so much as a porter to carry his bag.

Before too long, his curiosity got the better of him.

"So where are you heading so bright and early then?" the gruff driver enquired. "I was told not to sound my horn," he revealed with raised eyebrows, almost accusing Ted that something sleazy just had to be behind his dawn flit. "Just sit and wait, I was told, and you'd be out on time."

The balding man paused for a second, anticipating an answer that never came, but he didn't take the hint and instead took Ted's silence as his cue to continue. "And then out you popped, right on time, so c'mon old man, let me in on it! You look a bit too old, if you don't mind me saying so, to be making day trips!"

The last comment made the driver chuckle beneath his small round spectacles in a manner that reminded Ted a little too much of Heinrich Himmler. The similarity was so unnerving that Ted found himself quite unable to banish a sudden and irrational sense of hatred towards him, which had risen from the pits of his stomach. Had he not been in such a hurry to make the early train, Ted felt quite sure that he would have asked the driver to stop and would have walked the rest of the way, in spite of his age!

Instead, Ted decided that the annoying little aficionado would have to get by for the rest of the day without knowing where his first fare of the morning was creeping off to.

"Mind your own business and concentrate on your driving, why don't you!" Ted scolded. "I'm going to the railway station, that's all you need to know!" and with that, he sat back in his seat and closed his eyes in defiance.

On his arrival in the station forecourt, Ted found that there were a few minutes to spare before the train was due in. Yet he still managed to resist the urge to buy a newspaper for the first time in years, but he did succumb to a packet of mints for the journey. His train was on time and he was pleased to find that, despite the morning rush, he was able to get a seat to himself.

As the journey unfolded, the sense that he was heading into something that he could no longer deal with intensified, but with it there came a sense of destiny, a feeling of inevitability. For the last ten years, he had not lived, but had simply existed. An old man, alone, with only one friend in the whole world of any note and when that sole ally had finally departed this life, Ted had become acutely aware that his time was almost up.

Over the years, he had learned his lesson well, that for life to have any meaning at all, a man had to have some reason to exist. At times these last few years, as his body weakened and his mind retreated, he had almost lost sight of his. Sometimes, he would just sit and wonder how long there was to go, but he didn't contemplate his own death with fear or even with sadness. Death was the only sure thing in life and his life had been far longer than many that he could think of, and for that he remained thankful.

Now, in his final days, months or years, his life had a purpose again. He was about to cast a stone into life's eternal river and although the ripples might pass without witness, someone might just be washed ashore on the waves.

If things had gone as far as he suspected, then that someone's life may be in danger and that possibility, however slim, made the long trip and its repercussions worthwhile. Saving lives had once been his business and he had saved a few, especially during the war and in its immediate aftermath. He'd seen a few lost too and Joe had been a lot closer to joining that unwelcome roll call than anyone.

Unexploded bombs were a menace.

Ted had seen children maimed and crippled by them, but they were the lucky ones. Many more had been lost without trace; soldiers, like Joe and civilians too, as Ted knew only too well. Men of the Royal Engineers, specialist bomb disposal sections, Britain's 'death or glory boys', as they were known. Men that had risked and lost their lives to save the lives of strangers.

Would men today do the same?

Somehow, Ted doubted that they would.

Ted had got to know Lance Corporal Wilson as he recuperated from serious injury during the blitz. Ted's immediate prognosis was that the man would never walk again, but on that point, medical opinion was to be proved wrong. He was in an awful state, the explosion having blasted shrapnel into his lower body and one rather vicious piece had sliced a wound down the length of his right leg. Gangrene had been a distinct possibility and so antibiotics had been pumped into him, but for a few weeks it was touch and go. And then there was the fever.

The fact that the bombsite had been so close to the hospital may well have been the crucial factor in deciding Joe's fate. Had the bomb fallen further upstream rather than nestling in the soft mud around the bridge, it would have taken far longer for the medical corps to transport him through the carnage to the nearest hospital. An on-the-spot amputation would probably have resulted, the shock of which could well have killed him.

In any case, in the days that followed, the hallucinations that the young soldier had been forced to endure were, by all accounts, almost unbearable. During the first few days, the nurses had told Ted, during his frequent but impromptu visits, that Joe's nights were often restless. He would cry out over and over again and wake in such terror that sedatives had been prescribed on more than one occasion. Such manifestations were not uncommon during the war though and many people were not so lucky. At least Joe had survived his terrible injuries.

Ted's own injuries, whilst not physical, had not faded with the years. In many ways, the emotional carnage had proven even more difficult to bear and Ted had spent too long after the war, sifting through the wreckage in search of something to salvage of his life. In the end, when he had finally accepted that there was nothing there to find, he had somehow found the strength to start again.

Long before the train drew into London, Ted had fallen asleep as the effect of his expedition took its toll. But as the train neared its destination, he awoke to the unwelcome sight of another man's groin, positioned uncomfortably close to his face. The carriage was packed with motionless commuters and Ted realised with sudden regret that his timing could not have been worse.

It was the dreaded morning rush hour.

When the train finally ground to a halt, he lowered himself gingerly onto the platform, much to the annoyance of the waiting passengers who bobbed and jostled in the narrow aisle behind. Ted pretended not to notice as he hobbled towards the crowd that was building at the ticket barrier, like a medieval mob baying for blood. As he waited his turn with more patience than all his fellow commuters put together, he was left feeling distinctly out of place.

He remembered a London from another age. A city of bowler hats and pin-striped suits. Of bankers, businessmen and smartly dressed secretaries. Where people rushed to work, but still had time to pass the time of day with one another or to say, 'excuse me' or 'good morning'. As he made his way into the scrum that is Liverpool Street Station at eight-thirty on any weekday morning, Ted thought that he'd taken a wrong turning somewhere along the line and had ended up in Bedlam.

As he ventured out onto the main thoroughfare, he spotted a flower-stand through the crowd of bodies and on the spur of the moment, he decided to pick up a bunch of carnations. He was forced to shuffle through the flow of human beings to reach his target, but he found that playing the frail-old-man card worked quite well, especially if he pushed his stick out a few feet in front of him and, with an apologetic smile, tripped the occasional passer-by.

He bought a bunch of red ones, at an extortionate price, but something told him that his date was going to need a pick-me-up. In any case, carnations always reminded him of Lucy and that was no bad thing.

In the melee, he was unsure of the direction that he should take and after making several requests for help, Ted was fortunate enough to find one helpful young lady who pointed him in the direction of the Underground. She also advised him to get on a District Line train to Bow, but those directions had not changed in four decades and that gave him a strange sense of comfort. As he struggled across the concourse and into the funnel of stairways, his walking stick proved its worth again as he did battle with the commuters.

There was more buffeting and barging to endure, before he finally found himself heading east on the District Line for the first time in many years. As he passed through Aldgate and on towards Whitechapel, he closed his eyes, lest his sight should settle on some relic of another age, when an altogether different tube station had dissected the line on the old Whitechapel Road.

He'd been in touch with London Transport the night before, to remind himself of the nearest tube station to the family's home in the East End. He just hoped that Joe's daughter had not since moved from the address that she had given in her fateful letter and in that respect, he was in luck. The family hadn't left their long-time residence, but as it turned out, they may as well have moved to Australia.

As he stood shivering on the doorstep waiting for a response to his gentle knock, he became aware of the intensity of the cold for the first time that day. He'd caught another taxi from the tube station, even though it was a mere five minutes away, but even in his heavy winter coat, the chill somehow reached inside. He put it down to old age.

Just as Ted was about to knock again, a heavy-set man, who turned out to be Joe's son-in-law, answered his call. Ted was left shaking on the doorstep as he was forced to explain the reason for his visit through the gap between the doorjamb and the flaking red paintwork.

"Oh, so you knew the old man, did you?" Patrick Stubbs barked, a cigarette burning in his hand. "Well, I suppose you'd better come in then," he said somewhat reluctantly, quickly turning up the decibels to shout over his shoulder to his wife. The offensive man then slammed the door, only to slip it off the latch, before opening it again and retreating just a foot to let Ted squeeze inside.

"Did you hear me? We got company, one of yer dad's old army mates," he roared as Ted followed in his footsteps into their cramped but immaculate parlour. Ted did not bother to put him right on his assumption. "I thought it was the bloody carol singers again," he cursed. "I was about to tell 'em to sling their hook, thieving bastards!"

In sharp contrast to her husband, Joe's daughter was very pleasant and seemed happy enough with the flowers. She offered him a home-made mince pie with tea, which he declined on account of his diabetes, although a couple of Rich Tea biscuits were a welcome, but strictly forbidden, substitute.

At first, Ted found it hard to accept that the woman who cowered before him was the same bright-eyed girl that he had once known. He had last laid eyes on her at her sixteenth birthday party, when she had lit up the room with her laughter. It looked to Ted like she had not managed a smile much since then. She looked older than he had imagined she would, but as he quickly totted up the years, he realised with some surprise that she must now be in her fifties.

Any pleasantries that passed between them were short-lived and when a pause in the conversation became too excruciating to bear, Ted decided to breach the subject of their son.

"Does Terry still live here?" Ted asked quite innocently, but the question was met with a look from Patrick Stubbs that could have caused serious injury. "Only, I sort of promised Joe," Ted added, hesitating for a second before meekly riding out the rest of his pre-planned sentence, "that I'd look in on him, from time to time."

For a few moments, nothing was said as Patrick stared at his wife, until she looked away to inspect the spotless carpet that she had vacuumed only half an hour before. Eventually, and not unexpectedly, it was the husband's voice that broke the awkward silence.

"If it's him yer looking for, then you'll be disappointed," he snapped, taking a hefty drag on his third cigarette, but he didn't seem to be counting. "You've probably got a better idea of where that lazy sod is than we 'ave. He's been gone for twelve months or more, ever since the funeral, so you've wasted your time comin' 'ere if that's what yer after!"

Pat didn't even bother to ask Ted why he was looking for their son, or why Joe thought that his grandson needed a very old guardian angel. It was immediately clear that he just wanted him to leave, and in the circumstances, Ted was more than happy to oblige.

As he stepped outside, the temperature seemed to have dropped a degree or two more and Ted quickly pulled his scarf up around his neck and secured his top button as a last line of defence against the wind. He was suddenly aware of the pain in his knee, and he knew from bitter experience that, come the following morning, he would have to pay for this day's exertions.

Joe's daughter saw him to the door and made an apology of sorts for her husband's behaviour.

"I got your letter about my dad," she said, a little brighter now that she was out of doors. "I'm sorry that I never wrote back to you, but I'm not much of a letter writer," she confessed, "and we've had our own problems, as you can see. We've had another bereavement recently, just to add to our woes," she told him, sucking on her own cigarette for comfort. "My mum died two weeks ago and so I've not been at my best, haven't even found the time to put the Christmas decorations up yet."

"Oh, I am sorry," said Ted. "I knew Annie well, please accept my condolences," at which point, the distraught woman began to cry.

"I found a letter amongst mum's things," she explained, as if to deflect the attention away from herself. "It was addressed to you and so I forwarded it on, did you get it?" She seemed about to say something more until her husband's voice boomed from inside and so, after putting her fag out on the bare wooden windowsill, she turned to obey her master's voice without further hesitation.

"Yes, thank you, I received it," but sensing that time was short, the old man kept his conversation brief. "If you do hear from Terry," Ted asked quickly, "could you let me know?"

"We won't," she replied. "His dad will kill him if he dares show his face around here again!"

"But, if you do…"

"I know where to find you," she answered meekly. "Now I really must go and so should you, I'm sorry."

She smiled the kind of smile that carries with it a hundred different meanings, closed the door on the draught and cut off her chief tormentor's rising voice in mid flow. But even through the closed door, Ted still heard a thud that he didn't much like the sound of.

Before the roof had fallen in on their conversation, he had asked for directions to where his old friend had been lain to rest but was disappointed to learn that he'd been cremated and like many Londoners before him, his ashes had been scattered into the river.

He would have liked a final chat with Joe, but even that simple wish had been denied him.

As he made his way back to the tube station, he was left to reflect on a journey that had begun in hope, but like so many others in his life, had ended in disappointment.

Chapter Six
Fifth Lock

A man may seeme too just, too full of wit, but to be too good, never man was yet.

It arrived as expected, late on that Wednesday morning.

Jake spied its approach from the master bedroom and watched as it glided down the Avenue, occasionally winking at him, white and silver in the morning sunlight. As soon as he was certain of its destination, he sprang from the wooden window seat that overlooked the front of the house and leapt down the stairs, two treads at a time.

"It's here!" he shrieked, without expecting to hear much by way of reply.

His first company car and his reward for three years of graft and disappointment. One of life's milestones—like passing his exams, graduating from university with a useless degree or starting his first decent job in spite of it. He'd been crowing about it for weeks and finally here it was, his own brand-new BMW and the best Christmas present he'd ever had. It was only a basic model and according to his associates, it was *nothing to get too excited about*, but for a glorified salesman like Jake Harvey, it would do for starters.

As he opened the front door, he glanced back towards his wife who had looked up from her computer momentarily, before pulling the study door shut so that she could complete her conference call in peace. Jake thought he heard laughter coming from the tiny room and for a second he wondered if it was at his expense, but he told himself that he didn't care. This was his moment and no one was going to spoil it for him. He stepped outside and gazed up the short driveway and out through their wrought iron gates towards the still empty street.

He and Lisa had chosen the car together, although when it came down to a straight choice between the Audi and the Beamer, his wife had lost the argument.

She had been teasing him incessantly at his childish impatience, as continued delays in delivery had left him cursing his selection. Now that it had finally arrived, he was determined to bask in the glory of the moment and everyone who was anyone was going to know about it.

At the end of the longest minute of his life, the new car came to a stop at the top of the driveway. Its alloy wheels were raised high on the pavement and in the white light of that winter morning, it seemed to Jake that there was no-one behind the steering wheel. He used his hand as a shield, but the sun was so low that he could not see a soul in the light. Then he heard the conspicuous creak of a car door and the high-pitched rap of scampering footsteps, hurrying towards the rear of the vehicle. Yet the driver's identity remained obscured behind their overgrown hedge, which should have been attended to months before.

In a sudden flush of annoyance, he strode up the path to confront the delivery man, but on reaching the top he was surprised to see the sturdy frame of a fair-haired woman, standing with her hands on her hips just a few feet away from him. It was obvious to his now watching wife that the woman was merely going through the formalities of looking the car over before finally relinquishing responsibility, but something in her manner persuaded Jake otherwise.

In that moment, he became convinced that she had uncovered some problem with the rear lights in the course of her short journey and was now trying to work out how the car could possibly have passed through quality control in such a state. He felt a stab of panic, certain that his long-awaited status symbol was about to be ushered away before he'd even had the pleasure of showing it off.

"Good morning," Jake called out, expecting a civil response, but none was forthcoming. It was as if she hadn't seen him. "Is something the matter?" he shouted, a little more insistent this time, but still she didn't acknowledge him, as if she hadn't heard a single word he'd said, or as if he wasn't there at all.

Without further hesitation, Jake walked purposefully towards her, but her sights remained fixed on the car and as he closed in, he heard her mutter something inaudible under her breath. As Jake's right foot reached the head of her long morning shadow, she at last lifted her eyes to meet with his, but a second or two more passed into history before she finally stuttered into life.

"Hi, hello, sir," she mumbled, rather too loudly to travel the few inches that now separated them. "Mister, mister Harvey, is it?"

Jake nodded in confirmation, offering his hand, but finding it hard to offer much sympathy for her inexplicable behaviour. "Is there something wrong?" he asked, still certain that there was something amiss.

She paused for a sharp intake of cold suburban air, before reassuring her first customer of the day that all was well. "No, it's fine," she smiled, "no problem! It's just that," she started to say, but whatever she was planning on saying, it never materialised. "No, it's fine. It's fine!"

It was clear that she wasn't at all convinced, but there was the paperwork to take care of and after finally apologising for her lateness, she began with the ceremonial hand-over. "The traffic on London Bridge was diabolical this morning," she explained in a delayed attempt to make up for her earlier curtness. "Roadworks I suppose, though I didn't see any. Took me an age to get across, I reckon I'd have been here an hour ago if not for that!"

As Jake faked a modicum of sympathy with a withering smile, a copy of the corporate insurance policy passed between them, together with the card for windscreen replacement services and an online form that required his digital signature. Though he wasn't the registered keeper, it was his name that they needed as proof of receipt and he was more than happy to scrawl his mark across the screen as many times as she needed it, if it meant that he would soon be free of her.

"The manual's in the glove compartment," she said as he handed back her tablet. Jake motioned to move towards the driver's door, his eagerness to get behind the wheel getting the better of him, but she stopped him in his tracks, leaning in front of him to snatch the keys rudely from the ignition before he could retrieve them.

She juggled with them for a moment as if unwilling to relinquish control, until finally slipping the two gunmetal keys unceremoniously into his grateful hands.

"Thank you," he said more in relief than appreciation, as his fist closed around them. The moment had arrived at last. A dull incision of cold metal helped him dismiss the unwelcome woman from his thoughts, as his eyes took in his new pride and joy.

"Can you tell me how to get to the nearest train station?" the smiling woman intruded, seemingly a little happier with life and less perplexed now that her duties were complete.

"The nearest station is a good fifteen minutes' walk away," explained Jake and suddenly feeling a little sorry for her, he made a half-hearted offer of a lift. The thought of playing the Good Samaritan was not his main concern though. He just wanted an excuse to get behind the wheel without further delay.

"I'll be okay," she said, backing away from him and the car. "I could do with the walk." It was clear from her response that she was keen to vacate the scene as fast as her short legs would carry her.

"Are you sure you're alright?" he pressed, doing his utmost to appear concerned.

"Let me know," she said, ignoring his offer, "if you have any problems, with it."

"Oh, it'll be fine," Jake assured her, missing the point. "It looks great!"

"Let me know though, won't you, if anything crops up, I mean?" she persisted, reaching out to clutch his arm and to wrest his attention from the prize before him. "Here's my contact details," she added almost as an afterthought, scribbling down an additional number onto her firm's standard business card, which Jake took to be her own business mobile number.

"Thanks." He shrugged, tucking the card neatly into his wallet behind a photo-booth snap of an old girlfriend that should have been disposed of long ago.

"I will," he said, a little bewildered. "If anything should go wrong, you'll be the first on my list."

She sensed the sarcasm in his voice and feeling a sudden flush of embarrassment, she bid him an equally curt farewell, leaving Jake Harvey to discover for himself that all was not well with the vehicle that he would now call his own. When he looked up again from the seductive curves of his new car, she had reached the turn in the road, and seconds later had passed completely out of view, heading in the general direction of the local station.

For a few more seconds, Jake stood by the driver's door and stared after her, wondering to himself if she'd had a near miss on her delayed journey from the dealership on the south side of the river, which had rendered her unfit for duty.

"That must have been it," he thought out loud and with a wry smile added, "Either that or she's a few bricks short of a bungalow!"

"What was that?" his wife called from the doorstep; her new fluffy slippers visible beneath her matching purple dressing gown. "What's it like, is it nice?"

"That's what you call 'service with a shake' babe!" he shouted back, but Lisa shook her head and shrugged her shoulders to indicate that she couldn't hear him, before rushing back towards the sound of her office ringtone. Jake wasn't disappointed to hear that familiar but instantly forgettable jingle, for it meant that his new possession could now receive his undivided attention. He wasted no time and in seconds, he was hunched inside the luxurious leather interior of his new motor car.

The driving position needed immediate adjustment to accommodate his six-foot frame.

His hand delved deep beneath the seat to pull at the lever and using all of his weight, he slid the seat back until his feet were comfortably balanced on the cushioned pedals. He ran an uncertain finger across the endless array of instruments; the leather-topped gear stick, the electric window controls, the settings for the air-conditioning and the Bluetooth entertainment system. He breathed in the sumptuous scent of a freshly registered motor vehicle and his eyes were lost in facts and figures that beckoned to him from behind the steering column.

The figures on the milometer hung ominously at 000066.6, but in that moment, the implication of the numbers failed to register.

Having made himself comfortable, he reached up to adjust the rear-view mirror when a dull glint of metal caught his eye against the black upholstery of the passenger seat. Something was tucked into the crease between the padded seat and the backrest, and at this distance he guessed that the ditzy driver had dropped some loose change in her rush to get away. As he leaned over and pulled the object unwillingly into view, he realised with some astonishment that his guess had been only half-right.

It was a coin, but it was not a familiar one and he almost dismissed it as some worthless foreign shrapnel, until its date came into view. As it did, Jake almost dropped it in amazement.

1663.

"Holy crap!" Jake blasphemed in the sudden understanding that the piece of metal in his hands was over three hundred and fifty years old. As he pondered its origins, he found himself wondering how many soiled hands had closed around it in that time?

It was clearly not from the Royal Mint as the coin bore no monarch's head, but the inscription was clear enough. IN SOVTHWARK stood proud around the circumference of one side and the words HIS HALF PENY were squeezed within a coiled circle, which was similar in its threaded pattern to that of his own gold rope chain from which his Saint Christopher's medallion hung. As Jake flipped the coin nonchalantly over, the initials TR came boldly into view. The letters were embossed, like hardened arteries, on the copper surface of the coin opposite the date and at its centre, the raised ridge of two oars were crossed, as if in preparation for some ancient crucifixion.

Without thinking too much about the possible consequences, Jake slipped his new-found piece of history into his pocket and turned his mind to the more pressing needs of the day.

Or at least he tried to, but for a few minutes he could not recall the chores that needed his attention, and his senses were clogged with misplaced feelings that crowded in on his own. When he tried to describe the experience later to his wife, the closest analogy that he would be able to come up with was a feeling of drunkenness, but that wasn't it.

It was more like a sudden seasickness had blurred his vision, distorting his sight in a kaleidoscope of images that danced and moved before him. Afterwards, he could only recall one of them.

A drifting abandoned boat.

The feeling passed quickly, a momentary urge to vomit that he would later put down to a 'funny turn'. It was vanquished only by the turn of the key and a delightful mechanical purr, that made him moan in response. But it was not to be an isolated incident and over the next few days, his mind would wander far from his own shores again and again.

Lisa had asked him to mail a few letters that morning and so, the post-box at the end of the next road was his first point of call on a quick tour of duty. He flung the assorted envelopes onto the passenger seat and then flicked the switch that deactivated the electronic handbrake. As his foot pressed down on the accelerator, he could hardly hear the engine at all and except for the sweetest sigh, it was difficult to be sure that it was even running. As he slid the car into first gear, his right foot flexing deeper onto the pedal, his nervousness was banished, although he still winced a little at the slight bump as its shining silver wheels eased gently off the kerb.

Silent childhood memories stabbed at the slight jolt; the seesawing sensation in the park, the one just across the street from where he was born and raised. A sickly somersault in the depths of his stomach, as the brightly coloured bench skimmed the hot concrete beneath. His long dead brother waving cheerfully at him from above, perfectly framed against an unblemished sea of sky.

He reached the end of the road a few moments later, disappointed that a neighbour had not been there to notice him behind the wheel, but he would be able to enjoy that proud moment before too long, he would make sure of it. There was nothing approaching from the right on their quiet suburban road, so he pulled away left and accelerated quickly to thirty miles per hour, but his joy was short-lived, and he was soon forced into a sharp stop as he came close to forgetting all about the post-box.

"Shit!" he cursed under his breath, grasping at the crumpled pile of letters, "almost forgot about you!" Jake plucked them from the warm leather of the passenger's seat and eased his way out of the car. It wasn't until he raised the wad of letters to the grinning pillar-box that he noticed the rugged pattern that was now strewn across them. It reminded him of a sun-baked riverbed after months of drought and each looked like it had been ironed flat, after being squashed under a significant weight.

But he didn't allow the moment to perplex him for long.

He always treated the inexplicable with contempt and this particular observation was not about to be an exception. He dismissed it without a thought and was soon back beside his new car, key fob at the ready. He didn't expect to meet with any resistance as he simultaneously pressed the black box and lifted the handle, but his fingers were left smarting, as the door refused to budge.

"Damn it," Jake shouted in surprise, shaking his hand in a bid to rid himself of the tingling sensation, as he realised that the car was already locked. He had never been a big fan of central locking, ever since he had managed to disable a hire car in the centre of Manchester on a busy Friday afternoon. It always seemed to be too easy to depress the control by accident, thus securing the car and enabling the alarm in the process. He pressed the alternate button a couple of times more and the central locking obeyed his command without further fuss.

After completing a brief circuit of the estate, he returned home, squeezing the car down the driveway and parking it firmly in gear. It was a habit that he had inherited from his late father, an extra piece of insurance just in case the car should unexpectedly slip from its mooring and slide forward the three or four inches, to smack up against the up-and-over garage doors. Then with the driver's manual in hand, he left the car to its own devices and set off towards the kitchen to work his way through the documentation.

However, before going into the quiet of the house, he felt compelled to take one final glance over his shoulder, as if he had been tapped from behind or heard the call of a familiar voice.

The passenger door was open.

It wasn't half-shut or just ajar, it was wide open, gaping on its hinges as if enjoying a joke at its new owner's expense. It struck him as strange, but he had a ready-made explanation to hand as whilst he had not opened the door on the passenger's side, the woman who delivered it must have, especially if she'd been mooching in the glove compartment for the manual.

She'd left the door clinging onto its lock and when he'd driven down his steep driveway, gravity had done its thing. It was simple and perfectly reasonable as explanations went, and he wasn't about to let himself think otherwise, even though the lingering impression remained that someone had just stepped out onto their path to follow him all the way home.

"Don't be daft!" he said out loud, as he crunched his way back up the gravel path and slammed the door shut, as if to teach his new charge a short sharp lesson. As his fingers snapped tightly around the controller once more and the sidelights flashed an instant mocking reply, his fidgeting smile came to a sudden stop as if he'd just been slapped by some unseen hand.

Nothing had happened, but there was something eating away at him, and just like the despatch driver before him, Jake Harvey couldn't quite put his finger on what it was.

He stood there for a moment in the doorway, until the cold got into his bones. Then he turned on his heels and entered the house, abandoning the car for the first time, giving it ample time to get accustomed to its new surroundings.

**

"So how is it?" yelled Lisa Harvey as she emerged from the cubbyhole that she called a study, her calls with the Asian head office complete for the day. She headed straight for their fully fitted galley kitchen to quiz her husband at the breakfast bar.

"Isn't it great," Jake answered as his wife kissed him hello. He didn't mean it as a question; its greatness wasn't in question! "Maybe we can go out for a spin in it later?" he added, her silence encouraging him to go further. "Do you fancy a trip over to the Smiths, we can drop off their Christmas presents?"

His wife didn't answer; the look that she gave him was answer enough.

Jake's best mate was not in favour anymore, ever since their infamous house-warming party when Steve had drunk too much red wine and had been sick in technicolour red all over the new carpet. They'd had to buy a huge rug just to cover up the stubborn stain.

They did go out briefly that evening, but only drove for a few miles. Both of them were tired and as another early start loomed, they decided to retire early for the night. It was getting colder and as they pulled up outside their suburban semi, a frost was already gathering on the grass. Fifteen minutes and one cup of cocoa later, at half past ten, they were side by side in bed and within five minutes, Lisa was in a deep sleep.

Jake felt himself drifting away, but his legs kicked him awake as he imagined falling from the car onto the road below and the jolt forced him to open his eyes before he hit the ground. That free-fall feeling was a sensation that he had experienced at irregular intervals, ever since boyhood. He figured that other people had to cope with strangers dancing on their grave, when sudden chills infiltrate the marrow of their bones, or some other such affliction.

He was doomed to trip over a precipice, to fall off a ladder or to go head over heels down a flight of stairs, whenever his body was just on the verge of sleep. There was probably a medical term for it, but whatever it was called, the result was always the same and his eyes would spring open just before the impact. Someone had once told him that if ever you hit the ground in these half-conscious moments, then you wouldn't wake up again. He didn't believe such tales by any means, but all the same, he wasn't all that keen to be the first in the queue to try it out.

It was then that the phone rang, but it wasn't that late and so the intrusion came as no great surprise. Whilst it wasn't uncommon for one of Lisa's endless collection of friends to call just before eleven for a late chat, there were one or two people that he had hoped not to hear from again.

As he pondered the possibility that one of his less memorable associates may have learned of his move south, he glanced nervously at his wife to see if she had been disturbed, before deciding whether to answer it or not.

He couldn't tell for sure, but he noted that her breathing was not as steady as it had been and so he would keep the conversation short and sweet. If they were looking for a chinwag, they were going to get short shrift from him. He leaned across and grabbed clumsily at the handset, but it slipped from his grasp and fell to the floor with a cushioned thump.

"Bugger!" he said through gritted teeth, as he rolled out of the bed, eventually reaching the phone after a bit more fumbling. "Hello?" he mumbled, but there was no reply.

The settling sound that greeted him hissed in a gentle rustling hush; quieter than dry parchment crackling on a fire or a line of tall trees bending in an autumn wind. For the second time in twenty-four hours, he found himself thinking of his childhood, listening with awe to a sea-shell's soothing sigh, as if in fond recollection of its former resting place.

It ended with a familiar click, and Jake was left fuming.

His fingers fumbled their way across the buttons, and after two failed attempts, he finally managed to dial the number that he hoped would reveal the identity of the late-night prankster. Even though nothing had been said, any unidentified call was unnerving at the best of times, and Jake took such invasions of his privacy personally. As the automated voice at the other end repeated the source of the call for the second time, Jake was none the wiser for hearing it again, but the first few digits suggested that it had been made from a mobile phone.

The number seemed vaguely familiar to him, but as he contemplated the long array and tried to match them up with his extensive list of shady friends, that sense of familiarity quickly dissipated into the darkness of the witching hour. As he hit the redial option in an action that he would later regret, he was primed for a confrontation, but the number rang out and another automated answer confirmed that there was no response.

He declined the invitation to leave a message and gently placed the receiver back into its cradle, hoping against hope that the disturbance had not awoken his wife or aroused her suspicions.

"Who was it?" his wife asked dashing any hope of a lucky escape. He pulled the king-sized duvet over his shoulders and let his experience do the talking.

"No-one babe, wrong number," was his brief but unconvincing answer, yet it seemed to satisfy Lisa who was soon snoring again.

Sleep did not come so easily for her husband that night.

Chapter Seven
Roger Lock

Thus they were scorned, despised, banished, excluded from the Church alive and dead, alive their bodies could no harbour have, and dead not be allowed a Christian grave: thus was the Countrye's kindnesse cold and small, no house, no Church, no Christian burial.

Terry's journey out of London was even more difficult than he'd expected and long before he reached his destination, a dark and brooding bank of cloud had devoured the early evening stars. Without a penny to his name, Terry had done his best to hitch his way east, but it proved to be a tall order for the scruffy, malnourished vagabond he had become. As he trudged along in the wake of a spiteful stream of cars and lorries that hissed and spat as they trundled past, his injured knee offered up a thousand reasons for him to give up and his feet had come out in monstrous blisters, but he steadfastly ignored them all.

The choice that he faced was a very simple one.

He could turn on his heels and return to face an uncertain but bleak future, or he could take another even less certain path. Whatever the latter held, it had to offer something more and so, the choice was made. It was a 'no-brainer', as his old friends in the city would have said.

At the outset of his trek that day, when the first rains had revitalised his heart and soul, Terry had purchased a ticket that allowed him back onto the almost impenetrable Underground system. When he had finally reached the last stop on the Eastbound Central Line, he'd already travelled well outside of his permitted limits, but the prospect of a heavy fine was the least of his worries. Without a second's thought to the consequences, he had leapt over the ticket barrier, ignoring the fading pains in his side, and quickly fled into the surrounding streets.

When finally, he could no longer hear the protestations of the ticket inspector, he had slowed to an awkward canter and then, out of breath and with his heart still pounding, he had begun to walk, limping along at a steady pace.

After a short while, Terry's nerves had settled enough to allow him to kick the by then familiar habit of glancing over his shoulder in anticipation of a pursuit, and he was only then able to turn his thoughts to the present. A few wrong turnings lay ahead, before he was convinced that the general direction in which he was headed was indeed the right one, and he was thankful that the heaviest of the rain had fallen further east. But it was scant consolation. He must have been invisible to the passing traffic and was forced to walk for hours before an HGV driver finally stopped and offered him a lift as far as the main road to Colchester.

Until then, he had walked alone along the busy Essex trunk road, indulging himself with thoughts of the past and at first, it was the good times that he'd spent as a child at his grandparents' house that he recalled. Looking back, he now realised that his mother's parents and the holidays spent with them, had been his only refuge from a drunken father and a long-defeated mother. And now, separated as they were by the passage of many long and unforgiving months, Terry found it strange to think of that man as his father.

As he walked along at an ever-decreasing pace, the fact that he was unable to piece together an accurate image of Patrick Stubbs in his head did not disturb him unduly. What disturbed him more, was the fact that no matter how hard he tried, the image of his father that fused together in his mind's eye was not blurred or indistinct. It was of someone entirely different.

It was of someone else.

A face that he didn't recognise, but still a face that he knew and one that, to all intents and purposes, belonged to a man whom he had once called Father.

His body was tiring fast now, and he knew that the sheer determination that had carried him thus far could not be relied upon to carry him much further. A couple of times, he had been forced to stop completely, as a coughing fit took hold and although such seizures were not unusual, the effort that was required to coax his legs forward after each debilitating convulsion was immense.

He could sense that he was coming down with something and although he hoped and prayed that he would be able to fight it off, he knew full well that another night spent out of doors would only serve to deepen the gravity of the illness. His whole body itched, the very seams of his donated clothes gnawed at him, and he was soon convinced that each item must have already been crawling with lice even before he'd made his selection.

As he stumbled on, the light began to drain away as the first rains fell and it wasn't long before another face crept from the shadows. Maybe it was the onset of darkness that had beckoned it from its lair, but whatever the reason, Terry refused to bid it welcome.

He shivered as a stream of ice-cold water trickled down from the hairs at the base of his neck and he shook himself vigorously, like some sopping wet dog. The distance that he had now managed to put between himself and the site of the previous night's horror was no remedy for his rising sense of dread, but he clung to the thought, as one gold tooth shone from the darkest recesses of his mind.

Terry knew that that he would never be able to flush that memory from his head. It was engraved on the inside of his skull, like some Neanderthal's nightmare, daubed with splintered bone in charcoal and ochre on the pitted walls of a dark cave. And yet the prospect of another night spent alone did not concern him unduly. There had been hundreds of those of late and the only difference on offer as the night closed in again, was a change of scenery.

Terry tried to recite his grandfather's words, the words that had come back to him so suddenly just the day before, but at that moment his memory banks were exhausted. Maybe too much had changed since the incident in the hide all those years ago. Or maybe whatever else his grandfather had said to him that day, had been lost on a young boy who had no knowledge then of what the old man had been forced to face years before. By his teenage years, Terry had long since stopped listening to the older generation and so, any stories that the old man had imparted in his later years would have been ignored, by and large.

Now Terry feared that he might have to pay for his youthful arrogance.

His only hope was his grandmother, but even that was likely to be a lost cause. The last time he'd seen her, she had been losing it a bit and he very much doubted that her memory had improved any in the intervening months. Maybe it was the cold or the wet or the fear of what the future now held for him, but Terry was suddenly convinced that talking to his grandmother was no longer the answer that it had seemed to be. But however slim the prospect now seemed, she represented his only chance to understand and if the worst were to happen, and she were to tell his mother that her only grandson had been to visit, Terry knew that mum would almost certainly put the unlikely visitation down to old age.

Terry didn't talk much to the lorry driver who finally took pity on him. The burly man wasn't too inquisitive either but simply seemed content to have some company in his cab on the long drive to the port at Harwich. Terry's cold was clearly worsening, and he found himself apologising to the driver when he sneezed for the third time in quick succession.

"There's some tissues in the glove compartment there," the driver pointed. It didn't seem like an invitation and so Terry quickly retrieved a couple from the torn and sullied box and vigorously blew his nose.

"I'd get indoors tonight if I were you, the weather forecast is for heavy downpours all night," the driver advised him in a sharp East Midlands accent. "You'll catch your death out there if you're not too careful."

"I'll do my best," Terry replied, a little embarrassed.

The driver gave him a concerned look that settled on Terry's badly fitting shirt and then nodded in uneasy understanding. "I'll drop you off here if that's okay," he said a moment or two later. "The main road to Colchester is just over there, you can see the headlights."

He thanked the driver, who had kindly shared a cup of warm flask coffee during their short journey, but this time Terry was right out of memories. The prospect of a few more hours spent hoping against hope that another driver would stop and that the rain would not return did not exactly fill him with the joys of an early spring.

It therefore came as no surprise when he was forced to endure the worsening elements for a further two hours, before he was able to lower his weary thumb again, by which time his fingers seemed to have frozen into a permanent fist.

The world weighed heavily on his shoulders as the car ground to a halt beside him, and Terry's legs bore the brunt as he crouched down to peer inside. As he nodded his approval of the destination and shuffled within, Terry stifled yet another sneeze, just in case the prospect of a flu-ridden passenger should put this Good Samaritan off his good deed.

"I can't take you as far as the town centre," the driver confessed, still hoping for some meaningful conversation in return for the short trip. "But I can take you to the junction with the A134, if that's okay?"

Terry made no attempt to speak, but just nodded. If it was conversation that the driver was looking for then he was to be disappointed. It was warmer inside than the cab had been and within a few minutes, Terry had fallen asleep and had to be shaken awake a full thirty minutes later.

"I thought you were dead for a minute there, mate!" the businessman said, clearly a little unnerved by the experience. "I've been shaking you for the last five minutes."

Terry apologised and made some sort of excuse. "I guess the journey has taken it out of me more than I realised," he said. But it was more than that, and what's more, Terry Stubbs knew it.

He was ill and he had a feeling that, this time, it was serious.

He heard the car door slam shut as he turned away and the blue Ford roared into the distance to leave Terry alone once more. At first, he had absolutely no idea where he was and found that he had lost all track of time. He decided to make his way towards the town centre, which was sign-posted at the traffic island where he had been marooned, but to Terry's disappointment, the lights that shone from the office blocks in the distance still seemed to be some way off.

Terry made an educated guess at the time and judging by the miserable queues of traffic that still lined the roundabout approach roads, the rush hour was only just beginning to tail off, but the temperature was already close to zero. He picked out a few markers in the distance that seemed to be positioned a few hundred yards apart and more than a little reluctantly, he began to drag his feet towards the town. As he walked, he counted the steps between each landmark. At first a telephone box, then a huge tree at the side of the road and finally a post-box. Each time, he tried to limp along that little bit faster in the hope that he would soon find the answers he was seeking.

The first signs of Christmas cheer beamed and twinkled from the surrounding houses and as he got nearer to the town centre, the municipal decorations added to the seasonal feel, with candles and reindeers, Santa's sleigh and the occasional jingling bell, shining down on him from every other streetlight.

It was the season of goodwill to all men, but not to Terry Stubbs, it would seem.

Terry walked with as much effort as he could muster, but his legs were not as willing to play the game. He tucked his hands into the overhanging cuffs of his sodden coat and pulled the neck of his turned-up collar together, but still the cold got through.

Finally, when he had almost decided to put off the search until morning and look instead for a local hostel, he finally got the lucky break that he needed. He had only been to the home once before and that was under protest. His grandfather had just been hospitalised, much against his will, for what proved to be the final time, and as it had looked like it was going to be a long stay, his parents decided that the best place for his grandmother was in care.

She had been virtually bed-ridden for at least a year by then and although the move into the home came to nothing on that occasion, once the old man had died, there was no denying the inevitable.

As he made his way along the busy road, he recognised a landmark that he had first seen on that previous visit, and it rekindled his fading hope that he might be able to find the retirement home before morning. For once, he found himself feeling some gratitude towards his faceless father for insisting on his help that day, but no matter how hard he tried, he just couldn't remember the name of the place and still the face of Patrick Stubbs eluded him.

Asking for directions would have been a little like asking where he might find a particular public house in the heart of Dublin, but once he was on the right road, the residence was surprisingly easy to find. It was hardly inconspicuous; an ugly red brick building, built in the early 1900s, that may once have been a mental hospital or something of that ilk. It just had that look about it and even from a safe distance, it still retained the same oppressive feel that Terry could remember from his last visit, which the large and sparsely decorated tree in the grounds did nothing to dispel.

As he slouched up to the door, hesitation gripped him and had someone not left the building at that very moment and waited courteously to let him through, Terry might well have walked away. As it was, he nodded in appreciation as they wished him a *Merry Christmas* and did his level best to ignore every pair of eyes that bore down on him as he slipped inside.

As he cut his way through the clinical air, he could sense that something wasn't quite right. He didn't know how, but he could feel that something was up. As he approached the desk, time seemed to drag out behind him and as the receptionist lifted her head ever so slowly from the book in which she was engrossed, he felt his body begin to sink and his legs gave way beneath him. The next thing he knew, he was being propped up in an uncomfortable chair, whilst three or four white-coated figures busied themselves around him.

"He's coming around."

"Do you know who he is?"

"Never seen him before."

"Where am I?" Terry croaked, the reflected lights circling from the tinsel decorations in blue, silver and green stars and without waiting for an answer he pleaded, "Drink, I need a drink." When he tasted water on his lips just seconds later, he couldn't help but be disappointed.

A few more minutes passed before he was asked, none too politely, to identify himself. Clearly, the improvements that Terry had made to his appearance earlier that day had not been good enough to fool the good people of the shires.

"I've come to visit my grandmother," Terry explained, pausing for a full minute to cough into his hand and then having to wait for a moment for another sneeze to subside. "For Christmas," he added for good measure, hoping that it would seem like as good a reason as any.

The sweet-scented nurse waited patiently and once he had recovered himself sufficiently to answer another question, she smiled ever so nicely and asked for the resident's name.

"Annie," Terry replied. "Annie Wilson."

His response was greeted with a wall of silence and a crossfire of glances, before a man in a badly fitting suit stepped forward and said, quite coldly, "That can't be right. If you were Mrs Wilson's grandson, you would know that she's dead, now stop wasting our time here and get out. This is a retirement home for the elderly, not a hostel for your sort!"

Terry sat in silence as the realisation of what the man had just said began to seep through.

Dead. He was too late.

Dead.

But the overwhelming feeling was not one of sorrow or regret; it was one of relief. For now, he could never know. Annie was his only source of information and the only voice that his grandfather had left. Now she had gone too, and with her had passed his final link to his past. It was as if the final thread of rope, which had once tethered his boat to the shore, had been severed and now the current was carrying him away to his fate.

"Come on, out!" the suit commanded, instantly flanked by a couple of orderlies in green overalls that seemed to appear from nowhere like a pair of oversized elves. When Terry did not move, they each stepped forward, grabbed an arm apiece and yanked him to his feet.

The force with which he was pulled from the chair had the same effect on Terry's powers of communication as the Heimlich manoeuvre might have on a choking man, but his explanations came too late.

They weren't listening.

"I've been away," he spluttered, but he was being dragged to the door. People were standing motionless, watching the bizarre episode unfold. An old man, who may well have been surgically attached to his walking-frame, was clearly enjoying the Christmas cabaret that had been laid on in the foyer that night.

"I didn't know, I've been away for quite a while," Terry continued, but he had already reached the outside world, where he was unceremoniously bundled back out into the night.

His head was still reeling from his illness and from the news that had been imparted just moments ago, so the words of warning that rained down upon him were wasted.

"If you come back, I'll call the police," the suit declared.

Terry had no intention of going back. There was nothing that they could do to help him now.

He sneezed again as the thickening sweat began to ooze from behind his ears. His back, which had never really recovered from the earlier downpour, was now soaked once more with the spreading perspiration and in the freezing weather, even the shirt on his back would quickly turn to ice.

Terry knew that he had to find somewhere to sleep, and soon. As the staff backed away, Terry caught the end of a conversation that he knew could spell even more trouble.

"…call her daughter, you know, just in case?" and after a moment of contemplation, "No, I don't think so, she's had enough to deal with lately without this crank…" but the voices soon faltered on the rising wind that hastened Terry's departure.

**

Eventually, Terry did find somewhere to spend the night.

It was hardly The Ritz, but even a comfortable bed at a top London hotel wouldn't have ushered in a restful night's sleep for him that night. A fever had taken hold of him and his whole body had become wracked with the worst case of pins and needles that he had ever been forced to endure. The cold seemed to penetrate deeper than it had ever reached, boring right through to the very marrow of his bones. He had stumbled across an unlocked public lavatory near to the central bus station. According to the notice, the block was officially closed from eight o'clock each evening, but vandals had smashed off the padlock and the door to the Gents hung ajar, rocking to and fro in the wind.

Terry shuffled inside and tried as best he could to ignore the invasive stench of urine that emanated from the saturated floor; he curled himself up on a cracked toilet bowl in the cleanest cubicle that he could find. He tucked his knees up beneath his chin and pulled the long seam of his newly acquired trench-coat tight around his legs, but the temperature had since plummeted to well below freezing, and the graffiti-strewn walls of the toilet block offered scant protection from the wind that now raged outside. In an attempt to encourage the night to pass by more rapidly, he began to read the hieroglyphic-like array of inscriptions that had been scrawled across the walls and door for future generations to ponder.

Various proclamations of undying love such as "Jazz luvs Sasha 10-7-96" or "Stevie 4 Josie 12-9-97" to name but two, whilst aged invitations for sex in a public place with sad middle-aged men accounted for many of the other acts of vandalism. Curled up against the cold in the confines of the cramped cubicle, he felt like an unborn baby trapped inside its mother's womb, listening in terror to the world as it raged outside.

But he was not the only occupant that night and as the first letter began to form on the pitted surface of the battered door, he felt each hair on the back of his throbbing neck stiffen, as his sight settled on the trail of an unseen quill.

The red ink scratched across the door's barely blue surface, its breadth broad, then fine like the calligraphy that he had learned at school, but this was no homework project. The scrawling hand crackled like a sharp stylus does when it reaches the end of a long play record. Each word formed slowly, but at first, the words made no sense, and it wasn't until the first sweeping line was at an end that Terry was able to comprehend something of its meaning.

Terry closed his eyes and kept them closed. He didn't want to see what his eyes were seeing. No, it was more than that! He didn't want to believe what was happening right before them. It was impossible. It just wasn't real. It had to be in his head, in his mind, an hallucination brought on by the fever that now had him firmly in its grip. He told himself that if he kept his eyes shut then it would go away, but he couldn't close his ears to the scratching, the sound of pen on parchment, the ancient sounds of records being written down for eternity.

"Dead Coarses carried and recarried still," he stuttered, forcing his chapped lips to open against his better judgement. "Dead Coarses carried and recarried still, whilst fifty," he waited for the next word to form. "Corpses," he coughed, "scarce, one, grave, doth fill."

As he read the line aloud for a second time, the rest of the verse poured forth at an impossible speed. It was like an outburst of emotion from a disturbed child who has been silent for too long. As each line was completed, it seemed to loom out at Terry, as if through some unseen magnifying glass, as his torso swayed from side to side on the plastic seat beneath.

> *With LORD HAVE MERCIE UPON US on the dore, which (though the words be good) doth grieve men sore. And o're the dore-posts fix'd a crosse of red, betokening that there Death some blood hath shed. Some with God's markes or Tokens doe espie, those markes or tokens shew them they must die. Some with their carbuncles, and sores new burst, are fed with hope that they have escap'd the worst: Thus passeth all the weeke till Thursdaye's Bill, shews us what thousands death that weeke did kil.*

Terry had seen enough.

He leapt from the pan and clawed at the door, but in spite of the absence of any lock, the door was jammed. It was as if a substantial weight was leaning up against it, but when Terry crouched down low enough to peer through the six-inch gap beneath, there was no obstruction to be seen. Frantically, his frozen fingers clawed at the edge of the frame as he tried in vain to tease open a gap from which he could gain some leverage, until he saw the rusted hinges on the left-hand side of the frame and the sight stopped him dead in his tracks.

The obstruction was on the inside.

He tried to scream, but the low sound that escaped from his lungs was, at best, a moan, which slipped easily away on the wind.

"Who are you?" he stuttered, his jaw clattering as he spoke. "What do you want with me?"

There was no answer and in the resulting silence, Terry tried to take charge of his own destiny for the final time. As he was about to launch himself up and over the top of his unconventional cell, his eyes settled on a single monogram just a few inches from his face. At first, it was represented just once amongst this vast array of faceless identities, but as Terry looked left then right, then up and down, over and over again, like a nodding-dog on an unmade road, the initials seemed to multiply before his eyes.

Eventually, he could see nothing but a single pair of letters, etched a thousand times on the walls and on the door, in the same blood red ink.

TR

And beneath each inscription, two simple words were forming simultaneously:

'was here'

Terry's breathing became short and sharp, an endless panting that kept an alternate beat with the drumming of the damaged wooden door at the entrance to the facility. The door banged incessantly against the blue-brick wall, as if intent on completing the vandals' handiwork itself. Terry placed his left foot up onto the ceramic rim of the toilet bowl and with one hand perched on the broken tiles beneath the tiny window and his good knee at the ready, he counted down the seconds to lift off.

But he never made it.

When he pushed with his left, his right foot gave way on the soiled floor and as he fell down on his haunches, a searing pain tore through his ankle and into his lower leg. As he lay there, cursing and screaming, the door to the cubicle burst inward, to smack against the frame that had held it in place just a few moments before. In, then out, then in, then out, as if the tiny cubicle were a living lung for the whole prefabricated block.

Maybe it was the synchronicity of the two sounds that conjured the ancient tune into life, but from somewhere deep in Terry's subconscious, the haunting chant seeped its way into another century. At first, it could have been a trick of the wind as it whistled through the broken pane of glass above the urinals; but then an unmistakable melody arose, and that caused the feverish Terry to look up from the concrete floor beneath his frozen feet.

The sullen tune echoed off the peeling walls and yet the symphonic effect might not have been unpleasant in more suitable surroundings. In his present predicament, it merely served to conjure up a merry-go-round of visions that span faster and faster, like skaters on a frozen river, until Terry could take no more. He turned as best he could and vomited until his stomach wrenched and bile leaked from the cracked corners of his mouth. As he raised his head, only one vision remained. That of a woman and a child. A woman in a grey dress and white shawl, rocking a baby gently in her arms.

The words were spoken rather than sung now, like some ecclesiastical chant, but that likeness could not have been further from the truth, and Terry's bloodless lips began to mouth the familiar rhyme that every child in every English playground has recited for hundreds of years:

Ring a ring of roses,
a pocket full of poses,
a-tishoo, a-tishoo,
we all fall down.

Chapter Eight
Draw Lock

*To praise my vices all the swarme of them, would flocke and all my vertues
would condemn. Much worse than Ravens is their flattery, for Ravens eate not
men until they dye, but so a flatt'ring knave may get and thrive, he daily will
devoure a man alive.*

Who's there?

Staring up at me as I stare down through this crimson veil.

Their foreign chatter drifts on a gentle breeze, but the tangled voices are
beaten back in a frantic rush of wings and then they are lost, far beneath the shrill
shriek that I am powerless to evade. Talons that tear like teeth to taste each tender
morsel of my mortality.

The narrow street below is awash with delirious eyes, that sway with the river
beneath and I am smothered by the sweet stench, that pours from the dead heads
of a dozen corpses. The acrid smoke from a thousand hearths billows between
my dumb companions, to conquer the poisonous pall that oozes from as many
necessary houses.

I can almost hear the cruel crunch of moist gristle from dry bone and the last
tear of taut skin from supple flesh has stayed with me. The final snap of tendon
forever echoes in the void and the deafening rip of dense muscle cleaves to me.
Yet all should now be silent in the face of death.

The furious choke of the noose bites tighter than before and the merciless
strain of the rack stretches me still. The torturous savagery of the blade cuts
deeper in this darkness and the eager promise of the executioner's axe has failed
me.

Their world stares back in horror and in awe as I remember mine.

And now, as I stare up through an old man's eyes at the myriad of stars that
once bore witness to that betrayal, I can taste blood again.

Chapter Nine
Nonesuch Lock

The hue and cry is out and I protest, though hee scape hanging yet hee shall be prest.

A confusion of noise drilled through the night's crumbling barricade. Cheerful voices, familiar jingles and the morning news headlines had already proclaimed the start of yet another working day, but in the half an hour that had passed since Lisa had left the comfort of their king-sized bed, Jake had not stirred.

Even allowing for their heavy floor-to-ceiling curtains, which may have cost a fortune in their heyday but were long since passed their best, it still seemed far too dark. The temptation to pull the covers over his head almost got the better of him, but when an annoying glam-rock song blared out from the radio, he forced himself to hit the shower.

Autumn seemed like yesterday, but those winter mornings, which he had always found so hard to bear, were now at their darkest. Each dawn seemed darker than the last and the journey home each evening felt longer with every passing day. Jake showered and dressed and made his way downstairs for an habitual cup of coffee and a glance out of the window at his new car.

He didn't take much notice of it then, but something struck him as odd, something that he would not be able to put his finger on until long after he he'd stepped out into the cold morning air.

"What was wrong with you last night?" his wife asked. It was clear to Jake that the underlying sentiment in his wife's apparent concern had more to do with her own restless night than his.

"You were tossing and turning all night, and you kept on taking more than your share of the quilt!"

"Well, that makes a change," Jake quipped, at which his wife only smiled and stuck out her tongue.

"Devil will get it!" he said instinctively, a strange saying that had been passed down through generations of his family. He'd heard his aunts say it when he was a kid, his mother said it more often than he cared to remember, and now he was saying it too.

"I'd like to see him try!" Lisa replied, grabbing a piece of buttered toast and racing upstairs to finish her final preparations for the day ahead. Jake feigned to go after her at which she broke into a run, squealing "you can't catch me!" as she went.

He almost followed her, finding himself strangely aroused by her playfulness, but he knew that she was in a rush and he was also short on time. He was also much too excited about his new car to get all that excited about his wife, at least until the novelty had worn off, which would most likely only be a matter of days if past history was anything to go by. Gadgets, holidays, new clothes and other fine things only ever filled the gap in his life momentarily, before he was off looking for the next thing.

It was just who he was.

"It's how I was made, baby!" he said out loud, but fortunately, no one was there to hear.

He called up to Lisa as he left the house a few minutes later and heard her shout a muted 'bye' and 'good luck' as he pulled the door shut behind him.

Travelling to work together over the last few weeks had proved difficult.

It was not something that they had ever done before and as neither of them were what you might describe as 'morning people', it had proved to be an uneasy arrangement. As Lisa was invariably late despite her early habits, he had often missed his preferred train and that had given rise to further tensions between them.

A thick coat of frost had settled on his car overnight, but Jake could not be bothered to stand and scrape.

So as soon as he was comfortably ensconced in the driver's seat, he turned the heating up to full blast, even though cold air would pour out around him for the first few minutes. It wasn't long before the ice had loosened sufficiently for the wipers to clear the necessary porthole in the rear window, through which he could see enough to navigate the drive. He reversed up and out into the road and as he accelerated away the edge had already been taken off the chill, but it wasn't until he had almost completed the fifteen-minute journey to the local tube station, that he realised what had puzzled him about his view that morning.

It hadn't been such a cold night after all.

None of the other drivers that he passed were peering out through a semi-circular patch of smeared glass, and those cars that lined the side of every street seemed completely clear of the frost that had encrusted his car. The morning was crisp and bright, but as Jake closed in on the station, he had seen nothing to suggest that the temperature had fallen so far below zero overnight.

It was a puzzle, but it was hardly supernatural, and it wasn't long before a rational explanation came to mind. Almost every other car that he saw on that short journey must have been parked in the direct path of the rising sun or kept snug in a garage overnight. It didn't ring true, but there was nothing else that he could think of to explain it, so he settled on it and moved on. He had more important things to be concerned about than a frozen windscreen or his late-night hallucinations.

Last night should have been spent collecting his thoughts for that morning's sales meeting. The meetings were a regular monthly occurrence, though this was his first and knew that he had to make a good impression. He had spent the previous evening reading up on the car, and so mental preparation was now his only option. Failing to prepare meant preparing to fail, or so an old manager had once told him, but he had a black belt in thinking on his feet. A grand master at winging it, or a born bullshitter to those that knew him best of all.

He would be okay.

Jake had been in the job for less than six months and the last few weeks had been hectic. Not only had he just started a high-pressure job, but he'd also moved his family one hundred and fifty miles on the strength of it. Now, whilst his 'family' only consisted of a reluctant wife and a very cantankerous cat; the resulting turmoil had still been challenging.

Lisa had found temporary work almost immediately as a paralegal clerk with a local firm of solicitors and the two of them quietly hoped that it might lead to something more permanent. Their house was rented from a rather dubious landlord, but they had been fortunate to find a property in such a prominent position and at such a reasonable rent. Needless to say, they had snapped up the chance and had signed contracts for a year. There was a get-out clause, just in case his job didn't work out, but that was something that they both believed would not be needed. He had a barrel of faith in his own ability, even if his wife of seven months standing sometimes needed some encouragement to share in his boundless self-confidence.

Some people thought him arrogant. Jake didn't.

That morning, he would need every ounce of his unshakeable nerve and so any distractions would have to be put to one side. He knew that he had to step up and he was faced with a baptism of fire. The recent announcement of the third quarter sales figures had been a disappointment to many and a shock to Jake. The fact that his team had not hit their own target was a slump that he would be expected to explain, despite his short tenure.

The thought of trying to convince his regional manager that the figures didn't represent a downturn was almost as unnerving as his recent dreams, but not quite! The second quarter had seen a record intake of hardware orders, which everyone knew was due to the efforts of his predecessor. In the days before his own semi-meteoric rise, he had enjoyed many a sleepless night, but where sex had fizzled out, the dreams had taken a firmer hold.

As it turned out, the morning passed quickly and the grilling that he had anticipated didn't really materialise, although he did have to suffer one or two jibes along the lines of *having his work cut out*. After lunch, he returned to his desk to find half a dozen messages from clients and a couple from colleagues, the majority of which seemed straightforward enough.

The ninth message was from the car fleet company requesting an urgent call. He spoke to a Deborah Gear, an unfortunate name given her company's product and after thanking him for ringing her back, she asked him if everything was okay with the car.

"Fine, no problems at all," Jake replied, fully expecting the girl to then thank him for his time and to move onto another customer, but another question followed, which was to reveal the real reason behind this apparent courtesy call.

"What time was the car delivered, Mister Harvey?" the girl asked, a trace of nervousness in her voice.

"Around eight-thirty," he informed her. "Why do you ask?"

The girl didn't answer his question straight away, as if she knew that her next question would satisfy his curiosity. "Did Miss Simpson get the train back into London or did she get a taxi?"

He relayed to the clerk the details of how the driver, whom he now knew by name, had refused his offer of a lift. "From what Miss Simpson said, she was heading for the train, but she could have jumped in a cab on the way there," he reasoned. "I've no idea what happened to her once she left our street," he added, sensing the defensive tone that had risen in his voice. "Why? Haven't you heard from her then?"

He was suddenly a little more concerned for the woman's safety now rather than for his failing reputation as the sort of man that lets a woman walk for fifteen minutes, instead of insisting on giving her a lift.

"She didn't get back to the office yesterday," the shaken caller informed him. "We tried to get in touch with you, but there was no reply on your number," she continued. "She wasn't at her flat, so we thought we'd wait and see if she turned up today."

They had already called the police that morning, the girl went on to tell him, and was clearly annoyed when he told her that the police had not yet been in touch. At least he knew now to expect a visit, but Jake was not disturbed at work again that afternoon and he was able to complete his remaining calls without further interruption.

The local police called at the house the following evening, in the face of unrelenting pressure from the woman's family, who insisted that she was just not the type to do a bunk! It did seem from the senior policeman's tone that Jake was under some suspicion, which he supposed was only to be expected given the circumstances. After all, he was the last person to see this woman before her disappearance, although the policewoman didn't seem all that convinced that he'd been involved. In fact, she did not seem to be too concerned at all for the wellbeing or whereabouts of this as yet unofficial missing person.

"Adults go missing all the time," she explained with an air of someone who knows she is wasting her time. "She'll turn up, they always do," the WPC added. "She'll be with a long-lost friend in Aberdeen or will have buggered off to the Canary Islands for some winter sun while we're left chasing our tails here."

It struck Jake that this particular policewoman, whose name had already escaped him, was not the most professional that he'd ever seen and from the expression on her colleague's face, she seemed to be getting on his nerves too. After explaining to them in some detail what had happened that morning, including Miss Simpson's strange behaviour, the policewoman did appear a little more interested in his version of events, but it wasn't to last. She asked him if Miss Simpson had given any indication of where she was going, or if she had said anything at all out of the ordinary.

"Only that she wanted to go to the train station, the nearest one," Jake explained. "She seemed nervous, I know that much," he recounted. "She seemed very wary of something and also seemed genuinely worried for me for some reason. Made me promise to call her if there was anything wrong with the car," but he could help them no further and when they pressed him again for more details, he decided that he'd been helpful enough.

He had other things to attend to.

"Sorry, I can't remember anything else!" he said, though it was clear from their reaction that this was not what they had hoped to hear. Still, they thanked him for his time and explained that it was highly likely that they would want to examine the car, sooner rather than later. The thought of letting his new possession out of his sight, even for a morning, made him visibly twitch; not because he thought that there was anything for them to find, but because he didn't want anyone else poking around inside it.

It was his.

After Lisa had seen them to the door, she turned to Jake, a little more fearful for the girl's safety than her husband seemed to be. "I hope she's okay," she said, "what do you think has happened to her? Do *you* think she's okay?"

To Jake it felt like another barrage of questions, when all he wanted was to put the whole thing behind him. "I've no idea," he snapped in complete indifference. "She seemed fine when she left, a bit spooked by something maybe, but she can't have just gone up in a puff of smoke, can she? She'll turn up, you heard what the policewoman said!"

"But aren't you even in the slightest bit concerned?" his wife asked, a bit at a loss to see him be so blasé about it.

"Not really babe," said Jake, a bit too honestly for his own good. "I'm sure she'll turn up and if she doesn't, well, it's nothing to do with me, is it?"

Lisa looked a little perplexed by his response, maybe even a little unsettled by it, as if she had just witnessed a side to her new husband's character that she had never seen before and wasn't too keen on seeing again.

"Well, I'm going to say a little prayer for her," Lisa announced piously.

"Can you say one for my quarterly sales figures whilst you're at it!" Jake chirped, and at that a cushion was flung across the room which hit him full square in the face!

"Hey!" he yelled jokingly.

"Pig!"

"Oink oink!" he squealed, scrunching up his nose and scratching at the floor like a wild boar, before chasing her up the stairs and into the bedroom.

This time his car could play second fiddle.

In the early hours of Friday morning, the phone buzzed into life, but he felt too groggy to summon up any meaningful anger and was still half-asleep, as he put the receiver to his ear and mumbled in acknowledgement. He repeated himself once more, as the fog that was milling around his mind began to clear, but still the annoying silence persisted.

In that moment he felt the sharp stab of panic in sudden and complete conviction that his past had just caught up with him, a lot sooner than expected.

The move to London had been a bit like a bolt from the blue. He had not planned it but had seen an advert quite by chance in a professional magazine and the prospect had seemed like the answer to a multitude of largely self-inflicted problems. His debts would be met by his vastly improved wage, his career outlook would see a significant improvement through his increased level of responsibility and Lisa's career prospects would be far rosier in London, where legally trained graduates tend to be in higher demand. And on top of all that, he could put some distance between himself and two ill-thought-out late-night liaisons.

He was beginning to wonder whether the caller had been cut off and was about to slam down the receiver for the second night in succession, when one word filtered gruffly down into his ear. A solitary word that confirmed someone was there, and that that someone knew exactly who it was that he was looking for.

"Cooper!"

The voice carried with it such conviction that for a split-second, Jake almost took the name as his own. But it wasn't a voice that he recognised and seconds ground past before it spoke again, and then the words came too quickly for his tired mind to take in.

"Some say we carry whores and thieves, tis true. I'll carry those that paid so, for my due. Our boats like Hackney horses, every day, will carry honest men, and knaves, for pay."

The anonymous caller then fell silent. Not a sound followed. Not a breath. But for a while longer, he was there. Jake knew it and more than that, he knew not to respond. He had a strong suspicion that it wouldn't be wise to challenge his poetic friend. Yet, despite his racing heart, his logical educated brain still insisted that it was just someone messing about. He tried to assure himself that it had to be one of his so-called mates, winding him up to get their own back for some past transgression on his part.

"Danny?" he guessed. "Is that you? Stop dicking around, you idiot!" But Danny was asleep in his own bed after a great night of wild sex with an ex-girlfriend of Jake's and had not spared a thought for his old friend and drinking partner for quite some time.

"Hello?" Jake asked again, almost too politely and returning the receiver to within an inch of his ear, as if any closer might be too close for comfort. "Who's there?" he continued, just a little more forcefully, but the line had died.

Whoever it had been had grown bored of his late-night games, but this time Jake didn't hesitate to dial the number for *caller ID* in the hope that the source of the call would have been recorded. He was in luck; the automated answer confirmed the source, but as Jake scrambled in vain for the pen that had disappeared from the bedside table, his wife began to stir.

"What is it?" she asked, alarmed by his restlessness.

"Nothing," he cajoled her, as he scratched at the surface with the blunt nib of a pencil stub. "Go back to sleep!" he ordered, which was one command that she was more than happy to obey. Jake turned away and crawled back into his chilled and now meagre portion of the bed, with the joys of their earlier sex a distant memory.

By the next day, he had convinced himself that it was just some weirdo who had decided to pester him at random. He checked in the phone book to see where the call had come from; the code was a Harlow number, and he racked his brains to think of anyone that he knew who might now be living in Essex. He had hit the redial button not long after the call was made, but the line was busy and after two more failed attempts, he had given up the pursuit in favour of a night's sleep. As he tried to read back his nocturnal scrawl in the plain light of day, the numbers were almost illegible, and he took that as his signal to leave it at that.

It wasn't worth the effort.

At the time, he failed to link his two anonymous callers together. The latest was clearly just a prank and so he paid it little mind. Some nutter with a poetic bent, waffling on about horses and knaves and although the second call had been the more inexplicable, it was the first that had continued to prove more unsettling. He was confident that the memory would fade into obscurity after a few hectic days at the office and so it would prove. Within a couple of days, even the hastily scribbled note would be thrown away along with the rest of the week's refuse.

Lisa didn't ask about the call at breakfast or at dinner, so Jake didn't see the point of worrying her, but there was something else that plagued him more than the nocturnal poet's cryptic message. Something that had disturbed his sleep for more than a week, ever since he had woken to find himself standing alone on the landing of their house at three o'clock in the morning.

He had dreamt of stairs again; the same ones, the same twelve steps that descend into the lap of a vast river.

Always bathed in a thick mist, always bitter cold and without exception, he is always the only one there.

Yet he knows for sure that he is never completely alone down there, and something in the pit of his stomach tells him for certain that he had been there before.

Chapter Ten
Pedlar's Lock

Here, Parents for their Childrens losse lament. There, Children's grief for Parents life that's spent: Husbands deplore their loving Wives decease: Wives for their Husbands weep remedilesse: the Brother for his Brother, friend for friend, doe each for other mutual sorrows spend, here, Sister mournes for Sister, Kin for Kin, as one griefe ends, another doth begin

"Where is he?" screamed the gaunt figure in the fading blue dress. "Where's my son?"

The nurse looked up calmly from the collection of incomplete forms that were neatly piled up on the reception desk and left the question hanging. "I'm afraid smoking is not allowed in here," she said sternly, pointing at the no-smoking sign above her head. As Jackie glanced frantically around for a suitable place to extinguish her cigarette, the desk nurse pointed to a half-filled cup of cold tea on the side of the desk and when Jackie complied, the nurse asked politely for the patient's name.

"Terry," the pale woman stuttered, more in need of nicotine than ever before. "His name is Terry. Terry Stubbs."

After a momentary pause, as the nurse scanned through the unusually large list of recent arrivals, she picked up a biro and returned a more sympathetic gaze in the direction of the distraught woman. "And you are?"

"His mother," Mrs Stubbs said. "Please, is he here?"

"This will only take a moment, madam," the nurse insisted in a soothing tone that had taken her years to perfect. "The doctor will see you as soon as she's able, so if you'd just like to—" but the sentence was cut off in its prime.

"Please!" Jackie Stubbs begged with more conviction than she had ever mustered in her life. "I haven't seen my son in more than a year. I had a call from a doctor at this hospital telling me that my son is here, and I'm not about spend another minute away from him! Now please, tell me where he is!"

The nurse was unfazed by the outburst, having seen much of the same every working day for the past fifteen years. Just as she was about to launch into another of her standard responses for such occasions, another more authoritative voice came out of nowhere.

"Mrs Stubbs?" An Indian woman in a long white coat had just stepped into the waiting room and as she approached, her lapel badge announced her credentials long before the two were formally introduced. "I'm Doctor Anwar," she said. "We spoke earlier."

"Yes," Jackie answered, instinctively reaching out to shake the doctor's hand, but she could wait no longer. "How is he? How's Terry?" she pleaded.

At first, no answer was forthcoming, and the doctor instead motioned her through the double doors that led off to the right of the waiting room. Finally, the news was imparted, but it was not what Jackie Stubbs had hoped to hear.

"He's not too good, I'm afraid, Mrs Stubbs," the doctor informed her in the clinically matter-of-fact way that only those in the medical profession have truly mastered. "He has a broken ankle, but that's the least of it. He's got pneumonia," the doctor continued with a little more compassion. Jackie sat down.

"It was most likely brought on by the intense cold over the last few nights, I'm afraid." She paused, partly in expectation of some explanation for the boy's plight, but when none was forthcoming, she continued, "I understand that he was found by a council cleaner this morning, in the public lavatories here in the town centre." Again, she paused for breath or for effect, but Jackie was too shocked to offer anything in return and so the doctor continued to bring Mrs Stubbs up to date.

"He was delirious when they brought him in. He's stabilised a bit now, but other than that, I can't tell you much more." This time, the doctor seemed less willing to accept silence from her beleaguered visitor. "I do need to know a few things from you, Mrs Stubbs, rather urgently, I'm afraid."

Jackie raised her eyes from the floor and the doctor was not surprised to see that they were brimming with tears.

"Was he on any medication? Any history of asthma or epilepsy, that sort of thing?"

"No," sobbed Jackie, quite unable to hold herself together for a minute longer. "Nothing that I can remember."

85

"If you could fill in the form as soon as you can, it might help."

"How did you know where to find me?" Jackie asked, ignoring the request.

"His wallet," the doctor answered more patiently than Jackie deserved. "His driving licence was all that was in his wallet, so we traced your telephone number from that address."

"Dr Anwar!" a nervous male voice intruded. "Can you spare me a moment please?" The doctor excused herself and pushed her way out through the Perspex screen that divided them, but her slim silhouette remained visible through the scratched plastic barrier.

Jackie stayed seated. There was no other option open to her, as her brain had been bombarded with a thousand thoughts that were now crammed into every corner of her mind, and so she was quite unable to engage her legs even if she'd wanted to.

Her son was going to die!

Her only son. The son she thought she would never have. The doctors had given up hope, even she had given up hope, but then she caught and nine months later, there he was, as large as life, a healthy bouncing baby boy. The family had been delighted, especially her father who doted on him all his life, and even Patrick had looked pleased, spending most of the evening in the boozer wetting the baby's head until the early hours.

Jackie pushed the thoughts away into the dark recesses of her mind, but even from there, the possibility that she was going to lose him continued to plague her. Her emotions were in turmoil. Her only son was going to die. The only child that she would ever be blessed with, dead before his twenty-first birthday.

It wasn't that they had wanted only one child, she had been desperate for more. It was just that they had tried for long enough before she had conceived and although she had been pregnant before, it hadn't worked out. She lost her first one after just three months of her term and it had taken two years for her to recover from her second miscarriage twelve months later, but inside, she had never really recovered. Her body had never mended properly and after many tests and further disappointment, she had come to accept that the fall had not just taken the life of her unborn daughter. It had also left her with little hope of ever having the large family that she had always craved, but God had given her Terry, a late but wonderful blessing.

Luckily for Pat, she had never recovered sufficient memory of that fateful day and could only remember that she had been struggling to carry the vacuum cleaner up the stairs. After that, all that she could ever recall was the face of an ambulance driver peering down at her, as she lay crooked and bleeding at the foot of their steep and narrow stairs. Over twenty years had passed since that dreadful day and in all that time, Jackie was sure not a single day had passed without a passing thought for that girl.

Her unborn child, her Mary Anne.

And now she was sure that her son was about to be taken from her too and she was equally certain that the blame sat squarely at the very same door. Only this time, he was going to pay.

Her fear of the unknown was now bound inextricably with the same cloying sense of guilt that had been with her all her life. When she had lost the first child, she hadn't been eating properly and she was well aware, even then, that she had been working too hard. According to her husband, she had also been overdoing it on the day that she slipped and fell for no apparent reason and carelessly lost another sibling for Terry.

Now, on the day that she was about to lose him, she had been more careless than ever.

As Jackie sat alone, torturing herself in a fit of self-loathing, she wished that she had cared enough about her son in the days before he had left, to have taken his side against the excuse-for-a-man that she had married. More than the fear of what the next few hours would bring, more than the spiteful sense of shame that she felt deep down inside, more than any other emotion she had ever known, she was filled with an intense hatred that coursed through her veins. An insatiable disgust for the man that she had called her husband for far too long. The man who had driven his own son out into an unforgiving world and maybe to his death. The man who, in a fit of temper, may have cost the life of his own daughter, aborted before her life had even begun.

The last thought proved too much for her to bear. She leapt to her feet, determined to find her son, to hold him once more, but she stood up too quickly, and as she swayed unsteadily on her feet, she was suddenly awash with memories of his childhood, which slowly merged into a single image.

A bright-eyed boy with a bright blue sailing boat.

The feeling was quickly extinguished, although it left her confused as the image felt misplaced, the memory unclaimed, as if it did not belong to her at all. As if the boy in that mental picture was not her own. As if he belonged to someone else.

She was almost unaware of the tears that were now streaming down her cheeks as she began an increasingly desperate search for Terry. But the doctor was gone. Jackie ran to the end of the whitewashed corridor, but there was no sign of the kind lady or of the scruffy male whose disembodied head had joined them in the room just a few moments before. Busy nurses and orderlies hurried by, but no one asked the increasingly frantic Mrs Stubbs what the problem was, or if they could be of any help.

Or if they did, she failed to hear them.

She retraced her steps at speed, jogging past an ailing patient who was clearly about to undergo some major operation or other. She gave him a sideways glance, just in case, but it seemed that the old man was already staring back at her. Even through her frenzy, the intensity of his unwavering eyes as they bore down on her from darkened hollows, sent an uneasy shiver dancing down her spine. As Jackie rounded another corner at some speed, an arm reached out and grabbed her. It was Dr Anwar.

"I was just coming to find you Mrs Stubbs!" the doctor scolded, clearly annoyed by the woman's jaunt. "I've just been to see your son."

Jackie didn't much care for the portentous tone in the doctor's voice. There was no hope in it.

"He's been moved to an isolation ward," she announced clinically, taking hold of Jackie's forearm in a gesture that was intended to silence any response. It worked.

"It's just a precautionary measure at this stage, Jackie, but there are one or two symptoms that I'm unclear about. I need to get them checked out."

"What symptoms? What are you talking about?"

"All in good time," the doctor responded, "but first I need that information you promised me. Tony," the doctor called, and the same shabby orderly came bounding up like an excited puppy. "Can you get Mrs Stubbs an in-patient form please, as quick as you can?"

"I need a couple of other things too, Jackie, if you don't mind?" The doctor took her silence as acceptance and went on with the same line of questioning. "Has he been abroad at all recently, to any of the more exotic countries?"

"I've no idea," said Jackie, unable to miss the disparaging look on the doctor's face, which seemed to demand some further explanation on her part. "He's been away from home for a while, he hasn't been in touch. I'm afraid that I've really no idea where he's been or who he's been with this past year or so."

She started to say something more, by way of explanation, but in the end, it didn't matter.

"Is he Catholic, Mrs Stubbs?" The question was unexpected, but its connotation was not lost on Jackie. The look that spread across the doctor's face as her question hit home was not unlike satisfaction.

"You think he's going to die, don't you?" Jackie Stubbs cried out and, at the sound of a confrontation, one or two heads turned sharply in their direction. "Is he? Is he going to die?"

There was a slight pause as the doctor readied herself with the most appropriate response.

"Right now, I'd say his chances are fifty-fifty, at best," she admitted quietly and taking Jackie by the arm again, but this time more gently than before, she added a rider. "And that's if we're dealing with pneumonia here. If it's something more than that then, well, I just can't say right now."

Jackie was quieter now, more solemn, as the realisation of what she was facing began to sink in. No amount of screaming or shouting was going to help Terry now. All that she could do was pray and so she clasped her hands together in a standing prayer to whichever God might be listening.

"Can I see him?" she asked politely, her hands still locked together. "Please, and yes, he's Catholic, but our family lapsed a long, long time ago."

"I'll see what I can do," the doctor answered, seemingly taking some pity on her at last.

Dr Anwar returned ten or so minutes later to find a seriously agitated Jackie Stubbs. Her face was crimson, her eyes almost bloodshot and her hands were shaking uncontrollably.

"I always knew," she stuttered through choking tears. "I knew, it would come to this." The doctor handed her a cup of water that she hoped would help calm her down and tried to reassure her, as gently as she could, that all was not yet lost.

"I've just seen Terry," the doctor informed her, at which Jackie looked up, clinging to the hope of a miracle.

"Can I see him now?" she demanded.

"He's been sedated, but yes you can," said the doctor. "But you can't go into the room, Mrs Stubbs." Jackie looked close to a fresh outbreak of hysteria at the news and the doctor felt that further explanations were necessary. "He may be infectious, you see. We think that he may have some kind of tropical disease, which has manifested itself as bronchial pneumonia, but there are other symptoms."

"What 'other' symptoms?" asked Jackie, dreading whatever answer was to follow.

"Like lesions on the skin, blisters almost. Swellings in the groin and armpit." She didn't need to go on, but she did so nonetheless. "He became very aggressive when we tried to move him into the isolation ward," she recounted. "Kept on saying that he shouldn't be here and after a while, he seemed to have difficulty breathing. Like he was having a panic attack. Did he ever suffer with those, Jackie?"

"No," she answered, handing over a partially completed form that was barely legible through the tear-smudged ink. "No, he was always very confident, a very outgoing sort of boy." And then she lost what little control she had managed to muster, as cherished memories of her son crowded too close to be ignored.

"Is there anyone else that we can call?" the doctor asked calmly, placing her hand on Jackie's shoulder. "Your husband maybe, or a friend?" At first there was no response as Jackie grappled with the thought of how she was going to tell her husband, and remembering the detail of Terry's apparent ramblings, the doctor suggested another potential companion.

"Or his grandfather maybe? Terry has asked for his 'Gramps' a few times," she said with a nervous smile. "Would that be your father, Mrs Stubbs?"

"Yes," she answered, recovering her composure for a moment at the thought of her dad, but still heavy with grief even after all this time. For her, time had been no healer. "But he's been dead for well over a year now, just before Terry left home actually." At first, it seemed that Jackie might continue with the explanation, but she didn't have the energy and with a defeated sigh that did not go unnoticed, she asked the doctor to call her husband.

"He should be home from work by now, so you can call if you like." A look not unlike resignation washed over her as she continued to mutter instructions to the good doctor. "If he's not there, no doubt he'll be in the pub, The Mourning Crown, in Bow, they have a website."

"I'll get someone on to it right away, Jackie," the doctor informed her. "And do try not to worry," she added calmly, "a specialist is on his way now and we'll do whatever we can, I promise."

**

90

Terry died at 6.40 pm that day.

In the end, it was peaceful enough, although for a time, his body had been wracked by a bloody coughing fit. Even in death, they wouldn't let his mother in to see him and she could only look in at him through a two-feet-square pane of glass. The nurses and doctors that presided over him were clad in masks and suits that looked like something out of a sci-fi movie and when it was over, another doctor who Jackie had not met before had led her away to break the news that she had so dreaded.

"I wanted so much to say goodbye," she sobbed as the new doctor stood by, impassively.

"We told him that you were here," he said, "he knew that you were here." But somehow, she doubted it. He had died like he had lived these past few months—alone.

It was then that her husband's unmistakable voice reverberated around the ward, but it wasn't to last. For a second or two, it was almost welcome for at least his words brought with them a return to reality that had been lost these past few hours. But when the meaning of the words dawned on Jackie Stubbs, she could take it no more.

"Right, where is the lazy layabout then? Wasting taxpayers' money, no doubt." His words trailed off as he saw the emptiness in his wife's expression.

"No," he whispered. "Dear God, no." He hardly had time to steady himself before she flew at him.

"You bastard!" she screamed. "You fucking heartless bastard!" In an instant, he had tumbled to the ground, taking with him a whole collection of redundant medical equipment that had been standing idle in the corridor. Jackie Stubbs was on top of him, for what was the very first time in their lacklustre marriage, and her fists were beating down on his chest and head like some deranged drummer's solo performance.

The attack probably only lasted a few seconds, but for Patrick Stubbs, the end could not have come soon enough. As a troupe of orderlies and doctors dragged Jackie quite literally kicking and screaming away from her cowering husband, he crawled into a corner and through deep irregular breaths, muttered over and over again, "I'm sorry, I'm sorry."

But this time, sorry was not going to be enough.

His nose was bleeding quite badly from the assault and his left eye would be black by the morning, as would his ribs where her fists had pounded hard. He did not know what to think or how to react, but even in his shock, he could not return the gaze of his wife who was propped up in a chair at the opposite end of the corridor. This time, there would be no going back.

It was the end, in more ways than one.

Chapter Eleven
Gut Lock

Fear makes them with the Anabaptists joyne, for if a Hostess doe receive their
coyne, she in a dish of water or a paile, will new baptize it lest it
something aile.

"It's a token!" Samuel Goldberg declared, as if his diagnosis should have been obvious to anyone. "And it's in remarkable condition, given its age," a fact that the coin's new owner had managed to work out for himself.

"I'll give you fifty quid for it," the over-eager collector insisted, reaching into his pocket to pull out his wallet in readiness for the trade.

"I don't want to sell it," Jake stated as firmly as he could manage. "It's just that, well, I want to know more about it really."

"Then go see a bloody historian and stop wasting my time," the older man snapped, thrusting the coin back into Jake's hand and swivelling around in his chair, as he turned his back on his unwanted visitor to focus his attention on a tray of nineteenth-century silver shillings.

Jake made no response and for a couple of seconds, the relentless hum of the traffic along the Charing Cross Road was the only sound. Just as Jake was about to leave, the man spoke up again, but he did not turn to look at his unwilling customer, as if he had merely a passing interest in Jake's presence. It was more than obvious that the collector's professional interest had been aroused. The man was hooked.

"How did you come by it?" he enquired casually, clearly suspicious of the young man who stood awkwardly before him.

"It's been in the family for years," Jake found himself saying without a second's hesitation, but the lie didn't stop there.

"My uncle died recently. He left a few things for me and this was amongst them." The story came too easily, as always, but on this occasion, Jake had to clasp his hands together to prevent them from rising up to cover his mouth as he spoke. Two months of intensive sales training had taught him the pitfalls of non-verbal communication, and Jake didn't want this sly old curator to get any ideas.

"Such items are rare. Very few survived; although occasionally, one turns up like this," Jake was informed. "Usually, they're in an awful condition as they've been lying in the river for centuries and get turned over by the tide, once in a blue moon. If you happen to be walking on the foreshore at low tide, you might just get lucky, but I haven't heard of a good one turning up like that for, well, years actually. In any case, this one's not been hiding away in the Thames, that's for sure."

"So, what is it, exactly?" Jake asked tentatively, hoping that he would show some pity on him and share an ounce or two of his privileged information. He was in luck. It had been a quiet day and a boring week and Samuel Goldberg rarely turned down an opportunity to show off his expertise to the less well informed.

"Well," he started to say, pausing briefly to file the tray of common shillings. "It was minted near to London Bridge," he announced, as if that were a matter of fact to the whole population of London and was about to continue when Jake interrupted him.

"What, the bridge that they shipped to America?" Jake asked and wished very soon afterwards that he had not.

"No!" Goldberg snapped, as if the mistake was a common one and one that he was fed up of hearing. "That was Rennie's bridge."

He paused for a moment and, for what seemed like the very first time, made eye contact with Jake and that most personal of interactions seemed to fracture some of the ice that had formed between them.

For a while afterwards, the edge in the man's voice seemed to fade and, after telling rather than inviting Jake to sit down, he continued with the impromptu history lesson.

"Rennie's bridge replaced the old bridge in 1831, but it was dismantled in 1971 to make way for the new London Bridge," he said, nodding his head in the rough direction of the river, which was a good twenty minutes' walk away.

Samuel Goldberg then snapped his fingers and held out his hand at which the coin was placed back into his grasp. "No, this was born close to the Medieval bridge," he purred, his expansive eyebrows rising up as he did so, but his overshadowed eyes were now transfixed. "On the Southwark side, you see," he added, pointing at the embossed lettering as if the point were of the utmost importance. A momentary pause followed as the slightly built man caressed the coin and narrowed his eyes, as if in remembrance of all those forgotten years to which this insignificant piece of metal had borne witness.

"Nineteenth-century 'vandals' destroyed the old bridge to make way for the boats, which couldn't get under the low arches and with it sank eight hundred years of our history." The man appeared to be physically shaken by the news, as if it had happened only yesterday. "Preposterous act," he scowled, studying the coin through his eyeglass and grimacing like a gargoyle as he did so.

"What were the coins used for?" Jake asked, but he would have to wait for the answer.

"You know something?" the curator asked of no one in particular. "When they demolished the remains of the crypt from Beckett's Chapel, which stood right in the middle of the old bridge, they just let what human bones were interred there fall into the river!" Samuel Goldberg shook his head from side to side, still staring at the object in his hands and Jake sensed that he should not let the man's obvious dismay go unanswered.

"Disgraceful," his unwary customer stuttered, in a desperate attempt to add something to the conversation, "but I guess that's the price of progress!"

At that, Goldberg's sea-grey eyes turned colder still and locked with Jake's until the visitor averted his gaze to look sheepishly at the parquet floor at his feet. Realising that he'd said the wrong thing, Jake tried to make amends, but it was too late.

"I mean, the blitz would have seen to it in the end, wouldn't it?" but there was no response from the disgruntled collector and Jake began to shift uncomfortably in his seat. "Or maybe the great fire? 1666 and all that?"

"There had been a fire on the bridge already in 1633!" Goldberg said as if everyone knew that. "It burned down half the buildings on the northern half of the bridge and they weren't rebuilt by the time of the Great Fire. Had they been, then the fire may well have spread across the bridge to the south side. The gap acted as a natural break, but the rest of the houses were consumed. You should have listened more at school."

Something had changed in Goldberg's demeanour and Jake thought that he would get no more assistance from him. He'd blown it for sure with his stupid questions, although he found it hard to understand how anyone could get so irate over something that had happened hundreds of years before his own birth.

"Sorry," said Jake instinctively, finding himself apologising as if the man were his headmaster and he was back at school, in detention after being caught doodling in his history class.

"De Colechurch went down with that church, although some would have you believe that his remains have been preserved in some old casket, but I don't believe it. The man who built the bridge in 1176, treated like common rubbish, and as for your other question, I've already said, it's not a coin," Goldberg scolded, "it's a token. They were made by tradesmen as small change for their customers."

For a few moments longer, Goldberg continued to explain. Maybe it was just the momentum of the tale, sailing on to its conclusion, but it was more likely to be simply the fading hope that he could still persuade Jake to part with this small portion of his supposed inheritance.

"In the seventeenth century, there was a general shortage of coinage in small enough denominations to make everyday purchases," he explained. "From the middle of the century, when the civil war began, until the restoration of the monarchy in 1660, the shortage of coins was at its height as none were being minted. During these years numerous tokens were made by all sorts of tradespeople in and around London and they came to be accepted as legal tender for a while."

"Before the Commonwealth, minting your own coinage was considered to be a treasonable offence and so, many tradesmen resorted to cutting silver coins in half or even into quarters to exchange for goods. You see in those days a coin's value was determined by the weight of the metal from which it was made."

"Isn't that where we get the 'farthing' from," asked Jake, at last having something useful to add.

"Exactly! The Farthing, or *fourth thing*, was a quarter penny, and though coins were later minted they started out like pizza slices of old pennies."

Goldberg paused for breath there, intent on ending his little recital, but it was apparent from Jake's expression that his thirst for knowledge had not been quenched and so, somewhat reluctantly, the man continued.

"I've not seen a token with these initials before so I can't tell you who made it, I'm afraid. The crossed oars indicate that it's a Waterman's token and in 1663, he would have plied his trade from the river stairs at either end of the old bridge." He paused for a moment to think and then his eyes grew wide, as he recalled a similar coin that had passed through his hands a few years before. "It had two sets of initials on it, if I remember correctly," he mumbled, rifling his way through two separate volumes of hand-written records.

"Yes, there was TR and JC, that's it. JC.

"That one was dated earlier than this, so if the date on your one is anything to go by, it was one of the last to be made. Charles II had been crowned three years before and official coins began to appear in larger numbers and in lower values soon afterwards." He paused to squint at Jake's newly found treasure through the eyepiece one last time, as if in need of final reassurance before committing himself.

"It's of tiptop quality. Yes. Superb. I'll give you a hundred, final offer, take it or leave it."

At first, Jake made no reply and after allowing him a couple of seconds to mull over the increased offer, Goldberg restated somewhat more forcefully, which seemed to shake Jake from his sudden trance.

"I'll, I think, I mean, I'll think it over, thanks," Jake mumbled and meekly held out his hand in anticipation of the token being returned. And it was, somewhat begrudgingly and although Goldberg was silent for a moment, his aggressive stance returned with a vengeance.

"Well, here's my contact details," he said, thrusting a small blue and gold business card across the desk. "If you do change your mind, I'd be grateful if you would give me first refusal, email is best," he said rather too sharply to encourage any such reciprocal behaviour.

"Yes. I will. Certainly," Jake lied. "I owe you that much for the information," he added with a nod and a forced smile. It was obvious that there was little sincerity behind it though and Goldberg muttered something to that effect as Jake stood up to go. It wasn't coherent enough to warrant a response and as Jake opened the door and repeated his thanks, the man did not even raise his head from the far more valuable set of coins that were now laid once more upon the desk before him.

But before leaving, Jake had one more thing that he felt compelled to ask and he knew of no one else who could provide him with the answer.

"The river stairs, you know, for the old bridge," he stuttered. Goldberg's eyes looked up to stare across at Jake, but his head remained still, like a snooker player, about to launch into a long pot.

"What about them?"

"Well, would they still be there? I mean, have they survived?"

"Of course not!" Goldberg scoffed. "They'd be almost as old as the Tamesis river itself."

"Don't you mean The Thames?"

"No, I *mean* Tamesis!" said Goldberg with a look that could have started a fire. "It's the ancient name for the river, its Celtic name. It means the *dark one*, if you're interested!"

"Oh, I see. That's a bit odd isn't it?" said Jake, confused, but Goldberg had had enough of educating the younger generation.

"I told you, the bridge was destroyed and both banks are now awash with office blocks, now good day to you, I've got work to do even if you haven't!"

As he stepped outside, Jake snuggled into his woollen scarf and turned up his collar against the cold. It was a sharp Saturday morning in the grip of winter, but he had the wind in his sails now and was determined to discover more about the coin's origins and the fate of the lost bridge. Lisa had gone to visit her parents in Manchester for the weekend and so he was determined to indulge himself still further.

He had always been an historian at heart, and so the urge was not entirely alien to him, but the next step was not so obvious and the real difficulty was knowing quite where to begin. After grabbing a late breakfast at a burger bar near Trafalgar Square, he decided to head to the site of the old bridge itself. From what he'd been told that morning he knew that any trace of it was unlikely to remain, but it was his only lead and whilst he didn't know for sure that the location of the current bridge actually marked the site of the original structure, it seemed appropriate enough that he should begin his search as close as possible to where the token began its life.

What he hoped to find out, he really had no idea, but for now Jake was happy to while his time away on an open-ended adventure. It had been obvious from the things that weren't said, that the token had some significant value to a collector, which was likely to be well in excess of the hundred pounds that he'd been offered. So, it made sense to investigate its history as much as possible, before making any decision on whether or not to part with it. In any case, in the couple of days that the token had been in his possession, Jake had grown rather fond of it, so much so that it was now firmly zipped into the back of his wallet for safekeeping.

After a torturous journey on the Underground, Jake resurfaced at Bank station some forty minutes later and followed the exit signs for London Bridge.

But when he finally emerged into the early afternoon light, his felt compelled to first seek out the approach to the old bridge itself, if such a thing were still possible. Jake figured that such an impressive structure must have left some mark on the concrete and brick of the city, however insignificant.

In practice, it was not all that difficult to find. Although the buildings in that part of London have been transformed in the three or four centuries since the Great Fire, which destroyed a raft of tightly packed timber-framed housing in just a few days and nights, the layout of the streets is remarkable in its tenure. In fact, most of the main thoroughfares of the city can be traced right back to Roman times, when the central district of Londinium was first laid down by slaves and artisans, and many still bear names that speak freely of their ancient purposes.

Bread Street, Milk Street, Vine Street and Wood Street to name but a few, and so it should have come as no surprise to Jake to find that his search was a relatively easy one. He started at the Monument, where another tube station goes to ground, an obvious place to begin any historical survey in this part of London. The column rises two hundred feet or so in remembrance of the Great Fire, from the site of St Margaret's church that was the first of many places of worship to perish in that fateful year of Our Lord 1666. Yet Jake found no reference to the bridge upon the metal plaque that adorns its base, but its location on the old roadway that still runs down towards the Thames was an obvious pointer.

Even so, he wasted the best part of an hour wandering aimlessly around the city streets until, quite by accident, he stumbled across his first clue. Less than a hundred yards away from the Monument stands the Church of St Magnus the Martyr, rebuilt by Wren after the fire destroyed its predecessor. In its churchyard, Jake found the answer to his first question. A simple inscription on the stone wall of the yard reads:

This churchyard formed part of the roadway approach to Old London Bridge, 1176-1831

As Jake paused to read the plaque once more, he looked around, expecting to see someone to his rear but there was no one. The hairs on his arms and neck had stood to attention as an icy blast breathed through the arch, as if from the long extinct shoreline that was now buried beneath offices and car parks. It was like reading someone's epitaph, chiselled by a stranger's hand into the cold marble of a headstone, as if the bridge itself had once lived and breathed.

He slipped inside the huge oak doors of the building's largely featureless facade, but even within the confines of the church there was no warmth to be had. He wandered uncomfortably around, staring at each of the impressive stained-glass windows that were unusually free of the protective grilles, which serve to keep the vandals at bay in most English churches. It was dark inside, but the cold welcome meant that he didn't bother to loosen his scarf or to unbutton his coat.

He didn't plan to be inside for long.

There was something about old churches that always left him glancing over his shoulder and up and down every pew, whenever he took the time to amble respectfully around one. It was as if he didn't really belong in there. He didn't find them at all welcoming, he didn't marvel in awe and wonder at their architecture and although their history always interested him, there was just something about these old homages to someone else's God that left him feeling unnerved. He wasn't at all religious, but neither was he an atheist, he just never knew what to believe or who to believe in, and so he'd always believed in himself first and everyone else last.

Until he came upon the marvel that was the Chapel of Saint Thomas a Beckett on London Bridge, its eternal image preserved in a portrait on glass.

Jake could even make out the etchings of the bustling houses, crammed in on either side of the bulging structure and the fast-flowing waters beneath.

He had struck gold.

"Impressive, wasn't it?" The gruff voice came from nowhere. There had been no patter of footsteps to forewarn him of impending company, and so Jake quite literally screamed. In the immediate aftermath, it all seemed quite funny, but in that split-second, Jake thought that it was the dead themselves who had spoken.

In reality, it was just the church warden, who seeing Jake's obvious interest in the church of Saint Thomas, had sidled up beside him to give this bewildered visitor the benefit of his wisdom. In those ten or so minutes, Jake learned of the chapel's vaulted crypt and of its complex roof, that was supported by ornate pillars of *breath-taking craftsmanship*.

"The 'brothers of the bridge' were free to decide for themselves how to run their day-to-day business," the warden recounted. "And by the end of the fifteenth century, they could keep the collections from their own services for use in the upkeep of the bridge." Although the warden's words were spoken slowly, almost with reverence, it was clear that each one was individually chosen and that this speech was well rehearsed. He wasn't finished yet. "The parish of St Thomas was the most unusual ward of medieval London and of any time since. It stretched from the great stone gateway at the Southwark end to the city limits and became what locals tended to call the 'Bridge Ward Within' long before it was formally adopted as such."

"What kinda people lived on the bridge?"

The new voice had an unmistakeable American twang to it, and Jake felt a little annoyed that his personal tour guide was no longer his alone to enjoy, as several other sightseers had strayed far from the usual tourist trail to join him.

"The houses were home to the many businesses and shops that lined the street across the river," the warden answered in the same considered tone. "Printers, merchants, leather workers, all sorts really. Some of the houses were very grand indeed, like Nonesuch House, which was erected without the use of a single nail and was imported ready-to-assemble from Holland," he chuckled. "A sixteenth-century flatpack, if you like!"

After glancing at his watch for the second time in quick succession, he saw that the day was passing him by, and so he moved to bring his unscheduled tour to an end. "In later years, after the reformation, the chapel on the bridge was desecrated," he added sadly, "and fell into misuse, initially as a grocer's shop and then finally, a common warehouse."

The sacrilege of this final act was not lost on the small gathering. The American man in the blue sports cap and polo shirt had the final word— "Shame!"—a response that seemed quite inadequate in the circumstances.

As the warden revealed the final chapter in the chapel's history, when De Colechurch's remains were dumped into the Thames, he did so with the same air of loss that Jake heard from the numismatic at Charing Cross – the sentiment seemed to be catching. Having listened patiently to the warden's tale, Jake was surprised to feel some of that bewilderment himself, coupled with an overpowering sense of sadness that he could not quite put into words.

"If you want to leave a small donation, there's a box at the back," the warden said, hoping to drum up some additional contributions for the cause. "Oh, and there's usually a model of the old bridge in the foyer, but it's loaned out to an exhibition at the moment; its due back soon so if you're ever in the area again, do drop in. It's well worth it!" The American couple said that they would, thanked the warden for his time and waddled from the church, each forcing a ten-pound note into the wooden box as they went.

"Expensive holiday!" said Jake, prompting a sharp glance from the woman. Despite Jake's new-found sense of sympathy for the lost architecture of London, he could only bring himself to part with a pound. Jake had never been into good causes; however good they were.

He wandered around inside for another half an hour, inspecting the inscriptions on the tombstones underfoot and reading the plaques, dedicated to heroic sons lost in distant wars. When he finally managed to tear himself away, it was late afternoon. The winter light was beginning to fade and as it did so, the rapidly falling temperature provided all the encouragement that Jake needed to call off his search for the day.

The short walk across the river to London Bridge station gave him the chance to see where the mighty bridge might once have spanned the Thames, and to visualise where Beckett's chapel would have been. As he dodged between the lanes of human traffic that poured like a football crowd across the New London Bridge, he felt a long overdue rush of guilt as he recalled the events that had surrounded his last trip to the capital, less than a year earlier. A business trip, on which he'd taken in an exhibition at Earl's Court, but which had also provided the perfect backdrop to an evening visit to the fleshpots of Soho.

He stopped at the centre of the bridge to stare out across the river, and for a while was content to gaze downstream at the familiar sights of London. The Tower, the HMS Belfast and Tower Bridge, with its roadway aloft to allow a tall ship passage upstream, the lights of Canary Wharf jostling for position in the distance.

As for traces of any medieval structure, there were none to be seen, so he continued on his way, occasionally pausing to gaze down to the swirling waters below. It was then that he caught sight of some familiar stone steps that led down to the water's edge on the southern shore, and something deep in his memory shifted and he was caught beneath. A long, thin, wooden boat bobbed gently at the river's edge; its mooring rope lassoed at the foot of the stairs. It was completely empty, save for two long oars and from Jake's bird's-eye view, they appeared to be laid out in the form of an x-shaped cross.

Jake straightened up, then backed away and would have continued on his backward journey—straight into the road and beneath the wheels of a red London bus—had he not collided with a couple of Japanese tourists who managed to stop him from becoming just another casualty of the hellish London traffic. He may have mumbled an apology then, but he wasn't sure one way or another.

Memories swarmed all over him, but none of them seemed to belong to him.

**

A few hours later, Jake sat alone in his sitting room, the house illuminated from every corner.

When the telephone rang, a few seconds passed him by before he felt able to answer it. Lisa's voice dragged him from his trance, but there was something in his wife's tone that seemed different, and it wasn't long before she let him in on her little secret.

"There's something I have to tell you, darling," she said almost apologetically. "I didn't want to tell you like this, but my mom guessed, so it can't wait until I get back, as you know what she's like, she's already telling everyone."

"What is it, love?" Jake asked, already nervous that he knew exactly what it was going to be, and even before she broke the good news, his hackles were already up.

"I'm pregnant!" she answered.

When the two of them recalled the moment a few days later, Jake would insist that he had only stayed silent for a moment, as he collected his thoughts in the face of such an unexpected shock. Yet Lisa would remain adamant that a good minute had gone by, before she had managed to coax a response from him.

In those intervening seconds, the world seemed dark and the lights that filled the room were lost in shadow. And eyes were everywhere. Staring out from children's faces.

Gaunt expressions. Lost features. Long dead. Long forgotten.

"How long?" Even to him, it sounded like he was asking how many weeks she had left to live. "I mean, when?" he said, trying to correct himself.

"We're due in August," she said, a little subdued. "Aren't you happy about it?" she asked, suddenly close to tears, until Jake answered in the way that he knew he should.

"Of course, yes of course, I am, babe. It's just a little, unexpected," he explained. "That's all!"

She laughed then and for a while longer they chatted about who they were going to tell next and what their reactions might be, but soon they said their goodbyes and as he placed the receiver gently back in its resting place, he found himself wishing that the explanation he had given was really that simple.

He wasn't ready to be a dad, not just yet.

Chapter Twelve
Long Entry

For he's the greatest murderer alive, that doth a man of his good name deprive, with base calumnious slanders and false lies: tis the worst villany of villanies, to blast a good man's name with scandal's breath, makes his dishonour long survive his death.

"There's a visitor for you, Mister Gallagher," the care assistant announced rather casually, as if the arrival of unexpected guests for this particular resident was an everyday occurrence.

"Who is it?" Ted asked, more in amazement than excitement. He'd had enough excitement these past few days to last him for the rest of them and would rather have been left alone, to catch up on the sleep that had begun to elude him again at night. "I'm not expecting anyone," he explained as he slowly pushed himself up out of the armchair, with the aid of the young girl who willingly took his weight on her arm.

Ted had been feeling a little under the weather recently. The excursion to London had hit him hard and he'd been unable to remember much about the journey home, but it had taken far longer than it should have, so much so that he had not made it back to the home until after midnight.

"It's probably one of your girlfriends, Mister Gallagher," the red-haired girl teased. "I hear you've got plenty of them!"

"Oh, away with you, Maisy," Ted replied, not altogether displeased at the girl's teasing. Her name was Daisy, but she didn't bother to correct him. In that place, you took whatever name you were given as nine times out of ten, by the next day, they had usually forgotten it again. Ted knew that there was only one likely candidate and as the door to the day room swung open, Jackie Stubbs wandered in, but there was something different about his old friend's girl today, in both her appearance and her demeanour.

Her manner was altogether more assertive, as if her life once again had some purpose, but the expression on her face told a different story.

"Ted," she gasped, as if he had been a favourite uncle all her life. "Ted, we have to talk," she stuttered. "I don't know what to do, I've got no one else to turn to," but as her voice began to break, she fell into his accepting arms. Another elderly gentleman put down his newspaper and allowed his reading glasses to slip down to the tip of his nose. His inquisitive eyes scanned the middle-aged woman from top to toe, but his interest was in the scandal and so, he made no attempt to ask what was wrong or to offer his assistance.

Ted gave his fellow resident an unwelcome stare and when that failed to work, he tried a different tack.

"Why don't you mind your own business, Mister Jones, and I'll mind mine!" Mister Jones continued to stare for a second or two more and then slowly raised the broadsheet newspaper back up to cover his eyes, but not his ears, from the ensuing drama. Ted then turned his attention back to the ailing woman. "Now come on, Jacqueline, whatever is the matter?"

"He's dead," she announced. Ted didn't really have to ask to whom she was referring, but he had to be sure and so he asked the question anyway. It was then that Jackie looked up to meet his gaze halfway. "My son is dead. Terry is dead."

Yet even in her grief she couldn't help but notice the neat bandage on his cheek. "What happened to your face?"

"Oh, it's nothing," said Ted, brushing aside her concern, "I cut myself shaving, that's all. Now don't mind me, tell me what's happened!"

Wearily, she recounted the events of the last few days. Ted listened attentively, nodding where appropriate and occasionally reaching out an arm or a hand when it seemed that his best friend's daughter might not be able to continue. Mister Jones's newspaper was now at half-mast and his reading glasses were, once again, teetering on the brink.

A sharp glance from Ted was not enough to persuade him to avert his eyes this time and Ted could not be bothered to take issue with him again. Later maybe, but right then, there were more important matters to attend to.

"So, you still haven't been allowed to see him?"

"No," she answered and burst into a fresh flood of tears. Mister Jones's newspaper was on his lap now and his glasses had been neatly stowed away inside the chest pocket of his crisp white shirt. "They won't let me in to see him at all. They won't even confirm when they will release him for his," she paused again to gather her composure, but it didn't work. "For…his…funeral."

Ted bent down as best he could and held her tight and she hugged him back as if he were her last friend in the world. As she burrowed her head into the sagging skin of his neck, he drew her closer still and inhaled the sweet scent of her damp hair, to usher himself back down Time's winding path, to an age when his future had seemed to be paved in gold.

Her hair, like so many other things in his life, reminded him of Lucy.

As Jackie sobbed in his arms, he concluded that it was finally time to tell his tale. She had to know what he knew if only for the sake of her sanity. If not, then forever more she would blame herself for the death of her only son, but Ted knew that she was not to blame. The likelihood had always been that someday, the past was going to catch up with Terry Stubbs.

"Jackie," Ted began, squeezing her arm gently in his arthritic hand, an effort that set off shooting pains all through his bony old fingers. "Jackie, there is something that I have to tell you and some things that I have to show you."

The bedraggled woman looked up at him through sad and weary eyes. Mister Jones's newspaper was now all but forgotten and his eyes were fixed firmly on the woman's legs, as she hauled herself ungraciously to her feet.

She caught the direction of his gaze as she righted herself. "What are you looking at? You dirty old man," she said, straightening her skirt as she did so. It was the perfect riposte. Mister Jones blushed the colour of a post-box as one or two of his lady companions in the surrounding chairs turned to look in his direction and right on cue, they tutted their disapproval. He wasted no time at all in gathering up his things and cowered out of the dayroom and towards his own.

Ted smiled with an air of intense satisfaction as he watched him go, and after the remaining myopic eyes had returned to their own business, he looked back at Jackie and raised his hand to ask for her assistance.

"I'm suffering a little bit more than usual today," he explained as she pulled him to his feet, passing him his elegant walking stick from beside the chair.

Ted could not help but notice the look of recognition on Jackie's face as she passed him the stick. He thought he knew what she might be thinking, and he felt that it warranted some explanation. He also reasoned that the diversion might help to calm her nerves a little, before he broke more news that she might not want to hear.

"It was a present," he explained. "From your father, a few years ago now."

"Yes," Jackie confirmed. "I know, although mostly when I think about Dad nowadays, I picture him in his wheelchair," she sighed. "My mother was in her forties when she had me," she went on and then said, almost too quietly to hear. "She always called me her 'little miracle'."

After a moment or two of respectful silence, Jackie squeezed the old man's hand as he pressed the stick to the ground and hauled himself upright. "No, I'm alright, Daisy," he insisted, motioning the young girl away with his free hand. "I'm okay, now that I'm on my feet."

The redhead raised her eyebrows and smiled at his unfamiliar visitor, pleased that this pleasant old man had a visitor at last and went off to tend to another, more needy pensioner, who was waving frantically at her from the other side of the room.

"My arthritis started early," Ted explained as they walked, "and when it did, your father and I were still in regular enough contact. He always carried this stick," he recalled, "ever since the war, he always had it." Ted paused for a minute to give his knee a rest and took advantage of the break in proceedings to finish his tale. "And on one of his final visits, he gave it to me. Said that he had no more use for it."

Ted shook his head and squeezed hard on the ornately carved handle-piece. "I'll always treasure it," he said, smiling at her. "Any odds," he went on after a momentary pause, refusing the opportunity to wallow, "let's find somewhere where we can talk more openly."

He gestured his guest through the main doors in the general direction of his room. "Too many prying eyes and ears for my liking," he winked as they headed out. "No, let's pick up some bits and pieces from my room and we'll go out and get a bite to eat," he added in a grandfatherly fashion, "You look like you might need a pick-me-up!"

**

"That's the only photograph I have of the two of us," Ted explained as he passed the dog-eared picture into Jackie's agitated hands. "Christmas '43. That's your father, on the left, he was only 20 or so," Ted said fondly.

"Where was this taken?" she asked, with a sudden air of interest that might have been lacking up until then. "It looks familiar."

Ted took the picture back and inspected it, in the hope that another look might jog his own memory. "It must have been a pub up your way somewhere," he guessed, "because I stopped with Joe and your family for the festivities that year. It was one of the best," he added with a sigh and took another gulp of stout.

"Where's that food?" Jackie asked impatiently and of no one in particular, although there was no one else seated in the heated outdoor eating area who could have overheard. They had chosen their meals from the regular pub-grub menu and not the festive one, as neither of them felt that a Christmas lunch was appropriate in the circumstances. "I've just realised how hungry I am. I haven't eaten more than a bite for two or three days now, ever since…" but she didn't finish the sentence. There was no need.

Involuntarily, she reached into the breast pocket of her jacket and broke open a new pack of twenty low-tar cigarettes, motioning the open box towards Ted, who made a makeshift cross with his two index fingers as if to ward off the devil himself.

"No, thank you all the same," he said none too convincingly. "If they smell fags on my breath when I get back, I will be for the high jump!" But still he watched Jackie like a child in front of a toy shop window, as she lit up and inhaled.

Ted forced himself to look away and up towards the back entrance to the public house, where a woman had just emerged with two steaming plates of food, which he deduced to be their order.

"It's just coming, I think," he announced, shivering a little with the cold in spite of the heaters, which stood like tall red sentries beside them.

"Are you two alright out here?" the waitress asked, concerned for the old man in particular, "isn't it a bit chilly?"

"It's not too bad!" Ted lied, gesturing at Jackie as he explained, "She was desperate for a cigarette so these days, we have to sit in the cheap seats! Not like the good old days. It would have been like a *pea-souper* in there in years gone by!"

"'fraid so!" the waitress nodded, too young for her parents to have told her about the London smog of the 1950s. "Well, there's room inside if you want to come in when you've finished!"

"She might be right, you know," Jackie conceded. "It is a bit chilly now the rain's stopped." But it wasn't long before they were each tucking into steak and kidney pie and chips, washed down with a cold beer. A good old-fashioned lunch to accompany a good old-fashioned tale.

"That must be a nasty scratch, Ted," Jackie observed, reaching over to gently stroke his face, an action that Ted found rather too familiar, but he didn't move his head away. "You need to be more careful!"

"So much for the safety razor!" he laughed. "It's not as bad as the bandage would have you believe! It's only a nick, but the doctor had a look at it for me and tidied it up, so no harm done." He started to peel off the patch and as Jackie started to raise an objection, it was off. "I like to let it get some air, so I've been taking the dressing off whenever they're not looking!" he sniggered, like a naughty schoolboy who's been caught smoking behind the bike sheds once too often.

The scratch had faded considerably in the intervening days, but it was still prominent enough not to be missed. The doctor had been concerned enough to insist on a tetanus jab, which Ted could well have done without. It wasn't the sort of scratch that might result from an hour spent in the garden pruning the roses, and it left Jackie feeling dubious as to his explanation.

"Shall we go inside?" asked Ted, taking the waitress's advice to heart. "I'm freezing my you-know-what's off here!" Jackie didn't object but took a final drag of nicotine from a last cigarette before rising to her feet.

"They weren't too keen on letting you out, were they?" asked Jackie, as she stubbed out the short-lived cigarette and made her way inside, her almost empty plate abandoned to whatever scavengers were lurking close by. Ted took the remainder of his pie with him, never one to leave food on his plate and a testament to the war-years' mantra of *waste not, want not*.

"Well, I disobeyed the rules, didn't I!" he said in a mockingly stern tone. "That lot would have been useful back in the forties. They could have run the camps up in Scotland. The Germans wouldn't have stood a chance!"

"When did you first meet my father?" Jackie asked as their laughter subsided.

"Back in 1940," Ted answered after a moment's thought, as if he could hardly believe that the years had gone by so quickly. "And in the circumstances, it's a miracle that our friendship ever got off the ground at all. In fact, it could have been over before it had begun." Ted placed a last mouthful of steak in his mouth and began to chew slowly, savouring each and every morsel. He had been lucky with his teeth. After all these years, he still had enough of his own to chomp his way through as much meat as he could get his hands on.

"I was in the Medical Corps," Ted went on. "I suppose I was what they would call today a 'paramedic', but without the green overalls. Much of our training was on the job, there just wasn't the time to spend years at college," he added with a wry smile. "There was a war on, you know!"

"There had been a massive explosion down on the river, near to where the previous London Bridge stood, you know, the one that they knocked down in 1971, before they put up that new monstrosity. Very good," he said to no one in particular, jabbing his fork up and down in the general direction of the cold pie, and then added, "You know, the one they sold to the Yanks." Jackie had heard the tale before, but she didn't know for sure, so she just nodded, and Ted continued on a seemingly more relevant tack.

"Anyway, we were sent down there after they told us that the Royal Engineers had been disarming an unexploded bomb, which had landed in the mudflats, but it was booby trapped as they often were and so the bloody thing went off." Ted shook his head again and Jackie could not help but notice that beads of sweat had started to form on his forehead. He wiped them away with a monogrammed handkerchief and attempted to blame it on the meal and the open fire that was now smouldering nicely at the far end of the room.

"Your father was down there and when we reached him, we thought he was a goner. The other one was dead, there was no doubt about that because his legs were ten yards away from the rest of him." The thought of which was enough to turn Jackie's recent lunch over in her stomach.

Ted apologised immediately for his insensitive remark, but Jackie raised her hand. "Please, go on," she insisted. "Really, do go on, please."

"Well, we got your father up to the ambulance, but in those days, there just wasn't the equipment on board to save him and his only chance was to get him to a hospital as soon as we could."

"Was he conscious?" Jackie asked. "Did he say anything?"

"Sometimes," he replied, "but none of it made any sense to me, not then." The hidden meaning was clear, and Jackie was quick to pounce on an equally obvious question in return.

"Does it make sense to you now?" she asked. Ted did not answer immediately, but slowly drained his glass. Eventually, he answered simply and firmly that it did, without moving his lips.

"Would you like another drink?" she asked, very much in need of another herself. "I need to nip to the loo, so I'll get them in if you like."

"No, let me get them," Ted insisted, reaching for his wallet once more.

"Certainly not!" insisted Jackie. "This isn't the nineteen forties and anyway, you bought the meal, so sit back down," she ordered. "Same again?"

Ted nodded and thanked her. As she walked away in the direction of the bar, he found himself admiring the female form for the first time in a very long time, until he was sharply reprimanded by the voice that lived in his head. The voice, as usual, was Lucy's.

Jackie returned a few moments later and as she settled the two glasses onto the small and weathered table, she turned the conversation towards a different theme. One that had been playing on her mind, ever since she had forwarded on her late father's letter a few weeks earlier.

"Why didn't you and mum see eye to eye, Ted?" she asked bluntly.

The question was well prepared, but it still came like a bolt from the blue for Ted, just as he was about to take a first swig of his fresh beer. As the rim of the glass reached his lips, it stayed there, finally completing the motion a second or two later, until his elbow was on a level with his chin. The glass was half-empty when it resumed its position on the table.

"It's a long story," Ted confessed without raising his eyes from the glass. "One for another day perhaps." For a few moments, there was silence between them, but Jackie was not to be put off so easily.

"Dad made me promise to contact you," she continued in the same suspicious tone, "about the funeral arrangements. He knew that there wasn't long to go by then and he said that mother would never get in touch with you, if it was left up to her."

Jackie was looking at Ted like an inquisitive Afghan dog, her head uncomfortably angled to one side so that her grey-brown hair hung untidily on her shoulder.

"Any idea why my mother held onto that letter of Dad's for so long?" she asked. Still no answer came, so she went on fishing for a reply. "Only, I found it stashed in a box of stuff when I was going through mum's things, you know, after her funeral."

"What sort of stuff?" Ted asked, his interest stirred and his nerves shaken.

"Memorabilia," she answered. "Medals, photographs, some of the two of you, some with mum. Letters, from you mainly, but also love letters from her to Dad." She paused for a second, almost as if she were waiting to see if the old man would physically lick his lips at the prospect of rummaging through her late father's memoirs. "Would you like to see them?" she asked at last, but although Ted nodded his head, he was only being polite. The medals he had seen, the photographs were stored away in his head and as for the letters, well, he knew what he had written and he had never much cared for Annie's opinion, whether written or in person.

"There's something else, something that I think you might be keen to take a look at, Ted," Jackie teased. "And I'm hoping that you might be able to explain it, because from the limited amount that I've read so far, it's all Greek to me."

"Explain what?" Ted asked, a little irritated at the suggestion that he might know more than he was letting on.

"My father's diaries," she announced quietly. "And some scrapbooks, from the war years."

For a time then, nothing else passed between them as they sat and stared at each other, like teenagers engrossed in some mindless game.

Eventually, it was Ted who spoke up. "Joe kept a diary?" he asked in disbelief. Jackie's smile confirmed it to be true and Ted could hardly disguise his excitement. Or at least, that's how it seemed. "What period? Which years do they cover?" he said, betraying his true feelings of trepidation at what might be contained within them.

"The war years, mainly," she replied. "The 1940's to be precise." And at that, Ted's expression changed from one of fatherly concern to an altogether different look. "I suppose it was how he got interested in journalism," she said, almost to herself.

"So, you know it all then?" he challenged, leaning back in his chair. "Your father was an excellent writer, as you know, so I'm sure that his diary is no different." She didn't respond in words, but just smiled once again and looked away, in remembrance of happier times. "Have you read them, all of them?" Ted prompted, clearly desperate to know of all that she knew.

"Not yet, but I think I've read the important bits," she lied, "but before I let you loose on them, I need to know what you know. So that I can make up my own mind." In reality, she had read only a few lines, but she had inherited her mother's distrustful nature and wanted to tease as much information out of the old man as she could before deciding if he was truly on her side. She had come to trust her mother's judgement, especially when it came to men, after failing to heed Annie's warnings about her own choice of husband.

She had also not been satisfied by his apparent unwillingness to explain why he and her mother had not been friends; her mother had been *her* best friend and so Annie's mistrust continued to cast a long shadow over her daughter's latest acquaintance.

"Okay," Ted replied wearily, taking another gulp of stout to lubricate his now dry throat. He then plunged a hand into each pocket in turn but was disappointed to learn that he had consumed his last mint some hours ago. "But don't expect the unabridged version, we haven't got time for that!"

"Whatever it takes, Ted," Jackie answered with more composure than she felt inside. "I've got all day and all night, if necessary," and then, as if in sudden recollection of her present predicament, added sorrowfully, "I've got nothing to rush home for, have I?"

"Joe was lucky not to lose his leg," Ted started, resisting the temptation to expend any further sympathy on his old friend's daughter and choosing to begin with a headline. "They said he wouldn't walk again, but he proved them wrong on that point too," he added with a wry smile before taking a more sparing swig of beer. "But for a while, walking again was the least of his worries."

"Within a week, they moved him to another hospital," he explained with his eyes firmly fixed on Jackie's so that he would not miss any hint of understanding in her face. "They said that he had experienced some 'complications' and that he needed 'specialist treatment'. Are they familiar words, Jackie?" Ted asked carefully.

Jackie didn't speak, but her eyes seemed to flash in recognition. When she finally averted them to inspect her fingers that were battling like a pit full of vipers in her lap, he continued with his tale.

"The London Hospital for Tropical Diseases," he proclaimed. "That's where they sent him, only he didn't know it. By then, your father was delirious. He was a bit of a celebrity in there though," Ted recalled. "He was the only serviceman under treatment who had not served in North Africa or the Far East and yet he appeared to be suffering from an unknown disease that, in learned medical opinion, was not of European origin!"

At last, Jackie's voice broke the stranglehold that Ted had held over the conversation. "What were his symptoms, Ted?" she asked, sitting forward in her chair, a trace of trepidation in her voice.

"Why?" Ted asked, wanting to check her understanding before he went on. "Are they not described in his diaries?"

Jackie gave a sharp and simple response that made it quite clear that they were not, and that she wanted to know what he knew without further delay.

"Lesions on the skin, blisters if you like."

And at that, Jackie took over, "Swellings in the groin and armpits?" Ted nodded. "Aggressiveness, difficulty breathing, that sort of thing?"

"Exactly that sort of thing, Jackie," Ted answered, knowing where her line of thought was heading. "Exactly the sort of thing that afflicted your son before…" Ted paused to think of a less painful word, but none came and so he said nothing.

She followed his meaning on what would prove to be a long and arduous journey, yet she knew that she had no choice but to climb aboard. "So, are you saying then that it's genetic, this disease? That my son suffered and died because of something that my father passed down to him?" Ted did not reply immediately so Jackie took that to mean that she was on the right track. "So why didn't I get it then, if it's hereditary?"

Ted shook his head and finished off his second pint of beer. "I didn't say that it was passed down from generation to generation. At least not in the way that you mean," but he could see that Jackie was now more confused than ever and that her confusion was starting to give way to anger. If she had inherited her mother's infamous temper, then Ted knew that he was in for a fight and so he did his best to repair the damage. "I think that it was the same affliction, but it's not in the genes."

"But my father didn't die, Ted, did he!" she insisted. "So, why did my son?"

"I don't know, Jackie, maybe his resistance was low, maybe he just couldn't fight it any longer, maybe they didn't get the antibiotics into him in time." He reached out and held her hand. "I don't know, but your father lived and for that, we must be grateful," at which Jackie pulled away from his grip.

"I fear that many others, over the years, may have been less fortunate." It was a cryptic clue, but Ted was clearly unprepared to share everything he knew, and that left Jackie with a feeling of frustration and mistrust for the man her father had always called *his best friend in this world*.

"Are you telling me the whole story?"

"I'm telling you enough for now," Ted answered, "it's too much for one sitting. We will need to meet up again and you need to read those diaries cover to cover. Once you've done that, let's meet up again and I will fill you in with the rest!"

She looked angry and felt that he must have had an ulterior motive, but he made it clear that he was not going to budge, and there was no persuading him otherwise. It was clear that she would have to spend some time with her father's legacy and once that was completed, maybe she would be able to coax from him the rest of his story.

"Well, if that's your decision, I guess I'll have to do as I'm told," she said, draining her glass and standing up as if to signal that their meeting was now at an end.

"Don't be like that!" sighed Ted. "It's for your own good."

He staggered to his feet, determined not to end their lunch date on bad terms. "Listen, my dear, once you've read what your father had to say then you will be much more likely to believe what I have to tell you," he said in an effort to reassure her that his intentions were honourable. "He kept that diary for a reason, you know!"

"What does that mean?" asked Jackie.

"It was for you," he said. "It was always for you."

Chapter Thirteen
Chapel Lock

Then comes a voyce with horror and of fright, thou foole, I'll fetch away thy soule this night.

Who's there?

Watching as I stumble down into the darkness.

Each wooden step seems to give a little beneath my feet.

The fourth croaks; a rusted hinge on an oak door.

The fifth grates; razor sharp claws on a pane of glass.

The sixth groans; a doomed ship on the high seas. And the next?

A gentle nudge and I am sinking; a condemned man who dreads the crack of the fall, yet the end doesn't come. All is submerged in the white mist when the voices rise again.

And then I plunge into the sickening depths. Filth fills my mouth where a final breath should be as I sink beneath. My legs are like lead and my arms betray me at the last.

One gold tooth, shining through the silt.

Hollows, where red eyes stare and snarl, as the swirling waters barge into my lungs.

You're mine.

I'm awake and his words slither from my lips.

My skin crawls with grease and my tongue flounders on a stranger's breath.

Chapter Fourteen

St Mary's Lock

Yet all that deare-bought Lechery would be, the greater brand of lasting Infamy, and though her Carrion Corps, rich clad, high fed (Halfe rotten living and all rotten Dead), who with her hellish courage, stout and hot, abides the brunt of many a prick shaft hot, yet being dead, and doth consumed lye, her everlasting shame shall never dye.

"Aren't you pleased?" Lisa stuttered, clearly on the point of tears.

For a moment, Jake couldn't answer. He just couldn't. He knew in his heart what his answer was, but he also knew with equal certainty what the effect would be on his pregnant wife if he was to share his true feelings with her. After all, his wife's parents were so pleased at the news, and so, he thought, should he be.

"Of course, I am," he started to say, pausing for a second to choose his words carefully. "It's just a little sooner than I expected that's all."

His wife looked up, still perilously close to breaking down again, but Jake's unconvincing explanation was doomed to failure.

"A month ago, you were all for it!" she reminded him sharply as the tears began to flow. "So, what's changed, Jake? Why have you suddenly become so…" She took a deep breath to select the most appropriate word. Then in a much more subdued tone, she shook her head and finished what she had hesitated to say, "…so bloody distant?"

The resulting hush drifted between them like a shroud that masks the living from the dead.

"I don't know babe," Jake answered more honestly than he had intended, falling back into the armchair like some worn-out drunk, his hands clasped to his head to hide his shame. Then through soiled palms, he tried to offer some defence for his sudden U-turn.

"I've not been sleeping that well," he pleaded, still searching for the excuse that might buy him some precious time to work out his defence. "You must have noticed that?" When his wife's expression told him that she had, he tried to force the point home. "Haven't you noticed?"

Lisa Harvey, who was still standing, nodded like a moody child and rubbed her weary eyes, smudging an unsightly trail of blue-black mascara across her flushed cheeks.

The sight brought about a less abrupt response than Jake felt prone to give. "I don't know what it is, darling," he said. "Really, I don't. It's just that lately, well, the future doesn't seem that bright to me anymore."

At that, his wife joined him on the sofa, never once taking her eyes off her husband as she picked up one of the embroidered scatter cushions and cradled it in her lap, as if in training for the months ahead. "What do you mean?" she asked him, somewhat bemused. "I thought your job was going really well. You've just been given a new car, for God's sake!"

"The job's fine, Lisa," he said, his tone perhaps betraying a deeper acknowledgement that something else was not at all 'fine'. "There's no problem with the job," he continued a little more sheepishly and immediately regretted the emphasis that had settled rather too clearly on his last two words.

Knowing that he would soon be called upon to explain himself again, Jake sprang to his feet and in three or four paces had crossed the room. He took out the crystal tumbler, which had been a wedding present from his best man and poured himself a shockingly large straight Irish whiskey.

"It's a bit early for that, isn't it?" his wife asked, knowing full well that her words would invoke an angry response.

"Not really," Jake replied more calmly than she'd expected, but still sure that a reprimand would follow. "Do you want one?" he asked a little too innocently for his own good.

"I'm pregnant!" No more explanation was necessary, but she raised her eyebrows and cocked her head for emphasis just in case.

For a full five minutes, neither of them uttered another word. Jake moodily sipped his undiluted drink with his eyes transfixed on the wastepaper basket in the corner of the room. Lisa's gaze did not waver either, but the tears had begun long before another word passed between them.

Finally, it was Lisa who could take it no more.

"So, do you mind telling me what the problem is, if it's not your precious job?" she sobbed, but Jake's eyes were unmoved. "Is it me?" she asked bluntly. "Have I done something else to upset you, besides conceiving your child?"

"Oh, for God's sake, Mary!" he screamed, but as soon as the unfamiliar name had burst forth into the chilled air of the room, it was if someone else had given the name life. It was Jake's lips that had moved all right, but he felt sure that the choice of name had not been his. His wife, however, was in no doubt, no doubt at all.

"Who the fuck is Mary?" she roared, quickly reaching the obvious conclusion.

For a second, Jake was just as bemused as his wife and all he could offer in his defence was a meek and hollow, 'I don't know', but it was the truth.

"And you expect me to believe that do you?" Lisa yelled. "Some tart at the office, I suppose!"

Jake could take no more.

He leapt to his feet and without another glance at his wife, announced that he was going out. The bulk of the whiskey was consumed in a single gulp and after snatching up the car keys from the top of the imitation Adams fireplace, he was halfway to the door before Lisa spoke up again.

"Where are you going?" she asked frantically, lines of anger etched over her now scarlet face.

"I don't know," Jake said again, and he didn't. He had no idea, but something told him that the car was his only sanctuary, and so he intended to drive and drive.

**

Her name should have meant nothing to him, but when Jake heard the newsreader's announcement, the penny, or more appropriately, the token, dropped with a clatter.

He could vaguely recall hearing on the previous evening's news that the body of a woman had been found on the north bank of the Thames and that the police were treating the death as suspicious. The news bulletin announced that the police had confirmed that the body was that of the missing car saleswoman, Melissa Simpson, and that a murder inquiry was now under way. A contact number for anyone who might have information that could help the police with their enquiries was also provided, but by then, Jake had shut out the unwelcome voice. For once, he was concentrating on the road, but he had no pre-planned route in mind and so, as he mulled over the consequences of this latest bombshell, he let his instincts be his guide.

His first reaction to hearing the shocking news should have been one of sorrow. A sense of great sadness for a woman who had lost her life too early and who would almost certainly still be alive, had she not had the misfortune to be the only available driver on that fateful day. Most listeners would have then reacted with anger at such a senseless murder and may have shed a tear for the girl at the thought of how she must have suffered. Finally, most would have simply been thankful that it was not one of their loved ones who had turned up on the morning tide that day.

But not Jake. He could only think of one person, someone very close to his heart. He was worried for himself first, second and last, as he was certain that he was going to be implicated in this sordid affair. If it were not for the token, of course, there might be nothing to connect him to her and the thought of coming clean to the police about it did cross his mind. After all, if it had belonged to her then someone, a close friend or a family member, may have reported it missing and if it was found in his possession, or if it was revealed as being missing, then a wily old curator on the Charing Cross Road could drop him right in it with one simple phone call.

However, he found that he'd become rather too attached to that tiny copper piece and the thought of parting with it, at any cost, filled him with dismay. In any case, he felt reassured in the belief that the coin had nothing at all to do with the dead woman. It could have been dropped by a production worker or by quality control or it could have belonged to the salesman at the local showroom; the sort of people who always go to work with three-hundred-year-old coins rattling around amongst their loose change.

Jake took no notice of the large green sign, which mapped out the routes available to him at the fast-approaching roundabout. As he tore across the give-way markings, much to the horror of an oncoming van driver, he quickly skipped into the inside lane to enable him to take the third exit, which Jake noticed was city-bound.

Yet no one had tried to claim the token, had they? The girl from the leasing company had not mentioned anyone who was trying to trace a lost coin, which any self-respecting collector would certainly have done. Jake knew that in the circumstances, he had nothing to gain and everything to lose by sharing what he knew with the police. He had no doubt that they would want to question him further, now that the girl had turned up in the worst possible way, but that prospect held no great fear for him. After all, it was finders-keepers and he was sure that he'd be able to provide an alibi to prove that he could have had no involvement in her death.

For a second or two, he allowed himself to wonder what Lisa would make of the news when she heard it. No doubt she would put two and two together and come up with five as usual, and then worry herself into a frenzy about the implications of wrongful arrest and so on and so forth.

Jake leant forward and turned up the heating. The temperature inside the car had fallen like a lead balloon as he closed in on London and the internal temperature gauge flashed at just six degrees centigrade. He could see his breath as it filled the gap between him and the windscreen and he willed the engine to warm up enough to banish the chill.

He was interrupted by a wolf-whistle that signalled that his wife had sent him a text. He ignored it. He hadn't set up his Bluetooth yet either, so voice activation would not have worked, even had he wanted to hear what she had to say. *Better not to know at this point*, he thought.

At a zebra crossing, he stopped to allow a pedestrian passage across the street, but the disconcerting figure to his left failed to take heed of the invitation. As Jake stopped and looked more intently at the hooded form, it appeared to have no intention of crossing the road, but just stood and waited, like a statue waiting for a command from some higher authority. The driver behind was displaying little interest in the sideshow, and a long blast on his horn persuaded Jake to ignore the marooned pedestrian and resume his mystery tour.

He drove on, not unduly unnerved by the experience, but he remained only dimly aware of the direction in which he was travelling. Soon enough, he found himself on one of London's main arteries, drifting inwards towards the capital. It seemed a natural direction to take. It seemed like the right direction. But to where he still had no idea.

The news of his impending fatherhood had come as a shock, but Jake could not fathom why it should have affected him so much. He had thought many times of how wonderful it would be to have a son, but now that the dream might soon become a reality, he had for no apparent reason developed cold feet. But it was more than that. Jake did not feel afraid for any financial reasons, he was not the squeamish type and so the birth held no qualms for him, and he did not believe that the sleepless nights could be anywhere near as bad as some of their more family-minded friends had suggested. Neither did he feel any real pangs of guilt at his past indiscretions, yet all the same, he felt a deep and intense dread at the prospect of becoming a father.

Was it the commitment that scared him? Maybe. Until now, it had been just him and Lisa and although they were newly married and happily so, should things ever turn sour, he had always known that both of them could walk away and no-one else would get hurt. All that was about to change.

Still, Jake knew that there was more to his apprehensive mood than any of these simple explanations could account for. Maybe it was all of them, a combination of factors that left him feeling bewildered and scared at the prospect of paternity, but maybe it was none of them.

He just couldn't explain it, so what hope was there that he was ever going to be able to explain it to his wife?

Another wolf whistle; another text or the same one as before? Jake resisted the urge to look.

He had thought of talking to someone about it all. Not a close friend, as he wouldn't want someone who would see his child grow up to know that he had harboured doubts about his commitment to his own child's life. That secret might be too juicy for anyone to keep forever. No, maybe he would talk to a counsellor or someone of that ilk. There was an employee assistance programme at work, all the best firms had them these days, and he was sure that they had such services available, at no additional cost to him.

It was inexplicable, but he seemed to be able to recall the experiences of fatherhood quite distinctly. Yet Jake had never been responsible for a child's welfare in his life before. He had never been considered trustworthy enough as a teenager to have been asked to baby-sit for a neighbour or for a family friend, and to his knowledge, he had not yet fathered a child of his own. Given his track record, the latter was always a possibility, but even allowing for such a mistake, it did not explain his sense of foreboding at the very thought of it. It was more than just a sense, it had become a deeply held conviction and as the car edged its way closer and closer to the city, it seemed to be becoming ever more entrenched.

His brother maybe? His dead brother? That could be it. Losing a sibling at a young age was bound to leave him fearing the same responsibility that he would have felt for his own flesh and blood, but the boy had died when he was very young, and he could remember very little about him. A couple of times at the beach, moments in the local park, the accident that had finally claimed his life?

He could feel that familiar animal instinct to protect, to shield and to nurture. A sense that is unbridled love woven with an unrelenting fear, that seemed to give way to images that continued to masquerade as memory. A child suckling at its mother's breast, an open fireside and a wooden clotheshorse, where a child's garments steam themselves dry before the roaring flames. A rocking chair where a mother cradles her baby and a brightly painted rocking horse, where a delighted child squeals in the early morning light.

In the distance, a confused late-night reveller appeared to be jaywalking along the white lines in the centre of the road, as if the broken dashes were arrows on the ground, placed there just for him to mark his journey home.

As Jake's car drew closer to the disquieting form, it slowly raised its arms until each was outstretched at his sides, like a high wire act at some macabre travelling circus. But as the car drew even nearer and just as Jake began to feel some concern for the man's safety, its outline seemed to sink into the very tarmac on which it paced. It sank as a stone crucifix might sink, if time had no say in the matter, into the damp consecrated earth of a churchyard, until all that remained was a black mound of cloth which in turn seeped into nothingness, as the wheels of Jake's car passed above it.

A horn sounded and Jake pulled sharply at the steering wheel to drag his pride-and-joy back onto the left-hand carriageway. He stared into the rear-view mirror, but the road to his rear was deserted, save for a couple of cars heading home or to the late shift at a local supermarket or call centre, yet still he turned around to look frantically at the empty streets behind him.

The signs for London had now disappeared, to be replaced with signs for Tower Hill, Shoreditch and Liverpool Street. Jake continued to steer as if at random, but he knew deep down that he was being lured somehow, down through the city of London and onwards, past The Monument, to the traffic lights that mark the approach to London Bridge.

The city was devoid of life. The only traffic was of the vehicular kind. There were no more pedestrians to be seen and even the drunks seemed to have found a home for the night. The traffic lights changed to amber and then to green, but the gleaming BMW did not move. And back to red. Another car pulled up alongside from which an impressed driver glanced across at the newly registered car and its motionless occupants. Again, the change in lights enticed the traffic to move forward, but Jake's hands remained fixed on the steering wheel, his eyes staring into the reflective glass and still, the wheels did not move.

Red. Red-Amber. Green. Amber. Red.

"Dead."

Jake had not spoken as the car came to a halt at the traffic lights, but he had heard the word.

There was someone else in the car.

Someone else, who had spoken. The voice did not belong to Jake, but his lips had moved as the word sounded out.

In the darkness behind him, something was stirring. The city in which he was immersed was brightly lit in spite of the hour and yet the rear seats of his car were bathed in blackness. It was thick and impenetrable, like peering into the depths of some primeval cave, or down into the belly of an ancient well that is drilled so deep into the bowels of the earth that its bottom sits far out of sight.

And then, it opened its eyes. Two spiteful, yellow, hate-filled eyes that spat out at him and all that Jake could do was look back in terror. But he did not turn around. Instead, he sat transfixed with his eyes staring at those eyes until it smiled.

One gold tooth, shining.

"You're mine," it hissed.

Jake's left foot released the clutch and his right floored the accelerator, although quite how he hoped to escape from the thing in his back seat in such a manner, he had absolutely no idea. It was instinctive. He was in flight. The lights were on red but fortunately for Jake, the crossroads were deserted, and when he finally summoned up the courage to look once more into the darkness behind him, there was nothing but new leather and the acceleration of reflected white lights that waltzed across the upholstery.

And lingering in its wake, a pungent odour rose from the spotless mats that sat tight in each footwell to his rear. A rancid earthy tang of rot, like a compost heap in the height of summer that wafted up to fill the space, forcing Jake to bring the car to a sudden stop, to allow himself to unbuckle and burst forth from his seat.

He had a sudden urge to vomit, that was only beaten back by the breath of fresh air, which he sucked into his lungs like a deep-sea diver who has just risen from the depths of the ocean. He stood astride the open door like that for a full five minutes, motionless and fearful of what might happen next, but nothing did.

All was quiet, all was calm, but his beating heart continued to burst from his chest, until a bike came steadily to a halt beside him, and a city policeman removed his helmet to enquiry politely of his intentions.

Trick of the light.

"Sir?" the leather-clad officer continued, a little perturbed at the lack of response to his initial questioning.

Trick of the light.

"What seems to be the problem, sir, you are obstructing the highway. Please get back into your vehicle or pull over to the side immediately!"

It was enough to spark Jake back into life, and the thought of his earlier dram or two of whiskey reminded him that a breathalyser test was just about the last thing that he needed. "Sorry officer, new car!" he smiled, as if that would be an answer to everything.

Trick of the light.

"Heard a funny noise, so was just investigating."

The officer seemed satisfied enough and luckily for Jake was more intent on finishing his shift than on filling out unnecessary paperwork. "Well, best be on your way then, sir!" he instructed, giving the car a cursory look over and making a note of the number plate. "Seems okay to me."

"Yes," agreed Jake, his feet already back in the driver's footwell, followed quickly by the rest of him. "Thanks officer," he said, raising his arm from the open door to wave an acknowledgement, as he pulled the door closed and coaxed the car back into life.

The lights were with him this time and he didn't hesitate, quickly moving off and checking to see that the motorcycle was not in pursuit, whilst doing his best to banish the fright that had just forced him from the car.

The smell was gone, but that face. TRICK OF THE LIGHT. *Get a grip, Jake.* "It was just a trick of the light, you idiot!" he shouted out loud, physically looking back over his shoulder to check that he was right. The rear seats looked back at him in unison.

Trick of the light.

Once more, his phone wolf-whistled impatiently and finally he answered its call, activating it with his thumb and ignoring the not-whilst-you're-driving warning, he glanced down to see a string of increasingly furious text messages from Lisa.

He pressed the speed dial to call her, but then instead of turning right at the next junction in the direction of home, the car continued on its way towards London Bridge and the river.

"I'm coming home!" he assured her.

"I'm sorry, I just needed some space."

"No, I'm not angry at you!"

"Of course, I love you babe!"

"I didn't mean for you to think that!"

"I'll see you soon, darling."

You're mine.

Chapter Fifteen

Queen's Lock

For infamie's colour dyde in graine, which scarce oblivion can wash out againe, as nothing's dearer than a man's good name, so nothing wounds more deeper than defame.

The funeral was a quiet affair.

Few tears were shed, as only a few people were there to mourn the tragic passing of such a young life.

His mother sat motionless as the coffin slid effortlessly through the heavy scarlet curtain towards the waiting incinerator. His father, sporting a purple and yellow black-eye, sat alongside his estranged wife for the last time, his hands clasped together in what may have been a silent prayer for his son, or more likely for himself.

A few of Terry's old school-friends hovered awkwardly at the back of the modern red-brick building, looking suitably solemn but clearly keen to get away as soon as the formalities were done with. A hastily stifled sob sounded from the right of the assembled mourners, where two unsuitably dressed young girls sat awkwardly. Jackie had seen them come in and recognised them both as former work colleagues of her son, whom she had seen on one or two occasions at weekends before Terry's disappearance. She found herself wondering how they had come to know of her son's death and of the funeral arrangements, but she was in no fit state to solve such a conundrum. Bad news clearly travelled fast!

Aunts, uncles and cousins – on his father's side – were all represented, as was their duty, and afterwards at the house, whenever Jackie or Patrick were in earshot, they all agreed that it was so sad for such a young man to be cut off in his prime.

"His whole life ahead of him," proclaimed a tall and rugged man in an inappropriately bright tie, with a solemn shake of his head.

"And so much to look forward to," an appropriately dressed old woman added, allowing the first speaker more time to devour the flaccid remains of a rather unappetising cold meat sandwich. But when each of the weary parents had moved out of range, the surmising and the rumour-mill started in earnest.

It wasn't long before Patrick succumbed to the temptation and did his usual disappearing act in search of more alcohol, and within the hour, most of the others had also made their excuses and left. Ted had chosen not to attend. He didn't feel that his presence would be appropriate, and Jackie had done her best not to appear offended by his absence. Soon only a handful were left and then the tears started in earnest.

"Why?" Jackie found herself asking over and over again, knowing full well that no answer was going to be forthcoming. Her neighbour just shook her head and said nothing that was of any use. Even when her younger friend raised her head to speak, something got the better of her and she clammed up again.

"They insisted that he was cremated, you know?" Jackie slurred, unaccustomed as she was to the amount of wine that she had already consumed, an almost empty wineglass still clenched in her fist. Her friend just shook her head and made some noise that may well have been intended as a word of concern or condolence, but somehow a coherent word failed to pass her lips. She just nodded and looking lost, waved for reinforcements from across the room.

"Don't stay for my sake, you know," Jackie prompted, sensing the woman's discomfort. "I'll be fine," she lied, suddenly wishing that she had invited her only real friend that day. Though she hadn't spoken with Dee for a while, and their letters had dried up as her own depression had taken a firmer grip, it would have been good to have had someone alongside her to support her in her grief. Someone that cared.

"Do you mind?" the woman asked, rather too eagerly. "Only I've got to get Dave's tea on, he'll be back," but she realised her fateful mistake in mentioning the imminent return of her own son and quickly thought of something else to say.

Then with an awkward wink of a wrinkled eye, she announced that she would 'pop around later, see how you're getting on'.

"Don't bother!" Jackie snapped back, the drink getting much the better of her. "I mean, don't worry about me. I'll be fine, honestly." The woman, who was dressed in a low-backed and tight-fitting black evening gown, which was more suited to a night on the town than a winter funeral, stood motionless. "Really, just go!"

Her furtive acquaintance of five and a half years' standing needed no further encouragement and with a curt smile and a passing squeeze of her neighbour's shoulder, the woman was gone.

"So, what now?" Jackie asked of the empty room as she slumped back against the threadbare cushions of her husband's armchair. "What the fuck now?" she muttered again and drained the rest of the lifeless Prosecco into the cheap cut-glass goblet.

**

The next few hours passed like a life sentence for Jackie Stubbs. She sat alone and in near silence, the only noise there was came from the neighbouring houses. An occasional raised voice or the high-pitched squeal of a child in the midst of a tantrum, but nothing that could drag her from the depths into which she had plunged.

To her everlasting shame, she found herself wishing that her son's identity had died with him. That his wallet had been lost or empty when he had been found, or that his body had never been found at all. For then she could have gone on, living out her monotonous life in the belief that he was still out there, somewhere. Living his life. Making his mark in the world, as she had always hoped he would, and she could have continued to live out her paltry existence in blissful ignorance.

She had coped with her only son's disappearance, but now that he was gone, truly gone, there really was nothing left for her. Not in that cold and empty house, not anymore. She had stayed in the belief that Terry would return someday and had never been able to face up to the awful possibility that things would never ever be as they once were. She had clung onto that vain hope for a year or more. Now even that faint prospect had finally fallen into dust.

Jackie strained her neck, to peer through the doorway at the round featureless face of the kitchen clock, that hung for dear life to the wall on which it had been mounted for ten years or more. It was almost midnight. Somewhere in her head she realised that Patrick had not yet returned, but she paid it no mind. He was no longer of any importance to her. Since the beating that she, for once, had administered, he was running scared. The coward that she always knew he was had surfaced and somehow, she didn't think that he would dare to raise his hands to her again, but she wasn't going to give him the chance to prove her wrong.

On the day after Terry's death, she had found herself marooned on the unwelcoming doorstep of their house in the early hours of another inhospitable morning. She had not expected to find her husband at home, but as she wandered into the dark room and closed the door behind her, the sudden illumination had revealed a sore and sorry-looking figure, slumped in his usual place.

Jackie had fully expected him to be drunk, yet when he spoke, his words seemed clearer than they had been in years, but it was too late for reconciliations. He had mumbled some kind of apology, but when she refused to accept it, he had quickly reverted to type and took two steps towards her, his fists clenched and his face enraged. Her words came right on cue, fully rehearsed and word perfect.

"You lay one more finger on me, you bastard, ever again," she had snarled. "And I promise you, on the graves of my children, I'll put a carving knife in your back some dark morning!" She had meant it, every word of it and Pat froze in his tracks, because he knew. He knew that there was no reason anymore for her not to be true to her word.

Following her mother's death, Jackie was soon to receive what was left over from the proceeds from the sale of the Wilson family home. The money had been earmarked to pay for the old lady's medical care for the rest of her days, but as it turned out, those days had been numbered. Of this, Jackie's husband was either unaware or he was too scared to mention it.

Rising property prices in East London following the extension of the Jubilee Line and DLR had seen house prices hit new heights, and now that much maligned development offered Jackie the promise of a new life. She had received the final probate statement earlier in the week and its contents had spawned the seeds of a new beginning.

Within the hour, she had packed and called a cab. A pile of bulging carrier bags sat stacked against a single battered red suitcase in the porch, all of which were crammed with an untidy pile of clothes, toiletries and minor valuables. And next to them sat two small cardboard storage boxes, which had once belonged to her mother and now provided Jackie with her only link to her family's remarkable past.

It took her a few minutes to transfer all of the quickly assembled packages into the waiting hackney carriage, as the small white plaque on the back of the vehicle proclaimed. But as the taxi driver slammed the boot shut, Jackie could not resist taking one last lingering look at the tattered house that had never, in her entire married life, felt like home. Her gaze strayed up to the end of the street where she had half expected to see a drunken man, rolling home after seven hours and God knows how many pints, but the street was empty.

"C'mon love, I've got another fare waiting!" the driver called, but instead of stooping down into the car, Jackie stormed back into the house, wailing an apology as she went. On her return just a few minutes later, the driver did not even attempt to hide his annoyance, as she bowed her head and shuffled across the back seat of the car.

"My phone!" she panted, holding aloft the seemingly unopened package as if expecting her unkempt chauffeur to be impressed. He wasn't.

"Where to?" he demanded gruffly.

She instructed him to head for one of the cheap hotels that had sprung up along the base of the North Circular road over the last few years and settled back into the seat for the short trip. Once comfortable, it was all she needed for her body to slip into a deep slumber that was so sudden, it was almost as if the lights had just gone out.

When she awoke, it was to the unsympathetic prompting of the taxi driver who seemed keen to get her offloaded as soon as possible so that he could move onto another more profitable fare.

"Will this do?" he asked, gesturing at the modern, two-storey motel in front of them.

"Yes, that'll do fine," she answered drowsily, her head throbbing with the after-effects of the afternoon drinking spree as she unzipped her handbag to pull out her purse. She asked how much and winced at the fare that she was quoted, but as she was not one to haggle, she retrieved a twenty-pound note and waved it in his general direction. He then opened the boot and dumped her shambolic array of belongings on the pavement.

"Sorry, I must have dozed off," she said embarrassed to admit it, but the driver wasn't in the mood for small talk and instead he just nodded, before squeezing his generous frame back inside the car. He had already turned out onto the main road as she turned the handle on the door to the glass-fronted motel.

To her astonishment, she found it locked. For a second, a wall of panic loomed as her obvious vulnerability, out there in the early hours of the morning, became all too apparent. However, those fears were soon allayed as a welcome surge of light lit up the interior – there was someone home after all.

The night porter opened the door and welcomed her inside, remarking on the lateness of the hour and the ramshackle pile of luggage that was stacked out front.

"We don't get too many late callers," he explained, seemingly glad to have at least one. "We get the odd one or two, coming up from the airport on late or delayed flights, but they usually head for town." He didn't ask her business or why she was out so late, although she thought that he must have been curious, and for that she was grateful, but the banter continued and although Jackie offered little in return, she managed to smile and nod in all the appropriate places.

Once the formalities were complete, he showed her to her ground-floor room and invited her to make herself at home whilst he brought her luggage through from the front desk. Ten minutes later and he was back at the door to room 17 with her belongings neatly piled up on a trolley, each of which was dutifully despatched onto the sofa bed.

One large tip later, when the door was shut and the catch firmly secured, Jackie was finally able to discard her shoes and relax. It was the first time that she had ever spent a night alone in a hotel. She thought of her husband, who would now be at home, passing the night in a drunken stupor on the sofa and unaware that the bed upstairs was empty, but she didn't think of him for long.

She considered taking on the dreaded instruction manual for the mobile phone, which had lain unused at the bottom of her wardrobe ever since her fiftieth birthday. The present had been a gift from her son, but as she turned it over to scan its many features, she remembered how Patrick had taken the gloss off the surprise by declaring it a waste of money for 'someone like her'. Someone without friends and now, without any family to speak of either. She pushed those memories away, placed the sealed box on the bedside table and snuggled down to a late-night movie or a talk show to help to pass the time.

But as she waited for the news to finish, her thoughts drifted away from the world's worries and back to her own. She had needed somewhere to get her head down for a night or two, and this plain, sparsely furnished room, would fulfil that need. In the morning, she would face up to the questions that had now reached siege proportions in her mind.

Although she had absolutely no idea where she would go or what she would do with the rest of her life, the prospect did not concern her unduly. It had been years since she had been able to put herself first, before her husband or her son, or latterly her ailing parents, and she realised then that her very own *new normal* was going to take some getting used to.

A barrage of worries did their best to unbalance her, each seeming more pressing than the last. Where would she live? Where would she work? Would she stay in London or move away completely? Would anyone even notice that she'd gone if she did?

Her mother's money would last for a while, but it wouldn't last forever.

So, when the weak winter sunlight started to stream through the undrawn curtains, it took her a little by surprise. She had not expected to fall asleep so easily, but as she pushed herself upright, a searing pain behind her eyes provided an unwelcome reminder of the previous day's excesses.

At some point during what was left of the night, she had managed to crawl beneath the covers, although she could not remember doing so, but she still woke up feeling cold and unprepared for the day ahead. As there was no clock in the room and her only watch was packed in one of the three carrier bags that had been knocked to the floor during the night, Jackie found that she had absolutely no idea of the time. Her body clock told her that it was getting late and judging by the noise of the traffic from the flyover outside, the rush hour was well and truly underway.

After filling up the kettle in the confined space of the bathroom, she left it to boil while she took a shower, discarding a dark pile of clothes that she realised had been in faithful service for nigh on twenty-four hours. The shower was cold, but it did the trick, shocking her system into life and kick-starting her day.

The click of the kettle was enough to drag her from the bathroom mirror, where the sight of her drawn and grey reflection had threatened to send her back into the clutches of depression. After vigorously brushing her teeth to make up for the previous night's break in routine, she dragged a hairbrush through her hair and closed the hotel-issue dressing gown around her, before heading back into the welcome unfamiliarity of the room. At last, she felt human again and to complete the trick, she breakfasted on caffeine with two complementary sachets of coffee and a trio of custard creams.

Then, making herself as comfortable as she could, she leant back against the tarnished headboard to watch the morning news. It was almost 9 o'clock and the headlines told of another earthquake in Greece, measuring six point something on the Richter scale, and a parliamentary scandal involving a prominent cabinet minister and half the occupants of a London brothel, both of which she paid little mind.

However, as the local news began, the top story caught Jackie's attention.

There had been a health scare in Essex and that made her look up from the pages of the free newspaper, which she had found shoved beneath her door as she emerged from the shower. A particularly virulent strain of influenza had hit an old people's home in Colchester and as the newsreader switched to a live report, Jackie was amazed to see a drenched reporter standing outside a too familiar red-brick retirement home.

"Twelve residents have been confirmed so far as being affected, Jean, and three have already died," a suitably shocked reporter informed the studio. "But they are hopeful that the outbreak has been contained. Antibiotics have been prescribed in all cases, although the chances for at least one more resident are thought to be slim. This is…" But Jackie had stopped listening. She sipped the last of her black coffee as she wondered if any of those suffering had been friends of her mum and with that thought in mind, she mumbled a silent prayer.

The week had been full of those.

Jackie had booked herself in for three nights and so she was in no rush to vacate with the other overnight guests. Instead, she unpacked a few of her things and repacked those items that she knew would not be needed straight away, and which in her haste to get away, had been bundled into the bags like a contribution to her local charity shop.

She even found time to break the seal on her trendy new telephone and after fifteen minutes of mild confusion, she was pleased to have deciphered enough of it to at least put it on charge. Once completed, her attention was drawn to the stacked boxes, which had seemed so important to her just a few hours before.

For a moment, she seriously considered trashing the lot, a symbolic gesture that would allow her to start her life afresh. She could recall moving them once before, when her father had passed away and her mother's final move had become permanent. On that day, she had made her daughter promise that she would not *go mooching through her things*, something that until this morning she had been able to resist despite the occasional urge to do so.

Just as part of her wanted to respect those wishes now that her mother was gone, this time she had more reason than ever to take a look and time on her hands to do it justice. Ted had thrown her down a challenge and if she wanted to get to the bottom of things, then she had some reading to do.

There was no time like the present.

As she began to rifle through the realms of memorabilia uninhibited, for the second time that week, she did so more thoroughly, but with half a mind on disposing of as much of it as she could. There was no room in her new life for sentimentality, or so she would tell herself as she sifted her way through a lifetime of someone else's junk. As two piles began to assemble on the bed, it became clear that the small mound that was set for the dustbin was not going to make much difference to her load.

It was the larger pile that she could not take her eyes off.

Photographs that conjured up sounds and smells from long gone summers, ugly ornaments which held precious memories within their clay and chipped enamel, and dated postcards which told their own stories, made up for much of the growing collection on the left-hand side of the bed. A small tin box contained further personal effects; a silver thimble engraved with the name Molly; a blue and white snowstorm from Brighton; a few medals from forgotten wars; and a small copper coin from 1663.

Unremarkable in everything but its date, the initials 'TR' were etched onto its surface and two long sticks were prevalent on the reverse. Jackie raised it to the light for the first time in who knows how long and found herself wondering as to its value, so she zipped it into the pocket of her purse for safekeeping and continued to reluctantly purge herself of her parents' limited legacy.

The second box had contained her father's diaries, which were now safely buried at the bottom of her suitcase. The rest of the papers from the box had been loosely bound with long brown treasury tags into various volumes, none of which were marked with titles. It was apparent that it would take some time to work her way through the contents and right then, she no longer had the stomach for the search, however intriguing their newspaper cuttings and forgotten headlines seemed.

Instead, she bundled them back into the box and turned her attention to the diaries, to which she had only paid only a passing interest a few days before. Having rescued them from the depths of the suitcase, she decided to first turn to the year of the accident. She reached for the volume with the faded gold inscription of '1940' and settled back in the room's excuse-for-an-armchair, fully intending to read it from cover to cover.

After only a few minutes, she was forced to admit that much of it held little interest for her. For a social historian, it would have offered a mouth-watering insight into life in the Blitz, but for Jackie, it was proving to be more tiresome than she cared to admit, at which she felt more than a little twinge of guilt.

Sorry Dad, she thought, which spurred her on for a little while longer. She was eventually rewarded, when she came across a series of blank pages, which spanned a period of more than a month from 17 March 1940 until almost the end of April. The next entry on 28 April 1940 proved to be much more relevant to the events of the previous few weeks and Jackie was soon engrossed.

28 April 1940

At last, I've got the energy to write again and I thank God that I'm still able to do that. The last few weeks have been hellish and I'm still not absolutely certain of what has happened to me.

I can remember the day pretty well now, although up until a week or so ago, there were still gaps. It's funny, but those bloody dreams have helped kick-start a few memories and I think I can remember everything now, although I still wonder whether some of it isn't the ramblings of a crank. I feel like I should write it all down, just in case it all goes again, or in case I take a turn for the worse. I just want people to know what happened so that they can make up their own minds. There will be people who will say that I bottled it, that I'm washed up, but I know I'm not and I can't wait to prove them wrong. Annie says I've done my bit now and that we should get away, but that's not me. I just can't run away. Not now.

I'm still here, in this blasted hospital, and although Annie has been in a few times, it's a long way from home and she can't make the trip right across London every day. Nor do I want her to. It's too bloody dangerous with Jerry's bombs blowing everywhere to bits.

We'd already been down to the river once that day to disarm a big bugger that The Hun had dropped right by Butler's Wharf. It was an easy one by comparison, lots of room around it and not too much digging to get at it. I was heading off to barracks for a wash-up when some bloke called from the bridge that there was another one, on the other side of the water. I told him that made it a BD2 shout and not ours, but he was pretty insistent and so I dragged the squad across with me and we did what we could.

I wish I'd left well alone, for the sake of Billy's family, and I'll never forgive myself for that. Gallagher has been in a few times since then. I think that he feels guilty, but he's been pretty useful. They need all the doctors they can get around here so to have my own private one has been a big help, I think.

I've thought about that day, time and time and time again over the past month and although I've been able to remember more and more each time, the pieces still don't seem to fit. I'll never forget poor Billy's face though. He knew what I'd done and he knew what was going to happen next, right before it exploded. His mum came in to see me yesterday. I didn't know what to say and I'm afraid that I lost it a bit. She told me not to blame myself, that he knew the risks, that she was proud of him. God bless you, Billy-boy.

Something wasn't quite right from the start. As we made our way down there, it was cold but as we got closer to the river, it got colder still and by the time we reached it, it was bloody freezing down there. The sappers had already dug down to it, shoring up the sides and securing the ladder as they do, and that meant that we could at least get alongside the beast. The water was pissing in through the walls though so the Jenny couldn't pump it out fast enough, so I told them to turn it off when I was ready to start in case the vibrations set it off. We knew that we didn't have much time so we did the usual preparations in record speed, drilling through the casing to get at the fuse and the gaine. My fingers were like sticks of ice and I couldn't understand why it was so cold on the north side compared to the other bank.

I called to Billy that we should pack it in as my hands were shaking too much, but when I looked up from the explosive, the mist had closed in and I couldn't see much even when I climbed out for a breather. And the bridge seemed so close from there that we figured an explosion would take it out, which would have crippled London, so we decided to get the job done. It was so quiet for a while that it wasn't hard to concentrate, but the condensation from our breathing was forming ice on the metal casing and as I looked across at Billy, he looked really scared.

"What's going on, Sir?" he asked me, but I just shrugged. I had no idea, but I just wanted to get it done so we could get out of there. I don't remember being all that nervous. I must have been, I suppose, but I think I put a brave face on it. I began to pull out the gaine, more by memory than feeling as I had lost all senses in my fingers by then. I could see numbers etched into the base of the unit and I called to Billy that it was a time-delay type, but he didn't respond and when I looked up, his eyes were fixed on something behind me. I had heard the scuffling and knew the sound of rats from many an excursion into the warehouses at the docks, but they didn't scare me like they did an inexperienced recruit like William James.

138

"What's up with you, Private?" I asked unsympathetically. "They're just furry rodents with overlong tails and that's all." Or something like that and I demanded the clips again, which he fumbled out of the bag. I'd seen this type of bomb a hundred times before and knew exactly what to do, but in the cold and mist, the bugger was proving difficult to reach. I could still hear the ticking and I knew that we were living dangerously, but then another sound began to drown out the countdown from the bomb and I guess that I began to get disoriented. It was then that something else distracted me.

I could just about see an object that was hidden inside the explosive housing and using the closed length of the clips, I eased it out into view. It was a coin. A coin with a date of 1663 and I almost dropped the bloody explosive when I read the date, but there was no time to think about it then, although how in hell's name it got inside I'll never know. Some munitions worker in Munich thought she'd have a joke maybe, but it would have been an expensive one—strange bunch, the Germans!

In any case, I shoved it in my breast pocket and somehow, it found its way here with me, although my jacket was ripped apart in the explosion that followed and I didn't see it again so how the coin made it, I suppose I'll never know.

The rats were swimming in the knee-deep water by then and clambering up and over the ordnance. I was more than a little unnerved by their size and by the sheer number of them. At first glance in the meagre light, they looked black and not brown and that worried me too, but I tried to put it out of my mind.

As I reached in once more to disarm the booby trap, something else caught my eye. A glint of light at the top of the shaft and as I slowly raised my head, I saw peering down into the hole at us a hooded form. It was the only visible thing in the mist that was sinking down into the hole and then it slipped back its hood and I swear to God there was no face. No face! Just a white skull and deep hollows where its eyes should have been and yet it smiled like a snake and a single gold tooth smiled down at me, and I panicked. The fuse slipped from my grip with the gaine still engaged – we had seconds to get out of there before the acid burned through.

The resulting explosion must have been heard for miles. Somewhere amongst the muddy debris was Billy – he had slipped on the final step and as I dived to the ground, he was still on his way out. I don't know why I didn't go too, but somehow; I was spared and for Billy's sake, I have to find out what happened that day. I have to. I might have dreamed the whole bloody thing and in one way,

I hope that I did because the alternative is too scary for words, but if I didn't and what I saw really happened then I have to get to the bottom of it, or I'll never rest.

Jackie put down the book and let the words sink in. It was the very last thing that she had expected. A horror story, is that what she was living through? A restless ghoul from a Hammer film or something? She allowed herself an unexpected laugh and then regretted it, in case her father was watching from somewhere. Her fingers moved over the rough fabric of his unit's red and yellow bomb shaped insignia, that had once been sewn onto the green sleeve of his tunic.

She picked up the book again and re-read the entry from start to finish, scanning through the first few pages and then revisiting the last, three or four times. It was incredible. It was unbelievable. Her father was not a superstitious man. He did not believe in ghosts and demons and hauntings; he believed in the here and now and yet, here it was. An experience in his life that went against all that she thought he believed.

It was discomforting to think that she didn't know him at all.

And so, Jackie spent most of that day reading through her late father's memoirs in the hope that somewhere in these volumes, he would have recorded his return to sanity and renounce his experiences of that spring day in 1940 as mere hallucinations, which could be explained by some scientific means. The fact that he failed to do so left her feeling wary and alone.

Gallagher was mentioned a few times, and it seemed that the two of them became quite close as time went on. However, no mention was ever made of the diagnosis that was obliquely referred to in his entries and that Ted had himself alluded to just the day before.

It was a tropical disease that had laid him low after the explosion, Gallagher had admitted as much. Something that he had picked up from the Thames or maybe from a rat bite. Something that had almost killed him as he admitted in a later entry. But there were no more mention of ghouls or unsightly skulls or any other paranormal experiences, and although he mentioned having nightmares at regular intervals, given the circumstances, disturbed dreams were only to be expected.

For a moment, she turned to the second box and to the bound volumes of research and articles that she had overlooked earlier, but it seemed less related to her somehow. A scrapbook of a series of deaths in the 1940s, with cuttings from the *Daily Standard* and *The London Evening Mail*, but in amongst all that death and destruction, even that seemed mundane and instead, a fresh hunger got the better of her. She made a snap decision to go out in search of food and fresh air and although she made a mental commitment to return to the task on her return, it was a promise that she would not keep.

A few hours later, she returned from the nearby shopping centre having feasted on a double cheeseburger and large fries, and as she closed the plain wooden door behind her for the night, her sense of abandonment was almost too hard to bear. She needed to hear a familiar voice, to see a friendly face, someone with whom to share her pain.

The mobile phone was fully charged now, and so she found herself turning to the only person she could think of. As she scrambled through the pages of her address book to retrieve the number she needed, she was almost overcome by a bout of nerves and as the recalled number started to ring out, her heart rate accelerated in time with the tone, but the sensation was short-lived.

"Hi," the recorded message chirped cheerily. "You've reached Diane Taylor. I'm busy right now, but if you leave me a short message, I'll get back to you as soon as I can."

Jackie almost ended it there, but she was caught out by the short beep and found herself muttering an excuse that was now being recorded.

"Hello, Dee," she started. "It's me, Jackie, Jackie Stubbs. Look, I'm sorry that I've not been in touch. No excuse really, but after last time, well, you know."

She paused for a moment, out of embarrassment more than anything else, remembering the fight that had ensued between the three of them, when her best friend since childhood had challenged her bully of a husband after a particularly nasty argument.

"Look, well, it's like this. I've left the bastard. I finally took your advice!" An out-of-place laugh came out of nowhere, as she found herself floundering for what else to say. "So now I'm on my own in a grotty hotel and, well I suppose I need a friend."

She left her new number and made her excuses and afterwards, she simply lay face down on the bed and cried herself to sleep.

For her son, for her mother, for her father, but most of all – she was ashamed to say – for herself.

Chapter Sixteen
King's Lock

Those are right Watermen and rowe so well, they either land their fares in heav'n or in Hell, I never knew them yet to make a stay and land at Purgatory, by the way.

The light has gone.

I watched the crimson sun leach the heavens red, but I am blinded in its wake and all I can be sure of is the bare mud beneath my feet.

A chilling breath heralds the swollen night and the sea's stench pours forth from my last banquet. All is silent save the wind, which gathers pace to wrap itself around me like a shroud. My arms are held fast and I am bound like a witch who is about to burn.

But fire will not be my executioner.

The tide scavenges at my feet and burrows beneath the treacherous silt between them to plant me deeper in the river's lap. My seared wrists choke as the tide turns against me, to whet its appetite on my flesh and to feast upon my soul. Too soon, the jostling river slavers at my chest and cavorts around me like a ravenous pack, impatient for the kill.

As the waiting water slips its noose around my neck, a smudge of light lays a broken path upon the waves, and I howl for my salvation.

A boatman's lantern seems to sway, and in its trance the water's leash draws taut and just for a moment, its relentless flow abates. And then even that meagre light is doused and in this sightless landscape, I scream for my deliverance.

And when I prise my precious eyes apart once more to seek some fading chance of life, they look upon another who is lost.

One gold tooth shining, where a human mouth once sneered. Two pared hollows, whence human eyes once peered. One ivory skull, which a human face once shared.

My breath cannot hold and the river rushes in as I strain and thrash against the biting cords. That barren mask still bobs beneath the waves until my lungs have burst and my eyes can see no more.

Now my sight has been restored and the whitest lights crowd the corners of my unfamiliar home. All alone, I stare into my estranged soul and pace the corners of my mind until the feeble morning stutters back to life and I can sleep again.

Chapter Seventeen
Index Wheel Lock

I care to please and serve my Master's will, and he with care commands not what is ill. I care to have them hang'd that careless be, or false unto so good a Lord as he. I care for all Religions that are hurl'd and scatter'd o'er the universall world: I care to keepe that which is sound and sure, whichever and for ever shall endure.

Jake Harvey woke up screaming and his words were as clear as the daylight outside his car.

"Trick of the light!"

And in his haste to put some distance between himself and the demons that had tortured him through the small hours, his flailing hand pushed firmly against the car's horn and the subsequent blare thrust him back into this world.

Jake's wide blue eyes bolted from left to right, but his head remained transfixed until, as if on the sound of a starter's gun, he spun himself around to rummage through the footwells behind him. As he sank back into the lap of the leather seat, his whole body shook from his white-knuckled fingers to his frozen feet, like a First World War veteran still suffering from the after-effects of shell shock.

It took him a full five minutes to regain a modicum of composure and even then, it proved difficult enough to persuade the ignition key to turn just one notch, so that he could let down a window and inhale a fresh gust of air. Then tentatively, he tried the door. To his astonishment, it opened with ease and like a greyhound bursting from its trap, he flung himself out of the car and onto the ground beneath. Jake's fingers clawed at the loose gravel, the grit biting into his flesh as he hauled his trailing weight, but whilst his left knee scraped against the uncompromising ground, his right leg held firm.

"Get away from me!" he screamed and turned one hundred and eighty degrees, until he lay floundering on his backside, with one torn knee of his once-beige trousers raised like a trophy above his head. He was writhing on the floor like a dumb fish ensnared on a barbed hook, with his left leg stabbing stupidly at the air, until his outstretched fingers finally latched onto the white metal of the gaping door. Then he heaved himself upright and thrust his hand inside the car to finally deliver his ankle from the clutches of the seat belt, in which he had become entangled.

As he scrambled away, his sight did not stray from the gaping door. After a few more stumbling yards, Jake's hands, then his legs and finally his back came up against the cold metal of another parked car, but still he could not sever the ties that bound his eyes to the scene before him. Instead, he let his hands lead the way, like a visitor to some strange house searching for the lavatory in the middle of a winter's night, until the tips of his fingers lost touch with the sleek contours of the anonymous vehicle, and only then did he turn and run.

It was still early, but whilst many of the day's populous were still to be found in the throes of breakfast or tucked up in their beds, the streets were busy enough. The market traders had been up and about for hours, their stalls already in position for the busy Friday trade and their goods piled high in readiness for the opening rush.

One of these early risers watched with interest as a dishevelled young man backed away from his badly parked car, and the very same observer arched his neck still further when the well-dressed but shabby-looking male turned and bolted along Borough High Street in the direction of Southwark. The street trader made a mental sketch of the suspicious character, just in case he was finally about to achieve his life-long ambition of being able to recognise a mugshot on a TV identity parade, and with this in mind, he took out his phone and called his wife.

Jake ran until he could run no more, which wasn't very far. In the shelter of a nineteenth-century railway arch, he ran out of steam and fell against the grimy concave wall, heaving on the cold air, but it could not keep pace with his sudden craving for breath.

His heart was pounding so high in his chest that even his Adam's apple vibrated with the force of it and to his own disgust, he was compelled to spit a sour string of phlegm, which dangled precariously close to his trousers, before nestling between the cracks of the pavement between his feet.

145

Finally, he allowed himself to slip slowly down the wall, to squat above the wet and littered pavement beneath. As fear tentatively surrendered to a sense of relief, Jake bowed his sodden forehead into his aching hands and dragged his nervous fingers through his hair.

When he raised his head again, the sight that greeted him could not have been more welcoming. From the opposite side of the street, a 'greasy spoon' café beckoned, and without a thought for the calories, Jake hauled himself to his feet; a little unsteadily he made his way across the still quiet street in search of the comfort food that he hoped would still his fractured nerves.

It wasn't until he caught the look on the proprietor's face that Jake gave any thought to his appearance, but as he placed an order for a 'full English' and a pot of coffee, he became acutely aware that he was not his usual dapper self. As he prayed for the earth to swallow him whole, he delved into his wallet and withdrew a twenty. Then, without waiting for his change, he shuffled off into the far corner of the room, stopping momentarily to grab a well-thumbed copy of a daily newspaper from one of the other tables. There were only two other customers crammed into the compact space between the kitchen and the door that Jake had just darkened, but both were so intent on demolishing their respective fry-ups that a naked customer would, in all probability, have failed to attract their attention that morning.

Jake did his best to settle into the hard-backed chair, which did nothing to aid his aching limbs, before scanning the pages of the tabloid; but he found it impossible to concentrate and even the sports pages could not hold his attention for long. Instead, the night's events turned like some macabre carousel in his mind, and the truth that still eluded him remained perched on the farthest steed from his own.

He had been on his way home; of that he was certain. He had spoken to Lisa and had calmed her down with an assurance that he would be home 'within the hour' and yet, here he was.

Not home.

Nowhere near home.

After the incident at the traffic lights, he had meant to turn right, to circle back in search of the Great North Road and the fastest way out of the city, but even as he failed to do so, he had known what he was doing. He could remember the lights of London Bridge as he assured his wife, even calculating in his head how long it would take him to make it back and yet all the time heading in the opposite direction. It was as if he'd been in a spell, captured by a snare, unable to escape from some unidentified foe that was reeling him in.

Trick of the light.

The words came back to him then, but he couldn't make sense of them, only the terror that the phrase now held for him. When he reached the other side of the bridge, he had told his wife that he loved her and would see her soon, before he had felt the breath on his neck. It wasn't a breeze from an open window, all the windows had been tightly shut. It was an old and long-dead breath that stank like the river itself.

Jake had raced away then, like a startled rabbit in search of its burrow, his foot to the floor and the tyres screeching in protest, but for Jake there had been no such sanctuary. Instead, he had found his way into a recently cleared building site, which doubled as an open-air carpark during the day, where the gates had been left open and where somewhere in the depths of his consciousness, he had decided to desert his newly acquired vehicle, for the night at least.

He had pulled up sharply at the back of the roughly laid out yard and even before the car had come to a complete stop, he'd already flicked on the hand brake. He'd turned off the ignition, withdrawn the key and slipped off the seat belt, as another minute passed.

Yet the driver's door had not yielded at his touch.

Immediately, he'd shuffled over to the passenger's side, but that door had also proved unmoveable. Jake would try each door again a dozen or more times before the night was through as he struggled to accept the ludicrous reality that there really was no way out of there.

Neither would the ignition respond to his command once the engine had stalled, as if someone else was the keeper of its key. But he was alone, just him. Definitely alone. He plucked up the nerve to look back into the seat behind and saw no-one. It was just him and his new car, but it felt like his tomb. A metal coffin that had been nailed shut with him still inside, still alive and still breathing and with a window seat of his own in which to while away eternity.

In the deceptive glow of the streetlamps, the car was well illuminated and for that small mercy he had been thankful, whilst the clattering lights from the occasional overhead train, also lent support in the perpetual battle to keep his spirits up, as the temperature began to move sharply in the opposite direction.

He picked up his phone, deciding on impulse to call his wife, to tell her of his predicament so she could arrange for the cavalry to come. But he was alarmed to see that the recently charged battery had been drained, the indicator standing at just 1% and now desperate to speak to someone, anyone, he called up the list of most recent calls, and that was when the phone gave up the ghost.

It was then that he'd let out an involuntary moan, a sound that at first was not even a word, but which built up in rising clarity, until it formed into two syllables that would have left no one in any doubt as to his situation. "Help, me!" But no one was within earshot, not even close.

Every now and again, he'd continued to try the doors, just in case his mind had been playing a cruel trick on the numerous other occasions, but each time he was left feeling bewildered and increasingly fearful at his continued imprisonment. Jake's rational mind had long since abandoned ship and beneath the yellow eyes of the scattered streetlights, he pulled up the collar of his coat and found himself longing for the sun to rise.

Jake watched as the warm air billowed from his lungs to coat the inside of the frigid windows in a simmering skin of condensation, like in a sauna, but without the warmth that might have made the experience a pleasurable one. He tried the doors. Still locked.

He tried the ignition. Nothing.

Jake stared into the depths of the rear-view mirror at the empty seat behind and then turned around once more to look again for himself. After a moment's hesitation, he wrenched the mirror from the windscreen and shoved it into the glove compartment where it would stay until morning.

He tried the door again. Locked.

A thick bead of condensation slithered down the window on the passenger's side of the car, like a trail of sweat seeping from a field hand's forehead as he toils in the midday sun. It stopped long before it reached the bottom and welled there for a moment, before turning ninety degrees for an inch or two, and then, in defiance of the known laws of gravity, began its upward journey that ended back where it had begun.

Jake watched in awe at the childlike circle that had been etched there and then the circle sprouted legs. The first moved straight down, again stopping before it reached the base of the window, whilst the second fell at an angle that was roughly sixty degrees to its significant other. At first, Jake was unable to make it out, but suddenly, he could see it.

It was obvious.

The letter 'R' had been scrawled on the chilled glass; its outline was ragged, and its width seemed roughly the size of a finger. It might have occurred to him then that help was at hand, for the intruder's handiwork at the very least should have offered up some hope for his release, but somehow Jake knew that a rescue was not on the cards.

Whoever was responsible for the inscription was not dangling the keys to Jake's salvation in his outstretched hand. As if to prove the point and in muted defiance of the choking sense of fear that brimmed inside his unconventional cell, Jake reached across and traced the outline with his finger. It was moist to the touch and as Jake's finger skimmed silently along in the wake of another's, his eyes grew wide and his jaw dropped, like a dead man's.

The inscription was on the inside.

Then, with frightening speed, another letter cut through the condensation. The initials 'TR' poured across the glass, so fast that Jake could not keep up and not once could he see a trace of the hand that was conducting this seemingly endless scrawl. When each inscription began to bleed, in Jake's tortured state he thought that he could see the faintest trace of red in every rivulet, which ran like blood down each pane of glass.

And then it stopped and other than that, he'd seen nothing, but he had heard plenty and it was the voices that, in the cold light of morning, he could not bear to recall. There was nothing to them at first, such that when his strained senses caught an essence of their meaning on the night breeze, it took but a few minutes to become convinced that the sound was just a conjuring trick of the wind. That same cold flurry then swirled beneath the car to rustle up the scampering shuffle of pattering feet to the front and rear, to his left and right, just inches from his tear-stained face.

"Cooper." The first syllable settled on the breath of air that had granted it life and the second faded on the wind that swept the word away.

It was just the wind, just the wind.

That's all. That is all it was. That's all it could have been.

One gust of winter, that gasped as Jake sobbed, sighed as Jake pleaded, howled when Jake prayed and spoke when Jake stopped.

Of course, he'd heard the name before, and he'd heard them too. Weeping and teasing in the belly of the night, but last night had been different.

For last night, he'd been awake.

"Full English!" the coarse voice bellowed from behind the counter. At first, Jake failed to realise that his breakfast was ready, but the next comment cut through the ambiguity. "Oi you, this ain't table service!"

"Sorry," spluttered Jake, catching sight of the grubby man brandishing a vicious-looking metal spatula and as quick as he could manage, Jake squeezed his way out through the packed maze of tables to collect his high-cholesterol meal. His feet were still numb, but he was grateful that the feeling in his hands had now returned sufficiently to grip the metal tray without fear of an accident.

"Coffee'll be over in a minute!" the unshaven fifty-something barked, but Jake could not bring himself to over-ingratiate, so he just nodded and laden with enough food to feed a family of three, he made his way back to his plastic-coated window seat. His hands had finally stopped shaking. As he tucked into the hearty meal that would keep him going well into the day, a sense of panic struck him like a runaway truck!

He had just abandoned a brand-new company car in a deserted south London carpark, complete with keys and a wide-open door to boot.

In the brightening morning light, as he took his fill of bacon and eggs washed down with strong sweet coffee, reality succeeded where fear had been Lord. And to add to that, his wife had expected him home ten hours ago. She would be frantic and there would be hell to pay. He had eaten breakfast like a king and from somewhere, he had regained some of his nerve. Either that or the very real fear that he would soon be incurring Lisa's wrath for another all-nighter now loomed larger than the night terrors that he had just endured. He bolted the last of the fried bread and toast, gulped down a final mouthful of diluted orange juice and instant coffee and ran out into the street.

Even from this distance, he could see that his car was still there, and his heart missed a beat as he broke into a temporary trot that lasted but a few yards. As he got up close, he slowed to a snail's pace and then almost stopped as he neared the rear of the vehicle. From where he was standing, he could see inside, and he could clearly see that the car was empty. Devoid of all life, like an empty coffin, which patiently waits for its one and only occupant to take up permanent residence. Jake was edging closer all the time, but he had to draw upon every ounce of his once considerable self-belief to exorcise the night's ghosts and peer in through the clear glass of the rear window.

His rising hopes for a lucky escape had been well and truly dashed.

The car door had been shut and at first glance, nothing else seemed amiss, but on closer inspection, he realised that he had not been so fortunate. The back wheel had been manacled with a bright yellow clamp and where the night's scrawl had dissipated in the morning sun, a police notice was posted.

He tried the door, but it was locked. He swore to himself at the irony and crouched down to peer inside at the wheel column, just in case his keys were still inside. They weren't. He made a mental note of the release number and swore aloud when he saw how much the previous night's trauma was going to cost him.

The nearby tariff board showed clearly that weekday parking in this prime location was a paltry £20 per day. Compared to the minimum fine and release fee of £250.

"Bollocks!" he cursed and cast a last nervous glance at the car, before trotting off in the direction of the river in search of a callbox. His phone was, of course, still in the car and right on cue, he heard it wolf-whistle after him, a timely reminder that Lisa was now at her wits end and more than a little furious.

It was also impossible.

The battery had been as flat as a pancake.

He finally managed to track down a working public telephone and his first call was long overdue. He readied himself for the verbal assault that was coming his way, but when it came, it left him reeling.

"Where the fucking hell have you been, Jake?" she screeched, giving him little time to respond. "I've been up all night, where the bloody hell are you?" She'd been crying, he could tell, and she was about to start again, but now it was borne of rage. "You bastard, where have you been?"

"I'm in town babe," Jake cried and for once, lies did not come easily to him. "If it's any consolation, I've been up all night too," he went on, trying his best to explain his predicament in a way that didn't sound rehearsed. "I've, well, it's been difficult!"

"Are you coming home then?" Lisa yelled as she choked back the sobs. "We've got to get this sorted out, today!"

"I know," agreed Jake. "I'm sorry for storming out like that," he said, "but it's not that easy. I've been clamped." He hesitated as he waited for the explosion at the other end of the line, but the fuse failed to ignite, and so he continued, "It might take me a while to get the car released so I can't say when I'll be back, but I shouldn't be too long."

"The police want to speak to you again," she said, as she quelled a final heaving sob. A pregnant pause followed on behind, which she clearly hoped might give him time to fully realise his predicament, but at first, he failed to catch her drift.

"That was quick!" he joked. "They've only just booked me. It was early this—" But she cut him off mid-sentence.

"Not about the car, you idiot," she snapped. "It's about the girl, the one that was killed. They want some more information, and they were not too chuffed when I said that I didn't know your 'whereabouts'. In fact, I don't think that they believed me at all. I think that they thought I was covering up for you. The way that you're carrying on, I'm beginning to believe them!"

"Oh, c'mon Lisa," Jake sighed. "What are you talking about?" But he was unnerved by her accusatory tone and like a blameless schoolboy in a class full of truants, he felt guilty in spite of his innocence. "Look, I'll explain everything when I get home. If the police call, tell them that I've been in touch, that I'm out on business and that I'll get back to them later. I can help them with their enquiries then."

"And the office called," she informed him casually. "They wondered if you were planning on going in today?"

"Isn't it Saturday?" an alarmed Jake replied and realising that it wasn't, he collapsed into a mild panic. "Oh shit, shit, shit!" he shouted, with another "shit!" for good measure. "Can you call in sick for me?" he begged. "I have to get my car unclamped and I have to wait for them to take it to the recovery yard, it's going to take all morning!"

"Too late, I've already spoken to them and told them that I don't know where you are!" his self-satisfied wife announced. "You'll have to do your own dirty work for once."

A few minutes later, Jake pressed the button for a follow-on call to get his car released. It took him the best part of an hour to find the yard and then another two before his car was ready and he was able to get back on the road.

His descent had begun.

Chapter Eighteen
Fourth Wheel Lock

And sure that wretched man that married is unto a wife dispos'd to this amiss, is mad to wrong himselfe at all thereby with heart-griefe and tormenting jealousie. If he hath cause for't, let him then forsake her, and pray God mend her, or the Devil take her

Once more, she awoke to the sound of traffic, but Jackie knew from the vigour of the daylight that penetrated the faded curtains with ease that the morning was almost gone.

In the reassuring fall of light from the window, Jackie could remember nothing of the nightmares that had wrested her from sleep, but the fear that had followed her into consciousness had been enough to keep her awake through the early hours. Now she found herself wishing that she had written something of them down, just in case there was any similarity to those that had haunted her father, and so it seemed, her son. But her memory had been washed clean and all that was left was an acute sense of foreboding. Something was going to happen, something that she knew might change her life forever.

She showered and changed and then called the reception desk and booked herself in for another night. After all, she had nowhere else to go and the cheap but comfortable room had proved more than adequate so far. Then she returned to her father's words and to his work.

First, Jackie retrieved the folder containing his research into their family's history. As she opened the binder and began to leaf through the meticulously arranged paperwork, she was staggered at the level of detail it contained. As she began her journey back through time, it wasn't long before the first revelation was revealed.

She'd had an uncle! Jackie had always believed that her father was, like her, an only child, but there, clearly printed in blue block letters, was the name. Terrence Wilson who was born in 1917 and who had died in 1943.

She had never been all that keen on the name Terrence and in the end, it had been her mother who had talked her around, no doubt at her father's behest. There was no mention of the cause of death, which was odd, given the nature of the exercise and scanning through the well-thumbed wedge of paper, Jackie noted that, in most cases, a cause of death wasn't always present. Given the year she assumed that he had died in the war.

Against some of this faceless array of names though, just a single letter 'P' appeared, and Jackie shivered at the prospect that the initial might well have stood for pneumonia. In retrospect, she thought that she could understand the omission.

Time had failed to heal her grief over her father's death and in her present state of mind, it seemed to her that the death of her mother and then so soon afterwards, that of her only son, would forever leave her in a state of mourning. The unmistakable flow of her father's handwriting was at first familiar and had brought with it some initial comfort, but that had quickly given way to anguish and finally, to a strange malevolence that would not leave her. It was as if her father was there beside her, urging her to read between each intricate line to reveal some dark secret that as yet, remained a mystery.

Against that armoury of emotions, she had to fight hard to keep the tears at bay, although she would lose that particular battle on more than one occasion. Still, she refused the intense urge to turn her back on the riddle that was laid out before her.

Her father had roughly sketched out the family tree on a large piece of what they used to call sugar paper, but the precise folds that drew and then quartered the manuscript, now threatened to cut the paper into four and also managed to obscure some of the detail along the joins. What struck her most was the shape of the tree; its branches were thin and few had grown into anything substantial, the majority just reaching a dead end long before the middle of the twentieth century or coming to an abrupt end in the war years. It looked unfinished, but she could not remember anything from her younger years to suggest that her father was working on such a monumental project, and he was just not the sort of man who would have given up on something that looked to her like his life's work.

As she edged her way down through the years and eventually through the centuries, she was amazed to see that the earliest date fell around the start of the eighteenth century. From there to the present day, and especially during the period 1750-1900, there had been many children. It was sad to see that so many had died in their infancy and from every branch of the family. If one or two survived to have children of their own, then they were indeed the fortunate ones. Jackie had little interest in historical matters, but she was aware that, in olden days, infant mortality had been very high. She could recall an article that she had once read whilst waiting for a train, or sitting in a doctor's waiting room, concerning the reign of Queen Anne. In that era, families had often been large in the hope that at least a couple of children would be lucky enough to make it past their teenage years. Indeed, she remembered that the Queen herself had given birth more than a dozen times and few of them, if any, had survived into adulthood.

With that in mind, she took another look at her own family tree laid bare before her, and this time, worked her way forward through the years, seeking the point at which the survival rate would take a turn for the better. It was unsettling to note that it didn't really do so. There were five children born to a Thomas Jacobs by 1875, three of whom were dead before any of them had reached their teenage years and two of these from the dreaded 'P'. The other two survived though, one boy and one girl.

The boy was to be her great-grandfather, who died in the Boer War, thousands of miles from home, in 1899. He had sired just one daughter, who lived to marry David Wilson, the grandfather that Jackie never knew and whose youngest son had died just after his sixth birthday. The girl also married at the tender age of seventeen a Peter Knowles and had three children, two of whom died in the Great War. But the youngest, a daughter called Louisa, was born much later than the two males, in 1905, and was married in 1929 to a James Harvey. It seems that they were blessed with two sons: Harold who was born in 1932 and William who arrived at the tail end of 1934. However, Harold never really knew his brother, as William was dead long before the onset of the Second World War in 1939.

There was also a carbon copy of a letter that her father had written to these distant relatives back in April of 1969. It was addressed to James Harvey at a residence in the West Midlands and although Jackie rifled through the wad of paperwork again and again, she could find no trace of a reply. The facsimile copy revealed little of substance and it was difficult to understand what her father's reason might have been for the correspondence, other than natural curiosity. In it her father had simply introduced himself and asked if the addressee would contact him at the stated address, which was their family home in the East End, as he had something that he wished to discuss. Another copied letter from later in the same year was a little more insistent and stated that it was in Mister Harvey's 'best interests' to get in touch, but as far as Jackie could tell, the request had gone unheeded once again.

So, she turned her attention to the next file. Its ageing treasury tags were stretched to their absolute limit by the thick wedge of paperwork, much of which was dog-eared and torn as a result of the over-zealous filing. One or two articles had been tucked loosely inside the binder and as Jackie lifted it clear of the box where it had lain undisturbed for so long, each leaf fluttered onto the bed. One was a cutting from a newspaper, although the identity of the rag had long since been lost, but even from her angle the headline was clear enough to grab her attention.

She quickly retrieved the crumpled piece of paper and raised it into the light. The print had faded considerably and although there was no date on the roughly hewn extract, the print type and the style seemed to place it sometime in the 1960s, as on the reverse side was preserved much of a rather harsh review of a concert by a pop group from Liverpool.

'Black Death Riddle' proclaimed the bold title and as Jackie read on, it became apparent that an outbreak of the terrible pestilence that had killed so many people across Europe in the fourteenth and seventeenth centuries had made a reappearance in some parts of Africa and in the Far East at the latter end of the eighteen hundreds. The article then went on to speculate whether or not it could ever get a foothold again in Europe and quoted a number of instances in recent history, when outbreaks had indeed been confirmed, including an episode in the tenements of Glasgow in 1907.

The second sheet that had broken loose seemed to support that pessimistic hypothesis, but this time referred to the disease as Bubonic Plague. The location though was even closer to home, as it cited sporadic concentrations of the disease in a Norfolk fishing village and in the port of Harwich in the early years of the twentieth century. This article was taken from a seventies magazine and Jackie noticed that it had been annotated in places in faded red ink, but the additional words were no longer legible. As she trawled through the seemingly endless offering of information relating to the greatest affliction mankind has ever known, Jackie Stubbs was truly overwhelmed by it all.

The latest piece of information seemed to hail from the last century, a research article suggesting that the great seventeenth century pestilence had in fact been down to an outbreak of pneumonic plague. Supposedly, it had spread rapidly in the overcrowded medieval city, as whenever an afflicted person sneezed, spores were released, which were then inhaled by another unfortunate victim. Bubonic plague, the author argued, was less likely to be passed from person to person and could only be contracted directly from the bite of a Black Rat's flea, and so was less likely to be responsible for the London epidemic than its pneumonic cousin.

At the very mention of the word, Jackie felt a cold hand clutch at her heart as the doctor's warning flooded back. The entry on Terry's death certificate stated pneumonia as the most likely cause of death, but Jackie had not forgotten the fearful look that dwelt deep in Dr Anwar's eyes on the day of Terry's death. She had always believed that pneumonia was a common enough complaint, one that could be diagnosed with ease by a trained physician. But there had been too many questions and not enough answers that day for the doctor to have been satisfied with that conclusion. As Jackie sat perched amongst that lifelong collection of dramatic cuttings, she knew that the answer lay all around her, but still she refused to ask the question.

This 'hobby' that her father had managed to pursue in secret for all the years of her life seemed to have an underlying motive that Jackie refused to entertain. As far as she had ever known, his journalistic vocation had never taken him to the tropics where he may have witnessed such things first-hand and, as a result, have developed a morbid interest of his own.

Nor had he ever demonstrated a penchant for family history and, as far as she could remember, had never expressed any desire to go off in search of any long-lost relatives. This rag-tag collection of press accounts and scribbled notes made no sense at all to her, but she knew of someone who could explain it.

Gallagher was the link. He was the only living person who could shed any light at all on her late father's work and she was determined that this time, he was going to reveal what he knew. Jackie wanted more than anything to understand why her father had been so clandestine in his research, and why he had not imparted some of this knowledge to his wife or to his daughter. Jackie felt sure, that had her mother known what the boxes contained, then she would have given her only daughter some clue as to her father's motivation, or if she had deemed it in the best interests of her only child, she would have destroyed the lot. Maybe, just maybe, through that knowledge, Jackie would be able to draw a line under the past and begin the painful task of rebuilding her life.

**

On arrival at the retirement home on the fringes of the Essex countryside, Jackie had not expected the brusque welcome that greeted her. The telephone was ringing, but the receptionist in the Santa hat and Christmas Tree earrings did not seem all that inclined to answer, and so Jackie strode up to the desk and asked if she could go through to see Edward Gallagher.

"He's to have no visitors today, I'm afraid," the receptionist insisted. "Thanks to that little flit of his last week, he's now very poorly and Doctor has given strict instructions that he is not to be disturbed!"

"But I really have to see him," pleaded Jackie. "Just for a few minutes, I promise I won't keep him too long."

"Absolutely not," came the stern reply that was out of keeping with her festive appearance. "He needs his rest, so if you would like to come back after Christmas, I'm sure that he'll be properly rested by then."

"After Christmas?" said Jackie in disbelief. "It can't wait until then. I have to see him today," she insisted. "Why don't you just ask him, I'm sure that he'll want to see me. Please."

"No," – it was clear that she was not about to negotiate. "Come back next week please, if the doctor agrees, but not before."

For a while, Jackie just stood and stared. The receptionist, for her part, continued with her routine, never once looking up from the neat pile of papers in front of her. Then, when Jackie approached the desk again and opened her mouth to speak, the receptionist simply picked up the telephone, which had been ringing off the hook for at least ten minutes and entered into a deep and meaningful conversation of her own.

It had taken almost two hours to travel up from East London by tube, train and finally by taxi and Jackie had no intention of making the return trip without some of the information that she was seeking. The trick was simply to bide her time and to wait for the present incumbent to leave at the end of her shift. At first, Jackie was in luck. An all-day café across the road afforded an excellent view of the home's main entrance, and so with a long wait in front of her, she made a detour via the newsagent and then settled down to wait for her opportunity.

It proved to be a long wait, but time did not drag as her thoughts turned back to the plight of her son and the only year of his life in which she had played no part. On his death, she had received his meagre collection of belongings, as there was no one else to claim them. There wasn't much to speak of, but her father's medal was amongst it all and as she waited, she took it out of her handbag and held onto it like a talisman. She tried to cast her mind back, to the weeks and months leading up to her son's departure, but there was little that she could remember.

She remembered the fateful day that he decided to drop out of college only too well though. That was a day that she would never forget. Her husband had quite literally hit the roof and she winced as she remembered how it was her that he had blamed for their son's change of heart!

It had been obvious to both of his parents that Terry was suffering, but they had put it down to stress and to the late nights spent in the city pubs after work. Even on those occasions, she had been woken in the early hours to find her semi-naked son stranded on the landing or halfway down the stairs in a semiconscious state and clearly frightened out of his wits; she had put it down to the drink. In his exhausted state, she had cajoled him back to bed, whilst the sound of her husband's snoring had drowned out Terry's forlorn attempts to explain.

One night, she had awoken to the sound of raised voices in the street outside and as she peered between the flimsy curtains, she had been horrified to see her own family brawling in the street, whilst the neighbours' curtains twitched in sequence at the spectacle. She had raced downstairs and ushered them inside before things took a turn for the worse, but only Pat had taken her up on it. Terry had turned and fled in a rage, but on that occasion he returned. And then, just a week later, her father had died and the rest, as they say, was history.

Four hours later, at almost five o'clock, a woman emerged from the home into the early evening darkness, pulled up her collar against the biting wind and shuffled off towards the bus stop. To the obvious relief of the café owner, Jackie wasted no time at all and after dodging her way across the now busy road, she made her second pass of the Christmas tree and through the doors of the old people's home.

And this time, her efforts were rewarded although as before, the initial response was to turn her away. However, Jackie adopted a different tack and her less confrontational style seemed to do the trick. It may have helped that on this occasion, it was a middle-aged man in residence at the front desk and he seemed more malleable than the ogre who had preceded him. He called through to the old man's room and as Jackie had predicted, Gallagher was more than happy to receive her.

But when she finally set eyes on her father's old friend, she realised that her adversary from earlier that day had been right to be so cautious.

Ted looked his age and older.

He looked exhausted.

The wound on his face had failed to fully heal and had broken out into a linear sore that spread right across his cheek. In fact, he looked like he was at death's door.

"Don't get up!" Jackie ordered as Ted tried his best to sit up in his sick bed, his hands shaking, and his breathing strained. "You look dreadful!" she gasped.

"I hadn't expected to see you again so soon, my dear," he croaked, completely ignoring her insensitive remark. "Delighted to see you though."

"It wasn't planned," she explained, "but I do need to talk to you Ted, quite urgently." He gestured for her to sit down and after a series of hand signals, which took a while longer for her to decipher than he would have liked, Jackie poured him a fresh glass of water. As the drink passed between them, she could see at close hand just how frail he had become, and his hands shook so openly and so suddenly that she was quite unable to prevent the accident that was about to happen. The excess water ran down the old man's chin, leaving a damp trail in its wake.

"Oh my goodness!" she said, fussing over the mess in a way that Ted found to be quite unnecessary, though not entirely unwelcome. "I'm so sorry, please, let me." And she sprang to her feet to fetch a cloth, which she then proceeded to wipe around his neck. The pitying look that formed on his face made her stop in her tracks. "I'm sorry," she muttered self-consciously, placing the cloth gently down on his lap. "Old habits die hard, I guess."

"Don't be sorry," Ted answered, taking her hand in his. "You have nothing to be sorry for, my dear. I, on the other hand, must apologise to you!"

Jackie said nothing, but instead, looked intently into the old man's eyes, as if searching for some clue as to what was about to be revealed, but there was

160

nothing there. No remorse, no sadness or anger or hatred. His eyes gave away nothing at all.

They were cold and empty.

Almost dead.

She could see in that moment why her mother had never warmed to him. Usually, on the rare occasions when she had gazed deep into the eyes of a friend, she had been able to gauge something of their character or of their mood. But Gallagher's eyes were devoid of feeling, almost as if there were no link between what they saw and who he was. There was no life in them.

"I know what killed your son, Mrs Stubbs," the old man said. Still her eyes never left his and although the sudden formality in his voice unnerved her, she failed to see a trace of the past through the windows to his soul. "Your son's death was not your fault," he announced, with clear emphasis on the negative. "Fate was always going to catch up with him one day, if you can call it that. Maybe it was more an inevitability or an inescapable finality," he pondered. "Or maybe Fate is the best way to describe it. I don't know, but I have been thinking about it for so many years now, and like your father, I still haven't truly figured it all out yet. Chances are that now, I never will."

Jackie could wait no longer, so she jumped at the opportunity to prompt him, lest he died before he could finish. "What happened to my son, Mr Gallagher?" Her tone was insistent and the return to formality was not lost on Ted.

"The same thing as happened to your father, my dear," he explained, but he no longer appeared to Jackie to be the kind and generous grandfather figure that he had once seemed. Now this old and dying man had taken on a new role; a harbinger of doom or maybe the grim reaper himself. "I believe," he started, but stopped abruptly to gather his thoughts before beginning again. "No, I don't believe it, I know it. Your father contracted a very ancient disease back then, which would have killed him had penicillin not been prescribed immediately."

The wind was rising by the minute outside and she could hear the branches of an overgrown tree as they tapped and scratched for attention on the windowpanes outside.

"I believe that your son also contracted what is commonly referred to as 'The Plague', but unfortunately, they didn't get to him soon enough."

Jackie was stunned. Gallagher had only confirmed what her father's notes had clearly hinted at, but to hear such an outlandish theory spoken out loud was a truth that she just was not ready to accept. She wanted to ask him a hundred questions. To understand what should have been done and how he could have been saved, but she knew that whatever answers he was to give, none of them could help her son.

Not now.

Not ever.

"It's unbelievable," was all she could say. "I thought it had been wiped out. I didn't think it was possible for anyone to get it anymore. There has to be some mistake!"

"No mistake!" the old man said with too much certainty for Jackie's liking. "It still exists today, and not just in a test tube in some locked-down laboratory either; it's never completely gone away, it's just been contained and as antibiotics become less and less effective, then the chances of another pandemic one day becomes less and less unlikely."

"Are you saying that this germ has escaped from some top-secret lab somewhere?" asked Jackie, missing the point by quite some margin.

"Not at all, Jackie," said Ted, "no, that's not it. I'm just saying it's not impossible that the disease is still out there, lurking, waiting for its next victim. It just needed a carrier. Or a deliverer."

The old man's words were too incredulous to comprehend and too outlandish to believe, and so she said nothing but did her best to bury her head in the drifting sand by turning to another line of questioning, one that was sure to put Gallagher on the back foot.

"Why didn't you tell me the truth about my mother?" she snapped.

"About what?"

"Why my mother didn't like you?"

"I don't recall," said Ted dismissively, before retreating into a convenient bout of coughing. It was a full minute before he could resume his defence, by which time Jackie had fetched them both another drink, with a half measure for him. "I don't recall giving you any answer! Did I?"

"No, but you said that the reason that you went to help my father was that you heard the blast and you came running," she said with an unmistakably accusatory tone. "Like a knight in shining armour!"

Ted smiled softly and then confessed, "I was never one of those, I'm afraid," slipping back against the untidy collection of pillows that had rucked up behind him. "I called to his crew from the bridge that there was another bomb and in doing so, I sent that young lad to his death, and I will never forgive myself for that. Never."

As he drew a long and rattling breath, the atmosphere between them seemed to lighten a little, as if something more than a coagulation of phlegm had been shifted. Now that the lie had finally been laid to rest, Ted thought it only right to reveal something more of what he knew.

"It wasn't my intention," he muttered quietly. "I have carried that guilt with me all these years. It has been my cross and I have borne it as best I could." He looked truly distraught and that was enough for now to build back the bridge between them. It would have been obvious to a child that Ted didn't have long left, and she suddenly felt that only she could lift his life's burden from him.

Or so she thought.

"It's okay," she smiled, but he did not reciprocate and so she sat back down and waited patiently for him to take up his tale again. She didn't have to wait too long.

"I saw the bomb and I called to his squad and like the good soldiers they were, they dealt with it, or at least they tried to." For a second, his eyes did not waver from the wall behind her, and it took all of her limited willpower not to turn around to check what he was looking at. "Your mother, bless her, never forgave me for that," he sighed. "Sadly!"

"So," he went on, "I took it on myself, as a doctor, to ensure that your father had as much care as I could manage." He said it proudly, as if his actions had in fact saved her father's life, and although he didn't say as much, it was clear from his tone that he believed he'd made up for that fateful intervention. "It wasn't my hospital, but in those days, there were not so many medical people to go around, and your father was very lucky to have one all to himself."

Jackie smiled at the thought and nodded her encouragement, though she'd heard the tale before.

"He wrote in his diary about the dreams, I take it?" enquired the old man boldly and when she nodded, he asked her, "And do you know what prompted them?" Again, she indicated that she did, but this time he held her gaze as if he were trying to read her mind. "And do you believe it?" he asked, challenging her to deny her own father's words.

Jackie thought for a few seconds before responding, and she chose her words with care. "My father was not a liar," she announced proudly. "Nor was he a crank, but if you are asking me in the cold light of day whether or not I can believe in monsters, then no, I don't."

Gallagher smiled a wry smile and shook his head, then rubbed an ailing hand across the white stubble of his chin, as if in contemplation of how he might convince her.

"You think that in his post-traumatic state, his tortured mind drummed up this horror story to, in some way, help him to deal with the loss of his comrade," he surmised. "Is that right?"

"It's one possible explanation!" she reasoned. "Anyway," she said, putting the ball back in his court, "why don't you tell me why you do believe it!"

"Okay," he agreed, taking as long a draught of the now tepid water as was possible in the circumstances. "Though I wish I had a cigarette."

"I thought you'd given up?"

"I hadn't had one for years, until recently," he lied. "One of the other residents offered me one in the garden and, well, no one was looking. Old habits do die hard, I suppose."

"Well, I've just given up, again." Jackie informed him with an unconvincing shrug. "New start and all that, you know." Her lie came easily too, but she tried to tell herself that there was some truth in it, despite the ten pack that was tucked inside her handbag. Maybe it was out of concern for the old man's health, or out of her mother's spite that even in his last few days on this earth, she could yet deny him one of the few small pleasures to which he was still clearly addicted.

"Your family is being stalked!" Ted announced, in a sensational attempt to banish his irrational craving. "And not just you and your son and your father," he continued, "but your father's father and his brother and, in my humble opinion, for many generations before!"

Gallagher waited a moment for the incredulity of what he was saying to sink deeper beneath the spreading creases of Jackie Stubbs' forehead. "And their ancestors in perpetuity!"

"Stalked?" she scoffed. "Stalked by what, by whom?"—and then, as Gallagher's drift began to float in towards her— "Oh, I see, by that monster-thing!" At the thought of it, she laughed out loud, but Gallagher wasn't laughing, although after a while, the thin trace of a smile did gate-crash his ancient face. It was a knowing smile, a victorious smile, the kind that belongs in the back room of some smoke-infested gambling den in the early hours of a Saturday morning. He had the winning hand.

"We carried out some pretty exhaustive research," he recounted, "after the war. It was impossible to do that sort of thing during the war, the records were in such a mess and if they hadn't been bombed out, there were so few people about to assist on such 'trivia' that it wasn't worth the effort," he explained. "And in any case, we were both too busy!"

"Then after the war was over, I moved out of London for a while and left your father to it." A tear seemed to well in his eyes and he pulled out a tissue from the box on the bedside table and vigorously blew his nose to cover up the sudden lapse in his emotional control. "There were too many memories for me then," he added. "I missed my wife too much to help rebuild the city that had killed her."

He shook his head in disbelief as he looked across the room towards the modest desk by the window. Jackie followed his line of sight and then, on seeing the photo frame, stood up to gain a better view.

"Can I see?" He nodded, but Jackie had already started on the short journey across the room. "She really was beautiful!" she said quite sincerely, carefully raising the silver frame into the light.

"She was," replied Ted, "in many, many ways." After a momentary pause to ask for yet another refill of water, he went on undeterred by the all too obvious deterioration in his wellbeing.

"Had she lived," he said sadly, "I have no doubt that we would have emigrated to Australia or Canada and had we done so, my life might have turned out very differently."

"Really?" asked Jackie, glad for an opportunity to change the subject. "Did many people do that sort of thing in those days then?"

"Lucy used to tell me that they were crying out for medical professionals in America and in Australia or New Zealand and we had no family to speak of."

"But she died, and I stayed," he said solemnly, with his stiff upper lip almost visible beneath the words. "He wouldn't let me move away you see. I was too important to him!"

"Who wouldn't?" asked Jackie. "My father?"

"Joe wanted to move away too," he said, taking the discussion down a different path, "did you know that?" Jackie said that she didn't, but Ted was adamant. "Yes, he wanted to go up north, said that he had some distant relatives up there."

"Oh yes, I did see something about the Midlands," she said, remembering the family tree that had revealed just one surviving branch to the family that her father had traced so carefully. "So why didn't he go then?"

"In the end your mum wouldn't leave the East End!" Ted told her. "Who knows," he speculated, "had she agreed, all of your lives might have worked out for the better."

"So, what exactly happened to Lucy? If you don't mind me asking?" She immediately regretted her insensitivity, but there seemed no point in retracting the question and after taking a moment to collect himself, Gallagher took as deep a breath as he could manage and began to recount his tale.

"It's quite simple really. I was late home one night," he explained. "Lucy decided that, as it was such a clear night, she would walk up to meet me at the bus stop. It was a mile or so from our lodgings and unfortunately, Jerry had decided to take advantage of the bomber's moon." For a minute he was quiet, and though Jackie said that he didn't need to continue, he raised his hand and insisted that he would go on.

"When the air raid warning started up, the nearest shelter was at the old St Mary's Underground station, on the Whitechapel Road. The station had been closed a year or so before the war started, but it was converted into an air raid shelter in thirty-nine. So that's where she went," he recalled solemnly. "And that is where she died. I'll never forget the day. Twenty-second of October 1940."

The passing of eight decades had clearly failed to heal and he drew a heavy hand across his face to hide the tears that were welling there. "I didn't know, of course. I got home very late because of the raid, and I couldn't understand where she was," he said as he began to tremble.

"It was the landlady who told me that she had gone out looking for me, so I went looking for her. Searched all night too, but when I saw the devastation, I knew deep down that she was gone. It was three days before they pulled her out. There was hardly a mark on her."

"I'm so sorry," said Jackie with as much feeling as she could marshal, but Gallagher did not raise his head. "Why were you so late home that night?" she asked, already believing that she knew the answer.

He looked up, a knowing look in his eye. "I was with your father! He wasn't very mobile after the, you know what, and as it was so difficult to get about the streets – there was rubble everywhere – we were so often together that they called us 'Flanagan and Allen'."

After that, there seemed to be little else to say and Jackie was about to make her excuses and face up to the prospect of another night in a motel bedroom, when Gallagher motioned that she should stay a while longer.

"There's more that we need to talk about!" he said. "I've not finished yet so put your coat down and make us a cup of tea!" She didn't put up much of a fight and if the truth were told, she had begun to enjoy his grandfatherly company, the like of which she had never known. As she fumbled her way through the assorted items in the old man's locker, he went on with his tale. She found the tea bags underneath a large white hooded robe that had seen better days, but which reminded her of the outfit that the KKK had made their own in 1960s America.

"Milk? Sugar?"

"Yes, please, but just the one sweetener please," Ted replied. "I'm on rations!"

"I came back to London in the 70s," he recalled. "Looking back, I don't know why, but I can remember having to. It was like being hauled back really, although I needed a change of career and so I followed my nose, so to speak, and settled back in Islington for a while."

"Did you and Dad keep in touch while you were away?" Jackie asked.

"No," replied Ted. "We had lost touch unfortunately and I guess that eventually, I would have looked him up, but soon after I returned, we literally bumped into each other, on a bus of all things!"

Jackie smiled as the old man laughed. "We couldn't believe it and we both did a double take at first. It was uncanny!"

"Dad was quite mobile by then, I guess?" Jackie enquired, placing the tea gently down on the 'golden-age-of-steam' coasters beside them.

"Yes, he'd recovered surprisingly well," Ted recalled. "He had his stick, of course, but he was as good as he was ever going to get by then, except for the limp; the arthritis hadn't yet kicked in." They both smiled at the memory, but then Ted's features turned more serious again as he readied himself to reveal more.

"Your father was still suffering with the dreams and was often unable to sleep through the night," said Ted. "As we got to see more of each other, much to your mother's disapproval I might add, I suggested that we should try something that I had been using up north, to help people with all sorts of problems."

"Oh yes," said Jackie inquisitively. "What was that then?"

"Hypnosis," he remarked in an overtly matter-of-fact manner, which was clearly intended to downplay the highly alternative nature of this form of therapy. "I had enjoyed some success with it on occasions. People who wanted to stop smoking mainly as, by then, we were becoming increasingly aware of the long-term effects of nicotine, but sometimes for non-medical matters too." He laughed. "One time," he went on, "I even managed to help an old lady find her wedding ring. She had put it under the mattress for safekeeping and had forgotten all about it!"

"And my father agreed to this 'treatment'?" she asked a little too sarcastically, completely ignoring his amusing little anecdote.

"Don't scoff," Ted scolded, "but no, not at first. It took a particularly bad night or two for him to come around to my way of thinking, if I remember it well!"

"So, what did you find out?" Jackie asked, expecting to hear little of interest in return. She had to wait a moment or two before Ted imparted anything at all, and in the abrupt silence, the sound of the storm outside intruded once more on their summit.

"That the dreams are more than just nightmares!" And his use of the present tense was not missed by Jackie. "They are memories."

Jackie sat bolt upright in the chair and frowned. "Whose memories?" she prompted in disbelief.

"I believe that they are like race memories," Gallagher declared, but Jackie looked more puzzled than ever. "Memories that are passed down from generation to generation. What haunted your father and your son and, now if I'm not very much mistaken, you as well, are the memories of someone that lived and died almost four hundred years ago."

Jackie laughed out loud at the very suggestion. A deep raw belly-laugh, which only came to an end when it became apparent that her companion was not about to share in the joke. But still, it took some minutes before Jackie was able to bring herself under control and only then, did she feel any compulsion to take him seriously. "How did you reach that conclusion?" she smirked, a little angry that she was expected to take his ramblings as the truth.

"Because I know what he is, or rather, what he was," announced the old man and this time, it was his turn to smile, and he did so broadly. It was a sinister expression, which left Jackie feeling chilled to the bone. His very own crooked teeth, of which he was so proud, leaned this way and that as he grinned at her, with several gaps of varying sizes that offered a tiny glimpse into the dark void beyond.

"So," she asked tentatively, "who, or what was he?"

"On the second and final occasion, when your father had slipped out of this world and into the other, I asked him to seek out the source of his worst fears. But the man that answered was most definitely not your father."

"So, who was this man? What did he have against my father?"

"Nothing," Ted said, choosing to answer the second question first. "It isn't he that is stalking your family. The man that 'came through' was Jacob Cooper and it is his memories that have proved immortal. It's his nightmares that have kept generations of your family awake at night for the last four centuries!"

He waited as Jackie pondered the improbable and tried to accept the impossible. Then he played his final card. "What would you say if I asked you about the steps?" he asked, his eyes fixed on his target. "Or the river? Or the bridge?" Recognition burned in her eyes as he placed the final piece into place. "Or the face, the skull, the gold tooth?"

The misplaced dreams stormed Jackie's mind and her blood ran cold as each nocturnal vision found its way home.

"So why didn't my father warn me of this?" she asked, shaken by these latest revelations. "He would have told me!" she said, determined to convince herself of that simple truth rather than to believe in the old man's words.

"What was he supposed to say, Jackie? 'Have you started having any awful dreams, darling? Well, don't worry, they are the memories of a dead man and, by the way, there's something out there that's 'gonna get ya'!'" Ted did his best Count Dracula impression, in the hope that a classic character from a 1970s horror film might persuade her as to the truth of his tale.

In truth, it had the opposite effect and as she began to laugh, he quickly joined in, breaking the tension between them.

"So why did you stop? If it was going so well, why did you only do it twice?"

"It wasn't that we didn't try," Ted recalled. "We tried on numerous occasions to find out more, but we couldn't get through. It was as if it was being blocked, either by your father's own mind or by something else. The path was simply blocked."

Jackie shook her head in denial. "So, is that why he spent his later years tracing his family's roots?" she asked. "Was he trying to find this Cooper person?"

"Yes," Ted guessed, though he couldn't say for sure. "He did what he could to protect you, you know that!" Gallagher asserted. "He kept you away from central London as much as he could, and as I said, he would have taken you much further away if he could have persuaded your mother to go."

"Did she know about all this?" Jackie asked, seemingly horrified at the thought that both of her parents could have kept her in the dark for so long. She was relieved when Gallagher assured her that Annie had not known and just to prove that he wasn't lying, he pointed her in the direction of Joe's last letter, which Jackie had held unopened just a few weeks earlier. Jackie received it somewhat reluctantly, her expression betraying her somewhat blasé feelings towards its contents, but as she began to read it, she did so with intensifying concentration that verged on astonishment. Judging by the length of time it took, she must have read it more than once before she let it slip onto the bed.

"What did he mean, 'May God forgive us'?" she asked, clearly disturbed by it. "Forgive you for what?"

Gallagher sighed deeply. "For murder," he answered as if it were obvious and so matter of fact that he knew it would get a reaction.

"Murder!" yelled Jackie. "Don't be ridiculous, my father was not a murderer! No way! What are you suggesting, Ted?"

"Please," Gallagher whispered and gestured for her to sit back down. "Please, sit down, let me explain."

"I think you'd better!" she snapped, falling back down on her backside like a sack of spuds. "Go on then," she prompted. "I'm waiting." Gallagher cleared his throat but decided to dodge the question.

"Ever killed anyone, Jackie?" It was intended to shock and for a minute or two, it did its job.

"No!" she gasped, as if she were some beleaguered defendant, stranded in the dock of the highest court in the land. "Of course not! What are you talking about?"

"It doesn't matter, you see, whether or not it's war. A life is a life." He paused for a moment to gather his thoughts, but Jackie could see where his line was leading and so resisted the urge to hurry him along. "Just because some politician, or fascist dictator for that matter, tells you that the enemy are evil or sub-human or whatever, you never forget it, you see. You never forget their eyes. Their dead, all-seeing eyes. And the older you get, the more you think about it.

You just can't help it. I guess that your father was feeling, as I do, as if he was a murderer too!"

"He wasn't a murderer," Jackie said, as if her word was all that mattered on the subject, and Ted was not about to argue. She looked, once more, as if she were on the point of tears. But she had cried enough, and she steeled herself to see it through to its bitter end.

"So, what now?" she asked, drawing on every ounce of her mother's stoic resolve, whilst seriously doubting the words of this old man who looked every inch the candidate for advanced senile dementia.

"Leave London," Ted ordered her. "As soon as you can. Go away somewhere and start again," he muttered with an air of reluctance, as if he himself were in two minds about the advice that he was giving. "It's the only way. When I was away, I wasn't troubled, not at all..." But his words trailed off as he realised his mistake.

"You have dreams too?" She was shocked. It wasn't possible. "How can you have these dreams? We're not related, are we?"

"Not as far as I know," said Ted. "I hadn't had them for years, until recently that is, and I'm not troubled by the steps or the bridge, or the face at all."

"So, what do you dream about then?" Jackie asked, unsure that she really wanted to hear his answer.

"An execution," the troubled old man admitted. "A horrible medieval murder, where a living head is spiked above a wide river and crows feast hungrily upon the meat."

It was a vision that neither of them wanted to dwell on for long.

"Well, who is it that's stalking us, Ted?" she asked nervously. "Who?"

Ted looked up from his sick bed, shook his head and whispered sadly, "I'm afraid that your father never fully worked out the answer to that one, Jacqueline."

"What about you?" probed Jackie instinctively. "Did you work it out?"

For a second or two, the atmosphere around them weighed heavily, until eventually Ted's jaw dropped, but at first, he didn't speak as if he was scared that someone else might be listening.

Then, with a long and crooked finger, he beckoned her closer still, until she could almost taste his aged breath above the scent of hospital linen that seeped up from the bedsheets in waves.

"The waterman, my dear," he hissed. "It's the waterman!"

Chapter Nineteen
Third Wheel Lock

Unto these Thieves, my Thiefe doth plainly tell, that though they hang not here,
they shall in Hell.

"Let's go through this again, shall we?" the portly police officer suggested as he lowered his considerable bulk down onto the weary chair once more. "Tell me again. When did you last see Miss Simpson?"

"I've already told you!" groaned Jake. "I saw her just the once, when she delivered the car. I offered her a lift to the station, which she declined and, as I've already said, that was the last I saw of her." His eyes never left the policeman's as Jake repeated his tale for the third time, but the suspicion that was levelled at him from the other side of the desk did not waver.

"It's true!" bawled Jake. "Why don't you believe me? You've no reason to suspect me, have you?" Silence. "I don't have a criminal record. There's no reason to think that I would ever do such a thing."

"Everyone has to start somewhere," Jake's accuser replied, pausing long enough to tease out a reply from the beleaguered suspect.

"All I did was take delivery of my car, and that reminds me," said Jake, asserting what little was left of his authority. "Have you done your tests yet? You can't have found anything, because there's nothing to find," he insisted. "Well, have you or not?"

"I'll ask the questions here, sir!" the officer replied bluntly, knowing full well that forensics had failed to reveal anything that might be viewed as incriminating in a court of law. "It's your job to answer them."

"Happy to!" Jake sneered, slouching back as far as he was able in the uncomfortable hard plastic seat. The policeman's silence was like a red rag to a bull though, and Jake could not resist taking another charge. "Well!" he demanded. "I'm waiting."

As the verbal onslaught abated, another voice laid claim to the silence. "May I take five minutes to talk to my client please?" Jake's solicitor asked politely.

"I don't need five minutes!" Jake reacted angrily. "I've nothing to hide. Come on, let's get on with it!"

"Really, Mister Harvey," the sharply dressed lawyer protested, glancing from the accused to the accuser and back again. "Please, calm down, this is doing no one any good!"

"Get on with it!" Jake ordered and the police officer duly obliged.

"What puzzles me, Jake," he teased, "is why you've been behaving so strangely of late. Something on your mind, is there?" he asked. "Something that you need to get off your chest?"

"I don't know what you mean?"

"I mean why, when your wife had told us you were out on business all day yesterday, should your new boss tell us that you had not turned up to work – you didn't even call in sick they said!" Jake just looked puzzled. "I mean, why should you spend all night sitting freezing in your car in a south bank carpark and then abandon the bloody thing to go for a fry-up?"

At that, Jake's bewilderment became all too evident, because in the cold light of day he found that it was quite impossible to explain it to himself, never mind whilst under investigation. The stark reality of it was almost as frightening as his recent experiences had been. Almost, but not quite. As he sat there, awaiting the next line of attack, his thoughts strayed to the previous night's captivity and to the sense of imprisonment that had now returned.

He shivered until another voice dragged him back from the edge to deliver a revelation that at first was too terrifying to take in and too outlandish to accept.

"You and your friend were caught on the security camera," the officer explained. "Two security cameras, to be precise, and we know that you were in that car from just after midnight until after seven in the morning." He paused momentarily for effect, before putting more questions to his prime suspect. "What on earth were you doing there, and what happened to the other guy?"

The temperature in the room seemed to plummet as the last syllable was spoken, and Jake raised his hands to his ashen face to push his fingers over its contours in a long exhaustive breath. When Jake had finished shoving his hands across his greasy scalp, they came to rest on the crown of his throbbing head, as he fought to compose himself for what he knew would be seen as an evasive response.

"I wish I knew!" he answered feebly, but though it was the truth it wasn't enough and so he tried to explain what he himself did not yet understand. "I was on my own!" he stated emphatically, more for his own benefit than anyone else's. "There was no one else in the car." He was sure of it, but even so, he could not resist asking for confirmation and so, somewhat reluctantly, the timid question tripped off his tongue.

"Was there?"

"No, you weren't on your own and yes, there was someone there," the policeman informed him, "the tape doesn't lie, unlike you!"

"What?" Jake stuttered, sure of what he had heard but still he hesitated to ask what he wanted to know. Eventually, he could no longer hold back.

"What did it look like?"

DI Pearson laughed out loud this time and still smirking, he took up his opposing position once more and made a snap decision to enlighten his seemingly forgetful suspect. Reaching into the brown paper file, he pulled out two photographs that were clearly marked with the serial number and location of the street cameras. Both of the grainy black and white stills clearly showed two figures hunched in the front of a light-coloured saloon car, but as Jake got closer, he found it hard even to recognise himself, never mind his nocturnal companion.

The only distinguishable feature was a large wide-brimmed hat that seemed to stretch from shoulder to shoulder. Jake noted the time on both pieces of evidence; it was just past two in the morning.

"Was he there?" asked Jake, swallowing hard on a sudden flush of saliva that had burst across his tongue. "All night?"

"You tell me?" came the unrelenting line of questioning.

"I don't think so," Jake stammered. "I mean, I did think someone was in the car with me, for a while, but I didn't see anyone." His accuser looked blank. "No one, I promise, I was alone."

"So, what was it?" DI Pearson mocked. "It was a ghost?" he frowned, then smiled and then, on realising that it was not a joke, he frowned again in anger. "The boogie-man? An alien?" he shouted. "You'll be telling me that you were abducted next!"

"I-don't-fucking-know, do I?" Jake shouted, pronouncing each syllable as he did so. "I don't know what it was! Look," he said, trying a more reasonable tack. "I've just not been myself lately and, I've been feeling the pressure a bit. I guess that I just flipped out for a while there!" Not surprisingly, this apparent plea for empathy did little to satisfy his adversary's thirst for the truth, or the nearest thing that DI Pearson could get to it.

Judging by the treatment that had already been doled out by the members of his local constabulary, Jake guessed that he was probably the only real lead that they had come up with. Although his solicitor had assured him that what they had was circumstantial at best, it was equally obvious that Detective Inspector Mike Pearson was not going to let him go without a fight. Jake had already been informed that the forensic tests on the car were overdue and he found himself praying that they would soon come to his defence.

"That's not good enough, Mister Harvey!" DI Pearson scowled rising in his chair, as he too tried a different approach.

"Now come on!" he roared. "None of this adds up and you know it!" He pressed each palm down onto the veneer surface of the table, leaving a damp impression in their wake and pushed himself up on his toes. The table moved beneath his weight, but DI Pearson didn't seem to notice. He was about to play his last card and the atmosphere had to be right.

Harvey watched him like a hawk as he paced around the room, his sturdy girth restricting him to short, deliberate strides. A minute passed in silence, then another. Even Jake's excuse of a solicitor was showing visible signs of agitation and seemed on the verge of an objection, when DI Pearson finally rounded on the desk and placing his hands once more on its surface, he locked eyes with his suspect and made his move.

"Answer me this!" he ordered with a jerk of his head. "Why did you call Miss Simpson's number on the night the car was delivered?"

"I didn't!" said Jake indignantly, looking at his solicitor for some support, which was not forthcoming, and then back into the eyes of the approaching storm. "I don't know what you're talking about!" was all that he could muster in his defence.

"Oh no?" said the police officer, standing upright in triumph. "Then why does it show up on your telephone record?"

Jake was stunned. "It can't!" he objected. "It couldn't, it's got to be a mistake." But by now, he was close to tears and that fact was not lost on the man who wanted his confession to a gruesome murder.

"It can!" DI Pearson smirked, reaching into his pocket to pull an official telecoms company report from the breast of his leather padded jacket. The call was highlighted in yellow, and the time was clearly visible at ten minutes past ten o'clock on the night of the delivery.

"All destinations are recorded somewhere, Jake," DI Pearson snarled. "They might only appear on your itemised bill if they last longer than ten minutes or so, but the telephone companies are only too happy to help out the police in times like this!"

Suddenly, Jake sat up in his seat in victorious recollection and shouted, more loudly than he had intended. "No!" It seemed the easiest and most appropriate word in the moment. "She must have called me!"

"What?" asked DI Pearson, mystified by the response and so was quite unprepared for it.

"I…" Jake began before correcting himself and starting again, "We…had a phone call! We had gone to bed early and I was just dropping off," he remembered. "I hit the call back number! It must have been her." As he rambled on, Jake suddenly recalled with horror that tucked away in the back of his wallet, was the scribbled telephone number in question and he almost gasped out loud at the thought, should that item find its way into the wrong hands. Jake's lawyer was oblivious to it of course and sniffed a chance to get his client off the hook, as he intercepted Jake's next question, just as it was about to slip from his tongue.

"You will have a printout of her outgoing calls, I presume?" he asked calmly. DI Pearson was firmly on the back foot now and was more than a little flustered that he had not thought to check this detail himself, but all the same, he nodded to his hovering colleague who slipped from the room to check out this latest turn of events.

"Yes, we do have a copy," he admitted. The wind had been well and truly sucked from his sails, and suddenly fearful that the outcome of the last few days' work was not going to go his way after all, he suggested a ten-minute break in proceedings to gather his thoughts. DI Pearson left in a hurry, leaving behind him the file from which the two photographs still protruded. Jake stared at them for a moment, almost daring himself to take a closer look.

He looked across at his unfamiliar ally, to reassure himself that his solicitor was on the same page, and when he made no attempt to stop his telegraphed next move, Jake reached in and pulled out the stills. There was no doubt that it was his car as the plates were crystal clear, but due to the angle of the cameras, his face was partly obscured on both. However, the time, which was etched on each picture, confirmed that it could have been no one else.

As for the form beside him, there was no explanation.

None at all.

"Who was he?" his solicitor asked, clearly annoyed that he had seemingly been kept out of the loop by his client. Jake stared straight into the face of his defence.

"I really don't know!" he said without hesitation. "I was truly on my own." The response seemed to do the trick, but as Jake bundled the snaps back into the file, he caught sight of something that turned his empty stomach. Another photograph, but this time in colour, had slipped from the pouch and it bore an image that Jake would take to his early grave.

It was a head.

A bloody severed head. Lying on a bed of gravel or more likely shale, given the riverbank crime scene that was scrawled in blue ink onto the white frame of the picture. The face was not marked, and it was a face that he had seen before, when it was attached to the body from which it had been hewn. He put his hand to his mouth as he tried to speak, but no words could have summed up his horror at the sight of the girl's disembodied head.

At that moment, the door swung open, and another flustered constable swept into the room. "I'll have those, thank you!" she snapped and drew the assortment of photographs towards her, before withdrawing from the room once more.

"I get the feeling that you were meant to see those, Mister Harvey!" The lawyer smiled as the door closed, but Jake was not in the mood for games. He just needed to get out of there!

When they resumed twenty-five excruciating minutes later, the formalities didn't last long, and it was with more than a little reluctance that DI Pearson was forced to admit defeat, at least for a little while longer.

"Some of your story seems to hold water," he conceded, but he was even more confused by this latest twist and was determined to get just a little more blood out of this particular stone.

"So why was she calling you?" he asked hoping for a quick answer to this new line of enquiry. "Do you want to know what I think? I think you'd been chatting her up earlier in the day and she was calling you to take you up on the offer. How's that for a possibility, Mister Harvey?"

"Do me a favour!" Jake sneered, now feeling more confident that what was left of his evening was not going to be spent locked up in a prison cell for the first time in his life. "Have you seen my wife?"

"Yes," said the DI, "and we've spoken to her at length." He let his answer sink in, just enough to worry his suspect before taking another swipe at him. "And it never stopped you before though, did it, Mister Harvey?"

At that, Jake looked as guilty as he felt, and he couldn't bring himself to put on a show for the cameras.

"We know an awful lot about you, Mister Harvey!" the DI told him. "It's amazing what people will tell you when they think they are *helping the police with their enquiries*, and your friends were only too happy to help."

"What friends?" Jake spluttered. "Who have you been talking to?"

"We'll leave it there for now!" said DI Pearson. "Finishing the interview at 12.23," he added for the record.

"You seem to be in the clear, for now, Mister Harvey," announced DI Pearson as soon as the tape had stopped recording. So much so that Jake thought it must be just another ruse to put him off his guard before launching into yet another attack. "Oh, by the way!" he chirped, as if he were about to recount some amusing story about a mutual friend. "What did you think of the snaps?"

"Sickening!" was the first word that came into his head. "Just unbelievable! I didn't know. It wasn't reported in the press, was it?"

DI Pearson smiled knowingly, as his eyes weighed up the options. "The press doesn't always do as they please!" he said smugly. "There was an embargo on the reports. Her body was found in north London, in your neck of the woods actually, if you'll excuse the pun! It had 'lost its head'."

Jake recoiled at the man's poor taste, but it did not put DI Pearson off his stride. "It would be appreciated if you could keep that little piece of information to yourself for the time being. We don't want any copycat episodes now, do we?"

Jake wasn't sure if he was expected to reply, but if he was, his hesitation spurred his sparring partner on.

"Don't worry!" he said. "We'll catch the bastard who did this. And when we do, we'll see that he gets what he deserves! You can pick up the keys to your car at the front desk," he instructed him, without taking a breath.

"So, the car was clean then?" Jake smiled smugly. "What did I tell you?"

"Don't get too cocky, Mister Harvey!" DI Pearson threatened. "There's too much in your story that doesn't make any sense to me. You may not have anything to do with this investigation but you're up to your ears in something sordid and I intend to find out what it is!" he promised. "Don't leave town!" he ordered like some Kansas City sheriff, but that was the last that Jake Harvey would see of Detective Inspector Michael Pearson.

Once outside, Jake took possession of his new car for the second time in a couple of days but somehow it now felt soiled, as if its reputation had been tarnished by association. He told himself to get used to it and made his way home to face another, far more invasive, round of questioning.

**

The next couple of days passed slowly. His wife's mood had softened somewhat at the start of a new week, and although he had to remain on his guard for the occasional throwaway comment from the kitchen or stairs, he hoped that things were starting to settle down again.

Her parents had stayed for an hour, no more than that, just to make sure that she was okay and that he wasn't going to do or say, 'anything silly', as her mother had so neatly put it. After the initial bout of tears, they had both had the good grace to make themselves scarce, but unbeknownst to Jake, they had stayed local for a couple of hours more, just in case things kicked off again.

He claimed that he had 'blacked out' and that he had been heading home after their call, but somehow had continued to drive until he found himself lost south of the river. He hinted at something that had spooked him, saying that he'd been distracted by a noise in the car and that he thought he'd seen a face in the back as he'd crossed over the bridge.

"I woke up in that carpark cold and disoriented," he had told them truthfully, "and unable to remember how I got there, other than that I'd been scared out of my wits by something and couldn't get out until the sun came up!"

"Maybe the locks had been frozen?" Lisa had suggested, looking for an answer that they could both agree on, and although it was a reasonable one in the circumstances, the look that Jake gave her told her that they hadn't been. "Well, there has to be a logical explanation, maybe the central locking is faulty – you should get it checked out!" his wife had concluded, and Jake had found himself hoping against hope that she was right.

There had been no doubt in Lisa's mind that he had been through some kind of trauma. He was visibly shaken by whatever events had befallen him in the fifteen or so hours that he had been out of her sight, but his story didn't seem to hang together. Even she could see that it was full of gaps, and she still suspected

179

that he'd been out on a bender and had imagined the whole thing. At one point, she even wondered if he had taken some hallucinogenic drug or if someone had spiked his drink with one. She had said as much to him the morning after, but he had firmly denied it, claiming that after downing the whiskey at home, another drop of alcohol had not passed his lips – he had not been near a pub, so such a thing would have been an impossibility.

"I want to believe you, I really do!" she declared. "But really Jake, how can a brand-new car be jinxed? And you have always said that you don't believe in all that hocus pocus!"

"I don't," he replied but his eyes suggested that something had changed, and he was forced to admit it in his next breath. "Or at least I didn't, until this. But I had nothing to do with that girl, I promise you, nothing at all."

Lisa didn't doubt him on that point and even though she knew that he was not averse to a pretty face, this girl just wasn't his type. She knew in her heart that even if he had propositioned her, there is no way that he could have been capable of such an evil premeditated act.

Jake was not about to leave his fate in the lap of the gods, or in the hands of the police for that matter, and so after doing a bit of online research himself, he had come up with a plan that began on Monday afternoon with a call to his old university professor.

"University of South Staffordshire," came the well-trained response. "How can I help you?"

"Professor Percival Montgomery, please," Jake asked and waited as the internal number began to ring. In his university days, the professor's seminar group had been allowed to call him by his nickname, but it didn't seem right to ask for Monty and so Jake had stuck with his official title.

"Montgomery," the familiar voice answered rather too quickly, catching Jake off guard, so much so that he found familiarities difficult.

"Professor Montgomery," he spluttered at break-neck speed. "I don't know if you remember me. I graduated a couple of years back. Jake Harvey." He was about to provide his old tutor with further clues as to his identity, but none were required.

"Jake!" he boomed. "Of course, how could I forget! The best thesis I've read on the rise of Chartism in nineteenth-century England for many a year. How are you?"

For a minute or two, they exchanged pleasantries as old acquaintances often do, but it didn't take long to exhaust their repertoire and the professor wasted no time in coming straight to the point.

"Now what can I do for you?" he asked, fully aware that the sole intention of the call was unlikely to be to catch up on old times, but the bluntness of the question left Jake short of words once more. It had been a long shot to call this man and he suddenly found himself doubting the logic behind it. Just as the learned gentleman was about to prompt Jake for a reply, the younger man regained some of his composure.

"I've a coin that I would like you to look at, if you wouldn't mind. In fact, it's a token," he recounted, "and I think, well, I'm sure that I'd like to get rid of it."

The last line was an obvious lie, but he could think of no other reason for his seeking the information, other than the truth, of course, and that was something that he was not ready to admit to himself, never mind to his former tutor.

"Oh?" Montgomery responded somewhat suspiciously and then asked him if he'd had it valued. "I can recommend a very good man near Marble Arch, if you really want to sell it."

"No, thank you," Jake answered awkwardly. "I've already got a good idea as to its value. It's its history that I'd like to understand and what with you being such an authority on seventeenth-century England, it suddenly occurred to me that, well, you might be just the man for the job." Jake realised that the request may have been presumptuous and was about to add some more weight to his story, when the professor warmed to his flattery.

"Okay," he replied, unable as ever to turn down an opportunity to broaden his already extensive historical repertoire. "Why don't you send me a few snaps over by email, and I'll take a look at it later in the week, I'm away on business from tomorrow—" But Jake did not wait for the details.

"No," Jake snapped. "No, I'm out of the country later this week myself, on business," he lied, "and I really need to get things cleared up soon."

"Well, I can't spare any time sooner, I'm afraid," Monty protested, so Jake ingratiated himself still further.

"Please!" he pleaded in a more pathetic tone than he had intended. "I only need a few minutes of your time, it won't take long, I promise." But silence prevailed. "It's personal, you see."

"Can you send it over straight away then?" the professor relented. "I have a lunch appointment at one and I'm not in the office tomorrow, but I'll try to find ten minutes in between meetings if I can." He sounded put out, but all the same it sounded promising.

Jake said that he would and after asking for his direct email address, he wasted no time in composing the message, including most of what he had learned from Goldberg on Charing Cross Road and adding several close-ups of the coin for good measure.

Jake didn't have to wait too long for the response, but he must have checked his phone at least three times before he finally heard it ping and dashed back to the study to pick up the message. The message revealed nothing but was progress, of sorts.

CALL ME – 4 PM.

**

"Can you tell me anything more about it?" Jake prompted eagerly, as the two of them reconnected just after the hour, via FaceTime. "Anything at all?"

"Well, it's an unusual one, I'll grant you that!" the professor conceded. "I'd like to see it up close before I made any absolute judgements, just in case it's a forgery," he explained, "but it's certainly a rare find and it's probably worth a few pounds to a collector."

The professor did not say any more for a moment or two, but instead took off his glasses and strode across the room towards a wall full of books, passing out of Jake's view as he did so. He had pulled down a couple and began leafing through the index of the larger volume, before returning to the first in search of the reference. After a couple of minutes, he mumbled to himself in approval, put the first of the books back on the shelf and returned to the desk with the leather-bound book visibly readied at the relevant page.

"I'm surprised the man at Charing Cross didn't know this!" Montgomery scoffed, as he frowned in disbelief. "The coin is very rare indeed. Only a handful are known to exist and many of them were found on the North Bank of the Thames, just a little upstream from Cannon Street Station, close to where the old Walbrook stream used to flow in. The stream has gone underground now, of course, a long time ago, in fact, although there is a street that still bears the name, which follows a little of the old course."

"I've never heard of it," Jake admitted, playing along with the virtual seminar.

"Pardon?" Montgomery replied, clearly engrossed in the book and seemingly oblivious to the fact that his historical small talk might not be of any interest to anyone other than himself.

"Yes, it's a Celtic name, you know,"—but Jake didn't. "Yes, 'Wale' means *stranger* in our terminology and 'broch' simply means *stream*," he muttered, staring more closely at the entry in the volume before him. "It was the last bastion of the Celts in London. They were eventually driven out of the city, but 'Britons Brook', as it was also known to the invading Anglo-Saxons, was held in high esteem by the Celts for spiritual reasons mainly." Jake did not quite catch his drift and just as he began to lose interest altogether, the professor quite suddenly returned his commentary to the token.

"It's a Waterman's token," he said, "but you already know that, but do you know which Waterman?" He looked up at the screen over the rim of his re-installed spectacles in hope of an answer. "No, I didn't think so!"

"Thomas," he announced slowly, "Radclyffe," as if his voice were a recording on an old forty-five record that has accidentally been played at a long-play speed. The name lingered amongst the particles of dust that were illuminated in a sudden ray of winter sun that made the screen hard to look at. Jake said nothing, but as much as he tried to convince himself that the name was unfamiliar, he seemed to know it all the same.

"The two crossed oars suggest that Radclyffe had a partner in his business," the professor continued. "Watermen were either 'Oars', if there were two oarsmen, or 'Scullers' if there was only one. The Oars were faster but cost twice as much as the one-man boats and tended to be more stable when shooting the rapids beneath London Bridge," he told him, looking up to check that Jake was still on board with the recital. Jake returned his virtual stare with a blank one of his own, which Monty took to mean that further elaboration was necessary.

"At high tide, the level of the water on the city side of the river could be as much as five feet higher than the level in the Pool of London, so the river became a torrent through each of the arches. Most people would take their leave at the bridge stairs, and if they were travelling downstream, they would then re-board that vessel, or one of many others, on the other side. Many of the arches were called locks because of this and the Watermen tended to use St Mary's Lock, as this was the least precarious."

Monty again gave his one-time student a second to respond as he was wont to do in his lectures and seminars, an old trick that he often used just to keep his undergraduates on their toes. "Are you still with me, Jake?" he asked. "You look a little out of sorts." Jake assured him that he was fine and after a momentary pause, the professor went on.

"This token has a greater value than many that you will find for three reasons," the professor announced. "Firstly, because it's in mint condition," he explained and then added with more than a hint of suspicion that such a thing was unheard of in a coin of such impure metal. "Secondly, because as I've already said, it's rare. I've never seen a token bearing a Celtic symbol before, but that's what it looks like to me," pointing with glee to the circular pattern on the face of the coin. "It's either the Celtic symbol of eternity, or something very like it. It's very unusual." He coughed before continuing, "Quite risky for someone in those days, as the Catholic church was very sensitive to any suggestion of heresy, and Celtic beliefs would certainly have been viewed as such."

"And the third reason?" Jake prompted.

"Well, thirdly, and most importantly, because it has a tale to tell!"

Jake's interest had risen a notch and he edged forwards a little more towards his computer so that his face filled the professor's screen, so much so that Monty sat back in his chair. "Please, go on!" he prompted, but Monty needed little encouragement.

"Thomas Radclyffe was hung, drawn and quartered," he announced, as a storyteller might to a group of awe-struck kids around a midnight campfire. "His official crime was treason."

"What did he do?" Jake croaked. His mouth had dried up in anticipation.

"It was a time of religious persecution," Monty revealed, the phrase slipping off his tongue like the opening line to some literary classic. "You should remember that from your studies!"

Then he stood up and began to pace around the room, dropping in and out of view, as if before an expectant hall of eager students, his hands occasionally popping up from various angles around the screen as an accompaniment to the disembodied voice that sounded as clear as if Jake were in the room with him. "In 1661, an uprising in London, led by a chap called Venner and fifty or so

184

people from the Fifth Monarchist sect, had left 22 dead and the memory was still fresh when Radclyffe was accused of treason in 1663."

"But what did he do?" Jake asked again from the very edge of his seat, desperate now to know the crux of the story, but he was to be disappointed.

"I don't know, I'm afraid," the professor admitted. "All that is recorded here is that he was a religious dissenter of sorts and there were enough of them at that time, what with the Anabaptists, the Presbyterians and the like. I could do some more digging for you on the other side of Christmas, but not now unfortunately and not for a good few weeks either."

Jake was left crestfallen, as this particularly source was about to dry up.

"Sod it!" Monty shouted. "I've got a lunch appointment in ten minutes! Don't sell it!" he ordered. "Don't sell it to anyone and if you want to do some investigation yourself, the Guildhall Library is the place to go!"

It was something at least. A lead to follow. A line of enquiry of his own.

"And get yourself tidied up!" Monty shouted again at the top of his voice, before ending the call. "You look worse than you did when you were a bloody student!"

Chapter Twenty
Second Wheel Lock

Then when thou bidst the world thy last goodnight, squint upward, and cry,
Gallowes—claim thy right, to whose protection, thy estates I tender, and all thy
rights and titles, I surrender!

In the days that had passed since their impromptu meal, Jackie had read more books, browsed more webpages and checked out more genealogy sites than she had ever thought possible. It hadn't been an easy task and there was still much that she didn't understand, but she had discovered more than enough of significance to cast some considerable light onto her investigation.

During the course of Sunday afternoon, she had taken up a more convenient residence at the cheapest central hotel that she could find. It was, in fact, a new one, sitting right in the heart of the Square Mile, but at almost ninety pounds a night, there was a price to be paid for such convenience. In the evening, she had been held captive by her thoughts as she wandered through the quiet streets until, unnerved by the onset of darkness, she had returned to her room in the faint hope of a long and restful night's sleep. Indeed, she had slept into the early hours until, at four o'clock dead, she had awoken in a shivering sweat with the vision of a chalk-white face, just inches from her own. Thereafter, the unmistakable tang of salt, coupled with an uncomfortable smothering sensation that she feared might be akin to drowning, had ensured that sleep would evade her for the rest of the night.

Early on Monday morning, as she brooded over the growing disappointment that her lifelong friend had failed to return her call, it suddenly dawned on her that she had not checked her messages. Frantically, she had tried in vain to turn the handset on, but the battery was dead and as she reached beneath the dresser to jam the plug into the only available socket, her heart skipped a beat as the display flickered into life. A few seconds later a tiny icon popped up – an unopened message was waiting.

It was from Dee and Jackie's chest heaved as she heard her friend's voice for the first time in two long years.

"Jackie, why didn't you call me sooner?" she scolded. "I've been so worried about you. Call me, I'll leave you my landline number too, just in case," Jackie could tell from the tone that it was an order and not a request. "It's Saturday night now. Call me. Anytime, I mean it. Call me back, it's so good to hear from you. Love you."

Jackie took her at her word and pressed the newly discovered redial option. For what felt like a long time, the other end had just rung out, until finally a sleepy female voice chirped up and Jackie felt a sudden rush of guilt as she realised that, for most civilised people, it was still very early.

"Dee?"

A momentary pause followed, but it didn't last.

"Jackie?" Dee shrilled. "Jackie! Oh my God, where are you, are you alright, you are alright, aren't you?"

"Yes, yes, I'm fine," Jackie assured her, but Dee did not seem to hear.

"What has he done now?" she snapped. "Do you need me to sort him out properly this time?" She wasn't joking, but Jackie interrupted her mid-rant.

"No," Jackie insisted. "No, not at all. I've left him, for good this time!"

"Really?"

"Yes really, but look, I need to tell you so much, Dee. Life's been a little…strange lately." And as she started to explain, she realised it would be impossible to do it justice in a phone call. "I'll have to tell you all about it when I see you, it's too complicated and more than a little weird!"

"Where are you?"

"In London," Jackie said, realising that she'd need to narrow it down a bit. "In a motel in the city somewhere."

"Oh Jackie!" said Dee and based on her friend's previous message, she was imagining the worst possible accommodation.

"No, it's okay, it's not that bad, it's one of those travel jobbies, you know the type! Listen, can we meet up tomorrow?"

"Not tomorrow, no," Dee replied, clearly sorry to have to decline. "We are having a couple of days by the sea, me and Bill!"

"Oh, that sounds nice!" said Jackie, a little jealous, but it was Dee's turn to cut her off.

"We are only away for a few days though, so how about next Friday?" she suggested. "I can come to you!"

"That would be great," Jackie answered, knowing that she could make good use of the intervening days to complete her research.

"Where can we meet?" Dee asked, a little daunted at the prospect of a trip to London. "I've not been up to town for years."

"How about Moorgate station?" Jackie piped up, as it offered a simple direct line journey into London from the fringes of Stevenage, where her friend now lived. They agreed on a time and an appropriate meeting place, in a coffee shop just outside the station, and after exchanging a few more pleasantries, they said their goodbyes.

Jackie chose not to ruin the reconciliatory mood by mentioning the recent spate of deaths in her family and knew that the rest of her tale would also have to wait until her friend was with her in the flesh. Only then would she stand any chance of convincing Dee that she had not in fact gone insane since their last meet-up. With her mood lifted and with the whole day ahead of her, she found herself full of the joys of the season.

As she glanced across to the set of three large scrapbooks, bound together by a wide and frayed grey ribbon, it took her a moment or two to pluck up the courage to make a start. It was as if she knew that as soon as she opened them, she would find herself engrossed and before long, the day would be gone, buried under the forgotten headlines of a former age. She picked them up and pulled at the ribbon, but the knot was unmoved, fused into a ball after so many years and so she flicked the ribbon off each corner and slipped off the band.

All three looked identical in size and colour, although each had their own plethora of stains and dog-ears that made each one unique. There were no dates on the covers and so to check the years that each one spanned, she first had to open them to see inside. Not surprisingly, each one started at a different date; the first was September 1940, the second March 1941 and the third hailed from the summer of 1942. As she leafed through them at random, she was taken aback at the contents and couldn't help wondering what an expert would make of them all, should she ever find the time to drop them into one.

She made the snap decision to start at the beginning, as *it's a very good place to start*, and before long she was singing a jolly tune to herself for the first time in longer than she cared to remember.

The first extract was dated Monday, 9 September 1940, its headline very matter of fact—no spin, no gore, just the simple truth:

NIGHT BLITZ TIL DAWN—UNDERGROUND HIT, HOSPITALS TOO—EAST END DEVASTATED

An extract from *The Guardian* newspaper just a few days later on 10 September 1940 was also cut out and posted alongside this one, this time focussing on the East End. It gave a stark review of the lives that were lost as a direct consequence of the lack of shelters, as few of the terraced houses were blessed with basements, which had been impossible to provide due to the high level of the water table in the Thames basin. Jackie doubted that the headline told the whole story though:

DAMAGE CONSIDERABLE, BUT SPIRITS UNBROKEN—A VISIT TO EAST LONDON

Whilst some of the more patriotic broadsheets spun the line that Britain was standing up to their airborne invaders, what one paper described as our 'stiff upper lip', not all of them were toeing the party line as the headline from a left-wing newspaper spelt out on 11 September 1940:

RAIDS NEVER-ENDING—MANY THOUSAND DEAD

The story made for grim reading:

The official death toll is far higher than some would have us believe; the body count now runs into the several thousand as the government refuses to accept defeat.

Beneath, Jackie's father had added his own post-script that made it clear that he intended to keep a tally: *Who would notice another one or two amongst that lot?* was the question he had posed to himself and now, many years later, to his daughter. The bodies must have been piled high each morning, thought Jackie, though she had still not quite grasped her father's train of thought?

A vast collection of headlines crowded the pages of each scrapbook and once more, Jackie was left feeling overwhelmed at the prospect of finding out what it all meant.

HITLER LETS SATAN LOOSE ON LONDON
LONDON RAIDS RELENTLESS
NAZI BOMBS SPELL NEW PHASE OF LIGHTNING WAR

What the articles seemed to be saying was that the populace of East London were effectively sitting ducks for the Luftwaffe, something that her father may have been drawing attention to, as he had scrawled across the top of one page 'easy pickings' and on another 'didn't stand a cat in hell's chance'. In a couple of places though, her father had pasted in local street maps that covered the docklands region; Stepney, Whitechapel, Greenwich, Deptford and the Isle of Dogs were prominent in his research, each map colour-coded with the various bomb sites that had appeared following each night of the raids.

Jackie was astonished by the sheer number of explosions and found herself wondering how anyone could have survived such a prolonged bombardment, and how so many bodies would have been buried under the resulting devastation. There would have been no time for inquests or investigations into the causes of their deaths and little point in documenting whether people had died instantly as a result of direct hits on their homes or shelters. Falling masonry in the streets and flying pieces of shrapnel would have also claimed many lives, whilst the less fortunate ones would have no doubt been asphyxiated or have died from third-degree burns in the resulting fires.

People would have been dying everywhere and as that thought clicked into place, Jackie found herself on her father's wavelength, though it would take a while longer for her to tune into the voices of the past. Jackie got the general theme as she continued to leaf through the pages, looking through the volumes in no particular order and leaving them open at random on the bed to return to later. It was more of the same. A fantastic treasure trove for the military and social historian but, she was sorry to say, none of it was exactly *floating her boat*.

What did catch her eye however, as she glanced at the other volumes, was the handwritten names that had been scrawled beneath some of the headlines and annotated on the maps. Sometimes, it was just a name and nothing more, but in some instances, the name was underscored with some additional details. Often these hand-written notes seemed to be an account of the person's death, presumably as a direct result of the air raid. In some cases, there were even arrows drawn in red, pointing at a particular place on a street or at a factory, or a public shelter, presumably marking the very place where that person had met their end. She made a note of a few of them, just in case they did have some relevance to the family history research that was to follow.

One name did stand out though, and she was saddened to see it there amongst that most harrowing of rollcalls. The name of Lucy Gallagher, written in red and encircled in the same pen, an arrow pointing firmly at the site of the now defunct St Mary's Underground station in the Whitechapel area of the city. She thought of Ted then, and his terrible recollection of how they had brought her body to the surface, without any tell-tale marks of the dreadful direct hit that had taken her life, but still another casualty of Hitler's megalomania.

ST MARY'S DIRECT HIT—TERRIBLE DEATH TOLL

Screamed the headline from the *Daily Standard*, which included a picture of the devastated station entrance, the untouched Pavilion Jewish Theatre standing unscathed in the background, its name emblazoned beneath its arched tower in both English and Yiddish. The irony in the photograph was not lost on her.

She turned to the final volume for 1942-44, wondering for a moment if she was missing further volumes for the rest of the war, or if her father had managed to make peace with it all before the end. She started at the back and noticed that the last few pages were completely blank and that the volumes contained no mention of D-Day in June 1944, VE day in May 1945 or of any other victorious battles or military actions as the tide turned in favour of the allies. It was curious, as it stopped in the spring of 1944, with the same collage of letters cut from the headlines of the same newspapers. It was if his work was done.

It just said, several times across the breadth of the pages:

IT'S OVER

**

On Wednesday, Jake was finally forced to explain his unplanned absence from work, and he was left in no doubt as to what the consequences would be, if there was ever a repeat performance. He had managed to dodge the bullet for a couple of days by working from home on the Monday and taking the chance to set up several client visits on the Tuesday, but by the time Wednesday came around, he was summoned to the head office to see his boss who was in town.

It was made clear in no uncertain terms that the warning he was receiving was 'formal', a *first written warning* to give it its proper name. That fact appeared in writing later in the day via an internal memorandum on headed notepaper for full effect, but as the day progressed, it was clear that his unannounced absence had become the hottest line of gossip on the office grapevine. Everyone he met or spoke to seemed to know more than he did about it, and he was glad when the afternoon finally drew to a close and he was able to make his excuses and leave. As he made his way home, Jake worried that he should have stayed longer, just to show willing, but the plain truth was that he just had to get out of there.

The following weekend could not have come soon enough and after keeping his nose well and truly to the grindstone all week, when Friday night finally came around, he made sure to pick up an expensive bunch of flowers on his way home in the hope that they might help forge a lasting truce with Lisa. As was often the case of late, feelings had blown hot and cold all week and it was fair to say that relations were now balanced on a knife edge.

He felt like a convicted felon, out on parole after a ten-year stretch, and he knew that one more misdemeanour would land him right back in it. His nose needed to stay clean, and he intended to make sure it did.

They had heard nothing more from the police since his formal interview, though it was clear that he was still a *person-of-interest* and in the official parlance, he knew that he would be *assisting them with their enquiries* for some time to come. But the two of them had been grateful for the respite and although he was far from out of the woods, they at least had had some time to put things into perspective.

On his return from police custody, and once his well-being was no longer in any doubt, her manner had taken a turn for the worse and Jake had been forced to endure an onslaught that, in hindsight, was fully deserved.

Lisa had been none too pleased at his blatant inability to reveal the identity of the anonymous Mary and although she seemed to accept his excuse that it had merely been a slip of the tongue, it was clear that she had her suspicions, and she would return to the subject more than once in the days that followed.

The flowers did help dampen down that particular fire, but relations were a long way from restored by Saturday morning, when Lisa wished him a curt farewell before heading off for an early morning shopping trip with some old friends, to be followed by an evening performance in the West End, which left Jake free to pursue his own interests.

There was more than enough to keep him busy.

The Guildhall Library was his first stop, and having been fortunate with the trains, he emerged at Moorgate station just forty minutes after leaving home. The streets were dead and although a few tourists wandered up and down London Wall in search of the Roman city, it was generally deserted. Finding the Library was more of a feat, but after a couple of false starts, he managed to follow the trail of public signs right up to its unremarkable door.

There were several other researchers in-residence that morning, and as he joined the queue, he watched in surprise at the level of security, which required him to pass through an airport-style metal detector just to get inside. A sign of the times, he thought to himself, and a legacy of years of bomb threats and international unrest that made the financial districts of many cities a prime target for terrorism.

Jake waited impatiently for his turn, but once inside, he was almost overcome by the enormity of the task that lay ahead of him. He had jotted down a plan of attack during his relatively brief train ride and had decided that his priority had to be the origins of the token, but it no longer seemed that simple. Jake needed to know more about its maker, the waterman himself and of the Walbrook stream, which he now knew was nothing more than an underground water course. Then there was the bridge that had begun to hold some sort of spell over him, and which had dominated his sleep of late, but the feelings of longing that his dreams had invoked, almost of belonging, were driving him on.

He must have made for a bewildered sight as he dithered like a small boy in a sweet shop, so much so that one of the librarians was moved to put down the catalogue that she had been cross referencing with a collection of recent 'mudlark' finds, to offer her assistance to this overawed visitor.

"Can I help you at all, sir?" she asked, raising herself up on her toes from behind the broad and cluttered desk in an attempt to attract his attention. "Sir?"

she prompted waving and smiling, which had the desired effect as Jake was finally stirred into action.

"Yes!" Jake beamed as if she held the answers to all of his prayers in her white-gloved hands, and maybe to his nightmares. "I need some information," he asked a little too timidly, at which the young woman just continued to smile. Didn't everyone? "I'm looking for information on three things," and he spelt them out, but as she began to ask more detailed questions in order to narrow down his search, it became obvious to them both that he really had no idea.

When he mentioned the bridge though, her face lit up and she wasted no time at all in telling him to take a seat, whilst she fetched the portfolio of maps, drawings and artists impressions that the library had amassed over the years.

"Is there anything in particular that you were looking for?" she asked a few minutes later, manoeuvring the large black portfolio onto the reading table. Jake shook his head as she unzipped the collection and invited him to review its contents at his leisure.

"Well, just return it to me when you've finished, or to the front desk if I'm not around," she instructed, "and if you want to order any prints, they can usually be made available within the week."

Jake thanked her and wasted no time at all in getting to work and as he did so, that misplaced familiarity grew stronger. What seemed like memories jostled for position in his mind, as if he had discovered a set of long-lost holiday snaps from the halcyon days of his youth. However hard he tried, he could not pin down the source of these feelings, but as he read through the names of the arches that adorned the old bridge, he remembered the words of his old professor as he traced their trail across the Thames.

London Shore, at what is now the city side of the river on the north bank. Second Wheel Lock, where a water wheel once turned. Borough Lock, named after the ward of London, just a few hundred yards to the south. Index Wheel Lock, where another water wheel had once spun tirelessly for a few hundred years at least.

And so, it went on; twenty arches that had once spanned the great river for eight hundred years, and there, just north of centre, St Mary's Lock, where watermen had plunged through into the pool of London. The detail that remained was incredible to behold, so much so, it was as if he had been there himself, sketching the curvature of each arch and the dimensions of every battered buttress that protruded up from the tidal waters beneath.

He could feel the cold breeze on his neck and could hear the knock of the oars on the wooden hull of a boat. He could taste the salty spittle in the air and could hear the cacophony of voices and gulls from the wharf-laden banks and from the ramshackle houses high above his head.

In another world.

In another life.

"How are you getting on, Sir?" the girl interrupted from behind, forcing him to spin around in his seat to face her and breaking his train of thought.

"Yes!" He nodded, packing the collection away. "This is all great, but I think I've got what I need now." He carefully slipped the impressions back into their oversized wallet, before handing back the resealed case. "Just one more thing," he asked as she turned to go, "have you got anything on the Walbrook stream?"

"I should think so," she replied confidently and after placing the file back behind the desk, she ushered him back through the main hall and into one of the side rooms, which was quite unremarkable in its modest number of sparsely stacked bookshelves.

"If you'd like to follow me, all of the local geographic information on the topography of London is on those shelves," she pointed, "but if you are looking at historical events relating to the brook itself, then you might need to go back through to the main library."

"Great, thanks, you've been really helpful!" he said at which she gave a friendly smile, and he imagined for a moment that she was offering him something more than an efficient service. For once however, he was able to keep his urges in check as he forced himself to focus on the task in hand, though he couldn't resist another look at her as she walked away.

After almost two hours of painstaking research, he had unearthed any number of unusual historical facts, but he had jotted down just a few items of interest. The stream had disappeared by Tudor times, although it was suggested that the line of the now lost river ran into the Thames somewhere between the two bridges of Cannon Street and Southwark, but it was the ancient references that engaged him most of all.

The importance of the brook in Celtic mythology seemed an unshakeable fact, given the number of Celtic and Roman artefacts that had been unearthed from the riverbed over the years.

Included in that haul had been more than a few skulls, which it seemed, may well have been sacrifices to the fierce Gods that were believed to flank the river.

One article captured his imagination more than any other and although the author was not a name that he would remember, Jake found himself scribbling down some notes like the student that he had been not so long ago:

1) Walbrook stream – flanked by two hills, Cornhill and Ludgate Hill.
2) Celts may have likened these hills to their Gods, and later to Gog and Magog (statues can be found in the Guildhall itself) either side of their sacred stream.
3) Celtic God, Ogmios – sounds a bit like that that Cerne Abbas Giant down in Dorset, as it too brandished a club (though no phallus, so not the same thing). Human sacrifices and 'holocausts' seem to have been its thing though, just to keep him from wreaking havoc.
4) Hackney coachmen and Watermen on the Thames would swear 'by Gog and Magog' for protection – looks like they were seen as the seventeenth century 'boogeymen' by kids of the time.
5) Hatton's *New View of London* (1708) "apprentices … as frighted at the names of Gog and Magog as little children are at the terrible sound of 'Raw-Head' and 'Bloody-bones'" whoever they were!

The musty library seemed suddenly to be devoid of life, save for a faint scurrying, and in that vacuum, the room in which he was immersed seemed too deserted for his liking. The realisation made his stomach turn turtle, reminding him that he had not eaten anything of substance since his previous night's dinner. Skipping breakfast had seemed like a good idea at the time, but he was now doubting the wisdom of that decision, as he turned to the next item on his list.

According to one source, sacrificial attempts to appease the gods did not end with the onset of the modern age, going on to quote numerous occasions when such horrors have been repeated. Several sources spanned a very long timeline, but Jake did not have the time to investigate them all, and as he surveyed the material that was spread out on the desk before him, his sights settled on one particularly gruesome detail. He squinted at it through tired eyes to get a better look and was startled by the thud of a door that reverberated like ripples on a pond, up through his chilled feet from the floor beneath.

According to one book on crime and punishment in the underworld of London, numerous severed heads had turned up on the banks of the Thames over the years, although the exact locations were rarely recorded. Even as late as the

1950s, when gangland murders were blamed for at least two gruesome discoveries close to Southwark Bridge, the discovery of nameless decapitations seemed not to have been uncommon. As he revisited each entry in turn, he heard an indistinct scratching, though he only allowed it to deter him for a moment.

In the later years of the nineteenth century, when London was in the grip of Jack the Ripper's reign of terror, the head of a young man had been washed up close to the site of that ancient influx, by a group of poor children who were scouring the banks for pickings.

In that instance, a boating accident at Billingsgate had been cited as the official cause of death.

And again, in the early years of the twentieth century, a rare collection of thirty ancient skulls, proven by the isotopes in their tooth enamel to have belonged to a group of marauding raiders from Norway, had been found buried deep on the foreshore near to Queenshithe; each skull had been severed by the sharpest of Iron Age blades that had mercilessly sliced through their vertebrae like butter.

An ancient mass murder.

Nails dragging across wood.

Persistent. Insistent. The sound seemed to be speaking to him. Calling out. Asking to be acknowledged. Waiting to be heard.

The scraping scored through the silence of the sparsely populated library and Jake could bring himself to ignore it no longer. It was like trying to read a novel on a train, whilst an anti-socialite in an adjacent seat shares his favourite tunes through ill-fitting earphones. Yet the analogy was not a good one, as instead of being able to easily locate the origin of the incessant noise, he was left to scan the surrounding desks in a futile hunt for its source. When he returned his attention to his own table, it was clear that the irritating noise was emanating from closer to home.

As he stood with his hands upon the back of the wooden chair on which he had been sitting, he found himself staring at the untidy stack of papers, which he had shifted to the centre of the table in the course of the morning. In fact, it was several piles now, each roughly spreading into its neighbour like a pile of Sunday newspapers on a Monday morning.

The sound put him in mind of a termite mound on a nature documentary and an elusive itch that simply refuses to go away. Like cats at a scratching post or the mark of a sharpened nail as it is drawn across the wall of a wooden wharf.

He reached out towards the sound.

It stopped.

He sat back in his chair.

Grating.

Scratching.

Gnawing.

Jake couldn't stand it any longer and in one movement, he reached across the table and sent the papers flying in a single push, clearing the surface and scattering his day's reading onto the worn floor beneath. And as he stared at the display that was now embossed upon the once spotless centre of the table, he felt the cords in his neck draw taut and his veins run dry.

The shallow letters 'TR' had been carved into the wooden surface. Two large ornate inscriptions, both at least six inches square, were expertly hewn into the veneer. Yet the initials still seemed unfinished, as if a frame was yet to be chiselled there, to be filled with an entanglement of roses, vines or serpents, but time had caught up with the artist. Jake edged his way closer to the surface, stretching out his hand, fearful of getting too close to the scene of the crime, in case of splinters.

Or teeth.

He plucked up the courage to touch the letters, to trace their path with his fingertips as if their very trail might give him some answers. And to dispel any possibility, however remote, that his eyes were playing tricks on him, he allowed his index finger to trace each rough groove, its rugged edge still sharp against his flesh as if the surface had been gnawed by some savage beast. As he did so, another colder finger scaled his spine. It was his own sweat, seeping beneath his shirt like rain down a drainpipe,

Now the sound had ground to a halt, and all was still again.

Even the ubiquitous churning of the boiler and the incessant hum of the fluorescent lighting had been silenced as the day drew closer to an end and the building settled down for the night. He wasn't sure how long he had sat entranced at the sight of its monogrammed surface, but the light outside was now fading and as he fumbled for his jacket, he kept his eyes firmly fixed on the faceless vandal's work, before slowly slipping each arm into the sleeves.

Jake was trying to rationalise what he had witnessed a minute or an hour or half a day before, to convince himself that the table had already been like this before his arrival, but he knew it wasn't so. He also knew that his occasional sojourns to the shelves had not allowed enough time for a gifted craftsman to carve such an inscription. He placed his hands around his throat and massaged the strained sinews beneath his jawline, but his eyes kept returning to the desk and as he continued to ponder, he came to an unremarkable decision.

He had had enough for one day.

It was then that he noticed the rat. How long it had been sat there watching him, he had no idea. It was large, almost the size of small cat, certainly bigger than an average-sized rabbit and it was black, almost jet from its twitching nose to the base of its arched spine. Its tail was out of sight, curling over the top of the table-top where it was crouched, and it regarded Jake with eyes that suggested that it knew much more than it had any right to.

Now, rats had never bothered Jake much, unlike some people he knew who were terrified of them, but for him they were just large rodents with long tails. Little different to the common or garden hamsters, mice and gerbils that many children adore as pets and so he was not unduly alarmed by it; though he did resolve to tell the front desk on his way out, just in case they wanted to put some traps down. After all, a rat infestation would make short work of their manuscripts, should the rodents have a mind to, and after all these years of preservation, such an outcome would have been a crying shame.

It never occurred to him for a moment to consider that the arrival of a large black rat should have any significance to him. There was no reason for him to think so, but as Jake's hands returned to his throat, it was no longer the skin and tense muscle of his own neck that he could feel beneath his fingers. It was the time-worn skin of someone else's hands and as his faceless assailant tightened his grip, Jake's fingers squeezed in tandem to fight against piercing knuckles and flaccid skin.

The realisation that someone was trying to kill him was as sudden as it was shocking, and Jake was struck by the terrible realisation that he could no more force those alien hands away from his throat than he could run for his life. Instinctively, his fingers tore and clawed to be free from the vice like grip that had already raised him high up on his toes, but for all his frenetic struggling, he succeeded only to draw in the circle as his heels kicked at the ground.

Jake wanted to scream loud enough to wake the dead.

But what escaped from his closing throat failed to reach the nearest living person who was sat studiously at her desk in the very next room, oblivious to the act of murder that was close to taking place next door. Instead, Jake choked as he slumped to his knees, catching sight of the rat as it scurried away. Bile surged from his belly to clog his throat as his eyes bulged out of their darkened sockets and his tongue edged further and further from his gagging mouth.

Jake thrust his own arms back and forth to batter the legs of the intruder, in the fading hope that he might force his attacker to overbalance, but it was as if the man were cast in iron, so solid was his stance.

The crushing hands that were intent on taking Jake's life did not waver in their murderous intent. In his final throes of life, the foul tobacco-laced breath of his faceless attacker seemed more intense than ever, as if all of Jake's senses had peaked in his last moments. Jake kicked out aimlessly at the papers that were now strewn across the floor and from each white sheet a blurred black and white image now stared back.

A face from his past.

The face of his nightmares.

As his instincts began to fade on his last dregs of oxygen, bright white lights stared down like a thousand eyes on long black stalks. Each seemed to spin in opposition to its neighbour, like cogs in some huge machine that spun ever closer. As each golden circle swarmed into the next, a single awesome light burned down on him from above and in its warm embrace, Jake Harvey almost let go of this life.

Then it stopped and Jake's body fell to the ground, his hands still clutching at his neck, where someone else's fingerprints burned. The air rushed in to fill the void and his lungs were crammed to capacity on the unexpected influx of life, as he retched and writhed on the wood panelled floor.

From somewhere deep inside, he summoned up the strength to turn, onto his knees and then to drag himself up onto his feet, and as a door slammed shut in the world outside his head, he staggered forward, gagging and choking, out into the main entrance hall and on towards the exit. Jake hardly noticed the old gentleman, who in turn saw his approach too late and was bundled unceremoniously to the floor in Jake's haste to get out of the way.

As Jake burst out through the barrier, the alarm bells sounded, but the security guard was unprepared for the violent reaction that was about to befall him, as he did his duty by reaching out to grab the young man who seemed intent on one thing and one thing only.

Escape.

"Oh no, you don't!" he snapped, grabbing onto the cuff of Jake's coat as he reeled and dodged his way towards the street.

But Jake's determination proved him wrong and in a stumbling pirouette, he turned to slug the guard across the chin in a single movement. The uniformed man was already sprawling on the ground, as Jake completed the ungracious twirl and stumbled out into the sweet early evening air to run for his life.

And as he ran and ran towards the sanctuary of the waiting church, all he could think was this.

What a fucking week!

Chapter Twenty-One
London Shore Lock

Thy carkas and thy manners (that are evill), to Tyburn, Hangman, and (thy fire) the Devil.

At first, the solemn stone church seemed deserted as Jake staggered inside.

He had sought out the solitude of that holy place in a desperate attempt to calm himself, but an hour or more had passed since the savage assault and he was still a bag of nerves. There must have been many others where he could have found the sanctuary that he was seeking, but somehow, St Magnus already seemed like place of refuge for him and the thought of making the acquaintance of another did not occur to him.

It was like he'd been on autopilot, running into the arms of a trusted friend.

After fleeing from the library, he had first sought out a coffee shop where he had attempted to order himself a double espresso. But when it came to his turn to place his order, he had been quite unable to say a word and was forced to point like a child towards his drug of choice. After all that, the caffeine had failed to steady him at all and so, where mankind's medicine had let him down, Jake had turned to God.

In truth, his first instinct had been to head straight for the nearest police station or to stop one of the distinctive city police officers, but common sense had told him that any resulting assault charge was more likely to be directed at him. He also knew that should such a charge arise it would do little to assist his defence if the small matter of the girl's murder was ever to rear its ugly head again.

The soothing swell that rose up within the inner sanctum of the church, once the ancient oak door had settled back into its housing, held the clamour of the street at bay, and there in that settling calm, Jake's shattered nerves began to mend.

As fear slowly gave way to trepidation and then to unease, he raised his hands to his aching throat and allowed his ravaged body to rest up against the ornate and blackened oak pulpit at the back of the church.

Only then did he notice that he was not alone.

There in a plain wooden pew, just two rows from the elaborately carved altar at the front, an unremarkable figure was hunched. From his angle at the back of the building, it was difficult at first to determine whether it was male or female, but from the slope of the shoulders he hastily concluded that the form was of the opposite sex.

On closer inspection, an old-fashioned scarf of lace or silk that was drawn tightly around her head and a shawl draped around the shoulders, was a bit of a giveaway, but he was craving company and like a freed prisoner who has just drawn his first breath after years of confinement, he yearned for the touch of another human being.

Only a few yards separated the two of them, but Jake felt quite unable to muster up the courage to venture forward. After the day's trauma, he was genuinely worried that his legs may have ceased to function, but as he pondered his next move, she saved him the trouble.

She turned and looked straight at him, and her cold eyes held his in an accusatory stare that stayed for a second and was gone.

The moment was but a droplet in the vast ocean of time, but in that second, a spark of recognition flared. It wasn't as if he knew her, he was certain that he did not, but there was something too familiar about her to go unnoticed. He had met people before who had borne a striking resemblance to some film star or television personality and the likeness had often plagued him for days afterwards, until he'd either forgotten about it altogether or had placed the face, but this was different. It wasn't that she was a dead ringer for someone else, but rather that something in her features rekindled in him an image of someone that he had once known well, maybe even intimately.

Whatever it was, such minimal human contact gave Jake the kick-start that he needed and using the hardwood as a springboard, he pushed himself off in the girl's direction.

As he did so, something else caught his eye.

From behind him, a white-clad figure slid into view, slipping like a ghost from behind a heavy muslin curtain. Adorned in the robes of his chosen faith, he swung a golden orb like a pendulum before him and what little natural light was left within the sacred walls of the church hitched a ride on its arc.

It was time for Evensong.

His new acquaintance would have to wait.

On any other occasion, Jake would have left at this juncture, adverse as he was to any form of religious paraphernalia, but he found that he was quite unable to move from his appointed spot just a few yards away from the woman. Instead, he stumbled into the nearest pew, sat down and bowed his head, in reluctant acceptance of what was to follow.

As he listened in silent rejection of the word of God, he took from his wallet the ancient token and turned it in his fingers in a subconscious attempt to pass the time. At first, he only intended to take another look at it as a welcome distraction to the service, but as the priest performed his rites, Jake began to juggle the coin across the fingers of his right hand.

Left to right.

Right to left.

Balancing then flipping the coin through the shallow valleys between the fingers of each hand.

Back and forth. A party trick from his student days, when such things were more impressive and for a while, it proved its worth as a way to pass the time.

To his relief, the service did not last long and at the end, he was surprised that he felt some jealousy for these few faithful servants. For them, their God was their life, they had something to fall back on in times of trouble, something to cling to when the going got tough or when life's problems seemed insurmountable. The irony was not lost on him as he considered his own predicament, those of this world that were mainly of his own making, and those of late that were not.

His religious conversion was not on the cards though and he remained unmoved; his sluggish soul simply refusing to be saved, at any cost.

When the sign of the cross was made in the musty air to signal the clergy's retreat, Jake waited for the girl to make her move, but she stayed perfectly still as the handful of other worshipers received the blessing.

"And may the love of God which surpasses all human understanding be with you now and always," the priest relayed to the congregation. A benediction that even Jake could remember from his schooldays and he mouthed along with them, even allowing himself to speak the final word aloud.

He felt strangely comforted, but it wasn't to last.

"Amen," he muttered, though he did not form the sign of the cross as others did, but he noticed that the woman complied and even kissed the crucifix around her neck. Other than that, she remained unmoved, her head down and her hands clasped, seemingly lost in prayer.

Whilst Jake remained intrigued, he could see quite clearly that she was in the grip of some personal crisis for which the part of the knight was most likely already taken. But as he stood to take his leave, a distinct sob gave him the excuse he needed, and he was unable to resist the urge to satisfy his curiosity. Rediscovering all of his usual arrogance, he strode forward and in his softest, most sympathetic tone, offered her his humble assistance.

"Are you okay?" he whispered, or so he thought, but in the confines of the church, his cracked voice seemed to boom, and her expression told him all that he needed to know.

The intrusion was not welcome.

"I'm sorry," Jake coughed, his voice still hoarse from the assault. "I didn't mean," he said, attempting again to clear his throat, "to startle you."

"Please," she said after taking a moment to compose herself. "Please, go away."

Jake stayed put for a second or two more as he considered whether or not to continue, but despite the infuriating familiarity that she still inspired in him, he decided to take the hint and so, began to back away. As he turned on his heels, he heard the sharp snap of metal on stone and swivelled back around to look for whatever it was that he had dropped.

But the woman's reactions were quicker.

As she bent down to retrieve the small copper object, Jake watched as the unmistakable shock of recognition passed over her pale features and for the second time, she looked at him with accusing eyes that this time said 'thief'!

"Where did you get this, it's mine?" she said loud enough to be overheard. Jake was prepared for almost any reaction but not that one. But he knew that it wasn't really his and so he found himself wondering how it could possibly have belonged to her.

"No, it isn't." Jake recoiled as he tripped, knowing that he would be hard pushed to prove his claim if he was forced to do so. "It can't be!"

She chose not to justify her answer, but instead delved deep into her handbag.

After a full minute of burrowing, she pulled out a black leather purse from which she retrieved a small piece of white tissue paper. Jake watched bemused as she tore at the wrapping like an excited child on Christmas morning until, at last, another copper piece came into view. As the fading light kissed the dull metal, Jackie breathed a sigh of relief that her father's precious possession had not in fact fallen into this stranger's hands but was then left reeling at the game of snap that had just played out between them.

At first, the two of them just stared at the identical coins, that stared back at them from her upturned palms. It was as if she were weighing them up, before deciding which to discard as the fake. Jake was first to breach the respectful silence, but his first attempt to break the ice failed even to scratch the surface.

"Now there's a coincidence!" He smiled, uncertain of what else to say.

Jackie Stubbs did not share in his joke. It wasn't funny. "That's not possible!" she reasoned aloud. "How can that even be possible? Even the date's the same." She stared up at Jake, inviting him to provide some reasonable answer to her question, but he just looked dumbstruck, returning her blank stare with one of his own.

"Coincidence?" he said again, more sheepish this time, but he knew it couldn't be. It was a feeble attempt at an explanation and in the hush that followed, it seemed to him that the time was now right for introductions.

"I'm Jake Harvey," he announced, reaching out his hand, as if his name was of the utmost importance in their current stand-off.

"Jackie Stubbs," the woman mumbled, taking his firm hand weakly in hers for the briefest of formalities, her head still spinning from the mystery that lay before them. The name seemed familiar but at that moment, she was not in the slightest bit interested in figuring out why.

"Do I know you from somewhere?" Jake said, finally getting it off his chest, but once his question was out there, it seemed so patently flirtatious, that he felt himself blush. Jackie's expression required no explanation and Jake found himself looking for a cupboard in which to hide. It had been a long time since she'd been on the receiving end of a chat-up line of any kind, but even she had heard that one before.

"I don't think so!" she said haughtily, handing Jake's matching token back to him, before hauling herself to her feet. "And I'm old enough to be your mother! I have to go now," she lied and then again for good measure, "It was nice meeting you."

"I'm leaving too," Jake blustered, pushing the small copper object down into the depths of his pocket. "I wasn't intending to stay for the service, to be honest, I'm not even religious, I just got caught loitering at the back and it seemed rude not to. Where are you heading, maybe we can walk together?"

"Home," said Jackie. Another untruth, but she pulled on her coat and found herself wishing that that it was true. "And why should I want to do that?" She wasn't in the mood for small-talk and she wanted him to know it.

"I'm so sorry," replied Jake meekly. "I didn't mean to be so—" But it was clear Jackie Stubbs was not inclined to wait around, so Jake spoke up and deferred the thinking bit for later.

"I've not been myself lately," he confessed, like many sinners before him within the walls of that seventeenth-century church. "It's a lack of sleep, I suppose," he added, as Jackie picked up the pace, whilst he tagged along beside her like some embarrassing classmate from her youth.

"I've been suffering from nightmares, you see."

"Oh?" laughed Jackie, who had not planned to contribute any further to the conversation, lest it encouraged her new-found friend. "It must be catching."

"You too huh?" Jake smiled. "You don't look too bad on it though, if you don't mind me saying so." He was making things worse, and he knew it. He wasn't hitting on her, but even to him, it sounded like he was. "Better than me anyway."

As they reached the church door, and against her better judgement, Jackie aired what she hoped would be her last words of this short-lived encounter.

"Go on then!" she started, not really knowing what to expect in reply. Whatever it was, she didn't give two hoots for this stranger's insomnia. "What do *you* dream about then?"

As she struggled with the latch, she was somewhat surprised at his sudden reluctance to provide her with an answer, given the strange young man's previous willingness to openly impart his life story. As she tugged at the door, Jackie was relieved to find that her unwitting chaperone's attention had been diverted towards an intricate model of some medieval scene. Then, as the toes of her left foot reached the stone slab outside, but before her heel was flat on the ground, his lingering answer caught her in her tracks.

"Stairs," he whispered in a daze as she staggered away from the exit and back into the darkness of the church. "I dream about stairs, mostly."

Jackie allowed the door to slip gently back into its warped and twisted frame.

The very same coins.

The very same dreams.

Coincidence suddenly seemed to be an utterly implausible option. There had to be another explanation and if she walked away now, she might never know. If her story was somehow tangled up in his, then she had to know. It was a loose end that needed a tug, and she was inches away from doing so.

It was, as her mother would have said, her father in her.

And so, with some reluctance, she retraced her steps until she stood beside the forlorn figure who was now stranded beside the encased bridge, lost in thought or in his dreams.

The Old London Bridge stood before them.

A scale model of the lost wonder and it had encapsulated Jake. How he had missed it on his way inside he had no idea, as it was six feet from end to end, but he had been in such a daze as he had stumbled inside that he could have walked past an elephant doing a headstand and not noticed it.

Jackie watched as he ran his hand gently along the length of the glass display case, inspecting each tiny timber-framed building and the line of every boat whose delicately painted oarsmen seemed real enough to hail up at them from the river beneath. In the menacing lull, it seemed that those lost voices were calling still, and that locked within the glass case, the river scene was alive with the sounds of the long dead.

When Jackie finally spoke, Jake could have been persuaded that the voice had come from inside the glass display case.

"What do you mean, you dream of stairs?" she asked, a trace of fear in her voice, as if he were the source of her own night terrors and secretly hoping that he would take back his words as lies.

"What stairs?" she said, accusingly.

"These stairs," Jake was pointing almost before the words had left her lips and Jackie's gaze traced the line of his outstretched finger that stretched through the gloom towards one end of the precarious looking structure that was marked 'city end'. "These ones, or ones like them, I guess. I dream of a boat," he trembled, swallowing hard and with immense difficulty. "I dream of dying, of drowning. Of a face, a skull, with one shining gold tooth, that grins at me."

Jackie stared at him in disbelief. It wasn't possible.

"Jake," she said so quietly that she wasn't sure he'd heard her. She placed her hand on his shoulder and squeezed hard so that he would hear and understand what she was about to say. "So do I."

"Hello again?"

The two visitors jumped in tandem and turned in the direction of the disembodied voice that had no part to play in their newly formed pact.

"It's a very impressive model, don't you think?"

"Yes," agreed Jackie still shaking at the unexpected intrusion, whilst Jake just gave a lingering nod of approval. Had she known him better, she might have slapped him to make him stop, it was so off-putting.

"You were in here last week, were you not?" the short clergyman asked of Jake, his choice of words betraying his northern roots. Jake continued to nod, but he seemed completely unable to speak. "What brings you back, so soon?" But there was still no answer from Jake and so the man turned his attention back to Jackie, in whom he had already recognised a kindred spirit. "I trust that you enjoyed the service?"

"Yes," she answered eagerly, a little embarrassed at Jake's silence. "It was…"—the word was late arriving— "uplifting." The warden smiled, but Jackie sensed that he was ill at ease.

"I wondered if you keep any records here?" Jake piped up, taking the warden somewhat by surprise. He had learned from the library records that the church had been the haunt of many of the more righteous watermen, given its proximity to the river. More especially in the case of the man that they were both now seeking, it was once the gateway to the bridge and to the Thames.

"What sort of records?" said the warden, more politely than he thought Jake deserved.

"Births, marriages," Jake mumbled. "Deaths."

"Of course, BMDs as they are known in some circles, I believe," said the church warden. "When for? There's been a church on this spot for centuries, you know, so we need to narrow it down."

"Seventeenth century," Jake said. "Particularly the 1660s."

"Well," started the warden. "The great fire might have laid claim to many of the old church relics, but not those, I'm glad to say. They survived as they were kept in the crypt in those days."

"They do exist then?" asked Jake excitedly.

"Yes," the clergyman confirmed, "along with the records of Saint Margaret's Fish Hill Street, they go right back to the Middle Ages, but they are not held here anymore, and of course, many of them are online now as well. What's your interest?" he asked, still wary of the younger man's purpose. "What are you looking for? Family history, I presume, we get a lot of people in here looking for information, people from all over the world, in fact. Loads of Americans, you're not an American, are you?" He was looking at Jackie as he asked the question, and she quickly shook her head to indicate that she was most definitely not an American.

"No, I didn't think so, that's a relief, they can go on for hours when they start! As I said, all of them have now been digitised and are available on most of the major genealogy sites—the records that is, not the Americans!" he chuckled. "Chance would be a fine thing, eh!"

"I need to trace someone in particular," Jake interrupted, ignoring the amusing anecdote, "someone who lived around here and who was executed in 1663, for treason."

Although it was only seconds, the wait for a response was excruciating and Jake found himself looking over his shoulder not once, but twice, as if concerned that some uninvited eavesdropper might be taking an interest in their conversation. Somewhere in the distance, a door slammed shut, as if to give proof to the lie.

"It's possible," the warden reasoned, "but why this church? There were hundreds of churches before the fire. Wren rebuilt this one and many others, but many were lost without trace."

"He was a waterman," said Jake, his face flushed even in the dim light. "He worked on the Thames and his head was put on a spike on London Bridge." By now, both Jackie and the warden were peering a little too closely at Jake, with a mixture of bemusement and horror and so, Jake finished what he had started.

"Radclyffe," he announced, and he repeated some of the old coin collector's grudging recital from what seemed like a lifetime ago and his professor's grim lecture. "His name was Thomas Radclyffe. I'm not sure of exact dates for birth and death but it's most likely to have been somewhere in the 1620s through to the 1660s or thereabouts."

"We don't hold those records here anymore," the warden repeated. "They're too old and far too valuable as research materials for social historians to leave them cooped up in a damp old church."

"Where are they then?" Jake demanded in desperation.

"They are all held at the Guildhall Library."

"You can ask to see them and whilst you're there, they have some excellent records from 'St Botolph's without Aldgate' as well. You might be in luck if you can get access to those."

Jake looked visibly deflated and as the warden excused himself and left them to it, Jackie asked Jake for an explanation.

"Why such a long face?" she said. "You can just pop along there can't you? It's not far, I can show you," but Jake didn't need directions.

"I know where it is," he snapped. "I was there earlier today, but I don't think I'd be welcomed back."

"Why ever not?" asked Jackie. "What happened?" But Jake was not at all sure that he wanted to tell her the story and instead pushed past her and out into the cold evening air. Jackie followed him, but her interest had been piqued and she wasn't about to leave it there.

They clearly had a lot to discuss.

Outside a steady procession of cars sped along Upper Thames Street, as the two of them looked up the hill towards the light of the monument. The traffic was very heavy for the time of year, as late-night shoppers made a late dash towards the west end, but the pavements were quiet and the two of them were able to contemplate their next move in relative peace. Jake took the opportunity to recover his composure and Jackie thought it best to give him a moment or two to himself.

"Seems like the best place to start looking is online, isn't it?" said Jake, as he wandered back through the redundant archway. "I've never used it, but I know loads of people who have, and you see them advertised all the time on TV. It's supposed to be really easy!"

"I'm not very good with computers," admitted Jackie. "Been a housewife all my life and haven't even had my own mobile phone until now. I'm still struggling to get to grips with that!"

"Don't you have any kids that could show you?" asked Jake, but Jackie shot him a look that stopped that suggestion in its tracks.

"My only son has just died," said Jackie, still finding it hard to admit.

"I'm so sorry! I didn't know!"

"It's okay, why would you?" she replied, accepting his apology.

"Why don't we go and get a drink?" she asked, keen to learn more from him, even if it did all turn out to be an unhappy coincidence. "It seems that we have a lot to say to each other, starting with what in hell's name happened to your neck?"

Jake rubbed at his throat and realised with a sigh that he would again have some explaining to do when the day was over. "How bad is it?" he asked, fearful of the answer.

"It looks awful, even in this light," replied Jackie, his injuries ushering in unwelcome memories from her own abusive marriage. "What happened?"

"I was attacked. Strangled," he grimaced, his chest heaving in an unexpected sob. The memories were still fresh, but Jackie couldn't resist digging a little deeper.

"By who?"

"I don't know," Jake mumbled. "Some maniac, in the library," but it was his turn to overreact now and he didn't hold back. "How should I know who it was? Do you think if I knew who it was that I'd be here talking to you, I'd be down the station having him arrested for attempted murder!"

At first, Jackie backed off, a little unnerved by the rebuke, but she regained her composure soon enough and with a little more compassion, plucked up the courage to ask another question which she hoped would sound like concern.

"Have you been to the police?"

"No," replied Jake, refusing point-blank to elaborate, but Jackie held firm.

"Why not? You really should at least have it seen to by a medic, it looks really bad." She winced as the bruise was illuminated by a nearby streetlight. "Stop a minute, let me have a look."

She made him lift his head beneath the full beam and she gasped at the full extent of the purple bruise that was only just beginning to ripen. "You need to see a doctor," she insisted, but she could see that he was not in the mood to take advice from anyone, least of all a virtual stranger.

"I'm sorry," she said, "none of my business." And she made up her mind to call it a night there and then. As she looked around for signs to the nearest Underground station, it was Jake who brokered a peace.

"I'm sorry for snapping at you, I've had a very bad couple of weeks," he admitted. "Have you eaten?" he asked, hoping that the prospect of food would hasten a quick conciliation.

"Can you eat?" joked Jackie, instantly forgiving his behaviour in a moment that she would come to regret.

"I can try, but what I really need is a drink, I'm parched," he croaked. "There's a good gastro pub place over that way," he pointed, remembering a liaison with an old university friend that had ended with an ill-fated trip to a Shoreditch strip joint.

"But first, I have to call my wife."

It didn't take long and once he'd left a message to say that he'd gone out for a bite to eat—that she wouldn't receive until after the musical was finished—they were each tucking greedily into some complementary bar snacks as they browsed a Christmas menu in the appropriately named *Hung, Drawn and Quartered* pub at Tower Hill.

Jake made short work of his first pint and was already starting on his second, as they placed their food order at the bar. Jackie was no slouch either and was soon sipping her second glass of chardonnay, when their conversation turned from the mundane to the macabre.

"How often do you go to that church then?" Jake asked, fully expecting Jackie to be a regular churchgoer.

"I don't," she told him. "I do believe in something, but that was the first time I've been to church since…" stumbling over the words she was planning to say. "Well, other than funerals, I haven't been to church for ages. What about you, why were you there?"

"No," he frowned, answering a different question altogether, his throat a little easier than it had been. "That's the second time that I've been there, but not for religious reasons."

"The Bridge?"

A sudden roar from a nearby table drowned out his first attempt at a reply, as an inebriated crowd of office workers got their annual Christmas party off to a noisy start. The party-poppers had just gone off in a coordinated show of team spirit, and most of the coloured strings of paper had ended up in their drinks. Mayhem ensued.

"The Bridge," he nodded as the noise abated. "Since I first discovered it, a few weeks ago, it has become a bit of an obsession with me, I have to admit. I can't explain it, but it feels familiar, like an old friend." Jake looked across the table for a glimpse of understanding, but there was none and so he continued to explain himself, "That church is the only thing that's left to mark where the

Bridge was, and something is pulling me there. I don't know if it's the dreams or what it is, but after the attack, well, it just seemed like the right place. I don't know London all that well but anyhow, I just headed right for it."

"You didn't get lost?" Jackie asked in disbelief.

"No," said Jake, a little puzzled by it. "I don't really remember much about it, to be honest, I was in a bit of a daze, but I know I walked there."

"Did you have to ask for directions?"

"Not that I remember," said Jake, nonplussed. "I must have done, though it's pretty much a straight route down London Wall and then on a bit, so maybe I just got lucky."

"Why were *you* there?" he asked, but immediately wished he hadn't as her pained expression was answer enough. It took a moment or two to fade and after another mouthful of wine, she dabbed her lips with her napkin and sat back against the high back of the chair.

"My son," she said sadly. "It's still very raw."

"I'm sorry."

"It's me that should be apologising," she sighed. "He was on the streets for over a year. He left home after a row with his father, and I didn't get to speak to him again, not alive anyway." A rogue tear blazed a trail down her cheek, but it was quickly brushed away with the napkin that was now caught in a stranglehold against the half-empty glass. The sudden roar of noise from the bar next door told them that United had just scored, and Jake glanced across at the TV to see who'd got the goal, whilst she sank the last of the wine and watched as its residue trickled like tears down the inside of the goblet.

"Another madam?" the barman said, collecting up their empties in the process. Jackie ordered one for herself and the same again for Jake—there seemed little need to check, she thought she knew him well enough already.

"What did he die of?" Jake asked, but he was in no way ready for the answer that followed.

"Plague, apparently!" said Jackie as if it were still the 1600s and they had just stepped into some coaching inn after a hard day working in the fish markets or on the docks.

"Pardon me?" said Jake, almost choking on his beer.

"It was Bubonic Plague," Jackie reaffirmed a little louder than she had intended, at which a couple at the adjacent table turned to look and then turned their heads away, but whilst their eyes were averted, their ears remained tuned in over the continuing revelry.

"At least that's what a friend of mine thinks and although the doctors didn't say as much, I'm pretty damn sure that they weren't all that convinced by the official cause of death."

"Which was?"

"Plain and simple pneumonia," she said as her chest heaved. "Although they did tell me afterwards that if they'd gotten to him sooner…" But she couldn't finish her words and she trailed off, waving a hand in the air to excuse herself. It was a minute or two later before she felt able to continue with her tale and for once, Jake didn't try to take charge. "Had they reached him sooner, then the antibiotics would most probably have saved him."

Maybe that simple statement of fact was the reason why she had been unable to rid herself of the guilt that she was now living with every day. The alternative was to find herself a scapegoat at whose feet she could squarely lay the blame for the loss of her only child, but that was increasingly feeling like a long shot. At first, she had thought that her husband could fill that gap, but despite the pent-up anger that she felt towards that man, she had failed to stem the sense of self-loathing that was simmering deep inside her. She had no one to blame but herself. She should have left that excuse-for-a-man years ago and taken Terry with her.

"As if it really matters anyway what he died of," she said, pushing the thoughts away. "He's dead and I've lost my only son. I lost my mother a month ago and my father last year. And I've just walked out on my husband too. I guess that you could say I'm making a fresh start!"

By the look of her, her new start hadn't started too well but Jake just pursed his lips and quelled the urge to speak, lest he put his foot in it again. He had wanted to mention the impending birth of his own first child but even he could see how insensitive that would have been; when she asked him outright, he still couldn't bring himself to admit the truth.

"Do you have any kids?"

"No," Jake answered, but he knew that the answer he gave did not sound at all genuine and the elaboration that followed swiftly behind was an admission that even he wasn't ready to hear. "None and no plans either! I've only just moved to London. The last thing I want to do is to tie myself down with kids. There's still far too much that I want to do with my life." Jackie could not fail to notice his use of the singular throughout and as Jake became aware of the extent of his unforced dishonesty, he turned the spotlight back on her.

"Where do you come from?"

"The East End, born and bred," she announced proudly. "You?"

"The Midlands," he answered, but Jake was much more interested in her. "Whereabouts?" he asked. "I remember my father telling me that we had relatives in the East End of London."

The party at the large table by the window were now performing an infamous seventies Christmas classic in a loud and tuneless chorus, which the weary waiter and bar staff had now been hearing for the best part of two weeks. He didn't need to say anything as he placed their drinks on the table before them; the look on his face said it all.

"We're from Bow," she continued, but her interest had been aroused and as she remembered her father's research, there was some nagging recollection that she had to satisfy. "Where were your relatives from?"

"West Bromwich way, a place called Tipton," he admitted. "My dad had all the details, but he died from a heart attack in 2010, on a visit to London, as a matter of fact."

It was as if he had never entertained the thought that there may have been any significance to that business trip before that moment, and for a while afterwards, he allowed his thoughts to drift. It had been a massive coronary, a tree-feller of an attack, the doctors had said, so much so that he was dead before he had hit the London pavement.

He'd been there for a conference, though Jake could not recall the exact location and may have never known, the memory was such a blur. Jake had been in the midst of school exams at the time, which may have gone some way to explaining why he could remember so little about it all, but he remembered the chaos that ensued, his mother's subsequent breakdown and the way his life was turned on its head as a result.

"So, what will you do now?" he asked, pushing his own loss back into its box.

"I'm not sure, but the world is my oyster," she announced, without much conviction and flinging out her arms to illustrate the point, as the wine began to take effect. "I suppose I can go anywhere! I'm free!" But she didn't look like a woman on the verge of a new beginning, she looked like someone who was much closer to the end than she knew.

"What do you do?"

"What do you mean?"

"Oh, you said you were a housewife, didn't you?" he stammered, and thinking that he might be about to put his foot in his mouth again, he apologised without really knowing why. "Sorry, I forgot!"

"Yes, so am I," she said, reflecting on the wasted years, spent washing and cleaning for a man who was no longer part of her life. "Sorry, that is! I used to work before I had Terry, but ever since then, I've been at home. I haven't really given much thought to what I'll do about a job." And she looked pensive at the prospect. "I was a secretary before Terry came along, but some people were still using typewriters back then. I don't know much about computers!"

"Oh, you shouldn't worry about those," Jake reassured her. "They're a doddle. If my mother can use one, anyone can, believe me."

It was then that their main courses arrived.

As they each declined the pepper but accepted a healthy dusting of Parmesan cheese, they settled back to tuck into a generous helping of fresh pasta and an oversized Christmas-themed pizza. There were no prizes for guessing to whom they belonged, and the waiter got it right first time, as Jake's eyes bulged at the sight of the fifteen-inch deep-pan with extra cheese.

"Those tokens are a bit of a mystery, aren't they?" said Jake, as he tore his first slice from the monster portion. Jackie looked up from her food and judging by her blank expression, she had not understood, so he tried again. "Those coins of ours?"

"Oh those," she said. "What did you call them?"

"Tokens, didn't you know that's what they are?"

She shook her head. "Where did you get yours from?"

At first, Jake almost spun out the same line that he had fed to the police, but he made the snap decision that he had nothing to fear from telling the truth for once. "Believe it or not, I found it sitting on the seat of my new company car when it was delivered a couple of weeks ago."

"Really?"

"I know." He shrugged, sensing that she didn't believe him. "It's ridiculous, but there it was." He felt the weight of suspicion bearing down on him again and he could not help himself from embellishing it with a lie. "I reported it, of course, but no one knew anything about it! What about your one?"

"I found it amongst my father's things, when my mother died," she recalled. "I didn't think much of it, I must admit. So, what have you found out about it then? Is it worth much?"

"No, not much," he told her, as if he himself were still getting over the disappointment. 'A couple of hundred quid at most' and he went on to impart what he had learned as Jackie did her very best to look interested.

The wine was most definitely winning.

She was weary and found herself pining for her bed, albeit only a crummy motel single.

"They were used by Thomas Radclyffe, hence the initials," said Jake and that rekindled Jackie's interest.

"Well, that explains that then."

"Explains what?"

"Why you were asking after him earlier, in the church. I just didn't know who made it, that's all." But there was more to it than that and as she considered revealing more of her research, she decided instead to cut it short for the night. "It's just that, well, I would have thought that my father would have found that out for himself, especially if it was that easy!"

Jake frowned in mock rebuke. He had never said that tracking down the token's origins had been easy and for a second, he almost took Jackie's unintentional jibe personally. "I guess I just have good contacts," he said defensively, before continuing with his tale. "There were others that also had the initials 'JC' on them, as well as 'TR'."

"And who was JC?"

"Don't know for sure," replied Jake, "but I've got a feeling that I know what the C might stand for now. I think they must have once been business partners!"

"Oh?" said Jackie. "Well, go on then?"

"Well," started Jake. "You know about the dreams that I've been having, it's been worse than that actually…"—and he paused to drain his glass. "I've been having hallucinations too, during the day as well as at night." Jackie reached out her hand and Jake did not push it away, but rather he clenched it tight in his own. A little over familiar for a first meeting, she thought, but she did not object as she found that she was warming to the young man's company.

The 'work's-do' opposite was now starting to thin out as the more sober members of the team made their excuses and left, relieved that their torture was now at an end. The younger members, who were crowded together at the far end of the table, were now singing along to another popular Christmas melody that had last topped the charts in the 1980s.

"The initials 'TR' have figured in a couple of incidents, so there has to be a link there, it's too obvious, isn't it, and another name has cropped up too. I've had telephone calls and I've heard it, elsewhere."

"What name? What calls?" asked Jackie in quick succession, pulling her chair closer to him so that she could cup both of her hands around his. It was unlike her to be so overtly friendly, but after just an hour and a half of his easy company and the lion's share of two bottles of cheap wine, Jackie felt like she knew him well enough.

"Cooper."

Jackie's elbow caught against the table to knock her fork onto the tiled floor with a clatter.

"I've heard that name on more than one occasion these past few weeks and it's scared the shit out of me, I don't mind saying so."

"Jacob Cooper," Jackie slurred and then as the penny dropped, "That's the name that Gallagher gave me." Her voice tailed off as if she were going to say more but the words became indecipherable as her eyes became transfixed on the window to Jake's rear.

Jake shrugged. "Maybe. Could be, I suppose. Who's Gallagher?"

But Jackie wasn't paying him any attention anymore. She was staring past him into the distance. He could see the pink veins snaking through the white orbs of her blue eyes and her chipped nails now threatened to permanently scar the cold skin of his hands. Jake turned, just in time to see a ravaged face sneering in at them through a spittle-smeared pane of glass.

"Sorry, that scared the crap out of me for a second then!" she yelped, at such a volume that even the remnants of the Christmas party turned and looked in her direction. "It's just some homeless guy!"

"Bloody low-life," was Jake's verdict, but he didn't stop there, as he continued to share with her the benefit of his limited experience. "Most of them are on drugs or are alcoholics and those that aren't, are part of organised gangs run by the mafia." He was so sure that he was right that he interpreted Jackie's mute reaction as agreement, so it was fortunate that they were interrupted before he could elaborate further.

The waiter came over again, but this time Jake waved him away. "Are you sure you're alright, you seem quite shaken up?" he asked perplexed, as she shook her hands loose from his.

Jackie nodded and took a final swig of wine with her now liberated hand. "My son was on the streets for a year after he left home," she reminded him, fully intending to spark an apologetic response. "I didn't know but neither did I try to find him either, so I guess it's just guilt getting the better of me. Every time I see a homeless person now, I think of him."

"Oh," said Jake, wishing that the floor beneath would open up and swallow him whole. "Well, I guess there are exceptions!"

"There's a family friend," she said, ignoring his feeble attempt at a recovery. "His name is Gallagher. He knew my father during the war."

In spite of her misgivings, she then launched into her story, all about her father, about the diary and about his research into the Black Death and their family history. It took a while for her to finally get to the crux of it all, but Jake's attention did not waver and this time, he did not interrupt.

"My friend, Ted, would have me believe that my family is descended from a man called Jacob Cooper, who lived and died in the seventeenth century and who keeps me awake at night with his memories."

"What?" choked Jake as he put down his glass to cough like a trooper into his crumpled napkin.

"He hypnotised my father in the sixties, and so he says, they discovered that our dreams, my father's, my son's and maybe even yours it would seem, are all the remnants of another man's life."

"Does that mean we're related somewhere down the line?" wondered Jake, stating the obvious question, the one that they were both thinking.

"I don't know. It's possible I suppose; I was wondering the same. One thing that I've accepted now is that anything, absolutely anything is possible." She looked at Jake, as she carefully selected her next words. "And as if that were not enough, he wants me to believe that my family is being stalked."

"Stalked? By who?"

"He didn't know for sure or just didn't want to say, but he said that it's the waterman," said Jackie, looking up from her empty glass for the first time in a while. "That's what he said."

"So that's this Radclyffe fella then?"

"I suppose it must be," reasoned Jackie, but she was in full flow now and it seemed that there was more that she now wanted to share before the night was through.

"My father was not a quitter. If he had wanted to know something, he would have found it out, however long it took him. I think that Ted Gallagher knows more, but he has chosen not to tell me everything. At least, not yet anyway. All he would tell me was that it was 'the waterman', like that should really scare me or something!"

She tried to smile at the suggestion, but neither of them felt much like it.

"Well, we both have a waterman's token, don't we?" said Jake, but he didn't stop there. "This is too weird! I don't understand it, it's just too weird for words!"

Jackie agreed whole-heartedly, but she just shook her head as if she still couldn't bring herself to admit it.

"Whatever it is, my dad was on to something, I'm sure of it. I just wish that he'd explained it to me, at least if we knew what he knew, we might have a better chance of getting to the bottom of it all."

"Maybe he was trying to shield you from it?" Jake suggested. "To keep you distant from it for as long as possible?" The thought sparked an idea in Jake's mind, but it wasn't yet ready to be aired. It needed time to grow, like a seedling that has not yet broken through the soil.

She went on to relay the details of her father's work culminating in the letter that he had sent to his distant relatives in the Midlands and letting her fork fall into the large white bowl with the remains of her pasta.

"He sent the letter to who?" Jake asked, but he was not about to wait for an answer. "My great-grandfather was called James Harvey."

"He sent a letter to 'a' James Harvey," Jackie said, not wanting to make the connection, one that seemed too neat to be true. "I can't remember the address and there must be lots of James Harveys in the world."

"I can," said Jake. The address that he recited seemed familiar, but Jackie still wasn't sure.

"I'd have to check," she said, unwilling to accept it, on the back of everything else that happened. "I'm useless at numbers and addresses," she went on, suddenly desperate for a fix of nicotine. "But I am very good at names," she announced before launching headlong into a recital of her father's work.

"James's mother was called Louisa. She was born, oh, I can't remember when, but it was before the first war, and they had two sons. One called Harold, I think, and another called William, who died." But Jake stopped her there.

"My father was Harry, named after his uncle and my grandad used to talk about his Uncle Will, who died of TB when he was a kid." For more than a minute, the two of them said nothing. They just studied each other across the cluttered table in a desperate search for some sign of their distant kinship.

"Oh my God!" exclaimed Jackie. "The dreams. Yours really are the same as mine."

"What does he look like?" asked Jake; he wanted irrefutable proof that their dreams were linked. Not just similar, but the same.

The same places.

The same faces.

The same man.

"Who?"

"Radclyffe!" Jake prompted. "The one that is stalking you, I mean, us." Jackie was still in denial, but the assumption was a simple one. "It has to be him, doesn't it? Well, what does he look like, in your dreams?"

Jackie cleared her throat and brushed away a loose strand of hair, which had slipped from its clip. "Well, I never have gotten a really good look at his face, close up..."—swallowing a piece of Jake's leftover pizza. "I've seen, or at least it seems real enough to me, a skull staring out from beneath a hood. He wears a dark hat, like a rain hat, with a big rim. And a cloak of some sort." Jake was nodding. "And he has a gold tooth."

"Which one?"

"At the front." Jackie bared her teeth, as if she were about to growl and prodded with her forefinger at the tobacco-stained tooth that divided her left incisor from her front teeth. "This one, I think."

Jake nodded. "Ever seen him when you've been awake?"

Jackie sat in horrified contemplation at the suggestion.

"God no! Have you?"

"In the car!" Jake nodded, as the memory leached the colour from his skin. "At the traffic lights near to the bridge." But he decided not to mention the indisputable photographic proof that the police had provided, as it might have led Jackie the wrong conclusion about his character, or to the right one. He paused for a second or two as he found himself almost telling her the whole story,

222

and he had to mentally pinch himself just in case this were all just another bad dream from which he would soon wake.

"It was in the back of my car, and it said—"

"You're mine!" said Jackie, but Jake had not anticipated that the words had not been solely meant for him and he stared at her in awe, as realisation dawned.

"Yes!" said Jake fearfully, rubbing his temples with both hands, as if in hope that a genie might yet pop out of his head to take on the supernatural strength of their tormentor. "So, there's no doubt about it then, is there, but how can that be? How can we be having the same dreams?"

"I don't know, Jake," said Jackie. "But I'm scared. What did he mean by that? What's going to happen?" But Jake had no answers, so Jackie posed another question to add to their growing backlog.

"What the hell is going on, Jake?"

"I don't have a fucking clue," he admitted, "but I'm going to find out if it's the last thing I do!"

"Don't say that!" Jackie cautioned and Jake found himself wishing that he hadn't. "So, what does all of that make us then?" she asked, trying to lighten the mood between them. "I'm old enough to be your great-aunt, or something!"

"Don't be daft," Jake laughed, "you're not that old! Distant cousins, I suppose!" Jake frowned. "I guess this means that I better not ask you out on a second date then?"

Jackie did her best to ignore him as she tried in vain to make some sense of the mess in which she had become embroiled, but after fully five minutes of mental torture, she gave in. "Oh well," she sighed, looking on the bright side for a moment, "at least I've got something left of my family."

They were both quiet then, stranded in private thought and this time, there was no entertainment on hand to distract them. The party had now dissipated and though the table was still awash with an array of party hats and plastic tat, the only couple that remained were locked in a passionate embrace that had obviously been on the cards all evening. When eventually Jake piped up with a welcome change of subject, a full five minutes had transpired.

"Jackie," Jake pressed, "I still don't understand what you were doing in that particular church today of all days."

"My son was on the streets around here, I believe," she explained. "I found out that he used to pick up his benefits money at the post office on Walbrook, just off Lower Thames Street over there," she said, pointing in the general direction of the river. "I guess that I came down here today so that I could be close to him again. I really don't remember why I went to that particular church. I suppose that I needed some support! Something spiritual, as if I'm going to believe in all this supernatural mumbo jumbo, then the Holy Spirit seems a lot less far-fetched, if you ask me and I know that He's on my side!"

"And did it work?"

"For me, yes, it did!" said Jackie, sensing his cynicism. "God is all that I've had at times these past few years, even though I've never been what some would call a practicing Christian, it's always been here." She patted herself in the general vicinity of her heart.

"I'm sorry, I didn't mean to suggest…"

"I know," she said, "but it works for me. You should try letting your guard down a bit. There's a lot out there that we don't understand and the deeper I get into this crap, the more I'm beginning to realise that we have a lot to learn."

The waiter made a momentary appearance at the bar to call last orders and Jake caught his eye before he managed to sneak away again, to signal for the bill. "So Cuz," joked Jake in an attempt to draw things to a close. "Who is pulling our strings then, because it certainly isn't us, is it?"

"We need to talk some more," Jackie insisted. "Can you meet me tomorrow?"

"No," Jake said, knowing full well that another away-day would not help bridge the growing rift with his wife. "I really can't get out tomorrow."

"What about Friday then?"

"I could do the evening, probably, but I'll be at work all day,"

"Let's meet at Moorgate, say six o'clock?" Jackie suggested, giving him little room for manoeuvre. "I'll go to the library as it's not far from there. See what else I can find out, about you know who."

Jake nodded and after leaving enough cash between them to cover the cost of the meal and a generous tip, they both slipped out into the night. As they walked up the hill, towards another tube station, Jake slowed and then froze in his tracks like a hunter who has just set eyes on his prey, but his sight did not stray from Jackie's shadowy profile.

"Stop!" he ordered and as she turned to face him, he blurted out what he had only just realised. "I've just figured out who you look like," he gasped. "The reason why I was so attracted to you, back in the church."

"Other than my mature good looks!" she scoffed, but Jake was too excited to take any notice.

"We have a picture in our hallway at home. It's old, really old, from the twenties or thirties or something. I've only just noticed, but in this light and from the side especially. You look just like Louisa. My great-grandmother."

Part Two: The Descent

Chapter Twenty-Two
Bridge Foot Stairs

Yet rather than thou shouldn't a hanging want, I'de trusse thee up for naught were Hangmen scant, Nay I would doe it freely, and for nothing, and give thy wife againe my fee and clothing: which courtesy of mine, no doubt would move the creature's kindness to requite my love.

Wake up! He was dreaming. He knew he was dreaming, but he couldn't move, his hands were tied!

Get off me. Leave me alone. He's coming, running faster, getting closer. Who is it? I know who it is. Breathing hard – running – legs don't work, not moving. Standing still. Trying to speak, needing to scream.

"Wake me up!"

Get off me, not his face. Leave me. Alone. I'm dreaming. Legs like lead, buried in silt. Concrete shoes. Dark skies. Dark water. One gold tooth. Leave me be, I'm dreaming. Screaming. It's a dream, only dreaming. Run! Got to run. Run from the rats. The eyes. Beady. Biting. Black. Rats.

"Get off me!"

Crawling, slithering. No. Not again. Get away. Got to get away. Can't move, hands tied. Feet like lead. Weighted down. On my chest. Coin flipping, spinning, glinting, falling.

"No! Wake me up!"
"Wake up!"

"Jake, wake up!"

Shaking, dreaming, still asleep, need to wake up! Who is it? Who is it? Heads you win, tails you lose. You lose. You lose. Sinking. Lost. Melting into nothingness. Rising. Waking. Awake.

"Wake up, Jake!"

The bedsheets were drenched in sweat, it was still dark, it was still early.

"You were dreaming!" Lisa whimpered, a little shaken herself by the ferocity of his nightmare. "You were having a bad dream again."

Jake didn't speak, but his eyes darted around the room, the walls illuminated in the muted glow of his wife's bedside lamp. A droplet of sweat slid from his temple and he wiped it away with his free hand, the other propping him up on his sodden pillow. But it was tears that fell across his face and not sweat.

He was crying.

"Same fucking dream!" was all he could say in response.

"It's okay," his wife's soothing voice was in his ear. "You're okay now."

If only that were true, thought Jake.

For a while they lay there, side by side, not speaking, but it felt like he'd wet the bed, so much so that he wondered if he had.

Lisa, sensing his embarrassment, ushered him out.

"Go and make us both a cuppa," she said quietly. "I'll change the sheets, they're soaked!"

It was 4 am. He made a nature call on his way to the kitchen, taking a brief look in the mirror as he reached for the flush. He looked awful. As he navigated his way downstairs in the semi-darkness, reluctant for some reason to switch on the lights to aid his journey, he felt a sudden need to call Jackie, feeling certain that she too would be awake. That she too had been dreaming the same dreams, maybe even waking at the same moment, but he knew that she would be alone and without a bedpartner to shake her from her captivity, would she still be lost or in the clutches of their stalker?

He didn't know, but in that moment, he was actually scared for them both.

The kettle came to a boil, and he dropped a tea bag into each cup before drowning them in scalding hot water. He always added the skimmed milk last of all, something that Lisa would always object to if and when she noticed. She was strictly a milk-first type of girl.

Was it too early for a biscuit? Maybe he was better off making toast.

He wasn't going back to bed that was for sure, so he dropped a couple of slices of bread into the toaster and pressed down the lever.

There would be no more sleep that night, at least not for him.

**

Lisa came downstairs at just after seven, to find Jake already dressed and on his laptop, the white LED lights of their artificial tree flickering from the corner of the room. He had a lot of catching up to do and was working his way through over one hundred and fifty emails that had clogged his inbox over the last week, most of which weren't urgent.

"That was some dream you were having last night!" she said as she sat down opposite him. "Want to talk about it?"

He didn't but he felt he should and knew that if he tried to shut her out again, she would only get suspicious, so he opted for a sanitised version. "It's a bit hazy now," he lied, "but I was being chased and I couldn't move. I was frozen but I needed to run but I still couldn't move. The crazy thing was, I knew that I was asleep, and I was trying to shout for you to wake me up, but I couldn't make the words, like I was gagged or something!"

"You were shouting!" Lisa told him. "You woke me up, you were shouting so loud. I'm surprised you didn't wake up the street; you were screaming and moaning, but not really making any sense."

"It was horrible!" recalled Jake, shivering. "I've been down here since four-thirty, I brought us up a cup of tea and lay there for a bit, but to be honest, I couldn't bear the thought of going back to sleep in case it started again. So, I waited until you were asleep and then came down and did a couple of hours' work. I've been quite productive actually."

"Good," said Lisa, but she was clearly unsettled by his night terrors, especially as it was not the first time she'd been disturbed.

"Are you worrying about that girl, is that what it is?" she asked, digging a little deeper. "Or is it the bloke that attacked you the other night that's troubling you? Maybe you do need to see a doctor, get some sleeping pills or stress tablets or something?" It was clear that his earlier admissions had not convinced her of his innocence, and she harboured some serious misgivings about what he'd told her.

"Maybe I should," Jake agreed, much to his own surprise. "I need to do something, that's for sure, it's starting to get me down."

"Liar," she snapped out of nowhere and the force of it made Jake physically recoil. He knew that she hadn't believed him when he had blamed a bar brawl for the state that his neck was in; the suggestion that he would step in to stop a fight between complete strangers was just not in his make-up and even as he was spinning the tale, he had known that the lie would come back to haunt him. "There's something going on, Jake, and you'd better tell me now, right now, or…"—but she had not planned to deliver an ultimatum and so the threat that followed lacked any real conviction—"…or, I'm out of here!"

"Babe!" Jake objected, but the force of her rebuke had taken him by surprise, and he felt the need once more to tell her what had happened in all its gruesome detail. "Look," he stuttered, "it's like I told you before. I haven't been messing around."

At the very suggestion, his wife's eyes burned with anger, and she was quite unable to hold back the threat that followed. "I never said you had, what made you jump to that conclusion? Well, you know what would happen if you did, don't you! There'd be no second chances again, that's for sure, not after last time." The contradiction was obvious, but he knew the incident to which she was referring; it was old ground that he really didn't want to turn over again.

"That was a long time ago, Lisa," he pleaded in the general direction of the worn carpet tiles at her feet. "It was a drunken mistake, you know that!"

"Yes," she snapped. "I know, and I also know how often you get drunk!" Her eyes rested on his and they were locked in. "How much did you have the other night? More than a couple, I bet, and I hope you weren't stupid enough to drive afterwards?"

"Listen," he said with more composure than he felt. "Go and sit down in the lounge and I'll make us both another drink. Then I'm going to tell you everything from start to finish and you can make up your own mind." She started to say something in retaliation, but Jake raised his hands. "I know it's crazy, love, but I've done nothing wrong. Nothing. But you're right, the thing that is 'going on' is scaring the shit out of me."

Five minutes later, when the storm between them had calmed to the force of an autumn squall, he placed the tray of drinks on the nest of tables and sat down in the opposite camp. He had fully expected her to renew the onslaught, but she was more composed than he had seen her in quite a while. The pregnancy had begun to kick in during the last week and she had begun to suffer from a gruesome bout of morning sickness each day within an hour of rising. So, judging by the time, he had about forty minutes to clear the air.

"I can still hardly believe it myself, but I think I was attacked by something that was not of this world," he surmised. "I don't remember exactly when it started for sure, but I guess that it was a week or so before the car came. I had a dream. A nightmare, actually." And he cupped his hands around his mouth and nose to sneeze, as his words revived the memories that he had hoped to forget. Almost a minute had passed before he was able to resume the tale and in the intervening minutes, his wife began to feel nauseous a little ahead of schedule.

"I woke up on the landing, at the top of the stairs, to be precise."

"You mean you were sleepwalking?" she asked, a little unnerved. She had always found the very idea unnerving.

Jake nodded.

"But you've never done that before, have you?"

"Not to my knowledge," said Jake, pleased that his wife's concern had risen a notch or two at the prospect of his nocturnal wanderings. "I always dream of a river, of a boat,"—and he shuddered at the thought—"of wooden stairs that lead down to the water's edge."

His uneasiness must have been obvious, because to his surprise, his wife leant from her chair and squeezed his knee, as if to reassure him that it was, after all, just a dream. He smiled at her touch, but it was not enough to dispel the visions that had returned to haunt him again.

"And of a face," he added unwillingly. "A dead man's face, that has no skin, but still, it smiles at me, like it knows me. Recognises me. Like it knows who I am."

He must have been convincing, because he had said enough to entice Lisa to sit by his side on the settee, but the hug that she gave him was not enough to ward off the evil that he sensed around him. If only the familiar fear that he now felt had been just for show, but it wasn't and for once, Jake was not putting on a performance.

"If you've been having these bad dreams for a while, why didn't you say?"

"It's not just dreams," Jake cried out, knowing full well that he had only just begun to explain himself. "I've had a few, a few experiences, I didn't tell you the full story the other night, I didn't want to pile it all onto you."

"What sort of experiences?"

"Inexplicable stuff," he recalled, "weird coincidences, that sort of thing." This first attempt did not prove sufficient to persuade his wife that the magnitude of these experiences had been enough to explain his recent behaviour. His second attempt though did the trick. "Paranormal stuff."

"Like ghosts?" she asked with a mocking smirk. "You can't really be expecting me to believe that Jake? Can you?"

"I don't know, for sure," gulped Jake as he finished off his nearly cold coffee. "I saw, something, in the car, the other night."

"Oh yes, the face in the car," she laughed. "I thought you said that you'd had a blackout?"

"I know what I said," Jake said, but he was losing track of what he had already told her and what he had kept to himself. "I had two experiences, on the night that I didn't come home. As I think I told you, the police have a photograph of someone alongside me, but I saw it earlier, I saw it in my car and it wasn't just a face and it wasn't a reflection." But the very thought seemed to edge Jake to the point of tears and at that, Lisa's resistance broke.

"It?" she said, still unconvinced that there wasn't something else, but willing to give him the benefit of the doubt. "What do you mean by 'it'?"

"An apparition, a ghoul, something that wasn't there before but then was." He knew that he was doing a terrible job of filling in the blanks, and she was looking at him with a look of incomprehension. "I guess that I wasn't ready to admit it to myself, least of all to you."

"Well, let's just get rid of the car then?" It seemed like the easy way out, but her husband was quick to put her right.

"It's not that simple," Jake replied, making it clear that he'd already thought of it and had rejected that idea. "The car is leased for three years, but in any case, there have been other incidences. Worse things than that..."

"What other things? Things that you haven't told me?" she asked. "Worse than what? Worse than the invisible man in your passenger seat? Jake, you're not making sense."

"Do you think that I did this to myself!" he cried and pulled his sweatshirt up and over his still stiff neck. The purple bruise had not faded much, and the set of fingerprints were still clearly visible on either side of his battered neck.

"Of course not!" Lisa sobbed. "But why haven't you reported it to the police if you're completely innocent? Why haven't you been to hospital to get it checked out? Why did you lie to me, Jake?"

"What am I supposed to tell the police?" Jake heaved, quelling a sob as it crept from his chest. "There was no one there. I didn't see anyone," he recalled with a heavy intake of air. "The police already suspect me of being a murderer, they already think I'm a lunatic with an imaginary friend and are just biding their time before they arrest me again. They are not going to believe me if I tell them this as well!"

Lisa knew that he was right, but she was flummoxed by his story. "Tell me everything, Jake!" she ordered. "I want to know everything. Don't leave anything out to save my blushes. I want to know it all, last chance!"

"I was at the library, the Guildhall Library, at Moorgate…" Despite the warning, he could still not bring himself to tell her the whole story for fear of an assault charge, which was most likely to result in a criminal record and the loss of his job and prospects. Even though he might have argued a case for *diminished responsibility*, it was hardly in self-defence; he had punched a security guard square in the face when he was just trying to do his job!

That's how they would see it, he was absolutely sure of that.

"What were you doing there?"

"It's a long story, that's not important," he stammered, "but it's like someone's after me and I can't get away. I just can't."

"You should still go to the police about it."

"And tell them what?"

"That you've been attacked!" Lisa yelled. "For God's sake, Jake, they've only got to take one look at your neck to know that you're not making it up!"

Jake didn't answer, but just looked up at her like a guilty puppy, in acceptance of the reprimand. He knew that whatever answer he gave would not satisfy his wife, because nothing that he could think of was cutting it for him either.

"Well, I am taking you to see *my* doctor!" his wife commanded in utter disbelief that he had not already seen someone. "As soon as they are open, I'm making you an appointment. You really should have seen a doctor straight away!"

"That's what Jackie said," said Jake, ready to embark on the next chapter in the story.

"And pray tell, who is Jackie?" she asked sarcastically.

He knew as soon as he mentioned her name that he was in for a long explanation and so he began. "A long-lost relative, from the East End of

London!" Lisa's look said it all and so, Jake spent the next half an hour explaining the circumstances surrounding their meeting in the church of Saint Magnus, the things that they had talked about in the pub on Saturday night and all that he could recall that would help share his burden with his wife.

"That's who your mysterious dinner date was then!" smiled Lisa, trying hard not to let her natural suspicions rise to the surface. "I knew you hadn't been out on your own!"

"She's married," Jake added, knowing that it was only a half-truth but holding onto the fact that it was not an outright lie, at least not yet, but it didn't fully satisfy Lisa.

"Never stopped you before!" she countered, echoing the words of DI Pearson just a few days before, but she could see that Jake was on the verge of snapping and so she decided to defuse the situation before it got out of hand again. "So where is she now then? I'd like to meet her, this distant relative of yours!"

"She's holed up in some cheap hotel somewhere," he answered truthfully, which led him to reveal all. "She's left her husband, a bit of a pig apparently." But Lisa had reached the point of information overload and her morning sickness was about to bring their longest conversation in months to an abrupt conclusion. "She's the spit of my great grandmother," he added, "you know, the one in the picture in mum's hallway. It's uncanny!"

"I—" Lisa started to say something, but was stopped in her tracks, as she ran out into the hallway, reaching the small downstairs lavatory just in time.

The sound of her retching almost made Jake heave himself, and although he knew he wouldn't be able to make much difference, he scooted into the kitchen and poured her a fresh glass of iced water, with a splash of lemon juice. It was the only remedy that she had found to have worked, but there was plenty more in the pipeline before she would be able to keep it down and so Jake waited on standby for another ten minutes, until the moment had passed.

It was another fifteen minutes until she was sufficiently recovered to continue with their conversation, but by then, the day was moving on and a new working week beckoned. "It's just too far-fetched, Jake, isn't it? It just sounds so, so unbelievable, I'm surprised that you've been taken in. This woman, this Jackie, she sounds like a right fruitcake to me and by the sound of her family, we should keep well away from her. I mean, a drunk for a husband and a down-and-out for a son and all this stuff about her father and the Plague of all things; I think she needs help. And not yours either. Professional help."

"So how do you explain the dreams then?"

"I don't know. Maybe it's the power of suggestion," Lisa offered. "Maybe you both saw the same films on TV and it was playing on your minds."

"And what about the coins, the tokens, I mean?" asked Jake. "That's too much of a coincidence surely? Isn't that the proof that something unusual is going on here? I can't explain it; I've racked my brains to think of a logical cause; can you?"

She couldn't, but it was all too much for a Monday morning and they both needed to get on with their day. Lisa shook her head and patted him on the knee as if that was all she had left. "Let me think it over some more," she said, now having serious doubts about her husband's sanity. "It's all so strange we just need some time to think it through, logically."

"Maybe you could put it in a spreadsheet?" he quipped and at that, they both managed to laugh. She did love a good spreadsheet, of that there was no doubt and in truth, part of her thought it might be a good idea. Lay out the data. Look for the relationships. Maybe even see if she could work out a few formulae, though even she knew that that wasn't going to provide the answer to this particular brainteaser.

Her very next question mirrored his thoughts and he shivered at the prospect.

"So have the police been back in touch, about the murder?"

"No," said Jake as calmly as he could. "No, I hope that we've seen the last of them, but I don't think so somehow."

"Have they got anyone yet?" she asked hopefully. "It's been over a fortnight now; they must have some idea who did it surely?"

"I don't know," he answered to the best of his knowledge. "I don't think so; I've got the feeling that I'm still the chief suspect." But it was not a subject that he wanted to dwell on any longer. Unfortunately for him, Lisa had other lines of enquiry that she wished to pursue.

"And we still haven't found out who the lovely Mary is, have we?"

He knew that he was never going to be allowed to forget that momentary lapse in concentration.

"Who?" said Jake, pretending not to remember.

It wasn't a name that was familiar to either of them. but his wife knew that he knew to what she was referring, and she was not yet ready to let him off the hook.

"Lisa, for God's sake, it was a slip of the tongue," he pleaded. "I don't know anyone called Mary and the only person that I've ever known with that name was a girl at primary school whose mother didn't like me because I pulled her daughter's pigtails in assembly. Can't you let that one go now, please?"

"Okay," Lisa agreed meekly, reserving the right to change her mind at a later date. "I'll let you off, but if I..." but she didn't need to finish the sentence.

"I haven't, I don't, I wouldn't," said Jake, anticipating her line of thought and the threat that went with it and at that, Lisa nodded in acceptance.

"So, what happens now?" she asked.

To that, he had no immediate answer.

**

The day passed without further incident and the evening had almost drawn to a close without further conversation on the paranormal. Lisa was feeling tired, the pregnancy starting to take its toll on her energy levels, so she was relaxing in a warm bubble bath, her new favourite band blasting out an accompaniment. Jake was finishing off a few emails, having cleared several invoices for new orders placed that day, which he had managed to secure against all odds. For the first time in a while, he had a feeling that things were starting to get back onto an even keel, but his good mood was not going to last.

As he heard the cistern groan as Lisa topped up her bath with another splurge of hot water, the telephone chirped into life and as Jake lifted the receiver to his ear, he had quite forgotten his growing phobia of telephones.

"Harvey," it said. "Jake Harvey." It was a voice that he had heard before.

It was not a question that he felt much like answering.

"Yes," he admitted against his better judgement. "Speaking."

"How are you, Jake?" the caller asked without a trace of care for his wellbeing.

"Fine," was all that Jake could think of in response. "Who's this?"

"All in good time, Jake," it said. "All in good time. You need some help, Jake," the voice declared, "you need my help."

"Why?" Jake argued, "I don't even know who you are? Who are you?"

"How's your neck, Jake?"

"What?"

"Your neck! How is it?"

238

"How do you know?" Jake croaked. "How do you know about my neck?"

"I know a lot about you, Jake," the voice announced. "Even more than you know yourself, in fact. How have you been sleeping lately?"

"Better," Jake lied. "Better now, thanks," but Jake wasn't grateful for the question. "I want to know who you are, or I'm putting the phone down!"

"Don't do that, Jake," the voice warned, each crisp firm syllable constituting an order that was not to be ignored. "You'll regret it, believe me. I can help you, you see, but you must listen to me. Listen to me, Jake!"

"How?" Jake demanded. "How can you help me?"

"Do you want the dreams to stop, Jake?"

Silence. Of course, yes. What a stupid question.

"Do you want to stop dreaming about him, Jake?"

"What dreams?" he bluffed. "I haven't..." he started to say, but what little composure he had left slipped from his grasp. "I've not had any dreams!"

The laugh started with the faintest seepage of breath into the distant mouthpiece, but the transformation into a roaring guffaw was rapid. It was as if Jake had just delivered an absolute belter of a punchline at the end of a well-rehearsed joke, but Jake wasn't smiling.

He was quaking and it was a minute or more before the caller was able to ask the question again and this time, Jake did not deny it its victory.

"Do you want them to stop?"

"Yes!" Jake shouted. "Yes, yes, yes, you bastard! Okay? Do you hear me?"

"Those eyes, Jake, that face!" he teased. "That skinless smile. When did you last sleep through 'til morning, Jake? When did you last get through the night without a visitation?"

"Weeks," Jake admitted. "Three, four weeks, a month maybe."

"I can make it stop, Jake," it promised. "You can make it stop."

"How?"

"Just do as you are told, my boy," the voice explained. "Just do as you are told."

"What do you mean?" Jake sobbed. "I don't know what you mean."

"Of course, why would you, I haven't told you yet," he mocked. "But listen and you will learn. Listen. Listen very carefully to what I have to say."

"I'm listening. What exactly do I have to do?"

"Radclyffe only wants one of you," he informed him, "for now."

"What, me or Lisa?" Jake said, horrified.

"No, you idiot! Don't play the fool with me, Jake, you will come to regret it," the voice snarled. "You or Jackie Stubbs. He only wants one of you."

It was news that was always going to appeal to someone of Jake Harvey's self-centred disposition. What's more, whoever was at the other end of the line seemed to know Jake well enough to realise that such a tempting prospect would be too much for him to turn down.

"Who's it going to be, Jake? You? Or her?"

Jake did not reply, at least not directly, but he was sure that whoever was talking had not yet finished with him.

"What?" he pleaded, banging his fist on the wall as he did so and fearing that the assignment was not going to be to his liking. "What do you want me to do?"

"It's simple, Jake," he said. "I want you to deliver her, to me."

"What do you mean?"

"I mean, my friend, that I need her to be in a certain place at a certain time on a certain day," he explained, "but, for reasons that I won't bore you with, I am unable to do the job myself!"

"And if I don't?"

"Then you will dream, and you shall scream, and you will die," it said, as a familiar rustling hush descended to amplify the threat that hung between them. In the end, it was Jake who relented.

"What do I have to do?" he asked for the third time in quick succession.

It didn't take long for the instructions to be imparted and when he was finished, Jake knew exactly how to bring his difficulties to an end. He wanted to say no, he wanted to tell his caller where to go with his ultimatum, he even thought that maybe there was some way that he could trick his way out of it, but deep down inside, he knew that he would have to go through with it.

To save his own skin.

"And remember," the voice went on. "Your little local difficulty with the police. Should you fail to show up or should you fail in your task, then I'm sure that I could arrange for something incriminating to turn up, where you'd least expect it. Do you understand me?"

"Stop threatening me!" Jake snapped. "I get the message. Enough! You've got me hook, line and sinker, now just fuck off!"

"What an appropriate analogy and of course, I will stop, but by the way," the voice laughed. "I am always true to my word, Jake. Always."

Jake wanted to ask the caller how he knew such things, he wanted to scream abuse at his abuser before slamming down the phone, but he also knew that any such response would be futile.

"Yes," he replied reluctantly, "yes, I understand."

"Be there, by dawn, on the winter solstice."

There was an audible click and then nothing. Jake could have dialled call-back again to trace the origin of the call, he could have reported it as a nuisance call and had the caller tracked by the telephone company, he could even have reported it to the police. He had been offered a way out of this nightmare, a way to be free of the dread and despair that he had been subjected to for weeks and that were driving him to the brink of a divorce.

There was no alternative, however cruel it seemed.

It was a dog-eat-dog world, and Jake Harvey was a rottweiler.

His life was in danger, his wife's life was in danger and the life of his unborn child was too. He knew full well that what he had been asked to do was unspeakable, the order was evil, it was beyond anything that he had ever done before.

But in that moment, he made his mind up to do it and to bring this horrible chapter of his life to an end, for his sake and his alone.

Chapter Twenty-Three
The Plying Place

She in plaine termes unto the world doth tell, Whores are the Hackneys which men ride to Hell, and by comparisons she truely makes, a whore worse than a common Shore or Jakes. A succubus, a damned sinke of sinne, a mire, where worse than swine doe wallow in.

Jackie rose early and after a hearty breakfast in the restaurant, she had settled down in the hotel's small but perfectly formed business suite to continue working on her father's legacy.

It had taken her a while to master the online services and entering the phrase 'family history' into the search engine had brought up a plethora of helpful and not so helpful sites, including ones from prominent museums and libraries which she had quickly scanned and rejected. She'd been happy to sign up for a 14-day free trial on the most popular site, after reaching the conclusion that so many million users couldn't all be wrong, and so had begun her mission to track down the long-dead man who had apparently driven her son to his death. The thought still seemed incredulous to her, but it was a well-trodden path and her father's research provided her with a great platform from which to get started.

She had plugged in all of the names from his meticulously laid out family tree and was amazed at how quickly it built up before her. Jake's friends had been right, the site was really easy to use, so easy that even a technically naïve starter like Jackie Stubbs was able to get to grips with it in just a couple of hours. She wasn't ashamed to admit, even to herself, that by the time the tree was laid out before her, she was left feeling quite smug at what she had achieved in such a short space of time.

It was hard not to get side-tracked by all the hints that popped up within a couple of minutes of entering an ancestor's name, as the site's algorithms did their thing. Little flags to indicate that the database had found a matching record and before long, there were literally hundreds of them in her backlog. She had made the mistake a couple of times of diving into the details and ended up spending far too long on a some very minor branches. She soon realised her rookie mistake, and so decided to let them build; once all this was over, she would have herself a nice hobby that would keep her busy for years to come.

She became so engrossed in the task that time flew by and all alone in the neat office with no one to drag her away to make lunch or tea, or to fetch and carry for them, the whole experience was a delight.

The census records backed up the male bloodline, their marriages and some of the children that her father had already identified, but often the households were much larger than his records had suggested with very many children being born to each couple throughout the nineteenth century. Every time she reached back another ten years, she was shocked to see just how many had died, often in infancy and many more before they had come of age. The sense of continuity was very satisfying as she traced the names and ages from each of the registers as children were born, came of age and moved away. From 1911 through every decade back to 1841, she travelled back in time, with each one revealing a little more about the lives of her forefathers, their wives and children.

She was surprised to see how so many of them had stayed within the borders of the great city of London and heard her mother's voice remind her that *the acorn never falls far from the tree*, a favourite saying of hers. They worked in factories and warehouses, as stevedores on the docks, as shoemakers in the east end streets, as shipbuilders and as boatmen.

Boatmen.

The river was in her blood.

At least three times, she had come across names of men and boys whose calling had been a life on the Thames. All kinds of goods were ferried up and down the river, out into the channel and along the vast coastline of Britain. From coal and steel in the Northeast, to grain in East Anglia, cotton goods from Manchester, tin from Cornwall, her family had played their part in moving it along England's waterways, most notably up and down The Thames.

As she built up the picture of life in the growing conurbation that was to become the great metropolis that she had known growing up, it began to dawn on her that her chances of getting all the way back to the 1660s was far from guaranteed. Having skated back through time to the mid-nineteenth century and the relatively scant contents of the 1841 census, she realised to her horror that the censuses went no further; they had only been introduced for the first time in that year and prior to that date, there was very little way of knowing who lived where across the bustling streets of Bermondsey, Clerkenwell, St Paul's and Southwark. To add to her panic, she read in the research section that the official records of birth, marriages and deaths—the fabled BMDs—had only been started in 1837 largely as a way of supporting the new poor law, which had been devised just three years earlier.

For any earlier records, she had to rely upon the local parish records that were kept by each church, which varied widely in quality and availability. As she delved deeper into her history and the turn of the eighteenth century, the going began to get tougher, the records less regimented and the automated hints fewer, with many duplicated or mis-transcribed names. Digitalisation had made the process so much faster, but it wasn't without its pitfalls and the modern-day scribes often misinterpreted the names as they appeared in the historical record, leading to data inaccuracies and to several dead ends.

This was not going to be quite as easy as it had first seemed.

Through the 1700s, the names that her father had provided continued to come up trumps though, recognised by the database as *right name right place*, and giving her a great sense of satisfaction in the sheer bloody doggedness of her dad. She realised that it must have taken him years to compile in an age before computers. It also went some way towards explaining his regular trips to London at weekends, when she had thought that he was heading to a football match or to the museums, and she felt a pang of guilt that she had known nothing of his obsession until now.

In his notes, he had marked down numbers and references which she could see related to the original micro-fiche copies of the source documents, which she increasingly realised were going to be invaluable to her. That she would be treading in her own father's footsteps added a spring to her step at the thought that he had paved the way for her to complete his life's work.

If only she could talk to him just once more.

There was so much more that she now needed to ask.

The magnitude of the task grew with each passing generation and as she added her descendants and their families into her rapidly expanding list of names, she was utterly amazed at the speed with which the numbers piled up. The milestone of one hundred names was reached within an hour, five hundred within the day and by the end of her third day of sleuthing she was closing in on a tree that would be measured in more than one thousand souls. Parents and grand-parents, uncles and aunts and their brothers and sisters; countless numbers of cousins and second cousins spanning several generations that she never knew she had, but all of them, long since dead.

Having the backbone of the tree available had given her a massive head start and she had no doubt that without it her quest would have been impossible, but she knew that tracing each line of descendants emanating from just one man in the middle of the seventeenth century, would be like trying to find a needle in a haystack. If he had sired even a conservative number of offspring and they in turn had done the same across three or four generations per century, then the simple maths meant that the odds were stacked against her.

Five surviving children, each having five more who reached adulthood who then did the same meant that in each century, a minimum of 125 direct descendants would be added to the tree for every male heir and over four centuries, the numbers ran into many thousands. Add to that the opportunities for emigration – enforced or otherwise – and the possibilities that the new world had offered from the middle of the seventeenth century, with many people heading to the Americas and Australia, then in all likelihood she would have distant cousins across the globe.

But only if the children had survived to adulthood.

Her father's research had only focussed on one line, the line that stretched from him into the distant past. He had ignored or had not had the time or ability to look horizontally across the tree at the fate of the many hundreds of brothers and sisters in each of his forefather's generations, but the software threw up all those possibilities. It had begun to dawn on Jackie how easily this new-found hobby could become an obsession.

"Thanks Dad," she found herself saying out loud to no one in particular, a coy smile on her face. "You always did love a puzzle!"

**

The week passed by at a rate of knots, her days taken up by the mounds of reading and in hours upon hours spent in front of the hotel computer.

Despite another restless night, she sprang out of bed, reinvigorated at the prospect of meeting up with Dee that morning and the possibilities for further research that would follow. She showered, dressed and breakfasted in record time, reaching their rendezvous point a good fifteen minutes earlier than they had agreed, just in case the trains had proved favourable, and her best friend was already waiting for her.

She wasn't, and so Jackie had picked up a copy of the free morning newspaper from the vendor outside the coffee shop and treated herself to a strong latte, resisting the urge for a pastry so soon after consuming a plate of scrambled eggs in the hotel restaurant. She didn't have to wait long and the stalks on which her eyes were mounted caught a glimpse of her friend, as she dodged her way inside, and it wasn't long before the two made eye contact for the first time in many years.

She hadn't changed a bit.

Jackie began waving furiously and Dee, with unbridled joy at seeing her troubled friend for the first time in years, made a beeline right for her. As they hugged and screamed, one or two commuters tutted and griped their way around them, weaving their way towards the bustling counter intent on getting their first fix of the day. As for Jackie and Dee, they had no such worries—their only concern in that moment was for each other and the sheer amount of catching up they had to do.

"It's so great to see you!" squealed Jackie.

"I know," yelped Dee, "It's been so long I hardly know where to start!"

"Well, let me get you a coffee!" said Jackie. "Grab a seat, I'll be back in a sec." Jackie made her way to the counter for a second time in quick succession and returned a few moments later with a flat white and another latte for herself, plus a couple of Danish pastries for good measure.

"I didn't know if you'd eaten so I grabbed us one each!" she announced, wafting the divine scent in the air as if to emphasise the point.

Dee told her all about their recent holiday and the lovely weather they'd had, as well as all the wonderful sights that they had seen, but it wasn't long before the niceties were done with, and the conversation came full circle.

"How is the family?" asked Jackie, knowing that it would prove to be a leading question and when her turn came around a minute or two later, she decided to dive right into the deep end.

"Not so good actually," said Jackie. "Terry died just recently!"

Dee was horrified. "Oh my God!" she exclaimed. "Oh Jackie, I'm so sorry. I didn't know!"

Jackie had promised herself she wouldn't cry, but she couldn't help it and in the face of her friend's deep and genuine concern, she wept uncontrollably.

"It's been so hard!" she said, Dee's arm around her shoulder. "He was so young, but I blame myself, I should have been stronger!"

"No Jackie!" said Dee, her soothing voice providing a small blessing. "You mustn't blame yourself; it wasn't your fault!" But Dee did not know the whole story and so Jackie told her all about it, from the day Terry walked out to the day she was called to the hospital to watch him die. After that, it was hard to say anything for a few minutes and the two of them just sat holding hands, comfortable in the silence that only two old friends can enjoy. When Jackie was ready to continue, she brought her friend right up to date.

"And so here I am, spending my family inheritance on hotel bills and coffee shops!"

"And what about the stuff you mentioned on the phone, your family history thing?" asked Dee, keen to move the subject on to something less upsetting, or so she hoped.

"Well, where do I start with that?"

"At the beginning?" answered Dee. "We can sit here all day if we need to, that's what friends are for, aren't they? By the way," she added almost as an afterthought. "I want you to come to us for Christmas, I'm not having you being all alone at this time of year!"

Jackie tried to say no, that she was fine, that she was happy to be on her own after years of catering for a demanding family, but it was obvious that she didn't mean it and so she gave in without too much of a fight.

"I hadn't given much thought to Christmas, to be honest," she said, in fact it hadn't even crossed her mind. "Well, only if you're sure?"

"Of course we are!" said Dee. "So that's a deal, I'm taking you home with me tonight. I warned Bill that I'd most likely be bringing you back, so he's going to sort out a fish supper and we can sink a few bottles of red, just like the good old days!"

"Thanks Dee, that's so good of you," said Jackie, "but I do need to finish up a few things first and I have to meet up with Jake tonight, and so I won't be able to come with you straight away, sorry. But I will be on the first train out tomorrow."

"Who is Jake?" asked Dee, intrigued, wondering if there was already a new man on the scene.

"Do you want the long version or the short version?" Jackie teased, but her friend just shrugged her shoulders – she didn't have a preference either way. "Well, let's start with the short version and then you can tell me if you want to hear the long one!" smiled Jackie, trying to make light of the situation.

Dee nodded, they both took a mouthful of coffee and Jackie tried her best to find a way to explain herself in a few minutes rather than a few hours.

"He's a distant cousin of mine," she started. "Not sure exactly how he fits into the tree yet, but he's part of the branch that settled in the West Midlands before the war!"

"Oh no, not a Brummie!" laughed Dee and Jackie joined in. "Could you understand him?"

"Yes," laughed Jackie. "I could tell he came from somewhere up there, but I didn't need a translator or anything!"

"How did you meet?"

"Well, that's part of the mystery, to be honest," confessed Jackie. "It was a bit of a coincidence. He's been doing some research of his own and he ended up in the same church as me, down by the river near London Bridge."

"Whatever were you doing in a church?"

"Well, you know me, Dee!" said Jackie. "I've always had leanings that way. No, seriously, I found myself in the area after checking out Terry's old stomping ground and I just felt like I needed something spiritual. I saw it was part of the old roadway approach to the bridge and I kind of, fell inside, I suppose."

"So, what's all this about, Jackie? What's so important about the old bridge?" Dee pressed. "I assume that you're talking about the really old bridge, the one with the houses on it?"

"Yes, that's the one. They have an amazing model of it in the foyer of that church. Jake was transfixed by it and that's kind of how we ended up talking, and this is where it gets spooky."

At that, Dee moved forward on her seat. "Oh?" she said. "Well, you know me, I do love a good old-fashioned ghost story."

"Well, I don't know about 'old-fashioned'," Jackie answered with a shiver, "but it's certainly got all the hallmarks of a ghost story!"

Up until that point, Dee wasn't convinced that it would be anything more than a tragic tale of a broken marriage and an untimely death, but she could see that this new twist was not the script for a new work of fiction. As Jackie explained all about the tokens and the dreams as well as recounting Jake's experiences in his new car and at the library, Dee's expression became grave, and concern was soon written all over her middle-aged features.

"I did say that some crazy things had been happening!" said Jackie, recognising the look of amazement and not a little fear on her friend's face.

"And you're meeting him again tonight?" asked Dee. "Are you sure that's a good idea, Jackie? It sounds like he's in this thing right up to his neck and you hardly know him. You need to be careful, there are some right nutters about and how do you know for sure that he's not one of them?"

She didn't, Jackie admitted as much, but she had no intention of standing Jake up. "I need to see him again," she said, for the first time recognising the growing bond between them. "And I'm as much up to my neck in this as he is, although you should have seen the state of his neck after he was attacked!"

"Well, if you're sure," warned Dee, "but I want you to text me to tell me where you're going and what you're up to, and I want you to call me when you get back to your hotel tonight. Don't forget, or better still I'm going to call you at eleven and if I haven't heard from you by twelve, I'm calling the police!"

Jackie was flattered by her friend's concern and accepted the offer without objection.

"And make sure you've got your phone on and that it's charged at all times," Dee added insistently. "That way, I can call you wherever you end up."

Jackie assured her that she would and as she did, she glanced down at her watch. "Oh gosh, it's nearly midday! I've got so much to do at the library before tonight, I'm going to have to go, Dee, I'm sorry," but her friend was not about to be fobbed off so easily.

"Why don't I come with you?" she asked. "I've nothing better to do with my time and I've never been to the Guildhall. It sounds interesting. Isn't that where they've got a Roman amphitheatre in the basement?"

"Yes," said Jackie, "though that's at the Guildhall proper, which isn't far away. I'm going to the library, but if you get bored, you can always take a wander over there and we can meet back up afterwards!"

"I might just do that!" said Dee. "And I might just hang around long enough to meet this Jake fella, just to check him over. I'd like him to know that I know all about him."

"Okay!" Jackie submitted gratefully. "If it'll make you feel better, that sounds like a plan. We better be off; it's not far, and we can grab a sandwich on the way."

"It's those token things that I can't fathom," said Dee. "How both of you could have had them, an exact replica no less! Unless?"

They paused as they stood up to go. "Unless what?"

"Unless" Dee started to say, pausing again to think it through some more. "Unless they're his calling card?"

Chapter Twenty-Four
Walbrook

For I, whose credit n'er before was tainted, nor ever was with cheating tricks aquainted, to be by thee thus basely used and crost, and in the world my reputation lost, and all by thee that merit'st naught but banging, for sure I thinke, thou'lt n'er be worth the hanging.

It wasn't a long walk and so neither of them had time to bemoan the turn in the weather. Just a dog's leg off London Wall down between some nondescript office blocks and there it was, an unassuming building on the left-hand side of the street. It didn't look like the place where anyone would find the answers to their life's troubles, but that's what Jackie was hoping for as she and Dee made their way through security and entered their names in the registration book, each receiving a visitor's pass and reading permit in return.

They headed straight for the Manuscript section and following her father's notes to the letter, she retrieved the index card for volume 11361 from the clearly labelled drawers. Jackie had already decided that she would start with the faint and faded manuscripts that formed the seventeenth-century parish records of St Magnus the Martyr and St Margaret's Fish Street. She could see the afternoon stretching out ahead of them and found herself feeling grateful to have someone alongside her who could help her with a task that now loomed large. She hadn't been able to find the names online that she had wanted, prior to the onset of the 1700s, but the church records indicated that the family had lived in this vicinity, and so these churches remained the most likely resting place.

Fortunately for them both, the antiquated microfiche records had long since been digitised, so there was no longer a need to tackle the plates and rollers of the microfiche screens as her father had had to do many years before. Some of the machines were still in situ though and one look at them made her mouth an involuntary word of thanks to the heavens.

"What the hell are those?" a bemused Dee asked.

"The old microfiche readers!" explained Jackie. "The ones that my dad would have used when he did his research here in the seventies and eighties. Hopefully, we won't have to touch them!"

"Thank goodness for that," Dee replied. "They look like they need an instruction manual!"

"They probably come with one," Jackie chuckled. "I think we've got our work cut out without having to tackle those things!"

As they sat down either side of a large monitor, the screen chirped into life and Jackie entered her recently acquired reader number and password. She navigated her way to the BMD catalogue and quickly pulled up the records for the churches that she was most interested in. There was no search capability though and so unable to search by name, she settled down to browse year by year through the surviving records of both churches. She had been concerned to hear that not all years had survived and that a combination of flood and fire had laid claim to some of the original leather-bound volumes, but most were still available for the period in question and so, they crossed everything and pressed on.

"Here goes nothing!" she said, as if announcing the futility of her hunt to the world.

"Let's hope it's not one of the missing ones!" Dee quipped, not really understanding how it was going to work, but happy enough to ride shotgun.

Jackie started with the earliest surviving records, covering the years from 1557 to 1720 and containing a year-by-year account of marriages, 'baptisms' and 'burials', simply eyeballing the lists for the surnames they wanted to find. In places, the script was almost indecipherable, though not through any deterioration in the paper or ink, but simply due to the elaborate nature of the scribe's handwriting.

Some years were worse than others as the style changed whenever the clerk who was responsible for maintaining the record passed away or moved on, but as Jackie edged forwards through time, she couldn't help but be humbled by the painstaking accounts that were preserved before her eyes.

"Isn't the writing amazing!" exclaimed Dee, and indeed it was. Perfectly formed letters swirled and danced across the pages, the signature of a lost cleric from another age.

"What's the name that we are looking for?" Dee asked, in need of a reminder.

"Cooper," said Jackie, "and maybe Radclyffe as well though they both might have funny spellings, so we need to check the list carefully. Four eyes are better than two though!"

Dee was the first to spot one in amongst the ancient roll call and it was the name of Radclyffe inscribed that jumped out at her under the heading 'Baptismes Anno Domini 1645'.

"There!" shouted Dee gleefully, delighted to be able to contribute. She pointed at the point in the list where she had noticed the name and as Jackie looked closer, she was shocked to find that they may well have rolled a double six with their first throw of the dice.

"That can't be him, can it?" asked Jackie, amazed. "Right name, right sort of date, not sure about his wife but the father's name is the man I'm looking for alright. Thomas Radclyffe!" As she read the name out loud, she imagined that she heard someone in the depths of the library answer her with a "here!" as if she were a teacher completing her daily register.

It was hard to tell for sure. Halfway down the page, 'Radclyffe, Robert, son to Thomas Radclyffe and Mary, his wife, born May 21st'. Then another in 1647, a boy called Joshua on June 13th. As she continued her journey through the decades, she was aghast at the sheer number of children that Mary had borne, all nine of whom had been baptised in the old church in which she had stood just a few days earlier.

She knew from the online research that it was highly likely that some would not have lived for long, but from the list before her, it was impossible to tell, so she hoped for an exception to the rule and refused to dwell on the thought of such a cruel existence. Had she done so, then her emotional lock wheel, which she had worked so hard to hold tightly shut, would have cranked around once more and the gates that held her tears at bay would have been forced apart by the flood.

"So many kids!" said Dee, echoing Jackie's thoughts exactly. "Ouch!"

And so, they had moved on through the years, watching as the names passed before their eyes, until the annals of new-born babies came to an end. She decided to pass on the marriage registers that came next, believing that she had all she needed from her father's research and half a dozen pages further on the records returned once more to the year of our Lord 1557, and the register of burials.

As she began once again to peer at the contents that were unravelling before them, she felt like she was about to discover some long-submerged treasure from a maritime wreck. It was a strange feeling, but she had no doubt that she was on the right track and that in the hours that followed, all would be revealed about the life and times of two long-dead men, at least one of whom was refusing to rest in peace. Yet, as she sifted her way through the pages of history, she became increasingly alive to one solitary truth that still holds for all of mankind.

That a human life, which is so short and yet so full, should come down to this: just two or three preserved entries in a closely guarded volume of vellum parchment, the original of which no longer sees the light of day. Indeed, were it not for the studious attention of the clergy, in all probability there would be nothing now left to vouch for the lives of each living soul whose simple identities were now known to her. Just their names, worthy of their place in the annals of the church in which they worshipped all those years before.

All that was left of them was their good name.

But that at least was something.

"So many names!" Dee marvelled.

"And from just two churches!" added Jackie. "To think there were literally hundreds of churches all around here, let's hope that our man didn't move around too much!"

As their conversation quietened, all other sounds became drowned out in the crisp caress of old paper from the reading tables to their left. And each neighbouring turn of an old leaf seemed to substitute its essence to the screen before them, like an echo from earlier times.

"Oh, I just had a shiver down my spine!" Dee shrilled. "Someone must have walked over my grave!" It was a common statement, but the timing of it put their nerves even more on edge.

It took Jackie just a few minutes to decipher each set of scripts and to read aloud each timeworn name for her friend's and her own benefit, but she found herself cursing her luck at the absence of the one name amongst the list of the dead that she craved. The years passed them by at pace from the 1650s and into the 1660s until a name caught her eye and made her gasp in disbelief, but it was not a Radclyffe or a Cooper that stopped her in her tracks, it was her own.

"Oh, how horrible!" said Jackie, alarmed, "I don't believe it, look!"

She pointed to a line on the screen so that Dee could share in her horror. "Doesn't that say Jackie Stubbs?"

Dee was white. "It does!" she gasped. "Well, what a horrible coincidence."

Both of them were silent for a moment as Jackie tried hard to make her peace with the idea that someone with her name had died all those years before. The thought wouldn't settle though, and she found that she had to put it to the back of her mind and move on, as the possibilities and impossibilities were starting to smother her.

The name of Thomas Radclyffe was nowhere to be seen.

To her credit, she ploughed on undeterred, through the next annual and then into the plague year of 1665, where to her undisguised despair the name of Radclyffe was prominent, and it was on the rise. In 1663, there had been just four deaths recorded in total in the parish ledger, but still, not one of them related to the execution of Thomas Radclyffe. By 1664, the number had swelled to thirty burials and in the next, there were eighty entries in all.

The very same black emboldened names and as the age of each person was painstakingly recorded, it was clear that many of them had been but children. Names that she had seen recorded amongst the baptisms of earlier pages, who had once been welcomed into God's Kingdom within the walls of the church and whose memory was now but a crammed entry on the congested surface of an old journal.

She noted each name and date with a growing sense of despair.

The first mention of the name that she sought was not long in coming, but there was something odd about the entry, which made it stand out from the adjoining lines. As Jackie revisited the text, she realised that there was no mention of the father, none at all, as if all trace of his existence had been swept away. It simply read: 'James Radclyffe, son of Mary Radclyffe, buried Aprill 9'. It was to be by no means the last of its kind.

After she had counted out a sixth name from the left-hand column in the year 1665, she continued to trawl her way through each page in fear of the unpleasant truth that she suspected to be lurking there, a little further along the road.

"Did they all die?" Dee whispered, as if in witness to some grave historical tragedy. "I've counted six so far, I've been ticking them off my list of names from earlier."

Yet two names remained outstanding and as they compared their own scribbled notes, it seemed that the last-born sons, William in 1661 and then Jaromiah, who had been born early in 1663, had both outlived the great pestilence. Both had been born and baptised in the two years before their father's death and both were thankfully unaccounted for amongst the death registers of

255

the two churches. Jackie found herself praying that the children had survived, but in truth she knew that the state of the records for the remainder of that most tragic of years meant that she might never know for sure.

For much of the remaining months of 1666, from the time of the Great Fire onwards, those who had not perished would have been forgiven for letting their attention to detail slip a little, at least as far as the parish records were concerned.

The sheer number of inscriptions read like some Nazi camp from the twentieth century. As she reached the end of the third page for the year 1666, she reversed back three years and began again, just in case any of the names that she was seeking had eluded them the first time around. It turned out that between them, they'd been pretty accurate, but they had both become so focussed on their search for one name and one name alone that they had missed the name of Cooper amongst the list of burials, and its presence now took Jackie a little by surprise.

"Oh look, there's a Cooper!" she exclaimed. "A child called Elisabeth, registered as the daughter of Jacob and Mary Cooper, had been buried in the last month of summer in the plague year of 1665."

"Mary!" observed Dee. "Same name as Thomas's wife?"

The fact that both Cooper and Radclyffe had each taken a wife with the same Christian name did not strike Jackie as being particularly odd, given the religious origins of the name and the pious nature of people at that time. It did though offer another avenue for exploration and one that was destined to bear fruit. Before reversing the direction of her search still further, to look for evidence of her ancestral family amongst the baptisms and earlier burials, she sifted carefully through the remaining recorded deaths in search of further tragedies.

She half expected to find that she had overlooked an entry for Radclyffe's wife first time around but was heartened when no such name was forthcoming. However, her sense of relief at Mary Radclyffe's apparent survival was short-lived, as on the very next page, in the early spring of that most fateful of years, 1666, she did come across an entry and she could not help herself from speaking the name aloud.

"Mary Cooper," she shrieked loud enough to alert the attentions of more than one of their neighbours, who each looked up and stared at them, as if she had committed some cardinal sin for which there could be no forgiveness.

"What? She died as well?" asked Dee, with a pang of sadness.

"Looks like it," said Jackie. "Oh, that's so sad!" A sentiment on which they both agreed.

However, unlike most of the others that were listed there amongst that fateful list of burials in the year of Our Lord 1666, she was not shown as the wife of another.

Others that had died were listed there as husband of or son of or daughter of some other.

Mary was listed simply as 'servant to' a named body that Jackie was unable to fathom, such was the archaic state of the script. It didn't make any sense, but as Jackie began to go back again, revisiting the section on baptisms, she came to a hasty conclusion that seemed to fit the circumstances. It was a child that was listed there amongst the terrible catalogue of death, but she had found no corresponding baptism for a Mary Cooper in the church's archives; the only missing child from their list of baptisms other than the two surviving boys had been the identically named Mary Radclyffe.

"I'm confused!" Dee admitted. "So that's Mary who married Thomas who we have a death record for, a Mary Radclyffe born in the same year as Mary Cooper who we have dying in 1664. So, we have a birth record for Mary R, but no death record, and a death record for Mary C, but no birth record!"

"Exactly," agreed Jackie. It hadn't been too difficult to find the date of the infant Mary's baptism into the church. The child was born late in 1650 to Thomas and Mary, as she had been baptised in the October of that year and would have been a teenager when she was placed in service, a not uncommon career path, if you could even call it that, for girls in those days.

Of course, it wasn't possible; if Gallagher's theory was to be believed and Jacob Cooper was indeed her ancestor then there had to have been an heir, but there was no evidence of any children born to Jacob and Mary Cooper, other than the infant and as the century drew towards its close, no evidence that he had ever remarried after Mary's death.

"I guess that he could have left the area and remarried in a different church?" Dee suggested, at which Jackie nodded and scribbled down a few more notes to jog her memory later. "Is there any way to find out?"

"I could always do some more searching on the genealogy website when I get back," Jackie answered. "It's quite possible that he took on a younger wife, but there were no censuses back then so there's no way to search for the household."

"What about seeing if we can find out when he got married?"

It seemed like a great idea and Jackie immediately turned her attention back to the marriage register that she had put aside earlier in the day, but the day was passing them by and her appetite for the venture was starting to fade with the daylight. "Let's see if we can at least find that out and then let's go and grab a bite to eat and a drink. I'm famished; I don't know about you?"

She was about to feel like a fisherman who decides to have one last cast after a disappointing trip to the riverbank and makes the catch of the day, but at first, she was quite unaware of the revelation that was contained before her eyes.

Jacob Cooper and Mary Wilkes had been married early in 1664. A winter wedding, by the banks of the Thames, maybe a procession with friends through the cobbled and narrow streets of a medieval city that would soon be reduced to ashes.

That particular entry seemed to be an apt place to end. They had discovered so much they needed time to digest it, and although a written record of Thomas Radclyffe's fate had proved elusive, the talk of food had made both their stomachs rumble. They each took up a small pile of the reference books they had been given, most of which remained unread, and thanked the gentleman at the desk for his assistance.

"Any luck?" he asked.

"A little," Jackie conceded, reluctant to start an explanation of her quest this late in the day, but when he posed the question directly, her hand was forced.

"What exactly are you looking for?"

"A name," she answered truthfully, but without giving too much away.

"A man called Radclyffe," Dee chirped up. "Thomas Radclyffe. He died in 1663, but we are looking for more detail on his execution."

"Oh really," said the thin and wiry twenty-something as if he were on neighbourly terms with the very man she was seeking.

"Well, if he was executed, you could try another source," and he turned away to scan the library's extensive computer records until he found a reference to a recent paper on crime and punishment in the seventeenth century. "I'll just get it for you, if you like."

He returned a few minutes later, bearing a self-righteous smile that was almost as broad as the unexpectedly large file, which he quickly passed into Dee's expectant hands.

"What was his occupation, out of interest?" the polite young man inquired, but Jackie was already growing impatient with his questioning and was none too keen to answer another.

As it turned out, she was rather glad that she did.

"He was a Waterman," she said hurriedly, keen to get on with things. She was tired and more than a little hungry.

"Oh well, in that case, there is something else that might be of use to you," he announced, but it still took all of her mother's patience to wait for him to finish. "If he was a registered Waterman then an entry for him, and any apprentices, would have been made in the records of 'The Company of Watermen and Lightermen'."

At that, Jackie's interest was rekindled by the promise of the irrefutable proof of her Waterman's existence, but that fledgling flame was extinguished just moments later when the librarian recalled the year in question.

"You were looking at 1663, is that right?" and when Jackie nodded, his countenance veered back to one of genuine regret. "That's a shame!" he said. "The records are excellent from about 1680 onwards, but the earlier ones were mostly lost in the fire, and it took them a few years to recover. There are a few left, but they're far from complete and given the thousands of watermen who worked the Thames in those days…well, it would be like looking for a needle in a haystack, I'm afraid."

"Oh well," sighed Jackie, doing her best to feign disappointment. She just wanted to get finished and get out of there, if truth be told.

"This will have to do us for now then."

"Were the Magnus records of any use?" he asked, seeming to sense her urgency, which he misinterpreted as a natural desire to get down to business.

"Yes," smiled Jackie. "I know that most of his children died in 1665 and 1666, but there's no entry for his wife that I can see and none for him in the 1663 records either."

"Does it say what they died of?" he asked, and Jackie shook her head. Although, had it done so, she doubted at that very moment whether she would have passed on that piece of information, such was her compulsion to get the job in hand done with, as quickly as possible. "Most likely plague," he proclaimed, but he didn't look all that sure of himself. "It is unusual though to see full parish records for plague victims as at the height of the outbreaks, most of the bodies were dumped in lime pits at Finsbury, Blackheath or more likely Spitalfields or burnt in huge pyres. Summer months, was it?"

"Yes, mainly," Jackie answered, becoming unreasonably irritated now.

Jackie had never been a great reader. Even in her schooldays, she had failed to complete most of the classics and contemporary fiction that had been prescribed under the school curriculum and so, the contents of a research article filled her with apprehension. As Dee dumped the manuscript unceremoniously onto the desk and flicked on the reading lamp, her sore eyes objected to the intrusion and her head had begun to pound.

She told herself that this was to be their last undertaking of the day.

It was getting late.

The article was tedious. It was written by a professor of just about everything who seemed to have a complete alphabet of letters trailing after his unpronounceable name, but just as Jackie was about to give up and get out, she struck gold.

She had stumbled across a section on religious persecution and the range of punishments that had been meted out after the civil war and in the early years of the reformation. The crimes committed by these men and by a handful of women ranged from preaching on street corners to incitement to riot, but the severity of the punishment seemed barbaric.

As she read on, she came across the execution of a John James, a lay preacher whose particular calling was not listed, but it seemed that anyone who did not follow the prescribed Christian faith of the nation was liable to be punished. James was hung, drawn and quartered for preaching his own brand of Christ's teaching and so, it seemed, was Radclyffe.

There was only a short paragraph specifically relating to Radclyffe's death and it revealed nothing that she did not already know, but there was a footnote, which Jackie sought out without a thought for the rest of the man's ramblings.

It was like finding the key that unlocks the door to a vaulted room and Jackie was hoping against hope that she would not find it empty.

The reference led her back to another church that had stood at Aldgate, half a mile or so to the East of St Magnus. St Botolph's without Aldgate, to be precise where, according to the passage that she had just read, the dissenter Thomas Radclyffe had lived. Jackie could not understand why, when his children had been christened in the adjacent parish of St Magnus and when most of their deaths had also been registered there two years after his own tragic demise, that he himself should have come under the auspices of another ward.

She guessed that she might never know the answer.

"Let me have a look for that!" Dee offered, sensing her friend's urgency and now more confident in her own abilities. "You get on with the other stuff, I'll look through the burial records for the Aldgate church." Dee returned to the overeager librarian and asked to see the parish records for the year in question. Again, the records were now digitised from old microfiche, but she was to be left short-changed by their contents as his death was not listed.

A record of Radclyffe's fate continued to elude them.

The professor of everything's article had contained the precise date of Radclyffe's execution and so, as Dee was immersed for now in the records of other churches, Jackie turned her attention to what else the library had to offer. In the absence of an author's name or a book title on which to base her search, she selected the keyword option and entered that too familiar name.

A hundred or more entries were returned, and after scanning the first ten, she realised that she would have to be more specific. She added the date and then the one word that she hoped would prove decisive.

Only one article was listed as meeting all of her criteria and from the limited detail provided, it was impossible to tell whether or not its contents would be to her liking. The book was dated 1663 and began with the title, "*A narrative of the apprehending, commitment, arraignment, condemnation and,*"—the keyword— "*execution,*" but there was no clue as to the unfortunate victim of this justice.

The book was listed as 'Closed Access', but her initial fears that her interest in its contents would be denied were soon allayed, when the librarian simply asked her to complete a request slip. As she waited for the item to be retrieved, Jackie could hardly contain the sudden sense of anticipation that had closed its arms around her. She was again consumed by a certainty that all was about to be revealed and for once, her expectations were not misplaced.

As she skipped through the blank visage of the first age-old leaves, she was quite unprepared for the title page that loomed into view. The name that she had sought stood proud before her, bold as brass in an elaborate typeface that clearly hailed from another age.

At that moment, Dee returned from her fruitless search of the St Botolph record and was surprised to see Jackie looking so pleased with herself and a little disappointed that it had not been her that had made the breakthrough.

"What have you got there?" she asked, taking a seat alongside Jackie and reading aloud the title page, her voice reaching a peak as she blurted out his name.

"A narrative of the apprehending, commitment, arraignment, condemnation and execution of THOMAS RADCLYFFE, who suffered at TIBURNE, November the 13th 1663."

Jackie took up the reading, "With several occasional passages and speeches, faithfully collected from such as were eye and ear witnesses."

Dee had read on a little further and recoiled at the quote from Hebrews that doubled as a footer on the title page. "*By it, he being Dead, yet speaketh*—what does that mean?" she said, somewhat concerned at the choice of biblical reference. "From Hebrews chapter eleven, verse four, is that New Testament or Old?"

"New," answered Jackie as she shuddered at the words that were enshrined there, but whilst she did not expect to discover the reasons behind the author's choice of scripture, she could hardly believe what she had now unearthed.

At best, she had expected to uncover some ambiguous reference in a contemporary roll call of executions, but not this. Not a contemporary account of the man's trial and yet here it was, right before their eyes. A pamphlet produced in the months following her supposed tormentor's horrific death that would surely tell her all that she needed to know and more.

"But this isn't your ancestor, is it?" asked Dee, keen to understand.

"No, this is his partner," Jackie confirmed, "the man with whom he once plied his trade on the river. His fellow waterman!"

They bequeathed the first page to memory and read on, entranced.

To the Reader

For satisfaction of publick expectation (after much labour and pains taken) here is at last presented a NARRATIVE of the late Tryal, Sayings and Sufferings of Thomas Radclyffe, which as you will find, gives neither Gloss nor Descant upon the Matter, nor commendation of the person; but simply a plain account of some material passages and circumstances therein, and they collected with as much exactness as was possible, inserting nothing but what there have been sufficient evidence for.

The book was then divided into sections, each relating to a different day of the trial. They pressed on as carefully as their thirst for truth would allow in search of some clear indication of the man's guilt or even of his treasonable crime, but at first, every word that leapt up from the pages before them proved too much to take in.

His *ARRAIGNMENT* and *TRYAL*, *what passed the first day*—and then on the second and more briefly, on the third, followed by—*The Substance of the INDICTMENT*—and then, last of all—*The last SPEECH and PRAYER of THOMAS RADCLYFFE at Tyburn immediately before his execution.*

It was to the latter that she turned first. His speech was brief, but terrifying, and his words reached down through the centuries to claw at the dry flesh of Jackie's throat.

> *I have committed no crime against thee, nor against my God. I have done no wrong. But by all that is earth, by the wind and air, by all the fires in hell, I will be avenged. The Hangman said, the Lord receive your soul. Radclyffe replied, Anon, he will.*
> *The Sheriff and Hangman were so uncivil to him in his Execution they did not suffer the blasphemer to be dead before he was cut down; the Hangman, taking out his Heart whilst yet he lived, and burning his Members and entrails, returned his Head and Quarters back to Newgate, put in a Basket in a cart and from thence were disposed by the King, his Quarters to the Gates of the city and his Head upon the Bridge.*

"That doesn't sound too good!" said Dee in what was the understatement of the century, her hand hovering over her mouth in shock.

"Not good at all."

As if that gruesome account was not enough for any book to bear for all eternity, the author had also inlaid a transcript from the executioner's account of events. It was similar in style to the amateurish ha'penny-pamphlets that were commonplace in the early days of the printing press and which passed for the tabloids of their day. The columnist, in this instance, had not only provided his own sickening inventory of the circumstances leading up to the eventual death, but also described something of the atmosphere that had surrounded it.

As they sank ever deeper into that stinking pit of history, Jackie's heart thumped as if a boxer's jab was pounding at her chest and the roof of her mouth was as dry as old leather. Dee sat alongside, feeling like a witness to murder and starting to wish she had made different plans for the day.

They read on, but not aloud, as if to give it life again would be like some form of incantation.

The fayte of the traytor Thomas Radclyffe

Followinge the hangynge, aboute the ower of XI of the clocke in the forenoone, his bodie was cutte downe and putt upon the grounde. His soul had not departed and the sounde and stench of his tearing fleshe did make the crowde to turne. He sayd a fewe wordes, to sweare vengence on he who betray'd him, whereof he dyed.

The paygane's head was cutte oft his bodie, but in my blooded handes, his eyes were fill'd with spirite. At the brydge a grate storme did mayke the crowde to runne, whereof I spiked it on the grate stone gayte and left it to its grisly ende, but none did evere looke upon it for longe, until the crowes had pulled from it the eyes.

When the tyme was to brynge downe the sayd skull to put up the heads of other dreadeful wretches, the jawe did falle to the grounde and I did hear it speake. Couper. And I did kicke it from the brydge and into the filthie water.

Anno D XIXth Novembre 1663

An unexpected gasp escaped from Dee's lips, like the gas that pours forth from a corpse when death's call comes. "The Paygane? What does that mean?" she prompted nervously. "Does that mean he was a Pagan, as in not a Christian?"

"I don't know," said Jackie nervously, as she scanned every stroke and syllable of the text again, her sight finally coming back to the name where it settled and stayed.

But it wasn't the name of Radclyffe that leapt out from the foul description to stem the flow of blood in her veins. It was a misspelt Couper that caught her eye and that would stay with her long afterwards. She couldn't even bring herself to mention it to Dee who was still sat in awe alongside her, her hand over her mouth as if she was about to be sick.

"This is so horrible!" said Dee, incensed. "This can't be true, can it? Did they really do this sort of thing to people?"

"Yes," Jackie answered, in no doubt at all about its pedigree. "They sure did."

As they returned to the desk once more, it was clear that they had paid a price for her chilling discovery.

"Are you both okay?" asked another middle-aged librarian, as she circled around the desk to take Jackie by the arm. "You both look like you've seen a ghost."

"I might have," Jackie mumbled, averting her eyes in recognition of the inherent absurdity in her answer. "Is there any chance that I could have a copy of this?" she asked, as the world around her span in a pirouette of light and sound.

"No, I'm afraid not," the career librarian replied. "This is a very old book indeed and we don't allow any pre-1930 material to be photocopied. You can take a picture of it if you like, but flash photography is not permitted."

"Can I use the camera on my phone?" asked Jackie, expecting her request to be denied, but times had changed, and the librarian offered up no objection. In the end, Dee showed her how; she took several, just in case.

"Your colleague mentioned that you have some records of registered watermen as well."

It was Jackie's turn this time to extend their stay.

She was no longer that hungry.

"That's right," the woman confirmed in a rather more business-like fashion, "would you like to see them?"

Jackie hesitated for a moment and glanced down at her watch as if the time of day was suddenly of the utmost importance. Not only had she agreed to meet up with Jake, she also wanted to spend more time with Dee to get all of the day's facts clear in her head. "How easy is it," she asked, "to search for a name?"

"It's straightforward enough, but it could take some time if you want an answer today," the librarian explained, "but they're always available if you want to come back another time, we close in fifteen minutes."

Jackie and Dee exchanged glances and Dee was the first to shrug in indifference. "In for a penny, in for a pound?"

"Do you want to see them?" the bespectacled woman asked again as her customer dallied and this time, Jackie submitted to the inevitable. "They're all still on microfilm, but I can help you with that if it's only a quick search you're after. Do you have a name?"

The woman invited them to take a seat again at one of the archaic readers, Dee pulled herself a chair over and they doubled up in front of the old equipment.

"Cooper," Jackie answered. "Jacob Cooper—it might be spelt 'ou'."

"There might be lots of those," the librarian said. "It was a very common name back then, still is I suppose. You'll have to trawl through the dates, I'm afraid," she indicated. "There are no search engines with this stuff. What period are you interested in?" she asked.

"Late seventeenth century," Jackie replied. "From the 1660s onwards."

"Ah," the woman scowled, "the only thing you can really look at then are the Apprentice Binding Registers, which start in the 1670s. The Quarterage Books and the Register of Plying Places are only really useful for the eighteenth century onwards. Are they no good to you?"

"None at all," said Jackie, but something told her that the apprentice records might be worth a look. If Cooper had taken an apprentice, his name might have been recorded too.

"Thanks," whispered Jackie, "very much," and to her obvious disappointment, the woman then left them to it. Her fingers ached and her back throbbed, but she was sure that there, in that unforgiving chair, perched in front of a small and dusty screen, she really was on the verge of some great discovery.

She withdrew the insignificant reel from box 6289 and loaded it onto the dated 1970s technology. Judging by the leaflet that she had been handed, children had normally been apprenticed between the ages of fourteen and sixteen, although there were sometimes exceptions to that rule. As she scanned each page from the earliest records onwards, she was disappointed to see that the quality of the writing contained therein was not as good as in the church chronicles. Many of the names and details were hard to comprehend or had been scribbled out and rewritten in another hand, in another time!

She must have looked apprehensively towards the male assistant, who was suddenly at her shoulder, and he jumped in to offer the help that his colleague had stopped short of providing.

"Having trouble?" he asked, pressing her for further clues. "Who are you looking for again?" he asked and was surprised to learn that the focus of her search had changed in the intervening hours. Undeterred, he pulled up a chair. "And we were interested in the years immediately after the fire, were we not?" Taking her silence as concurrence, he leant across her to turn the wheel at some considerable speed through the years.

Several names appeared in fluorescent white on the up-lit screen before them and Jacob Cooper was just one of many on the list, his name preserved forever in a medium that would have been as foreign to him as his world was now to them. The entry was brief, but it told her most of what she needed to know. In the left-hand column, the name Cooper stood proud, the initial swirling like an entry in some monastic book of hours.

The date was clear enough, although the year had to be deduced from the chronological order of the volume, such was the stylistic nature of the writer's hand.

Aprill 16th 1677, London Brydge, Jacob Cooper bound his son, Jaromiah Cooper aged 14 yeares, for seven yeares beginning 16th Aprill 1677 [then in another hand] and approved by him dated 16th July 1677

"It seems that he was apprenticed to your Jacob Cooper there," her able assistant announced before peering more closely at the screen to make more sense of the subsequent entry.

"What about Radclyffe?" Jackie asked.

"No, nothing on him so far, I'm afraid," as if from a hundred miles away. "No, hang on, there is something here!" he exclaimed. "Well, it looks like your man Cooper took on two apprentices," but he didn't announce his findings and instead pointed Jackie towards the screen where she was able to read the entry for herself.

July 18th 1677, London Brydge, Jacob Cooper bound William Radclyffe aged 17 yeares, for seven yeares beginning 18th July 1677 [then in another hand] and approved by him dated 18th October 1677

"That's odd," said Jackie as she read both entries for a third time. "That's really odd!"

"What is?" said Dee, failing to pick up on the discrepancy.

"Well, first of all," she mused. "Why take on the son of his ex-partner as an apprentice, when he already had an apprentice?" But that was clearly not what had most puzzled her about the records that they had just reviewed.

"The first name of Cooper's son," she mumbled. "It's spelt rather strangely, but it's the same spelling as I saw in the Magnus records for Thomas Radclyffe's son and according to this," she gasped, frantically working her way through the mental maths after consulting the notes she had made, "he would have been the same age!"

"Chances are then," said the young man, seemingly impressed with their day's work, "that it's the same person."

Then Dee piped up, and from her tone she obviously thought she had cracked it! "So Jaromiah seems like a strange name, at least I have never seen it spelled like that, so if we assume that it is the same person then, isn't it obvious?" No one spoke so she finished the hypothesis for them. "Cooper adopted him as his son and changed his surname!"

"Okay," said Jackie, "but if he was christened Radclyffe then he was clearly Thomas's son so we have to assume that his mother was dead as well, though we can find no proof of that, so yes maybe our Jacob Cooper took both boys on as his own to save them from a life of poverty or the workhouse. But why did he change only one of their names, if it's the same boy?"

The assistant shrugged his shoulders and for a moment, there was silence between them, but it wasn't long before the librarian took up the search again. As Jackie and Dee remained lost in contemplation, he kept his nose firmly to the grindstone.

"Don't know when the boys died," he piped up a couple of minutes and a new reel of microfiche later, "but the young William was a waterman for many years it seems. Even took on his own apprentices, it would seem, later on in the century. No sign of Jaromiah in later years, but it looks like they plied their trade from the foot of the Old Swann Stairs by London Bridge; at least according to the list of plying places, that's where William worked out of, so it probably follows that their father did the same when he was in charge. I can tell you a bit more about his master as well, if you like."

As it turned out, he didn't need much in the way of encouragement.

"It looks like he went to war. Died fighting the Dutch."

"Why would he do that?" said Jackie.

"Watermen often did. They were usually pressed into service in times of war as they were able seamen, you see,"—and at that he smiled cannily. "I guess that they were the territorial army of their day." Although he laughed out loud, Jackie didn't and he soon realised that if he was trying to make an impression, the one that he was making was not doing him any favours. "Anyway, he was most likely press-ganged, most of them were."

"What does that mean?"

"Press-ganged?"

Dee filled her in. "It means that he accepted the King's shilling."

"Yes, that's right!" the librarian went on. "They would get a person, usually a waterman or sailor, blind drunk, give them a shilling and if they accepted it, then they would usually wake up halfway to France."

"That doesn't seem very fair," she answered stupidly.

"It wasn't," he replied, "but life wasn't very fair then."

"A bit like a token," muttered Jackie absent-mindedly, a thought that she would return to later. As she churned over the possibilities, there was only one that made any sense, although at first, she could not bring herself to believe it. Yet the more she thought it through, the more sense it seemed to make.

They thanked him for his help and as Dee started to gather her things together, Jackie couldn't hide her growing sense of excitement, which served to drag her back to the very place where they had begun the day's quest.

"I think I've got it, Dee!"

The register of marriages from St Magnus the Martyr in the middle years of the seventeenth century, a source that she had chosen to skim through earlier that day.

Starting with the year in which the first of the Radclyffe children had been born—1645—Jackie edged backwards in time. Month by month, she scrutinised every marriage registration, sometimes reading the names aloud quite by accident, as her lips mouthed each one.

Frequently, there were no entries for a while and then there were three or four marriages in a single calendar month, but there was nothing of note in 1644 and nothing either during the whole of 1643.

Just eleven weddings at the two churches, but none mentioned Radclyffe as the groom. As she scanned the list for 1642, she cursed aloud at the absence of the one name that she was sure would be there, but as she re-examined each one, another name caught her eye. As she studied the detail of the almost illegible scrawl that had passed for writing all those years before, the mis-spelt name of Radcliff was just about decipherable. But it was the maiden name of Mary, his wife, that was unmistakable in its clarity, and which burst forth from the page to trip the reader's eye as her sight moved across the ancient page.

Wilkes.

"I knew it!" she proclaimed, grabbing a bewildered Dee by the arm.

It was all starting to make sense.

**

As they walked out into the late afternoon air, Jackie allowed each piece to tumble gently over the mill of her mind, but whilst they weren't all yet flowing in the same direction, at least she could now see the general course in which they were headed.

As they took their seats in the pub opposite Moorgate station where she had agreed to meet Jake a little later that evening, she outlined her theory to Dee, who nodded her agreement at every step.

"Radclyffe's last surviving child, according to record at least, had been apprenticed to his old business partner after his father's death in a kindly act of Christian charity, you might say," started Jackie. "Assuming, of course, that the William Radclyffe listed in the records was indeed of the same line, but it seemed far too much of a coincidence for it not to be the son of Thomas and Mary Radclyffe, nee Wilkes."

"Makes sense," Dee concurred.

"Is it that surprising that the orphaned son of an executed man should have been taken on as apprentice by his former partner?" asked Jackie. "I mean, we know that that happened, but the fact that his fellow apprentice appears not to have been his brother, but his half-brother—now that would have been the stuff of scandal."

"I see," said Dee, her eyes widening. "So, what you're suggesting is that they'd had an affair; before they were married, Jacob and Mary had already been an item, whilst Thomas was still alive? Juicy!"

That Cooper had married the widowed wife of his ex-partner in the year after the execution was also clear from the marriage entries. But it also seemed, in the cold light of a twenty-first century evening, that a seventeenth-century affair had borne a son. A son called Jaromiah, from whom Jackie's family was descended. A son who had been christened Radclyffe in 1663 and whose name had been changed to that of his true father sometime after his mother had remarried in 1664, maybe even after his mother's untimely death just two years later.

"And maybe a basis for revenge," Jackie mused.

"Or for a curse!"

There were still many unanswered questions and more possibilities than they could fathom over fish and chips and a pint or two of real ale.

"Maybe Jacob Cooper had changed both of their names, but his eldest son had taken on his true father's name again in later life. Maybe Cooper had changed his only son's name long after his wife's departure from this life; had he changed one, but not the other during their short union, it would surely have given rise to rumour and reproach, had the real truth emerged."

Dee nodded in agreement. It certainly seemed possible, and the facts seemed to back it up.

"Maybe dishonoured and rebuked by his fellow citizens, his business had gone bust and leaving it to his sons, he had fled to fight in the war that would claim his life?"

Jackie needed to talk it over with someone else, someone who might be able to bring his own facts to the party. Just to get it clear in her own mind, if not for all of them.

And that someone was now late.

Chapter Twenty-Five
Wale broch

A married man (some say) has two dayes gladnesse, and all his life else is a lingring sadnesse: the one dayes mirth is when he first is married, th'other's when his wife's to burying carried

It was raining hard and Jake was late.

The cold winter rain clouds had hastened the onset of dusk within the city walls and there seemed little hope for any let up in the downpour.

Jackie had texted Jake with her suggestion to meet at the Moorgate pub, and she was mighty glad that she had, judging by the rain that was now falling in stair-rods outside. She watched as commuter after commuter did battle with the elements on their way to or from the trains, taking refuge from the storm beneath the bowed awning of a nearby coffee shop or fighting to control their umbrellas in the gusting wind.

One particularly cheap umbrella had performed miserably in the squalling rain as a sudden gust of wind left it horribly disfigured, its owner grappling in vain to restore it to its natural state, before finally giving up and dumping the bat-like pile of flapping skin and sinew in a litter bin, just across the street from the window seat in which she and Dee were perched.

"How much longer do you think he's going to be?" asked Dee anxiously, concerned at the growing lateness of the hour.

"I'm not sure," Jackie admitted, a little embarrassed. "I hope he's still going to turn up. I've texted him a couple of times, but he's not replied. You should get off, you know, I'll be okay."

Dee was tempted, but resisted the suggestion, preferring instead to wait a few more minutes just so she could clap eyes on him and draw her own conclusions. "No, I can wait a bit longer," she smiled. "There's another train at 8.45 that'll get me home for half past nine and Bill will pick me up from the station."

"Well, only if you're sure," Jackie answered, no less embarrassed at keeping her friend waiting. "Give it ten more minutes and then leave me, I don't want you to miss that train."

He had used up nine of those minutes when Jackie, peering down at her watch for the last time, caught a glimpse of him as he emerged from the jaws of the station and dodged across the road towards the pub. She lost him again in the huddled crowds and upturned collars, but a few minutes later, the door to the pub swung inwards and he came stumbling in, out of the filthy night.

"He's here!" announced Jackie as Dee stretched her neck over the tops of the crowd, just to get a better look at him.

"I'm really, really sorry, Jackie," he pleaded as he arrived, the rain running like an ancient stream down the contours of his face. "I had to work late. I overslept and I didn't get to my desk until ten. My wife thinks that I'm still at work."

"Hello!" Dee piped up.

"Oh hello," said Jake, surprised that they had company.
"Don't worry, I'm not staying," Dee informed him sternly. "I just wanted to get a good look at you, to check that your intentions are honourable, if you know what I mean?"

"She's only joking," said Jackie, trying to brush off the apparent rebuke, but Dee had other ideas.

"I'm not!" she said. "You'd better see that she gets home safe!"

Then turning to Jackie, they bid each other goodnight. "Don't forget to text me later and call me in the morning, to tell me what train you're on. It was lovely to see you again."

Jackie nodded and beamed back at her. "I will, love, speak to you later, thanks for coming down, I don't know what I'd have done without you!"

"Who was that then?" asked Jake as soon as they were alone. "If I'd known that you were going to bring a chaperone, I'd have come with an armed guard."

"Don't be stupid!" blurted Jackie. "She's a friend, that's all, and she knows everything. Can you blame her for being suspicious, but stop avoiding the issue, why are you so late?"

"What do you think?" he snapped. "I had a terrible night, didn't get to sleep until about four and had to get up for work just after six. I was out in the car most of the day, God only knows how I didn't have an accident! I almost fell asleep at the wheel twice and when I got back, I thought I'd grab a quick shut-eye—and slept for three bloody hours!"

She gave him a look that said *I don't believe you*, but he was adamant.

"I'm really sorry to have kept you waiting," he said. "I got here as fast as I could, honestly."

"I'll let you off," she conceded, "but you owe me one!"

Jake smiled suggestively and this time she hit him a lot harder for his trouble.

"What was that for!" he cried.

"Never mind what that was for," she said, "let's get down to business, we've got things to talk about!"

After a few more traded insults, Jackie returned to the research in which she had been completely immersed for what seemed like forever. She found herself feeling distinctly disappointed that, at the end of what had seemed like a marathon of reading and research, the sum total of her efforts came down to just a few minutes of explanation. It didn't seem like much, but between them, the pieces were edging closer together.

"They were definitely partners then?" asked Jake.

"I don't know for sure," Jackie replied, "but they both certainly existed at that time and Cooper was registered as a Waterman in the 1670s and Thomas's son too from 1680 onwards."

"But not Thomas Radclyffe himself?"

"Well no," Jackie frowned, as if that fact were too obvious for words. "He was already dead, wasn't he? Keep up, for God's sake, Jake!"

"I'm sorry," said Jake, stifling yet another yawn, which this time threatened to get out of control. "It's been a long day."

"You're telling me!" nagged Jackie. "Now listen."

Jake put his hands under his chin in his best '*your wish is my command*' pose, a task that he himself had never quite mastered.

"C'mon Jake, this is serious!" Jackie snapped, at which he took another gulp of beer, folded his arms in submission and tried hard not to smile.

"It seems that after his execution, most of his kids died, most probably of plague and that the two that survived were both apprenticed to Cooper, who we think we might be related to!"

"I wish we weren't, but yes, that's how it would seem!"

"I just think it's strange," she said, "that his kids should die of plague and mine is suspected of it, don't you?"

"What are you suggesting Jackie?" Jake said, as he drained his glass. "That this dead man somehow infected your son?"

"I'm not saying that at all!" she replied. "I'm just saying that it's another bloody coincidence and to be quite honest with you, I'm sick of them. There's something sinister going on here and I don't care how crazy it seems, Radclyffe and Cooper have got something to do with it. It might be only circumstantial evidence, but I'm sure of it now."

"Go on," Jake encouraged. "I agree by the way; I think you're on the right track."

"The two boys were listed as Radclyffe in the church records," she read from her hastily retrieved notes. "William was apprenticed to Cooper in 1682, according to the binding records, as was a Jaromiah, but..." and she paused to drain the last of her own drink. "His surname had been changed to Cooper, but not his brother's, just Jaromiah."

"So?"

"So," she shouted. "So, what's the chances of there being two boys with a strangely spelt and unusual name, both the same age in the same vicinity! It has to be the same boy and if so, why did Cooper only formally adopt the one child of his business partner and not them both?"

"I still don't see what you're driving at!" Jake parried, refusing to see the evidence that was just inches from his face.

"Jaromiah was Cooper's son!" Jackie said triumphantly. "It's the only thing that fits. Mary and Cooper had a fling, she fell pregnant and then it all went pear-shaped, but here's the real proof." She pulled herself closer to the table and nearer to Jake, before imparting what she believed to be the crucial evidence. "Cooper married a Mary Wilkes, in 1664."

"Okay?" Jake repeated, at which point Jackie beamed.

"So did Thomas Radclyffe, 22 years earlier!"

"What?"

"Yup!" confirmed Jackie. "It's got to have been the same person. The two marriage entries also show her as being the right age each time. It all lines up!"

"They had an affair," Jake concluded out loud. "And then Radclyffe gets executed? Convenient or what?"

"There's more," Jackie went on. "Jacob and Mary had a daughter who died, most probably of plague, but the son that she had when she was married to Radclyffe must have been Cooper's. It must have been, I have been unable to find any other descendants and if we are descended from him then it must be from Jaromiah," she insisted, but Jake continued to play devil's advocate.

"It's all a bit convenient though, isn't it? It seems too neat to be true!"

"If not, then why did his name appear as Cooper in the binding records?" she asked, ignoring his disparaging remark, but visibly disappointed by his apparent lack of support. "All spelt with a 'U' by the way," she added almost as an aside and one that he failed to pick up on.

"In *what* records?"

"Never mind," she snapped, "that's not important, but it has to be the same Jaromiah and if it is, then there's the motive."

"Motive for what?"

"For what Radclyffe had against Cooper," she hollered, slapping her companion hard across the thigh. "C'mon Jake, I'm being serious, it all fits." Jake did his best to appear to be working things through and as he did so, he posed another question of his own.

"I thought that such things as extra-marital sex were not condoned in those days?" It was a simple statement of fact and Jackie guessed where his line was leading. "If she was an adulterer, why wasn't she kicked out? If your theory is right, not only was the affair overlooked by the community at large, but they were even welcomed back into the fold of the church, with open arms! That doesn't seem very likely to me."

For a minute or two, Jackie stayed silent, as she worked through the cycle of events, but then it was as if a switch had been flicked. Her eyes lit up and she almost stood to attention to deliver her next deliberation.

"Not if her husband, her ex-husband, had done something so bad that all the sympathy was with her," she said triumphantly.

"Like what?"

"Like being a religious dissenter!" she shrilled, as if the severity of the crime was obvious. "The church would have wanted *him* to be the outcast. She would have been the victim; just think about it for a minute. Married for over twenty years to a man like that. I tell you, that's it, I'm sure of it! She even stopped using her married name—she was a widow when she remarried, but the name on the marriage register is her maiden name, as if even the memory of Thomas Radclyffe had been erased from history, or as if their marriage had been declared null and void."

Jake was too tired to argue the point, but in any case, he could not think of any meaningful counter argument and so he had no choice but to concede the ground. "Maybe," he surrendered. "Maybe you're right, so what else have you got?"

"Well," said Jackie, returning to the facts. "Radclyffe died in November 1663, that's unquestionable, but she died at the height of the plague, most probably of the Black Death itself, and Cooper died at sea, fighting the French, or was it the Dutch. Anyway, the two boys were all that was left of that family at the end of the century."

"It all sounds pretty far-fetched to me," Jake concluded, unhappy that he had been upstaged, or as if he had other things on his mind. "So why did Cooper let this William kid live? Why didn't he just let him die on the streets; it wouldn't have been difficult, would it?"

"I don't know," said Jackie as if the thought had not occurred to her. "Maybe he felt guilty about it all. Maybe he wanted to have a brother for his son and after all, they did have the same mother. Although she was dead by then, of course!"

"So, you said."

"Oh, I don't know," said Jackie, dejected. "Maybe he was just a good guy, you know, there are still a few of those even nowadays, so maybe there were more of them then, I don't know."

"I know what I want!" said Jake, rising to his feet, an empty pint glass in hand. "Want another?"

She was in no mood to decline. In fact, she was ready to drink the place dry and as she only had a short walk to her residence, there seemed to be no harm in over-indulging for once.

"Double G and T, no ice, thanks," said Jackie, more than a little deflated by her comrade-in-arm's lack of support.

When he returned a full ten minutes later after spending at least nine of those watching the closing stages of the football, Jackie had her phone at the ready and did not look up as Jake shuffled back onto his perch.

"City are winning!" he beamed, but Jackie wasn't interested.

"Really," she said. "I hate football. Take a look at this," she said, offering him her phone on which the post-reformation document was displayed.

"What is it?"

"Just read it." He did and then he read it again and then for a third time, just for good measure.

"Christ!" he blasphemed. "Where did you find this?"

"It doesn't matter where I found it, but it's an account from the time from people that were there," she yelled above the sudden noise from another gang of office workers who were making short work of a round of pre-Christmas drinks. "People like his wife and partner, amongst others," she added as the voices subsided.

Jake nodded, but he wasn't listening. He was too busy trying to coerce his exhausted brain into one last effort before the day was through, as he scanned the account of the execution.

"Well, that's that then," he said, refusing to discuss Jackie's theories any further. "He swore vengeance on his partner. His partner was Cooper. We're descended from Cooper. We're fucked!"

As the words left his lips, Jake tried to convince himself that he had nothing at all to worry about, especially if he followed the instructions he'd been given to the letter. No one had died in his family of late. Sure, he'd been a little under the weather lately and there had been a few sleepless nights, but he had decided to put all of that down to lifestyle.

Stress management, as the consultants called it, was the answer to his recent problems. Ghostbusters was not. Yet still, as he turned the caller's demands over in his mind, it felt like an easy way out, and if all this turned out to be true, it felt increasingly like his only way out.

"I'm going to talk to Gallagher again," Jackie decided on the spur of the moment.

"Oh yes, the hypnotist," Jake scoffed. "The man with the stalker theory!"

"Well," Jackie said, wondering if she could face going outside into a howling gale for the sake of a cigarette. She decided that it wasn't worth it and dropped the pack back into her bag. "Do you have any better ideas?"

Jake didn't, but as Jackie slipped away to find a quiet corner from which to make the call, even the final throes of the football match could not distract him from his thoughts. When Jackie returned, he was none the wiser for his ten minutes of solitary confinement.

"Any luck?"

"No!" said Jackie, clearly puzzled.

"What's up?"

"He's not there," she said concerned. "They say he's gone. They're very worried about him, obviously. Asked me if I knew where he was. I don't think they believed me."

"What, they think that he's absconded with you?" Jake laughed. "That's rich!"

"Well, I'm the only visitor he's had in years apparently," she said sadly. "Until I turned up a few weeks ago, he was just a frail old man waiting to die. He still is, but he's a damn sight more likely to die outside in this weather." At that moment, a look of horror dawned on her face, and it did not go unnoticed.

"What's wrong, Jackie?"

"Oh no!" she bawled. "He will have gone to my house! Patrick will swing for him, especially if he's drunk, and without me there to say anything, he'll be permanently drunk. Shit!"

Jake did his best to look concerned, but it was short-lived.

"Unless …?"

"Unless what?"

"You know that you owe me one!" But it wasn't a question and Jake's expression quickly changed from one of confusion to one of utter resignation.

"Go on then," he said, realising that he really had no choice in the matter. "What do you want me to do?"

He came back too soon to have been effective.

"No answer," he informed her.

"I'm not surprised," she admitted, "he'll be down the pub. You'll have to try again later around midnight; he'll most likely be back by then and remember!" she commanded. "Act concerned when you do. You're supposed to be the manager of an old people's home, not some used car salesman."

Jake checked out the time on his phone; it was past ten o'clock and he seemed to be getting increasingly agitated at the prospect that Lisa would be waiting up for him again. Jackie could not fail to notice, and she acted quickly to keep him from making a quick getaway.

They had more to discuss.

"Another one?" she asked him, but before he had time to say no, she was already well on the way to the bar. "Same again please," he heard her say as he found himself admiring her from behind. He hadn't thought of her in that way before, but in the hazy light of that good old British institution and with a couple of pints inside him, Jake felt the same familiar stirrings that had caused him to stray so often in the past.

"I've been thinking," said Jake, when she returned with their drinks, moments later. "About the tokens. There must be some significance there, don't you think? You have one, recently discovered amongst your father's things, so he had one too. I have one, but what about your son? Did he have one?"

Jackie shook her head. "Not that I'm aware of. His things are back in my room, but of course, he didn't have much and if he did ever have one of these token things, it would have been easily lost or stolen, or more likely sold."

"Well, quite," said Jake, "but say that he did. What then?"

"I don't follow," said Jackie. "What do you mean?"

"I mean, I found mine quite by accident, but it was as if it were meant for me. Your mother or your father never told you that such a thing existed; why not?"

"It wasn't important enough, I suppose!"

"Not important," Jake gibed. "Your father's life was tracking down this thing. All of his research into the plague and his quest to trace your family back to that time and that copper time capsule was not important enough? C'mon Jackie, give me a break."

"Okay then," smarted Jackie, annoyed at Jake's rebuke. "All my father's research is back in my room. Boxes of the bloody stuff. Why don't you come back with me now and let's see if we can't piece this thing together once and for all, if it's all so bloody obvious!"

Jake thought about it for all of two seconds. "You're on," he shouted, "drink up, let's go!"

"Bloody hell, give us a chance," Jackie complained. "I've only just got the round in."

**

The weathered collection of cardboard boxes was piled on the floor to the side of the queen-sized bed, on which Jake was a little too quick to perch. Jackie remained on her feet and seemed more than a little uncomfortable at the situation in which she now found herself.

"Would you like a cup of tea?" she asked nervously.

"Coffee would be nice," replied Jake, just to be awkward.

"Okay," she said, trying desperately to avoid a meeting of eyes, which might have made the situation distinctly more perilous for them both. "There's *Nescafe* and *Gold Blend*," she relayed to him as she rummaged through the paltry supply of instant drinks, but Jake just waved his hand like royalty towards her.

"Dealer's choice," he said in a sadly suave fashion that even Jackie recognised for what it was.

The water was quick to come to the boil and as Jackie had disappeared into the bathroom, Jake attended to their drinks. He paid especially close attention to Jackie's, taking the opportunity to slip something into the white ceramic cup, stirring it vigorously into the bargain. As Jackie emerged from the en-suite, she was sure that she saw a guilty look pass across his face, but to her eternal regret she paid it no mind.

"Thanks," muttered Jackie suspiciously as he sat back down on the bed, but she had already come to regret her invitation. She tried to tell herself that she had been motivated by the simple desire to unravel the mystery in which she had become embroiled, but deep down she knew, as he did, that signals had been exchanged. Now though, in the bright lights of a hotel bedroom, Jackie felt cheap and desperate, and she wasn't all that fond of either feeling as she attempted to hasten Jake's departure.

"Why don't we do this tomorrow?" she asked more in hope than expectation and when that failed, she tried to set him off on another train of thought. "Your wife will be wondering where you've got to."

For a moment, the reminder seemed to do the trick, as he took a short swig of his hot drink, but to Jackie's despair, he failed to take the bait. Instead, he peered inside the first small box and withdrew a small wooden casket.

"Those were my son's things," Jackie warned him, the tears welling in her eyes again, but whilst most would have heard the possessive undertone in her voice, Jake did not. Either that or he chose to ignore it as he pulled out item after item and dropped them onto the bed between them.

"What's this?" he asked, dangling the World War Two medal on its dull chain from his fingers.

"It was my father's," said Jackie, wishing that she had left it in her handbag and breathing deeply to ward off the fearful edge that had crept into her voice. "He gave it to Terry before he died." Jake looked up, sensing the rising emotion in Jackie's voice and as he did, their eyes did meet and in her cold stare, Jake finally recognised the naked fear that lay behind it. And he smiled.

If was meant to reassure Jackie, it didn't.

If it was meant to comfort her, it didn't.

All that his leering smile achieved was to put her in fear of her life and if she hadn't already recognised the stark reality of the situation that she had unwittingly helped to create, at that moment she saw in his smile all its dreadful possibilities.

Even if she could have reached her mobile phone, Dee would be too far away to come charging back to save her, and there was no telephone to hand to call the emergency services or even the front desk for assistance. Rooms with telephones were no longer a requirement of the modern-day business hotel. The hotel was virtually empty and so, no one would hear her, should she decide to scream.

Or should she be forced to.

Jake gave the impression of someone whose interest was on the wane, but that was only true in part. He was inspecting the medal, holding it up to the light and then turning it, just a fraction, so that it flashed like the summer sun on a discarded bottle.

"Come over here, Jackie," he said menacingly, but she didn't budge an inch and he looked genuinely surprised by her resistance. "Come on," he insisted, in the way that a small boy might encourage his best friend to follow him on a forbidden adventure. "I want to show you something!"

Jackie edged her way across the room, silently praying that he wouldn't touch her. "What?" she said brusquely from what she hoped was a safe distance.

"Look," he pointed, angling the medal again so that the unnatural light caught on the edge of the carelessly drilled hole. The metal that reflected was not silver, as it should have been, but copper. "There's another coin inside, you can see the rim." Jake was genuinely astonished. "Did you know that?"

Jackie didn't, but her thoughts were also heading in the same direction.

"What do you make of that then?" he challenged her, an edge of superiority in his voice. "I think that there's a little something hiding away in there and do you know something? I think it's desperate to get out." Jackie received Jake's underlying message loud and clear.

"I think that you should go," she insisted, reaching for the damp jacket that he had flung over the back of the chair as he had entered the room. "I'm tired, it's late and I've got things to do tomorrow, even if you haven't." She did her best to exert her own authority over him, to show him who was boss and although it had sometimes worked with Patrick when he was sober, the success rate on other occasions had proved to be painfully disappointing, especially for her. She blinked hard to ward off the threat of a flashback that she preferred not to recall, but the rapidly shelved memory made her want to retch.

"Don't you think it's odd," he surmised, ignoring her plea, "that even your son had one of these things?" Jackie said nothing, but Jake did not allow her reserve to put him off the trail that he was now blazing. "I've got one. Your father had one and now you have one too. And it turns out that your son had one all along! Now that can't be a…what do you call it?" as he pressed home his point. "A coincidence."

"But that was my father's," said Jackie, bemused. "He gave it to Terry when he died, which means that he had two!"

"Or that he was just keeping this one warm," Jake speculated, "until his grandson came along to claim it?"

"That's ridiculous," argued Jackie, momentarily forgetting the predicament she was now in. "You mean that it was meant for Terry all along? But how did it get in there? That's crazy!"

"Well, maybe, but why not?" reasoned Jake. "If you can believe any of this crap, why not believe that this thing that's after us has got the intelligence to plan ahead; years ahead in fact. It's probably got descendants of its own that it could influence somehow, I don't know how it got inside there." Jake paused to gather his thoughts, but he wasn't quiet for long. "Say that these tokens are in some way the link and that we have accepted them when they were given to us, what if we have somehow accepted everything that goes with them. What if it's like inviting a vampire into your home in its human form or like, I don't know, accepting the King's shilling or something!"

"What?" Jackie interrupted. "What did you say?"

"When?"

"The King's shilling. Why did you say that?"

"Well," Jake said dismissively. "I don't know. It just seemed appropriate. It was like a binding contract, when someone accepted the King's shilling. There was no two ways about it. There was no way out of the deal."

Jake was pleased that his makeshift theory had clearly made a good impression on his host, but she was puzzled by his choice of phrase and in spite of her obvious unease at Jake's intentions, she somehow found the nerve to press home her point.

"It's just that the librarian mentioned the very same thing," she recalled. "That watermen were often, *pressed* I think he called it, by accepting the King's shilling." Having successfully side-tracked Jake for a moment or two, she found herself hoping against hope that he would now be more open to her next suggestion. "Now I really think that you should go, Jake, it's getting really late; gosh, it's gone eleven already!"

When he smiled and nodded, Jackie's sense of relief was immense but as he raised himself up to his full six-foot frame, her vulnerability became all too apparent to both of them. Jackie held his surprisingly heavy coat aloft, inviting him to just slip inside it, as if after a satisfying meal at an expensive West-End restaurant. As she waited for him to oblige, she thought she saw a trace of concern in his eyes, but it was only temporary and as he strode gamely forward to snatch the coat from her hands, she could see that he was not about to give in so easily.

"C'mon Jackie," he hissed. "You didn't invite me back here for coffee and biscuits. I saw the looks."

"No, I didn't," she said fearfully, as an embarrassing crimson rash began to burn around the top of her all too visible breastbone. "Not from me, I want you to go now, please." She was close to tears, as she realised too late that she had completely misjudged him. He was not, in fact, a nice guy. He was not a nice guy at all. Dee was right and Dee was her only hope.

"Well, I haven't changed mine, *Jackie*," he spat, using her name as if it were an insult. "In any case, at your age, you won't get any better offers!"

It was probably the smile that did it, but the chuckle that followed closely behind didn't help matters and when he burst into a peal of goading laughter, Jackie lost her grip on reality.

"You bastard!" she snapped, but the half-hearted punch that she aimed at his chin landed on his shoulder, where it remained. As she flung her free hand in a similar fashion, he caught her fist in his and spun her around in a swift move that might have made a dance tutor proud.

But this was no dance hall.

And he was no teacher.

Jake rammed her forearm up to rest against her shoulder blade. "Is this what you want?" he hissed. "Is it?"

"No," she cried, "please stop, please," but Jake was no longer listening. He forced her down onto her knees so that her stomach was pressed against the lip of the bed and her tights were quickly laddered as her knees scraped against the rough surface of the carpet tiles.

Jake's forearm ground into the small of her back as he forced her upper body flat onto the bed and with his muscular legs, he kicked her knees apart.

He wanted her to be scared.

He needed her to be terrified.

He left her where she lay and slumped back down into the chair in the corner of the room. For a moment, he almost changed his mind again, but instead, he grunted like a pig and headed into the bathroom, leaving the door open to block her route to the exit, should she be brave enough to try an escape.

She wasn't sure why he'd not gone through with it, but Jackie didn't waste any time thinking about his motives. She grabbed her phone and texted two words to the only person that she knew would come running.

HELP

ME

When he returned, Jackie had done what she could to right herself, but her skirt was torn where the button had been wrenched off and her tights had been laddered. She had propped herself up by the headboard, her nose was bleeding and her mascara had run amok. But in spite of the terror that she was feeling, she could hardly keep her eyes open.

"You best get some sleep," he commanded, "we've got to be up early in the morning." Jackie was still too dazed and terrified to take in the meaning behind his words, but when she didn't answer, he couldn't resist another opportunity to exert his physical dominance. "Oh, didn't I tell you," he teased. "I'm taking you for a little trip in the morning. We're going down to the beach, but don't pack your costume, because you won't be needing it!"

"Please," Jackie begged. "Please, just let me go."

Jake picked up an outdated copy of a daily newspaper that a cleaner had overlooked and sat down to read. "Get into bed," he thundered. "We're away before sun-up, and don't try anything. I'm staying put, right here, all night!"

She did as she was told and slipped fully clothed beneath the covers, but she didn't sleep. Instead, she listened. She listened to his breathing, feeling sure that after his previous sleepless night, he would not be able to make it through another.

She wasn't scared of him, but she was scared of what was coming.

She felt sure that he had something planned and that most likely it would end in her death. With everything that she had read, seen and heard the last few weeks, with the death of her son and the circumstances surrounding his final days, she felt sure that Jake was going to be instrumental in her own demise, but if so then she was determined to take him with her.

As she tried her best to stay awake, he put the television on and turned up the volume, switching immediately to a 24-hour news channel and watched intently as if he was waiting for a particular item. There had been another outbreak of a deadly disease in China and the authorities were busily building several hospitals on the outskirts of Beijing at breakneck speed. The newsreader was clearly worried, but the health authorities were confident that it could be contained.

He switched channels before the Asia correspondent had completed her story and Jackie almost screamed when she saw Jake's own face staring back at them from the TV screen.

Police are keen to interview Mr Harvey in relation to the disappearance of missing delivery driver, Melissa Simpson, whose body was discovered on the banks... but she didn't get to hear the rest of the piece as he hit the off button and immediately started to pace around the room.

"Fuck, fuck, fuck!" he said repeatedly. His ringtone whistled at him, and she could hear him fumbling in his pockets to turn it off, swearing to himself as he did so. "I didn't do it," he kept saying over and over. "It wasn't me; it wasn't me!"

She sensed an opportunity to goad him into making a mistake and she decided to chance it. After all, what did she have to lose? She sat up in the bed and looked straight at him.

He was a snivelling wreck of a man, if he was a man at all.

"You cowardly bastard!" she spat at him.

"Shut up!" he screamed. "You can shut the fuck up!"

He was losing it and if he did, then she might just be able to get away with her life. It was a faint hope but that was better than no hope at all, and she grasped at it.

"What kind of man are you?" she asked him outright, guessing at some of his other misdemeanours and judging by the look on his face, none of them were too far wide of the mark. "You cheat on your wife at every opportunity; if you can't get it or take it, you most probably pay for it. You can't face up to the responsibilities of parenthood, so you run away and play at being a big boy in a big job with your big car, but all the time, you're just a scaredy-cat little coward!"

At that, he launched for her, but this time she was too quick for him, and she leapt from the bed, screaming for her life in the hope that someone in an adjoining room or outside would hear her cries.

She reached the door and pulled at the latch, just as he caught up with her, which was when he heard her mobile phone ping and he realised with dread that someone else was onto him.

"Who is that?" he snarled. "Who is it?"

"I don't know!"

"Is it that bitch from earlier?" he guessed, knowing that Jackie didn't have many people in her life to come to her rescue, as he pulled her closer into his clutches. "Well, show me then!"

He held the upper hand now and she knew that she had no choice if she wanted to survive the night. She withdrew her phone from her pocket and shaking, she entered her code to display her messages. A single message from Dee that left him fuming.

WE'RE COMING. WHICH HOTEL?

"Give it here!" he commanded, grabbing at the handset and typing in a random reply with one hand, a skill that he had perfected over many years of one-handed driving. He didn't even know if the 'Minerva' hotel existed, but it sounded convincing enough and it would put them off the scent for a while at least.

It was then that the drug that he had slipped into her tea took full effect.

At first, he thought that she was faking it, but as her legs gave way beneath her, she began to weigh heavily in his arms, and he let her fall to the floor in an undignified heap. The whole thing took just seconds and within a minute, Jackie was laid out unconscious on the carpet tiles.

He took the phone from her grasp and slipped it into his pocket. It was well past midnight. He glanced out of the window at the storm that was raging outside and figured that he still had time.

He had done his research.

Sunrise was not until after seven and so he did not want to get to the scene too soon, as without shelter in these conditions, it would be treacherous underfoot and the longer they were out there, the greater the risk that someone would see them and raise the alarm.

He knew what he had to do to get her down to the river.

He had hoped not to have to use the sedatives, but she had left him no choice and she would now need a few hours to sleep off the effects, before he was able to frogmarch her the short distance to the river.

But at least now she was quiet and the chances of him being caught out by a fellow resident complaining about the noise had been eliminated.

He'd been lucky. She had foolishly not told her friend exactly where she was staying as there were dozens of hotels in the area, none of which would be that forthcoming with their guest list, even in an emergency. He figured that he had a few hours to spare, but he knew that he would have to be even more careful as they left the building.

The police would have been alerted and would be in the vicinity, on the lookout for a deranged male dragging a female through the dark silent streets of the city. He would have to leave a little earlier than planned, but he calculated that he still had time to carry out his plan to perfection. So long as the other geezer kept his side of the bargain.

He didn't expect to sleep at all, but he set his alarm just in case he dozed off and settled down in the armchair to while away a couple of hours with only the TV and a comatose distant cousin for company.

Chapter Twenty-Six
Tamesis

For if a woman be to lewdnesse given, and is not guided with the grace of Heav'n; she wille finde opportunity and time, in spight of watch or ward, to doe the Crime.

For the first glorious second in the twilight world of a new day, life seemed to have some hope in it again. For the first time in weeks, she had not dreamed of ghouls and monsters or of her own watery grave.

In fact, she had not dreamed at all.

The feeling was akin to the first breaths of morning on the day after her father had died. Like the very first moments of the new dawn after her mother's death. Like the first instant of consciousness the day after her son's funeral, but as her nervous system flickered into life, she was unable to ignore the simmering sense of dread that had forged its nest deep in the pit of her empty stomach.

As her eyes grew accustomed to the gloom her sense of disorientation spiralled out of control. The strengthening contours of the room pulled in all the wrong directions and as she turned to face the darkness before the dawn, an all-too-familiar silhouette provided her with a rude awakening.

Her resurgent memory had not failed her.

All of it was true.

"Get up!" he shouted again through gritted teeth. "Get dressed or do whatever you have to do. We're leaving."

It was clear that he was not in any kind of mood to be reasonable and as she scurried obediently into the bathroom to render herself as presentable as she was able, her instincts told her just to play along, for a while at least. As far as she knew, he had no weapon of any sort concealed about his person and there was nothing in the room that might meet that need. So, all she had to do was to hang on in there and then create merry hell the very second that she set eyes on another living person in the world outside.

She washed her face, gingerly dabbing the corner of a wet towel against her bruised nose and battered cheek and did her best to scrub away the long black scars of make-up from beneath her swollen eyes.

Her arm was throbbing and at first, she could not recollect the cause of the injury. As her fist closed around her toothbrush, the searing pain that shot up her arm like an illegal drug dragged the unwanted memory kicking and screaming from the closet where it had been hidden. The strained ligament in her shoulder was just the first of many injuries that would make its presence known that day and it acted like a catalyst for every other ache and strain, real and imagined.

An angry voice from the room was enough to enforce their silence for a while longer.

"C'mon, you've got ten seconds," he roared, persuading her in an instant to forget about her dental hygiene for another day. She hobbled out into the trashed room with five seconds to spare, her head throbbing, still groggy from the after-effects of the drug.

"I need to change my clothes," she said meekly, at which he raised his hand, palm upwards, as if inviting her to do so, but he made no attempt to vacate the room. When it was clear that he fully intended to watch, she grabbed the first garments that came to hand from the top of her suitcase and bundled them on with little regard for her appearance, but Jake wasn't satisfied.

"Trying to draw attention to yourself?" he asked accusingly. "Get dressed properly. We've got a long walk and I don't want you standing out like a sore thumb." He leapt to his feet and for one dreadful moment, Jackie was convinced that he intended to hurt her again, but he had another more immediate calling. "I'm going to take a leak. When I get back, you better not look like a dog's dinner!"

For a second, Jackie seriously considered making a run for it, but as she rapidly weighed up her options, it was clear that she couldn't risk it. The bathroom was right next to the locked exit, which she would have had to pass at speed to stand any chance of escape.

She would just have to bide her time.

Jackie was grateful for the small mercy that he had elaborated during his call of nature, as she had time to make a presentable selection from what few clothes there were that didn't now need washing or ironing. When he emerged, she took his silence as approval.

During his absence, she had frantically scanned the room in what she knew to be a futile search for a weapon of some kind. But as she looked around, all that she could see was her father's papers, scattered across the carpeted floor like litter after a sold-out rock concert. His diaries were shredded, the boxes upended, and all his painstaking research had been torn asunder, as if in some sacrilegious rage. When Jake returned, he could not fail to recognise the look of pure hate that Jackie hurled towards him like a javelin. To attack her had been a despicable and cowardly act, but the violation of her father's memory seemed to charge Jackie's hatred for her distant relative to the point of overload.

"Nothing in them," he smirked. "Waste of bloody time reading them really, but it helped me pass the time. You should be grateful to your old dad," he said with a sinister grin. "Whilst I was stuck into those, I wasn't able to get stuck into you!"

She didn't give him the satisfaction of a response, but her eyes didn't stray from his sickening leer as he strode across to the door where his jacket was hung and retrieved a worn and battered book from the inside pocket. He opened it carefully, as if its contents were primed to leap out like a Jack-in-the-box, but then to Jackie's astonishment, he tore out a few pages and rejecting the rest, he dumped it onto the floor with the rest of the night's debris.

"Treasure map!" he said sarcastically, picking up her coat and flinging it towards her.

"Where are we going?" she asked, trying not to sound afraid.

It didn't work.

"To the river," he said without hesitation.

She had no reason to doubt him. "The river?" She trembled, fearful of his motives. "What's at the river?"

Maybe he had a boat moored there and was planning on making a getaway, but as she thought it through, the whole proposition seemed to belong to the script of a spy movie, and he just didn't fit the part of a secret agent.

"Here," he said, holding out the offending piece of paper that he had just ripped from the reference book. "It's a map," he jibed, as she struggled to open the folded sheet to its full extent. Not surprisingly, it was a map of London. On it marked in blue ink were a selection of rivers and at the top of the page, the heading should have explained all: 'The Lost Rivers of London'. Jackie was none the wiser as she glanced from corner to corner, taking in the names of old streams, some of which she knew well, like the River Lea and the Fleet, and others that she had never heard of before.

"It was in my pocket, when I made my excuses at the library," he sniggered boyishly, an act that was quite out of keeping with his character, which only served to intensify Jackie's rising terror. "I remember picking it up, but I don't know how it ended up in there. Anyway, I'm glad it did, because it's going to come in handy."

"But—" Jackie started to say, but it was Jake who finished her sentence for her.

"But where are we going?" he mimicked in a voice that was pitched significantly higher than his own and pulling a childish face as if to emphasise his point, he filled in the blanks. "Do you see the stream marked 'Walbrook'?" he prompted, continuing the patronising tone. "Well, take a good look, because that's where we're going. Satisfied?"

"Is it still there?"

"What do you think?" he scoffed. "Now," Jake bellowed, so forcefully that Jackie froze in fear of retribution for anything that she might have been about to say, "When we leave you will do as I say, do you understand?"

"Yes."

"What?"

"Yes, I understand," louder this time.

"Because, if there is any funny business, if you try to cross me just once, you'll be in for a bigger surprise than you bargained for," and he opened the side of his coat like an old-fashioned watch salesman, displaying his wares on the streets of London. Except that it wasn't a line of timepieces that adorned the blue-lined fabric on the inside of Jake's jacket.

It was a knife. A wooden hilted knife with a handle that jutted out two inches at the top of his pocket, which had sliced through enough for an inch of gleaming metal to be peeking out at the base.

It had been there all along.

All night and in the pub and as Jackie stared in disbelief, Jake cocked his head and beamed.

"Oh Jackie," he said ever so sweetly. "And you thought that I'd struggled down in the rain just to see you, eh? C'mon, time's getting on and we have to be there before the sun's up." He grabbed her roughly by the hand and yanked her to her feet, screwing up the map and stuffing it into his hip pocket as they approached the door. Jake opened it, but although he pushed Jackie out first, he held her hand firmly in his so that her fingers were crushed like pencils in a child's case.

It was just before six, according to the pale-faced clock in the foyer and as they passed by the reception desk, Jake gave his hostage's fingers another little squeeze just to keep her mind on the job. As it was, the porter was dozing and it wasn't until they had pressed the exit switch that he began to stir, by which time Jake had pulled back the door and had followed Jackie out into the early morning air.

Jake looked up to the sky.

It would be dark for a while yet on this the shortest day of the year, but he was still anxious that the sun might somehow rise sooner than he had been led to believe it would and he didn't want to be late.

He couldn't afford to be late!

"Let's get a move on!" he bawled, directing her down a side street that came out on London Wall.

"That way," he pointed, recalling from memory the map that was now buried amongst the sweet wrappings and tissues that always seemed to remain in his pockets for months after their useful life was over.

There were only a few people milling about, which was only to be expected at such an early hour. Street cleaners and manual workers from service companies, but few of them were primed for a chat and most looked close to sleep as they shuffled towards an early start. Jake sensed that Jackie was about to make her move. She had tensed up and was no longer mindful of the route before them. When for the third time, she glanced to her left and then quickly to her right, Jake made his move to dissuade her from making one of her own.

"Try anything and I'll let you have this!" Jackie felt the sharp bite of the knife in the side of her back as he pulled her into the broad doorway of a sportswear shop. There was no one to see them. The back street that they were on was deserted and for someone who did not know London all that well, Jake had clearly done his homework. "One false move, Jackie, and it's goodnight from me. Do I need to say anymore?" Jackie shook her head and stifled the rising sob that threatened to give her away.

In front of them, one of several office blocks towered above their heads, its dim emergency lights illuminating a few of the floors to give rise to the optical illusion that each was hovering above the other like some modern-day Indian rope trick. Onwards they went, ducking through alleyways and side roads, some of which were quite unknown to Jackie, but Jake seemed to be working on autopilot, tracing an ancient outline of a city that he had known all his life, or from a previous one. He never once stopped to consult the map, but just held onto Jackie as if she were a small child on her first outing to the bright lights of the city.

Jackie spotted the sign for Threadneedle Street as they hurried on and just minutes later, they were rushing past the Royal Exchange, where another hectic day of high-end shopping was still a few hours away. Jake pushed Jackie before him across the familiar circus where one or two cars dodged and threaded in their opposing paths, enjoying the freedom of the nocturnal streets.

The sky seemed to be lighter although it was still dark, and the streetlights still had some life left in them. Jake sensed that the faintest hint of light was starting to be seen above the skyscrapers, but a more ominous sky was about to descend.

"Walbrook!" Jake blurted triumphantly, as if until that moment he was beginning to doubt his own ingenuity. St Stephens was crammed in between the offices on the left-hand side of the crooked lane and as Jake bullied Jackie down the old, cobbled route and across Cannon Street, their downward trajectory suddenly became more acute, beneath which an ancient stream ran its course. For the first time, Jackie thought that she could smell the age-old stench of the river, but Jake didn't flinch as he pushed on towards his destiny.

"Keep going!" he ordered with his arm straight out in front of him and his hand firmly perched on his victim's shoulder, such was the decline in the road which led down to a much busier stretch that intercepted their path. As they waited for a break in the traffic on Upper Thames Street, Jake gripped his hostage as if his life depended on it, just a few yards from the edge of the pavement. He knew, as she did, that they had reached the last leg of their journey. The river was but a few hundred yards from where they stood and both captor and captive knew that if she were going to make a run for it, she would have to do it soon.

"Now!" Jake shouted, but her reactions were too slow for his liking and so he dragged her forward with such force that, had she stumbled, she would have been forced to trail like a sled behind a slavering pack of dogs. She didn't fall, but her screams did not go unheard. A couple of weekend workers heading for an early start in the nearby skyscrapers looked across to see a middle-aged couple in the grip of what looked like a full-blown battle.

Neither man lingered for long though.

After all, time was money.

"Stupid bitch!" Jake swore, the sinews in his neck taut and sore beneath his own fading bruises. "Either shut up or I'll finish it now," he raged as his fingers delved frantically inside his coat in search of the blade. Jackie had stopped screaming, but she couldn't stem the flow of tears and Jake had no time left to malinger. The dawn was almost upon them. He dragged her past the iron railway bridge, where the pigeons were just beginning to contemplate the start of yet another day of scavenging, and continued straight ahead, down a nameless street and on, towards the beckoning river.

"What are you going to do?" she sobbed, as he pulled away the flapping strip of police tape and forced her over the barrier that barred their way down to the muddy banks beneath Cannon Street Station. Several identical police notices were pasted to the walls in the immediate vicinity and Jackie's eyes flitted from one identical word to the next. Just above the black and white face of a middle-aged woman, a six-letter word that she could not bring herself to dwell on for long.

MURDER.

"Please, don't hurt me," Jackie begged. "Please, let me go."

"It's not me you should be blaming for all this," he countered as he clambered over the railings to join her on the other side. "I'm not the one that filled your head with all of this crap."

"What are you talking about?" she screamed, as the cold drops of rain began to fall.

"Move!"

"What is going on?" she sobbed.

"Just move," Jake thundered, prodding her painfully in the small of her back, but he had forgotten his own strength and she fell over with the force of it. "Move," he yelled, but she was already on her feet and scrambling. "Upstream!"

"Which way?"

"Right," he barked, pushing her a little less forcefully with the butt of his free hand as he wiped the drenched hair from his eyes with the other. In the gathering storm, it had become more difficult to gauge the onset of daylight, but as Jake glanced down at his smart watch, he could see that the sunrise was still officially some twenty minutes away.

"Why the rush?" Jackie cried out. "Why is it so important to get there before the sun comes up?"

"Because I said so," the bully bellowed. "Before sunrise on the winter solstice, that's what your man told me! Now let's step it up, come on!"

As they broke out into the open from beneath the relative shelter of the railway bridge, they were forced to battle against the full might of the eastern wind as it surged up the channel and with it, the merciless winter storm gnawed at their skin. In the distance, Jake could see the outline of a figure, poised on the banks of the river, his arms aloft and palms upraised to the sky. As far as Jake could tell, Jackie had not yet spotted they're not entirely unexpected guest.

"Please Jake," she pleaded. "What is going on?"

"I had those phone calls traced, you know," he shouted so that she would hear him though the boisterous wind. Jackie said something in reply, but it was of no significance and Jake feigned not to notice. "They were traced to a retirement home, in Essex." This time, Jackie shrugged the objecting hand away and turned to stare straight into his smiling face.

"You were right," Jake teased, "about Gallagher, he wasn't telling you everything." Jake couldn't be sure if she was crying or not, such was the sudden intensity of the driving rain, but if he had been a betting man, he would have wagered a ton or two on the fact that she was. "He told me the full story and we weren't far off, not far at all, in fact. Come on, keep going," he insisted, grabbing her by the shoulders, but Jackie was not so willing or able to follow his orders anymore. When Jake pulled the knife into full view and pressed it up beneath her chin, she found another gear from somewhere, and as she turned around and trundled on through the deepening mire, she spied the form that Jake had spotted minutes earlier.

"Who's that?" she cried out, no longer knowing if the real fiend lay up ahead or right behind her.

"You'll find out soon enough, just keep moving. I tell you what, I'll tell you a story, to keep your spirits up, how's that?" It wasn't a question that required an answer.

"Gallagher told me where to come and when. He said that we'd be welcome, especially you. You see, this Radclyffe bloke is keen to have his revenge; I think you worked out why, but he only wants one of us, for now. Now I figured that if

I can get through this and then get away, somewhere nice, away from London, I might be able to live to a ripe old age, just like he did and like your father did."

Jackie was dumbstruck. She couldn't believe that Ted would have betrayed her family after all that they had been through. She didn't believe it, but right then she understood nothing.

"You see," said Jake, doing his best impression of a decent bloke, "it's you or me, babe, and I tell you something for nothing, it ain't gonna be me!"

There was to be no let-up in the rain, but although they were now almost upon their target, Jackie was no closer to recognising the tall figure in grey. As they closed in, it raised a hand for them to stop, like some bewildered traffic cop on location and then pointed, out into the rising water.

Jake followed its line of sight but at first, he didn't see the linear array of ancient wooden piles that, like so many others, had been driven into the riverbed a few hundred years before. The hooded figure did not raise its head but swivelled around to turn its arm towards the shore where an open rucksack was drowning in the rain. Jake caught on and ran back to retrieve the bag, but as he turned back towards the river, he was horrified to see that Jackie had taken her opportunity to flee in the opposite direction.

In the circumstances, he could hardly blame her.

"Come here," he yelled. It wasn't an order that he expected her to obey, but she didn't get far. As he charged after her, her legs were quickly bogged down in the gruelling silt and Jake was able to produce one of his meanest rugby tackles to stop her in her deepening tracks.

"Stupid," he gasped, "stupid, stupid. Get up!" But she had had enough of orders and chose instead to lay face down in the stinking mud, which, like her, would soon fall victim to the rising tide. She had smelt the putrid stench of silt and sewage before, but this time it was not the stuff of dreams.

So, he dragged her. First by her injured arm and then by her hair, until finally she staggered unwillingly to her feet. Jake didn't need to wait for his orders. He had guessed the man's intentions.

"Stay there!" he snarled, but Jackie's legs felt like they were shackled already, and she chose instead to reserve her energy for another opportunity that she prayed would come. He returned with a long length of thin rope, which he did his best to hide from view until he was almost upon her. As he came nearer, Jackie peered up towards the rail-bridge to the East and then towards Southwark Bridge to the West, but in the rain, each bridge was shrouded in its own peculiar veil of mist. It was almost impossible to make out the streetlights on the Western bridge and although she could see that a train had arrived on the platform above their heads, any human faces were lost in the gloom.

And so was she to them.

"Back up," Jake shouted, the rain careering into his face. "Walk backwards," he bellowed, gesturing with his hands as if he were helpfully guiding a car into a parking space.

When she glanced behind, she immediately guessed what he had in mind.

"No!" she screamed. "No Jake, you can't! No!"

It was the stuff of nightmares; her own nocturnal visions, which had finally come to pass. As Jake struck her once and then plucked her from the waves to slap her again, she found that she was too exhausted to fight for her life, so she did the next best thing and thought ahead. As he pulled the ropes tighter, she drew her whole body taut until every muscle and sinew was stretched to bursting point. When she was finally bound like a witch with the rising waters lapping at her waist, she coaxed her muscles to relax. But although the ties no longer seemed so tight, each sodden cord remained strong enough to hold her captive and with that, her fading hopes seemed all consumed.

As Jake turned around to accept the plaudits from his grateful redeemer, he was not expecting the full force of the blow that greeted him. The thick worn blade of a boatman's oar swung like a medieval catapult to strike his face so hard that it smashed his nose as if it were a piece of ripe fruit. When he eventually recovered consciousness almost ten minutes later, his bound arms were no longer at his command and his tongue was smothered by a rancid piece of cloth that had been jammed into the yawning cavity between his throbbing jaws.

The water was drooling at the underside of his chest and the brooding skies had called a coup against the dawn.

It was almost time.

The sky was a patchwork blanket of grey and black, but its eastern fringes had already been breached by a fresh surge of light from the invisible sun, which remained out of sight at the furthest reaches of the meandering river. The incessant rain had added its meagre measure to the burgeoning tide, but as the condemned stared up towards the foreboding heavens their frantic prayers went unheard.

Jackie had worked her mouth free of the nauseous gag that Jake had failed to secure in his haste to please his new-found master, but it was too late for words.

As the tide closed in around her neck, she screamed out in a seemingly endless volley of noise as she struggled in vain against the nylon ties that secured her to the oak post. At that moment, she thought of her father and of her mother and of her son and she prayed aloud that she might see them all again. Her chest heaved beneath the waves, but the water was freezing, and she was now only faintly aware of the vicious incisions that were burning tracks ever deeper into her wrists, waist and legs. She could see the grey robes of the mysterious man, his arms aloft, his body consumed by the waves up to his scrawny midriff.

"Please," she begged through gnashing teeth, her lips blue with cold as she made her final plea. This time, his preparations complete, he turned to face her. As he lowered his hood to reveal the face beneath, her heart shuddered, as instant recognition plundered her weary body and ravaged mind.

"Ted," she mouthed, but the words may not have made it.

The tears did and then she recovered her voice.

"Gallagher!" she screamed, his name skimming over the surface of the water towards him like a sea snake. "You bastard!"

She turned her head as best she could to look at Jake, but his eyes were shut tight. His jaw was grinding against the cloth's unwelcome occupation, either in defiance of the cold or in some muted prayer for deliverance.

The prospect of his death did nothing to placate Jackie's fear. She knew only too well that her own time on earth would soon be at an end, and she felt no empathy for the pathetic excuse for a human being with whom she was doomed to die.

She was about to scream again, when someone else's words boomed out across the Thames and with each syllable, the sky seemed to darken another shade. The words came from Gallagher, but the voice did not belong to him. Nor did the energy that was powering his every unwilling move.

"I am earth," it boomed, its arms aloft so that his body formed a perfect Y-shape against the ashen grey backdrop.

"I am fire," it howled. "I am wind. I am water." A clap of thunder roared all around them and each sharpened shard of rain seemed to quiver as it poured down upon them. "I am the bearer of knowledge from the time before time," Gallagher's mouth proclaimed, "and I will be avenged!"

A fork of lightning split the sky and in its passing illumination, the river's backdrop was transformed. As the sun began to burn through the relenting mantle of cloud in the east on the winter solstice of the Northern Hemisphere, an altogether different bridge had formed a barrier to its lower reaches.

The Shard was no longer visible, as if it wasn't there at all.

As if it had never been.

A span of irregular stone arches spread like the inverted turrets of a fort and above them, a line of bustling houses stood shoulder-to-shoulder above the life-giving river.

"O mighty Tamesis," the man who was Gallagher proclaimed. "O sacred stream. Bring forth thy vengeance on my brother's seed." Another peel of thunder split the air and as the rain pelted like spears in an archaic war on the surface of the water, this most unlikely of priests was lost to Jackie in the reflected spray. "O bountiful Danu, princess of life, God of the water. I gave you the head of an innocent. Now take these sinners so that I may be avenged."

Once more, Jackie looked across at Jake. This time, his eyes were open, as was his gagged mouth, until a sudden precession of waves laid siege to them both and the water stormed the makeshift gate of gagging cloth for the first, but by no means the last time.

Jake was choking now and as the realisation that the experience was literally just a taste of things to come, he shook his head violently, his eyes bulging in a fit of unbridled terror.

The unnatural swell that rose again and again across the surface of the water left Jackie in no doubt as to the one most likely source for such a wash. Even in the Reaper's grip, she had not yet lost her sense of reason and she prayed that such inner calm would prove to be her saviour.

"Help!"

There had to be a boat, somewhere nearby. A boat that had just sailed past, its crew oblivious to her presence in the awful weather. She was sure of it.

"Help me, someone, please help me!"

For a moment, she was filled with hope at the faintest chance for life, but when the prow of a small wooden vessel slipped into view through the unrelenting rain, she did not feel a surge of relief pulsing through her veins. A single occupant was crouched in its belly and as it raised its head, Jackie closed her eyes.

She didn't need to see it.

She had seen it before.

300

When she opened them again, the vision was gone, and as Jackie turned her head back towards the shore, the last thing that she had expected to see was the familiar face of a family friend just a few feet from her own, but Gallagher was not focused on Jackie. He waded deeper into the water, out towards her assailant of just a few hours before. The old man's extra height kept his shoulders above the water, but when he reached her not so distant cousin, even he was forced to tread water. He didn't stay for long. Just long enough for Jake to recognise him too, but it wasn't his face that Jake found familiar at first.

It was his scent. The faint aroma of cheap aftershave, that Jake had inhaled once before, in similar circumstances. In the library, when ancient hands had closed around his neck, but once the link had been forged, recognition burned in his eyes.

When Jackie saw the look of terror on Jake's face, she could know but half of his story, as his last hope of redemption moved away from him and closer to her. Gallagher reached out a hand and placed it gently on her forehead, and as his middle finger pressed firmly between her eyes, the tangled words of some ancient incantation left his lips.

Then as his hand fell back gently into the water, a look of recognition lingered on his face and for a second, she saw the old man that she had known. The man who had been her father's staunchest ally and yet the man who had betrayed them all. As her last hope began to back away, she seized on her last chance for redemption.

"Gallagher, please!" she shrieked. "You can't do this," she sobbed. "Ted!"

He stopped, motionless in the water like an ancient Briton out spear fishing in the once fertile estuary. Jackie chose her words as carefully as her fear would allow. "Ted, you said that you would never forgive yourself," she heaved, "for my father's accident. Now you've a chance to put that right." She was frantic now that the end was so close, and the right words no longer seemed so easy to come by. "To save his daughter!" she yelled instinctively. "To save yourself!"

For a second, she was convinced that she had got through to him, but her hopes sank into the deepening depths of the river, as he resumed his arduous journey towards the London shoreline.

"No!" she sobbed, "no, please, don't leave me here!" She turned again to look at Jake and when she saw his face, she screamed again and again. This time, she could not stop. Jake's mouth was below the waterline now and as the waves began to seep beneath his bloodied and flaring nostrils, his head contorted as his body raged against the terrible fate that awaited her.

"Edward!" the voice roared, her lungs straining with the last efforts of life. Jackie found herself looking around for the source of the sound, to see who had succeeded where she had failed.

Gallagher was standing stock-still, just a few feet from the water's edge and when he turned, the look that he shot her was not unlike sorrow. The voice had been female, but it had been deeper than Jackie's, more mellow, less accented and yet, the words had come from her mouth. She knew that for certain.

The tide would soon surmount her.

Jackie's head was now angled backwards in the water, the wooden post nibbling at her neck and as she waited for the final few tidal inches to consume her, she closed her eyes for the last time and waited for her life to pass before them.

It was then that she felt a tug at the cords around her wrist. Then another at her waist and finally, she sensed that her legs were free. She had lost all feeling in her limbs, such was the intensity of the cold, and when she looked at the hand that had floated up to the surface, she did not immediately recognise it as her own. And then she felt another pull and she was gliding through the pungent water, her feet dragging on the turbulent silt at the river's bottom. Behind her, she could still make out the stub of the oak post and beneath it a dark mat of what she knew was Jake's hair, but which could easily have been mistaken for seaweed.

As she came ashore, she stayed where she fell for a minute or more, crouched on her hands and knees in just a few inches of water. Eventually, she fell back on her haunches and raised her head to stare straight at the body of her tormentor turned saviour. He was lying awkwardly on the sand, just a few yards away from her, but as she pulled herself up, her legs gave way, and she was forced to crawl like some amphibious creature towards his crestfallen form.

When she finally reached him, she gently slapped his limp cheeks with the palm of her throbbing right hand and when he did not respond, she assumed the worst. As she sat slumped on the ground, with this aged man beside her, she was quite unable to make sense of the full armoury of emotions that were frantically laying siege to her mind. Until he moved. It was just a finger, which curled and lengthened, but it was something and Jackie slapped him hard across his upturned cheek in a final act of defiance.

She found that she liked the feeling, so she did it again and again.

"Ted!" she yelled. "Ted, I want some answers! Don't you die, you shit!" she sobbed. "I want some answers!"

"Lucy, I'm sorry!" he whispered, but it was barely audible. The rain had stopped now, and the wind had died away enough for it to no longer be a hindrance, but he was so weak that his voice would have been lost on the most forgiving of breezes.

"I'm not your fucking wife!" she screamed. "I'm Jackie! Jackie Stubbs, your best friend's daughter, remember?"

He did.

She could see it in his eyes.

"I was a prisoner, just like you!" he implored her, but Jackie didn't hear him. "He gave me the strength to be here, to do his bidding and now, I will die, and he can do no more."

"What?" she bellowed. Then more quietly, she asked again, "What did you say?"

"I am a descendant of Thomas Radclyffe," he confessed. "I never knew," he sighed, coughing up a spatter of phlegm onto the polluted sand. "Until the last few weeks, I never really understood it myself. I was used, just like you."

"I don't understand," said Jackie angrily. "Is that why you sent my father down to the river? You wanted to kill him?"

"Not me!" Ted pleaded, as a tear rolled down his bleached cheek, where his fading scar had been cleansed by the salty water. "Not me. Him." He stared at Jackie as he said it and then did his best to push himself up, but he was soon out of breath at the effort and so he lay back down, on his side, this time to die.

"I didn't know then who I was. I truly thought that I was helping your father. We both had dreams. We thought that we were somehow linked, but we didn't know how. I left London to get away from it and I did, for a while, but he wouldn't let me stay away. I had no choice."

"What do you mean?" stormed Jackie. "Of course, you had a choice. You didn't have to come back. You could have gone anywhere!"

"Like your father, you mean?" Ted rallied. "Like your son?" Jackie bowed her head, but she no longer had the energy to fight. "None of us had any choice. It was like a spider and a fly. Once you stepped inside his web, it was only a matter of time before he reeled you in. Once he's inside your head, once you've accepted his coin, there's nothing you can do. Nothing."

"So why didn't you kill my dad, back then?" she urged. "Why did he let him live?" But she could see that he was slipping away, and she was determined to bleed him dry before the Otherworld could have its prize. "Ted!" she yelled, shaking him by the shoulders with all the strength that she had left. "Edward Gallagher, I haven't finished with you, I haven't finished!"

"Not long," he muttered, his eyes parting for the final time. "Not long now. I don't know," he spluttered. "Don't know why he got away. Maybe Radclyffe's spirit had been reborn, don't know," but his words had trailed off and Jackie was unable to make them out. "Be grateful that he did. Be grateful."

"So why was I spared then? Why did you have a choice? Why didn't you let me drown, like that pig?"

"It wasn't until my wife spoke…" But his words trailed off for a second or two as he regained a little of his fading strength for a final time. "Then you spoke to the man I was, in this life," he said sadly.

"I chose to set you free, not him."

A hundred questions still needed answering, but she could see by the rapid dilation of the old man's pupils that there was little time left for many more. She didn't need to ask the first of them.

"Thomas Radclyffe," Ted continued, his face as white as fresh fallen snow, "was a pagan. He was executed because he was betrayed and the man who gave him away,"—Ted paused—"was his partner, Jacob Cooper. He took his wife and his business, but he made one fatal mistake."

"He let his son live?"

"Yes," the old man confirmed, as his failing lungs hauled in a deep and ailing breath. "He took on Radclyffe's only surviving son, as apprentice, and in so doing he preserved the Radclyffe line."

"So?" Jackie asked, still bemused, her body trembling.

"Radclyffe's belief was an ancient belief, what has become known as 'Celtic', far older than what has come since. They believed in reincarnation." Ted stopped for another drag of air, but little seemed to reach his lungs and as his words began to waver, his head lolled with the effort. The world was doing cartwheels as the sun climbed higher in the clearing sky.

"Ted," Jackie yelled. "Ted, what else?"

"They believed that the soul is immortal, as long as your lineage survives. That the spirit, the sidhe, is born again and again in a man's descendants and when…" he gasped, "when the spirit is not in human form, it lives, as his does now, as a malignant force, in the Otherworld."

"The Otherworld?" But Jackie was no longer the sceptic that she had been in her own former life.

Ted nodded and closed his eyes.

It was almost a full minute later before they sprang back open, for the very last time.

"He made me do terrible things," he wept, his fingers rising to paw at the bruised and oozing sore that still dissected the chilled white flesh of his face. "He made me kill, for him." His last words would puzzle Jackie later, but there was no time left for any more cryptic clues.

"What now?" she asked, fearful that his answer might not be to her liking.

"Get away!" Ted commanded. "Get right away. There's nothing to keep you here. You might be safe, Cooper's line cannot continue through you, you're too old now to have another child."

He was lying flat on his back now and the mucus on his lungs was beginning to choke the life out of him. "But I don't know if that is all he wants," he coughed. "It's the ultimate revenge, you see. Cooper may have won in one life, but Radclyffe wants to end his line, forever."

As Jackie contemplated her next question, the old man's legs kicked against the searing pain, each straighter than they had been for years. With a weak and trembling hand, he clutched at his chest, until his legs pulled up and his body curled into the foetal position from which he had been born.

"It's not over," he whispered, but those words were not to be his last. His last filled Jackie with a sense of awe and joy and a tragic sense of loss. It was a simple word, just a simple name.

It was recognition.

It was a greeting.

"Lucy."

For a few minutes Jackie just sat and cried. She wasn't sure for what or whom. In truth, her tears were for them all: her father, her son, her mother, for the old man too and last of all for herself. Somehow, Gallagher's life had been the most tragic of all. As she stood to go, her eyes came to rest on a fading pattern of footprints, which seemed to trail from the water's edge to the body before her.

Small footprints.

Children's footprints.

In itself, one fresh set of unclaimed prints was unnerving enough, but as she cast her net further afield, many more littered the surface of the shoreline to form a seemingly perfect circle. Some were already beginning to fade, beneath the still rising tide, but at least two thirds of the circle remained. A countless array of tiny footprints, and with one exception, none of them had a trail. There were just there, placed in the sand as if they had landed from somewhere above and, their business concluded, had lifted off again.

The thought that they might still be there, poised like tiny statues upon the soft sand, watching her every move, provided Jackie with all the impetus she needed. She might have stayed to contemplate their fate, but a shrill breeze hastened her retreat and not wanting to face the unenviable task of explaining to the police why there were two dead bodies in the Thames that morning, she turned hastily away.

As she stared down at Ted for the last time, she made a silent promise to call the authorities, if only to put a name to one of the bodies that they would find washed up as the drizzle cleared.

But it was a promise that she wouldn't keep.

She trudged towards the putrefied steps and hauled herself up, gently pressing her chapped feet upon the viscous green slime with her numb legs trailing behind her, as if an encrusted anchor was manacled to her ankle.

As she placed her foot on the final tread, she felt the unwelcome brush of fur on flesh and looked down just in time to see a river rat scurry away from the rotting carcass of a large fish.

She almost screamed, but she had done enough screaming for one day.

Instead, she looked up into the eaves of an overhanging house, its wooden beams black with age, and was surprised that she could not see through to the inside, so thick were the leaded lights that made up the window. As Jackie hauled herself up and stepped out into the enclosed street, she gasped at the sight that met her eyes, as carts loaded with hay trundled by and a herd of pigs snorted past on their way to slaughter.

Then her eyes began to focus on the people, their haggard faces and strange costumes, with posies of flowers thrust about their mouths to ward off invisible noxious fumes. Men on horseback dressed all in black sporting tall hats and white lace collars, half-starved children begging in packs like dogs and creaking carriages jostling to be next to cross the bridge, but none of these were her undoing.

For Jackie, reality came in the form of a man in a long black cloak, a square hat perched on his head, as he crouched to exit through a tiny door at the base of a nearby timber-framed house and stepped out into the covered street to face her.

A mask that completely covered his face, with circular peepholes stitched unevenly around its eyes, and where his nose should have been, a curved and blackened beak carried with it the unmistakable scent of lavender.

It was the Plague Doctor.

Epilogue

It was a crisp November morning.

The low early light had only just surmounted the barricade of buildings to the east and was now skimming its way over the timid waves, as if a thousand stars had burst out across the slimy surface of the water.

The child shrieked with delight as the brightness glittered like stardust, stretching out his hands in the innocent belief that he might be able to gather their aura up within them. His mother held him tightly in her lap as the boat rose up and then gently fell back at the mercy of the river.

It was the first time that she had been on board the riverboat and it had been almost two years since she had last ventured this close to the site of her late husband's terrible end. Yet she had arrived in town more than an hour and a half ahead of schedule and so, with little thought as to what lay in wait for her on the opposite bank, a little jaunt downstream seemed to offer a welcome diversion from other more morbid pursuits. And if she were to be a little late for lunch, well, her friend would surely understand.

After all, toddlers could be hell at the best of times!

The boat was hardly full and only a handful of people had clambered on board at the mooring near Cannon Street; a businessman in a sharp suit, just visible beneath his full length winter coat, stood impatiently at the stern; two American tourists in their fifties, or maybe a little older, sat with outspread maps discussing the day's agenda; and two smartly dressed Japanese gentlemen, who may have been on a sightseeing trip too, but as they were unmoved, there was no way to tell for sure.

For all of them, their plans for that day would not be fulfilled.

The accident investigators could not agree as to the cause of the disaster. Even two years on, no conclusion would be reached as to why an apparently seaworthy vessel had gone down in such circumstances.

When finally, the dark river relinquished its hold at low tide, they had been surprised to find no evidence to support the initial view that a collision with something unknown had holed the boat below the waterline, with such force that it had sank within a minute.

After the final hearing at the virtual inquest in June of the following year, the chief investigator, a Dr Jack Thompson BSc PhD, was recorded as saying:

It was as if something had physically pulled the boat down to the river's bed.

The captain himself had been unable to attend the hearing on medical advice, but the inquest absolved him of all blame for the deaths that day. The inquest board had concluded that there was no negligence on his part, or on the part of the riverboat authorities whatsoever and so an *open verdict* was recorded.

He recounted the captain's report that the boat just upended; he had felt the bow lift up out of the water and then the whole ship had just sunk beneath the waves. The death toll could have been much worse, but for a passing ferry boat that had been on the scene within minutes and whose crew had rescued five of the more fortunate passengers.

The captain and the ticket inspector had managed to swim ashore and after immediate treatment for shock at the nearby hospital, were released with a clean bill of health, at least physically. The same could not be said for a young mother and her fifteen-month-old child. It was said that the mother had drowned in a frantic search for the boy, but that was only supposition, as she did not come out of the water alive.

In fact, she was dragged out less than an hour after the tragedy had occurred and was laid out on the muddy northern bankside, next to the stairs that led up onto London Bridge. A policeman's coat was used as a temporary shroud until the coroner arrived to officially pronounce that Lisa Harvey's life was over.

A crowd of onlookers watched in awe and horror, as the body bag was hauled up the stone steps and out into the waiting ambulance. A passing youth hollered an unwelcome addition to the disrespectful din of midday traffic:

"Bring out yer dead!"

His friends laughed and went on their way, hands in pockets and life before them, but whilst the words may have been in extremely bad taste, nothing could have been more appropriate in the circumstances.

One of the unfortunate passengers, who had managed to swim ashore with relative ease, had informed the police that a woman and a little child were amongst the ill-fated party. That simple fact was confirmed by the ticket inspector, who was inconsolable on hearing the news that the child was missing. Just hours earlier, he had made faces at the smartly dressed baby who had hidden his eyes and smiled at the man in the funny hat.

The child's body was never recovered. An unusual fact in that a missing body will usually turn up somewhere along the river, even if it reaches the Thames Barrier, a few miles downstream. But on this occasion, there was no sign, even after the riverbed was dragged and teams of divers searched the murky water for some grisly sign.

Nothing.

Well, not quite nothing.

Nothing had been uncovered, at least not officially, but one of the divers had been lucky enough to find himself a little piece of history, whilst searching through the silt and mud.

"A perk of the job," he told his wife, "just like a mudlark."

A single gold tooth. Perfectly preserved.

The way he found it had been quite remarkable. As he sifted his hand through the silt at the bottom of the river, in search of something that would help the enquiry, it had just come floating up before his eyes.

"Quite remarkable!" he would tell his friends and family that evening and for years afterwards.

"Quite remarkable indeed!"

Acknowledgements

Inspiration for this work of fiction came in a large part from the little known but extensive *'All the Works of John Taylor, the Water Poet'*, reprinted by the Spenser society in 1868-78 and viewed at The Guildhall Library in the City of London – since reprinted by *Taylor & Francis (Books) Ltd. UK and Franklin Classics*. The bridge itself is well documented, but I relied upon sources from Peter Jackson, *London Bridge: A Visual History* (*Historical Publications Ltd.* 2002), *A Thousand Years of London Bridge* by CW Shepherd (*John Baker Publishers Ltd.* 1971), *Old London Bridge* by Patricia Pierce (*Headline Book Publishing* 2001), Bridge, Church and Palace in Old London by John EN Hearsey (*John Murray Ltd.* 1961) and Old London Bridge by Gordon Home (*John Lane Ltd.* 1931). The amazing church of St Magnus the Martyr also features in my story and the pamphlet by John Wittich of the same name (*Beric Tempest*, 1994 and *Oyster Press* 2012), was an invaluable source of its history. I'd also like to acknowledge the wonderful 1987 model of the old bridge by the late David.T.Aggett, that is available to view in that church, as featured in this book. *The Lost Rivers of London* by Nicolas Barton (1ˢᵗ edition *Leicester University Press* 1962, republished by *Historical Publications Ltd.* including the 3ʳᵈ edition in 2012) and provides insights into the lost Walbrook stream, whilst Chris Ransted's work on *Bomb Disposal in World War Two* (*Pen & Sword Books Ltd.* 2017) was very useful. The Mysteries of Britain by Lewis Spence (*Rider.* 1928, republished by *Senate* 1994 an imprint of *Tiger Books International* and *Home Farm Books* 2008), provided me with the information on Gog and Magog as well as Edward Hatton's New View of London (*R.Chiswell and J.Churchill*, 1708) Michael Dickinson's book on *17ᵗʰ Century Tokens of the British Isles* (*Spink & Son Ltd.* 2011) and a similarly titled, *17ᵗʰ Century England: Traders and their Tokens* by George Berry (*Spink & Son Ltd.* 1998) shed light into that narrow window of history. *The Chronicles of the Celts* by Peter Berresford Ellis (*Avalon Publishing* 1999) and *The Black Death – a biological reappraisal* by

Graham Twigg (*Schocken Books* 1985) gave me the necessary background on those key topics. The Dissenters by Michael R Watts (*Oxford University Press*. 1978) provided some background, whilst a small pamphlet that I came across in the Guildhall Library many years ago was my inspiration for the fate of Thomas Radcliffe and it is with respect that I remember the unfortunate preacher John James who met that terrible fate all those years ago:

A narrative of the apprehending, commitment, arraignment, condemnation and execution of John James—closed access, Guildhall Library, A.94. no.80

Back cover print: *The Great Frost Fair of 1676* – Painting by Abraham Hondius, reproduced with kind permission of the Museum of London and the front cover silhouette of *The View of London Bridge 1632*, by Claude de Jongh, Yale Centre for British Art which is in the public domain.